Praise for Denmark Rising

"Barry Clemson's historical fiction novel Denmark Rising portrays the spirit and tactics of nonviolent resistance … Denmark Rising is a warm, engaging look into the practical use of nonviolence against an aggressor. It's a story that lingers long after the book is closed."
Janine Latus, author of the international bestseller "If I am Missing or Dead"

"Outstanding historical authenticity and beautifully detailed emotions of the participants during the occupation of Denmark by the Germans during the world war two era. This is truly a page-turner novel."
Richard L. Earls, author of *Timetrap* and *The Grapevine Hole*

"I could hardly put it down. I started yesterday morning and finished in the wee hours today. Your descriptions of the nightmares was so real it seems it must have come from personal experience. It is a good, good book. It is a book of power, real power, spiritual power. Thank you for writing it!"
Harold Confer, author of Finding and Creating Saints, and three books of poetry and Director of Ufufuo, Inc., a group of international and interfaith volunteers involved in rebuilding and recovery after natural disasters and domestic terrorism.

"Great read! A nonviolent resistance movement in 1940s Denmark confronts the Nazi invasion force. Surrounded by the horrors of occupation, Barry Clemson tells an uplifting story of a people who refuse to be crushed and who refuse to adopt the violent methods of their oppressors."
Joelle Presby, Naval Officer

"A workable manual for nonviolent resistance cleverly disguised as an entertaining and intriguing novel. A good read that provokes thought about the way the world does business and how we might do it differently."
Richard Hostetter, Master Carpenter and Healer

"While Denmark Rising is a work of fiction, it is true to the spirit of the people and the events. Had Denmark offered non-violent resistance to the Germans, it would have occurred just this way."
Frieda Landau, military historian and author of *Airborne Rangers*

"Unputdownable. Expect the characters to grab you from the start and drag you into this epic battle of wills. You'll care about what happens next as

much as they do and you won't be able to help yourself wanting to shout a warning or lend a hand. You'll feel the intensity of mass co-operation and wonder why people cannot unite so effectively today.
Or, after reading this book, perhaps we can?"
James Greyson, Founder of BlindSpot and Author

"Ladies and gentlemen, please welcome the birth of a classic. In Denmark Rising Barry Clemson has created a remarkable and action packed story about the power of a non-violent movement used by the Danish against Hitler's Nazis. Told against the backdrop of World War II, the stories of young and old, scared and brave, Gentile and Jewish, Danish and German blend seamlessly together in a novel that offers an amazing and rich tableau of ordinary people discovering the essence of their moral center or the depth of their depravity."
Sheri Bailey, award winning playwright and CEO of Juneteenth VA

Denmark Rising

Barry Clemson

Cybernetica Press Inc.

Norfolk, VA

Dedication

To

Fannie Lou Hamer

and the

Student Non-violent Coordinating Committee (SNCC)

for demonstrating that

Freedom is a state of mind,

not some external circumstance.

Cover design and illustrations by Beth Vinson.

Library of Congress Catalog Card Number: Pending
PCN number: Pending
Cataloging-in-Publication (CIP) Data: Pending

ISBN 9780984160501
Published by Cybernetica Press, Norfolk, VA, USA
Printed in the United States of America
First edition August 2009
Second Edition December 2009

Contents

EUROPE UNDER
NAZI OCCUPATION

FINLAND

Helsinki

Leningrad

Tallinn
ESTONIA

DEN

holm

Moscow

LAVIA
Riga

BALTIC SEA

LITHUANIA
Kovno

Tula

Vilna

Minsk

EAST
PRUSSIA

SOVIET UNION

POLAND
UNDER
GERMAN
RULE

Warsaw

Lodz

Kharkov

Stalingrad

Plaszow
Cracow
Tarnopol

Kiev

Auschwitz

Lvov

UKRAINE

Rostov

HEMIA
ORAVIA

SLOVAKIA

TRANSNISTRIA

Budapest

HUNGARY

CRIMEA

ROMANIA
Bucharest

b

ROATIA

Belgrade

BLACK SEA

SERBIA

Sofia

Sea

BULGARIA

Istanbul

ALBANIA

Ankara

GREECE

TURKEY

Athens

Crete

Cyprus

NEAN   SEA

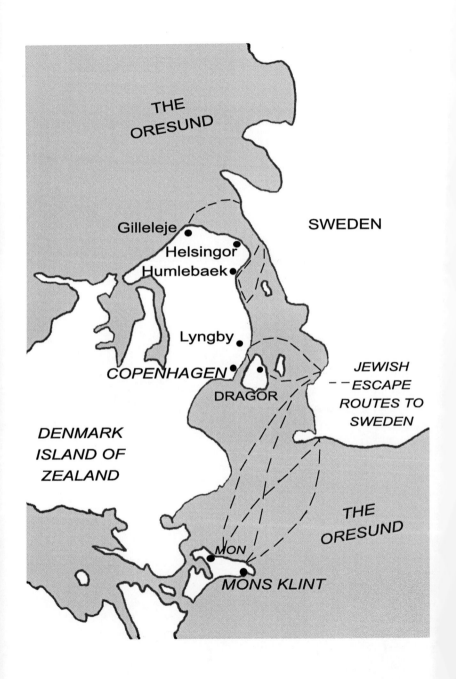

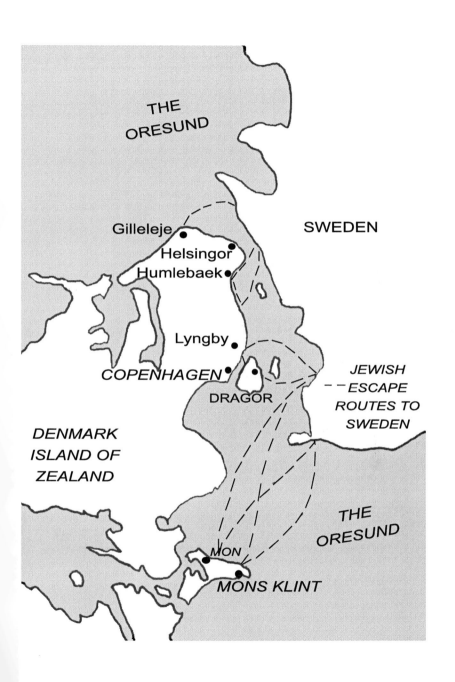

Glossary of German Terms

Aryan: According to Nazi ideology, the Aryan or Aryan-Nordic race was the master race and all others were untermenschen, the sub-humans.

Blitzkrieg: Literally, lightning war. Hitler's armies used a highly mobile form of mechanized war to bypass supposedly impregnable defensive formations (e.g., the French Maginot Line) and quickly overwhelm conventional armies. Blitzkrieg relied upon concentrating tanks and artillery and moving so quickly that their enemy couldn't recover quickly enough to attack the flanks as they drove through.

Corvettekapitan: The captain of a corvette (a small warship). Roughly equivalent to a US navy Lieutenant Commander.

Frau: Courtesy title before the surname or professional title of an adult woman.

Fuhrer: Leader or guide, used by Hitler as a title and as part of the title for other high level Nazi officers.

Fuhrerbefehl: Fuhrer's edict, a sacred edict by Hitler that could not be changed.

Fuhrerworte: Literally, Fuhrer's words, the title of a satirical book published by the Danish resistance to ridicule Hitler, the book infuriated many of the 2000 Nazi officers who received it through the mail.

Grupleutenant: A literal translation is group lieutenant.

Judenfrei: A Nazi term used to designate an area free of Jews.

Judische Frage: Literally, the Jewish question, this was the Nazi shorthand for "How do we get rid of the Jews?"

Kapitanleutenant: Equivalent to the US Navy rank of Lieutenant.

Lebensraum: Literally, 'living space', the room needed for a nation's expansion. The concept justified, at least in their own minds, the German invasion of the neighboring countries. Introduced by Friedrich Ratsel in 1896, the term became a central concept in the propaganda literature of the Nazis

Luftwaffe: The German air force.

Mein Kampf: Literally, My Struggle/My Battle, the title of Adolf Hitler's book. It combines elements of autobiography with an exposition of Hitler's National Socialist political ideology, including his poisonous racist views that all peoples except Aryans (i.e., "pure" Germanic stock) were inferior sub-humans.

Reichfuhrer: Literally, a leader of the state. Both a title and the highest rank in the SS (Schutzstaffel). Heinrich Himmler was the Reichfuhrer-SS.

Schnaps: German Schnaps is clear, colorless, and is distilled from fermented fruit (mainly apples, pears, plums, and cherries), is bottled with no added sugar, and normally is about 80 proof.

Schutzstaffel also know as the SS: An elite corps of combat troops (literally, "protective shield") formed originally within the German Nazi party as a bodyguard for Adolf Hitler and other Nazi leaders and led by Heinrich Himmler. The SS carried out most of the Nazi atrocities during Hitler's reign.

Swastika: The official emblem of the Nazi Party.

Untermenschen: Literally, under man, sub-man, sub-human; a term from Nazi racial ideology used to describe "inferior people", especially "the masses from the East," that is Jews, Gypsies, Slavs, homosexuals, Soviet Bolsheviks, and anyone else who was not an "Aryan" according to the contemporary Nazi race terminology.

Wehrmacht: The regular German army, made up mostly of draftees.

Zichorie: Chicory, the root of the Chicory plant is ground up and used as a substitute for coffee.

Glossary of Danish Terms

Amalienborg Castle: Home of the King of Denmark.

Bispebjerg Hospital: One of Copenhagen's leading hospitals, very active in the rescue of the Jews.

Danmarks Nationalsocialistiske Bevægelse: Danish Nazi Party, they supported Hitler and opposed the Danish resistance.

Det kan man ikke: a phrase that many Danes used to explain their reaction to the Nazi persecution of the Jews, it means "that is not acceptable!"

Faelledparken: A big popular park in the middle of Copenhagen, used for generations for big meetings.

Kobenhavns Radhus: Copenhagen City Hall.

Kobenhavns Universitet: Copenhagen University.

Kroner: Unit of Danish currency. In 1940, one kroner was roughly equivalent to about 21 cents.

Oresund: The bay separating Denmark from Sweden. It varies in width from a few kilometers to more than thirty kilometers. The Germans mined parts of it and heavily patrolled the rest during the war.

Pladhausen: Danish for city square.

Radhuspladsen: the square at City Hall.

Sarny, Sarnies: Danish for sandwich, sandwiches.

Schalburtgage: Cultural sabotage, the term referred to the campaign by the Danish Nazi Party in which they destroyed Danish cultural sites in retaliation for actions by the resistance.

Skæreost: Danish for sliced cheese, usually a buttery creamy white cheese.

Stikker: informer, a Dane who collaborated with the Nazis, many stikkers belonged to the Danish Nazi Party.

Studenternes Efterretniingtjeneste: Student Information Service, an underground equivalent of our Associated Press that functioned throughout WWII to supply news to the Danish underground press.

Sukker: Danish for sugar.

Tallit: Jewish prayer shawl.

Tzitzis: The tassels on a Jewish tallit (prayer shawl).

Visitationen: The office that allocated patients to hospitals in Copenhagen.

Zichorie: Chicory, the root of the Chicory plant is ground up and used as a substitute for coffee.

Part One: Opening Moves

April and May, 1940

Chapter 1. The Danes, April 9, 1940

"Arne, get dressed. Hurry up, we have to go to Amalienborg Castle."

His father's command made no sense. The alarm clock showed 4:45 a.m. on a Tuesday morning. The King's castle? We should all be going to work in a few hours.

Arne slipped into his pants and rushed to his parent's bedroom where his father was buttoning his shirt.

"What's going on?"

"The Nazis are invading. Everybody is going to the castle. Be prepared to spend most of the day."

This can't be happening, Arne thought. Isn't Hitler satisfied with the countries he already has?

He dashed back to his room. Let's see. My rifle, a canteen, some sandwiches. By the time he finished dressing, his mental list was complete.

When his mother came downstairs, the sandwiches were nearly finished and his rifle, a full box of cartridges and his canteen were all on the kitchen table.

"You can't take the rifle," his mother said.

"What do you mean? Aren't we fighting them?"

"Not with guns."

"What?"

"Arne! You've heard us talk about this. No violence. Get your camera, though."

"I don't see how that could work."

"Leave the rifle, we'll explain on the way."

The explanation-on-the-way didn't happen.

They lived about ten miles north of the castle and, like most Danes in 1940, routinely rode bicycles to get around Copenhagen. Arne's father barely started explaining Operation Total Resistance when he had to stop. There was too much traffic ... at 5:00 a.m.

An hour later they arrived at the square in front of the castle and realized that the numerous bicycle racks were already full.

"We'll chain the bikes together … leave them here," his father said.

While his father locked the bikes together, Arne looked around. Hundreds of people were in front of the castle entrance and more were pouring into the square from all the adjoining streets.

'Look, I don't have time to explain it," his father said. "Just remember, our national policy is nonviolent total resistance."

"How come I never got any of this?"

"Everybody eighteen and up had a briefing. At seventeen, you were too young."

"Great. The Nazis invade and I don't have a clue."

"Arne, just follow along with everybody else. I'll tell you everything as soon as we can talk. Okay?"

Arne nodded, only slightly mollified.

"What do we expect to happen? Why are we here?"

"Sometime today the Nazi commanding general will arrive to see the King and the Prime Minister. We're making sure there's a big audience for the general's arrival."

Arne couldn't see the point. They were being invaded. And everybody in the city was just standing around waiting for the conquering general. Was everybody too chicken to resist?

"I'm going up front." Arne figured that he would at least get a good view of whatever was going to happen.

"Arne, wait. Stay with … ," Mother started.

"Let him go. He'll be okay," Father said.

* * * * * * * * * *

Fritz Clausen was sound asleep when the German bombers flew over Copenhagen and dropped tens of thousands of leaflets. He threw open his bedroom window and crouched there, looking up. Planes were everywhere … just above the buildings.

Fritz thrust out a hand to ward off a falling object and by accident caught it … only a piece of paper.

He glanced at the paper and almost shouted aloud. Hitler's moving! At last. Maybe we'll get a little more respect now.

But why hadn't they told him? Breaking my ass as leader of the Danmarks Nationalsocialistiske Bevægelse since 1933, the same year Hitler came to power. Maybe now we'll get past two percent of the vote and three seats in the Danish parliament.

No time for sulking. Go find the German HQ and offer our assistance.

Clausen skipped breakfast, put on his best suit, sprinted out his front door … and came to a dead stop. Instead of the usual morning traffic going in all directions, everyone was headed toward downtown.

"Excuse me," he said to a walking man. "Where's everyone going?"

"Oh, you didn't get the word? We're going to Amalienborg Castle."

"What for?"

"Why, to show the damned Nazis we're not afraid of them. To show support for the King. To stand up for Denmark, that's what for."

"Well, I'm … " Fritz bit off his angry reply in mid-thought. He had to think about this. The location of the German HQ would be general knowledge soon enough. In the meantime he would listen to the radio to find out what was going on … and call his lieutenants, make sure all his people were ready to act.

* * * * * * * * *

Thorvald Stauning, Prime Minister of Denmark, after a late night bout of insomnia, had been asleep only an hour when the special phone rang at 4:22 a.m.

Vald reached for it in the dark and dropped the receiver. He threw the covers back, swung his legs onto the floor and turned on the light. Retrieving the phone, he answered it.

"Yes? This is Vald."

"This is Command Central. Prime Minister Stauning? Is this the Prime Minister?"

"Yes. What is it?"

"I'm sorry, sir. Sorry to call so early, but the Germans are invading. They've crossed the border in force, sir. Several divisions, moving fast. And there's a major naval force approaching the capital."

Vald couldn't think. What will we do? How can we get through this? For several seconds he fought waves of nausea that threatened to erupt into vomiting.

"Sir? Are you there? Sir?"

"Yes … I'm thinking," Vald's little lie took enormous effort. Command Central remained quiet. Finally Vald remembered their preparations and he asked the critical question.

"Is Phase One of Operation Total Resistance being implemented?"

"Yes, sir. We started Phase One thirty-five minutes ago. We're now on the second wave of calls and are pretty much on schedule."

"Moellar? Did Moellar get off. And his support people?"

"Um… Give me a second to look at the board … Okay, Moellar is in Sweden already, most of his people have been notified. We're still trying to contact a dozen or so, but most of them are either on the way or already in Sweden, sir."

"Thank you. I'll be in my office in twenty minutes." Vald hung up.

"The Germans. I kept telling myself they wouldn't do it." Hanne, Vald's wife, was sitting up, eyes wide, hand pressed to her mouth.

Vald wanted to comfort her, to reassure her that everything would be all right but she knew what Operation Total Resistance implied. He took her in his arms and wasn't sure which of them was doing the trembling.

Vald, still in his pajamas, called his telegraph office and walked the duty officer through the process and the secret code words that authorized sending a special set of telegrams to the key heads of state and media outlets around the world.

Vald dressed in a severe charcoal grey suit, half way brushed his teeth, and didn't notice that he still had toothpaste in his beard. He grabbed his trench coat and turned to Hanne.

She dabbed at the toothpaste in his beard with a corner of her robe. He enfolded her in an embrace and they clung to each other. He kissed her, hard, said, "I love you," and dashed out of the house.

Vald arrived at his office in Amalienborg Castle at 4:44 a.m. King Christian met him at the door dressed, as always, in his formal uniform. Vald's first job under Operation Total Resistance was to let the rest of the world know that Germany had broken its word by invading them. He followed up his telegrams by calling Franklin Delano Roosevelt, President of the United States.

Roosevelt came on the phone almost immediately and, on hearing his voice, Vald once again marveled at the warmth the man projected even over transatlantic phone cable. Vald kept his report of events short.

"It seems, Mr. President, that Hitler has decided to invade us in force. We have a large Nazi force coming overland and another one by sea. Remember, our plans include the press in your country."

"Prime Minister, I will do everything in my power to publicize Hitler's actions. I think it may help my people wake up to the threat. Look, I want to think about this and get the right person, but I'm going to designate one of my people as a press-liaison for Denmark. I'll have them contact your office later today."

Vald thanked Roosevelt and called Churchill. He made four more phone calls and then had nothing more to do.

Vald hated waiting, had never been good at it. Getting people to work together, working out compromises among political enemies … that's easy. But a Nazi General … wish my hands would stop trembling. Not nearly so brave as I had imagined. This guy might kill us. How the hell are we going to manage?

Chapter 2. General Himer

General Kurt Himer, chief of Staff of the German armies occupying Denmark, strode down the gangplank from the troopship Hansestadt Danzig and onto the dock in Copenhagen harbor at 6:37 a.m. on April 9, 1940. The ancient Citadel guarding the ports of Copenhagen had fallen to his troops an hour and a half earlier … without a single casualty. His landing force had occupied the entire harbor area without firing a shot. Very strange. Why no resistance?

Still looking straight ahead, he extended his left arm to the side and behind. His aide, hovering behind his left shoulder, put the little black notebook into his hand. He wrote "Occupation proceeding flawlessly. Reconnaissance trip last week highly effective." Again without looking, he handed the notebook in the general direction of his aide. The aide took it instantly.

The only resistance General Himer's forces encountered was an unarmed patrol that stood on the dock in front of them and ordered them to leave.

His army coming overland had yet to fire a shot. They also were confronted by an unarmed patrol and were also ordered to leave. Both patrols were taken prisoner. Strange and stranger ... Why were the Danes not armed as proper soldiers?

Putting this anomaly out of his mind, General Himer gave the order to march on the seat of the government and secure the rest of the city. Then, back on board the troopship he enjoyed a leisurely breakfast. It seemed that the Danes might not cause any trouble.

At 8:33 a.m. Himer's aide told him that all reports indicated the city was secured and quiet. Faster than even our most optimistic predictions.

"Get me a full report on the Danish merchant marine fleet," Himer said to his aide. "Name, tonnage, and current location for every ship."

The Danish fleet had almost no offensive capability, but it had 230 ships with roughly 5500 sailors and a combined capacity of 680,000 tons. Hitler was anxious to use it to help in importing the critical minerals needed for war production and, so far, it was unaccounted for.

Himer sipped at his coffee and considered the situation. The Danes must be cowards ... not one soldier or sailor or marine even tried to defend their country, not one. Good. Denmark can make major contributions to the war effort immediately. The Fuhrer will be most appreciative.

Himer finished his coffee and glanced at his watch. Time to meet with the King and Prime Minister.

Preceded and followed by crack Schutzstaffel (SS) units, Himer drove toward the Amalienborg Castle, the King's palace. No one on the street. Everybody's hiding in their basement.

About a kilometer from the castle, Himer began to see people walking and cycling, all going the same way he was. More and more people.

The convoy entered the square in front of the palace and came to a dead stop. Hordes of people, probably several thousands, jammed the far half of the square. And more arrived with each passing second.

The palace steps and the wide porch leading to the entrance were clear of people except for a dozen Royal Guards and several religious leaders in full robes.

My God. People on balconies, at windows, on flat roofs overlooking the square. All of them silent, waiting, watching. Eerie .... A band next to the steps ... playing Beethoven's Ninth Symphony?

Were the Danes all crazy? Didn't they realize they'd just been conquered? Too craven to put up a fight, they should be cowering somewhere ... they're right here, looking at me. Maybe they intend to attack. No weapons in sight ... and there're many women in the crowd. Even children.

They're up to something. This calm can't be real ... when will they start fighting back?

Only fifty soldiers, not enough for this mob. Shouldn't show fear ....

Himer rolled down the window and leaned out.

"Lieutenant. Clear a path for the vehicles. Use no more force than necessary."

"Yes, sir," the lieutenant saluted. "Sergeant Grimsky. Twelve men, fixed bayonets, clear a path to the palace."

Grimsky's men walked forward, bayonets at the ready and the crowd parted. The convoy followed until they reached the palace steps.

Himer blew out his pent up breath. The steps remained clear and the Royal Guard still stood at attention in front of the main entrance. Why are the clergy just standing there at the top of the steps? What are these crazy Danes up to?

Chapter 3. Arne Sejr at Amalienborg Castle

Arne left his parents near the back of the square and moved off toward the castle steps. Progress soon slowed to a crawl, people were packed shoulder to shoulder. By dint of a little shoving here and there, Arne continued to move toward the palace steps.

"Excuse me, sorry, didn't mean to step on your toes," Arne said.

Ten minutes of rather determined wriggling, shoving and downright rude behavior finally brought Arne to the front row, right in front of the Royal Guard.

"What are we waiting for?" Arne said to the man next to him.

"The German General will come to see the King. We're here to show support, to let them know we aren't afraid," he said.

That's pretty weak, Arne thought, but he didn't say anything.

Time dragged and then just stopped. Arne's irritation, excitement, and frustration all drained away, to be replaced with a sort of sleepy stupor. Around him, the citizens of Copenhagen waited.

* * * * * * * * * *

Hours later Arne realized the Germans had arrived. A ripple passed through the crowd and a passage opened to Arne's left, just big enough for the German vehicles. A large black sedan, preceded and followed by trucks, stopped right at the steps, just a few feet away.

A soldier jumped out and went up to the officer commanding the Royal Guard.

"I'm Aide to General Kurt Himer, Chief of Staff of the German Army," the soldier said in German. "General Himer is here to see the Prime Minister and the King."

"I am Colonel Jensen," the middle-aged officer had a chest full of medals and spoke Danish. "You are in Denmark illegally. You must leave immediately or you will be arrested."

"We give the orders here," the aide said, this time in Danish. "You have no choice but to cooperate."

"You have no authority here. Leave now."

"I can have you shot if you fail to cooperate."

"Shooting me will change nothing. You are here illegally and must leave."

Arne watched the aide hesitate, then go down the steps and get into the car. About a minute later the door opened and an officer wearing many, many medals got out.

Arne stared. So. That is the enemy. General Kurt Himer. He doesn't look so formidable.

Himer took his time climbing the steps, with the aide right behind him. He strolled up to stand in front of Jensen and then spent about twenty seconds simply staring at him. Ha! Jensen is staring right back, never averting his eyes.

Himer extended his hand in the direction of his aide who quickly gave him a small notebook. Himer wrote something and gave the notebook back to the aide.

Himer locked eyes with Jensen again.

Arne couldn't make out what Himer said, but it sounded like German.

Jensen just stared at him and said nothing.

Himer raised his right index finger like a spear until it was right in front of Jensen's face.

"I will see your King now," he said, in German.

"We don't understand German," Jensen replied in Danish. 'You are here illegally and must leave immediately."

Arne almost laughed aloud. Most Danes were fluent in German.

"I will see your King now," Himer said in Danish.

"Who are you?" Jensen said. "Do you have an appointment?"

"I am General Kurt Himer, Chief of Staff of the German Army. I will have cooperation. Take me to see the King now."

Jensen stared at him for several long seconds and Arne was smiling, enjoying the General's obvious irritation.

"Are you the head of the occupying army?" Jensen said. "Are you violating the non-aggression pact? Are you admitting to being here illegally?"

Himer, with a snarl, yanked out his pistol and pressed it into Jensen's forehead.

"You will take me to your King NOW! Or you die and someone else takes me."

Arne involuntarily took a step forward and the man beside him clutched his arm and commanded, "Don't interfere. Just watch."

"GENERAL HIMER," a clergyman on the left said.

Himer, still with the pistol at Jensen's forehead, looked at the clergyman.

"General, I am the Bishop of Copenhagen. Colonel Jensen is merely doing his job, just following orders. As a good Christian officer, I know you can appreciate another officer following orders in a situation of great difficulty."

"This officer is interfering with the Fuhrer's orders and, if he continues to resist I will execute him for treason."

Jensen paled and sweat popped out on his forehead, but he didn't move.

"General, perhaps you didn't notice," Jensen's voice shook a little. "There are a great many cameras focused on us right now. Do you want the entire world to see you murdering me?"

Arne snapped his camera up and aimed it at Himer and Jensen.

General Himer looked around and his gaze stopped at a balcony off to the right. Arne followed Himer's gaze and saw a professional camera crew with a movie camera and telephoto lens.

Well, this isn't going at all the way the General expected, Arne thought. This is kind of fun. Wonder what he tries next?

Himer put his pistol away and then did nothing at all for a few seconds.

"Now, look," Himer said in Danish, sounding very reasonable. "I'm here at the head of an army. We have occupied the entire country. Like it or not, I am now in charge. The King will have to see me."

"You may be in charge of your army, but we do not grant you any authority over Denmark or any of its citizens or any of its land," Jensen replied.

Arne noticed that Himer swelled up a little … and his face got red.

"Regardless. I will see the King if I have to tear the palace down."

"Would you like me to get you an appointment?" Jensen asked.

"I will see him now!"

"The King is not in at the moment," Jensen replied. "Would you like me to check his calendar?"

Himer's mouth gaped open. Arne wondered how long it would take him to remember to shut it.

"Make me an appointment for this morning."

Arne was impressed that Himer managed to make his voice sound quite normal.

Without a word, Jensen turned and marched into the palace.

General Himer turned to look over the square which was now full, a sea of people, packed shoulder to shoulder.

Arne felt a great exhilaration. Delaying and humiliating Himer was a victory. A small victory but one to savor nonetheless. Arne began to fantasize a tsunami of people, a great wave that would rise up and wash the square clean of invaders.

Himer's shoulders were drawn up so that he seemed to have no neck. It might have been imagination, but Arne thought he saw a shudder pass through the General and then he was descending the steps, moving with haste. His aide followed so closely Arne thought he was stepping on the General's heels. Both of them ducked into the car and, in spite of it being a warm day, they quickly rolled up the window.

It seemed a long time later but Arne's watch said only three or four minutes passed until one of the King's aides came out and very slowly walked to Himer's car. The window rolled down.

The aide spoke in a loud voice so that many of that great mob heard the King's message:

"King Christian Rex, Monarch and Ruler of the sovereign nation of Denmark, will arrive in his office at 11:00 a.m. It pleases him to see the petitioner, General Himer, at that time."

Without waiting for a reply, the aide turned and started back up the steps.

Himer's convoy started out even before his window was rolled all the way up. Arne thought the crowd was hard-pressed to get out of the way of the lead truck.

Arne was momentarily elated. Humiliating a general is great. But the damned general has all the guns and has just conquered our country. We need to do something ... something drastic, something to force the Germans out. The adults are fools if they think the Germans are going to be defeated with this weak-kneed nonviolence. We're Vikings ... Vikings fight.

Chapter 4. Himer and Vald

Vald gulped pills to calm his nausea, crossed and uncrossed his legs under the desk, leaned forward on his elbows, then leaned back in his large leather covered swivel chair. Again and again he grasped his full beard and ran his hands down the length of it, pulling at it.

"I too am nervous, my friend," Christian sighed. "Get your fidgeting done before our enemy arrives. Remember, you are a Viking, and we bow our knee to no one."

Vald managed a small smile. "I'm glad I have a little acting experience … I shall try to appear unafraid."

Vald could feel Christian's eyes, studying him. Christian is right to wonder about me, I wonder about me … I'm not sure I can do this.

He got up and went into the small bathroom and looked at himself in the full-length mirror.

The best suit money can buy … and I look like I just lost a wrestling match. I'll bet my shirt-tail is out too.

He continued to pull at his full beard while he studied his reflection. Oh, well, Christian is elegant enough for both of us.

Vald went back to his seat, clasped his hands together and willed them to stay in his lap.

"Excuse me, sir," Christian's secretary entered the room. "General Himer is here."

Before either of them could respond, Himer himself strode into the room, his own aide just behind him. Vald sat at a rather imposing desk on the left. Christian was in a large throne in the center of the room. Both Vald and Christian remained sitting.

Himer glanced around the room. There were no chairs so he was forced to remain standing.

"I am General Himer, appointed by the Fuhrer himself to protect you from invasion by the Allies. What is the meaning of this reception? When you insult me, you insult the Fuhrer. It will not be tolerated."

"You invade my country and then dare to complain about how I greet you?" Christian said.

"This is not an invasion. My strict instructions are to protect Denmark from invasion by the Allies. We have come to protect you, we have come in friendship and peace."

"Ah. As King, I thank you for your concern, however, there are no Allied troops anywhere near here. You may depart at once."

"My orders are to protect you. The Allies may try to invade at any time and we are here to prevent that. In return for our protection, we require certain materiel from Denmark."

The King bolted to his feet, ramrod straight and proud.

"I will never submit. Denmark will never submit. We are Vikings. You may occupy our land, but you will get no assistance from us, no cooperation, nothing but resistance." Christian sat down and glared at Himer until the man looked away.

"Mr. Prime Minister, you control the affairs of state," Himer said. "I need your full cooperation."

"General Himer, my orders are clear," Vald said. "There can be no cooperation with any foreign occupying army. I'm afraid I can't cooperate."

Vald thought Himer looked confused.

"You are conquered. We have control of your major cities and in a few more hours will control the entire country. Your cowardly forces fled before us and we occupied you without firing a shot. You have no means of resistance. You will cooperate."

"Our forces are anything but cowardly, they did precisely as ordered," Christian spoke evenly. "You may occupy the country, but we will not cooperate."

Himer wheeled and stallked out of the room. A minute later he was back, breathing harshly. He stood there glaring at them. They heard hasty footsteps leaving the outer office and then two soldiers returned with three of Vald's staff members.

The soldiers ushered the three men into the office at gunpoint, made them kneel in front of Vald's desk, saluted Himer and left.

"Do I need to begin executing traitors?" Himer looked from Christian to Vald.

Vald's throat was dry and his traitorous stomach churned.   Say something, fool! Respond, don't let him shoot our people.

Vald could find no words and remained mute.

"You think to coerce Vikings?" Christian said. "You think an evil act will gain our cooperation? To save their lives, I will tell you, here in private, anything you wish to hear. You will still not have my cooperation. You will never secure Denmark's cooperation."

"Well said, my King," Vald cleared his throat, finally able to speak.

Himer snatched his pistol from its holster and shot one of the kneeling men in the back.

The man fell on his face, his legs working as if he were running. The other two shrank away from their wounded comrade. The secretary shrieked and fled down the hall.

The wounded man tried vainly to rise from a widening pool of red. His breathing sounded loud in the silence and rapidly turned to a liquid bubbling as his lungs filled with blood.

King Christian dashed from his throne to the stricken aide, turned him over and cradled his head. A moment later, the man shuddered and died.

The vile smell of the man's relaxing sphincter filled the air. Vald, hand pressed to his mouth, struggled not to throw up.

Christian gently lowered the dead man's head to the floor and stood up, facing Himer.

"So. The brave general shoots defenseless men in the back."

Himer raised the pistol to Christian's face. For long seconds, neither man moved. Finally Himer lowered the pistol and looked at Vald.

Vald, sweating, took a harsh shuddering breath. His hands were shaking badly and he clasped them together, willing them to be still.

"What do you want of us, General?" Vald spoke.

"I thought you would see reason when I explained it properly. The Fuhrer will be pleased." Himer smiled and looked at his aide. "The orders for Prime Minister Stauning."

"These documents contain your orders. The Fatherland requires specific assistance in the form of minerals and other raw materials, food, and manufactured goods. Also your merchant marine fleet. You will execute these orders immediately and with all deliberate haste. The documents also include our liaison officers for each of your ministries and industrial sectors. By 11:00 a.m. tomorrow, I require you to have ready the names of the liaison person on your side for each of these organizations. Any questions?"

Vald pressed his lips together. There was nothing to say.

Himer glanced at Christian and walked out of the room.

A moment later Vald went to the door and looked out. The Germans were gone.

Vald slumped into his chair and held his stomach while tears ran down his cheeks. How would he tell the dead man's young wife and three children? It's too much …

"Swen?" Christian called. "Did you get everything?"

"Yes, everything." The voice came from behind one of the walls. "I got still photos, the movie camera was going the whole time, and we have it all on audio tape. We're off now, it will be in Moellar's hands and at the news service before the end of the day."

"Excellent. Good work, men." Christian turned back to Vald and rested a hand on his shoulder.

"Are you all right?"

Vald shook his head no.

Christian's grip tightened. "Listen. We did what we had to do. The situation is developing as expected."

"Yes … but watching him die … watching that butcher … it's hard."

"So far we have one casualty. Imagine what it would be like if we had a conventional defense."

"Okay, okay, I'm going to be all right," Vald swiped at his tears. "I hope we're not the next casualties."

"Humph. Not likely. They know killing either of us would cause major riots. Not to mention worldwide awful press. Fortunately for us, the Nazis want to appear honorable and civilized before the rest of the world."

Vald picked up his telephone and called the police to come and get the corpse, then called maintenance to come clean up the mess.

"You can handle the meeting with the senior staff?" Christian said. "I think I should take my usual ride through the city … it will re-assure our people."

"I will manage."

Vald walked into the auditorium full of the government's senior staff members at precisely 1:00 p.m. He recounted the morning's incidents, emphasizing the number of citizens in the square, the heroics of Commander Jensen and the fearless demeanor of King Christian.

"I cannot begin to express my emotions," Vald said. " Himer's a butcher … he showed no emotion whatsoever in killing my aide. On the contrary, he was smugly satisfied that I was horrified and distraught. I believe the Nazis will kill whenever they think it will benefit them to do so."

Vald paused.

"I don't mind admitting that the Nazis terrify me. I suspect that many of you share my feelings. Nevertheless, you have given me a role and I will play it. Likewise, each of you has a job and you also will find the courage and fortitude to do that job. Fortunately King Christian is resolute and fearless and an inspiration. And our people are magnificent. I hope each of you were able to see them in the square today."

Vald's audience burst into cheers and clapping. Many of them sprang to their feet. Vald waited until they grew quiet.

"Tomorrow, at 7:00 a.m., the radio and newspapers will report on General Himer's crime. We expect him to be furious … absolutely beside himself and ready to do mass murder … and to arrive here shortly thereafter. I want the building empty. No one inside, no exceptions. We shall give him no one on whom he can vent his anger in private. You are, of course, invited to be in the square with the rest of Copenhagen."

After a few questions, Vald ended the meeting and went to see the widow of his murdered aide. From there he went home, wanting nothing more than to be with Hanne. His stomach bothered him all night and he hardly slept at all.

* * * * * * * * * *

While Vald met with the senior staff, King Christian followed his usual route, on horseback, through Copenhagen.

Christian was not nearly so calm as he appeared. He needed the ride. The routine ... the horse moving under him ... early flowers ... the smell of the harbor ... the seagulls. Salute my countrymen, keep up morale.

A German patrol. Humph! Saluting me. Ignore them, don't even see them.

Christian stopped to talk to four Danish men.

"The Nazi General murdered one of our staff people this morning," he said. "Tomorrow, don't go to work. Be in the square by 7:15."

Christian stopped to talk so many times that his ride took him three and a half hours instead of the usual 55 minutes.

Chapter 5. General Himer as Celebrity

General Himer was lost in thought on the ride back to his quarters aboard the troopship Hansestadt Danzig.

Damn that Jensen Royal Guard son of a bitch! Strangling him would be pleasant ... first the struggle for breath, then the eyes bugging out, finally loss of consciousness and death. But that would be too quick, that one deserved a slow death.

"Hans," he said. "Have Lieutenant Juhl arrest Colonel Jensen. He can make up some pretext. Jensen deserves some very special attention."

And that pipsqueak king. They should put him under a platform and slowly pile rocks on it until he suffocates ...

The expression on that fool Staunings' face ... he probably never saw anyone die before and he about crapped his pants. That one at least would give them no more trouble.

When will the real resistance start? Clearly the Danes are planning something. Where will they strike? The troops must be kept on full alert. Can't relax, must be ready to crush the attack when it comes.

By the end of the day, Himer had the reports from his media corps. The major newspapers and the national radio station had been contacted and had the policies requiring German clearance for stories on military affairs and anything to do with the occupation.

Himer went to sleep that night with only one nagging worry ... he still had no information on most of the merchant marine fleet. He anticipated praise from his Fuhrer for the speed and efficiency with which he had taken Denmark.

* * * * * * * * *

Himer's satisfaction lasted most of the way through breakfast, until Hans, handed him several newspapers and immediately left the room.

Himer looked at the newspapers. The headlines and pictures took up the entire front page. Nazi General a Murderer. Nazi Barbarian. Himer Kills Innocent.

The pictures were worse. Firing into the back of the kneeling aide. The aide lying in a pool of blood. Pointing his pistol at a defiant King Christian.

Damn! Hitler wanted to appear to be protecting the Danes, wanted to present an honorable face to the world. Lucky to escape Hitler's wrath with a mere demotion … God help me Hitler might shoot me!

By God, he wouldn't go alone. These Danish bastards would pay.

"Hans! Get in here. Now!"

"Yes, sir," Hans leaped to attention in front of him.

"Arrest every newspaper and radio official in the country. Send troops to occupy the offices of every damn one of them. Get me an escort of three hundred troops. And at least four tanks. Move. I want it NOW! All of it."

General Himer, with his escort of four tanks and three hundred SS troops, headed for Amalienborg Castle. He'd wreak vengeance on King Christian and Prime Minister Stauning. A fantasy of slowly killing them unrolled in his mind.

The convoy slowing caused him to look around. They were still several blocks from the castle. The streets were full of people. What were these crazy Danes up to now?

They arrived at the square in front of Amalienborg Castle. The square was packed with people.

"Keep moving," he ordered. As people moved out of the way, the convoy of trucks and tanks drove, slowly, to the steps of the castle.

Himer's aide opened his door and he got out, pausing to look around. Just the same as yesterday. Cameras, Beethoven, clergymen and all. No, not quite the same … the King and Vald stood at the top of the steps, with ten clergymen in full regalia. Himer smirked. The King was rather short and slightly built, all in all a physically small man. Once again dressed in that ridiculous formal uniform.

A dozen Royal Guardsmen stood at attention in a row just below the top of the broad steps. A different officer was in charge today.

It wouldn't do to lose his temper in public. Calm, stay calm, no matter what. He strode up the steps, followed closely by Hans.

The Commander of the Royal Guard didn't move.

Himer had the choice of running into him or stopping. He halted one step down from the man.

"Get out of my way. I will see Prime Minister Stauning," he said in German.

The officer looked at him blankly. "I don't understand German," he said in Danish. "Who are you, and what do you want?"

Of all the gall! They wouldn't … couldn't … How dare they show him such insolence? What could they hope to gain by this charade.

Himer badly wanted to shoot this stupid, obnoxious, incompetent, roadblock of an officer. But the cameras, they were everywhere. No. He'd have to wait to kill this fool.

"I am General Kurt Himer, Chief of Staff for the German Army," he said in Danish. "I am here to see Prime Minister Stauning."

"Prime Minister Stauning is expecting you," the officer stepped aside.

What the hell is going on? Why is Stauning out here in public?

He walked the few additional steps until he was one step from the top, just below Vald and King Christian. Neither of them spoke.

A pain shot through his left wrist and he realized his hands were clasped rigidly together as if he were strangling something. He took a deep breath and unclasped his hands.

"Prime Minister, you disappoint me," Himer said. "I had thought you a man of your word … I thought we had an agreement yesterday."

Vald, cleared his throat. "We had no agreement. You shot my aide in the back, made a little speech, thrust some papers at me, and left. I agreed to nothing … in fact, I made no response at all to your demands."

Himer stared at Vald as if seeing him for the first time. The fool needed a good barber and a tailor. His full beard was actually blowing in the wind and his suit was rumpled. Apparently he needed another lesson. But it couldn't be administered now in front of all these cameras.

"Your news media disobeyed direct orders and are being shut down," Himer said. "The printing presses and radio transmitters will be confiscated and the managers punished. Your orders remain the same. You will follow them or I will remove you from office."

"General Himer," King Christian said. "You have no authority to remove our Prime Minister."

"I can arrest him. I can have him shot for treason."

"No, General," King Christian said. "You might shoot Prime Minister Stauning, but you will not be able to make a charge of treason stick. He is not subject to your authority but to that of the Danish parliament."

"Do not play word games with me, old man. I am in charge here, and Prime Minister Stauning has his orders." He looked at Vald, "Is that clear?"

Vald said nothing.

"Prime Minister Stauning. Are your orders clear?"

"Yes," Vald said.

"Will you carry out those orders?"

Vald cleared his throat, started to speak, then cleared his throat again. "I am forbidden to do so. No."

Himer turned to his aide.

"Detail a squad to Prime Minister Stauning. Keep a minimum of two men in his presence at all times. They go with him to the toilet, watch him when he bathes, sit next to his bed when he sleeps … all the time! If he makes love to his wife, they are to be there. They will be with him twenty-four hours a day, seven days a week."

Himer waited until a squad rushed up and positioned itself behind Vald.

General Himer beckoned another squad leader and whispered something to the man. The officer saluted and said, "Yes sir."

A moment later Himer turned to leave. He walked into the back of the Royal Guard officer, knocking him forward and down several steps right into the waiting arms of the squad leader.

"Arrest him," Himer snarled. "For assaulting a German officer."

The squad leader and two of his men hustled the Guard officer into a waiting truck. Himer stalked back to his car. The driver gunned his engine, the stunned crowd parted and the German convoy with its captive drove quickly out of the square.

Himer almost laughed aloud. The Gestapo would teach the insolent dog of a Royal Guard officer to treat German Generals with more respect … before he died he'd regret his insults. The officer would die, in agony, that was for sure.

As for Vald and Christian, they could be as stubborn and suicidal as they wished. He would bypass them and deal directly with the factories, shipyards, and farms. The orders were easy to prepare; the liaison officer had already been assigned to each industrial group. They would go directly to the people who actually ran the factories.

Himer prayed that the Fuhrer would be too preoccupied with other matters to worry about Denmark for a week or so. If he could get large shipments of critical materiels moving right away, perhaps the Fuhrer would overlook his public relations disaster. He would start with agricultural products and raw materials. Stripping Denmark of its food and metals, he'd have it on trains to Germany within three days.

A half hour after returning to his office, Himer handed the relevant orders to Hans for transmittal. He asked for a report on the arrests of the newspaper and radio managers.

"We have arrested no one so far," Hans stammered.

"Why are you having trouble?" Himer asked softly.

"Herr General, none of the managers are in their offices. We're looking for them, but it's going slowly. So far we haven't found any of them."

"Hans," General Himer spoke even softer than before. Hans paled noticeably.

"Why is it going slowly? What is the difficulty in finding these men?"

"We haven't been able to find anyone's address. Their offices don't seem to have personnel records on file, and no one will admit to knowing the addresses."

Himer gritted his teeth. A good, efficient German office would always have the addresses for its employees. Danish offices might not be as efficient ... but this was not credible ... these damnable Danes were engaging in another conspiracy. He'd break their spirit ... and this time there would be no embarrassing pictures.

"Schedule a meeting tomorrow at 10:00 a.m. for the officers in charge of the media," Himer said. "We'll make examples out of a few of these newspapers. After lunch, I want reports on how the shipments of food and metals are shaping up. "

Before Hans could reply, a secretary knocked on the door and handed Hans a telegram. He glanced at it and wordlessly passed it to Himer.

From Ribbentropp. So soon. No chance to do anything, no chance at all. He ripped it open.

> General Kurt Himer,
> You are hereby relieved of command. Your replacement will arrive shortly. You will take no further actions of any kind other than those routine actions needed to maintain your troops.
>> Joachim von Ribbentrop, Foreign Minister

He read the telegram again, still not really believing it. How could these sniveling, cowardly Danes have done this to him?

What now? What will Hitler do to me?

Himer spent the next two hours preparing the orders to stop the crash program of securing food and metals and to put his army at marking time. When all else was finished, he summoned a senior Gestapo officer.

"You have an officer from Christian's Royal Guard in custody."

"Yes, Herr General, we do."

"The man insulted me and then assaulted me. I expect him to be questioned with the most extreme methods possible. You will make him talk and I expect you to be finished with him no later than forty-eight hours from now."

"Yes, sir. Are there specific questions we should ask him?"

"No, just general questions. Ensure there is no trace of him afterward."

"Very good, General, we shall be finished with him quickly."

"Not quickly. I want you to be very thorough. I am sure the questioning will take most of the forty-eight hours."

"Ah. Yes sir, I understand."

"Good. The Danes will make inquiries about their officer," Himer said. "In about a week, in response to their inquiries, tell them he was released after two days of questioning. Be a little vague about exactly where he was released."

The Gestapo officer saluted, did a snappy about face and left. Himer knew the Gestapo man and suspected he would personally carry out the torture.

General Himer had no other official duties that needed doing. After giving orders not to be disturbed, he drank almost a quart of whiskey before passing out on the floor.

Professor Hal Koch Journal, April 11, 1940

The world continues to underestimate Hitler. His charisma and paranoia make him dangerous enough, but his blitzkrieg of tanks and mobile armor is a big innovation in warfare ... so far it has run around or simply smashed every army that opposed it.

He warned us. His book, Mein Kampf, laid it all out ... the concept of the Aryan as the "superior race", the untermenschen as the inferior races, and the divine right of the "superior" German Aryans to use force in seizing as much land as they want for their lebensraum (living space). He even argues the insanity that the untermenschen actually benefit from being enslaved by the Aryans. He baldly states his desire to eliminate Jews and gypsies.

The other great powers, America, Russia, Japan and China seem quite content to sit back and allow us to butcher each other.

And now all of Europe is plunged into chaos, war and terror. Hitler's blitzkrieg smashed Czechoslovakia without working up a sweat and defeated Poland in 27 days! And now he snatches us and Norway with hardly any effort. We can only pray that Belgium, France and England will prevail in resisting the Nazis.

Chapter 6. Ten Commandments

The crowd in front of Amalienborg Castle dispersed as soon as General Himer left. By the time Arne and his parents arrived back home, Arne's elation at General Himer's humiliation had ebbed away. He couldn't see how nonviolence was going to achieve anything against the Nazis.

Arne's father had to go to work and went immediately to bathe. Arne helped his mother fix a big breakfast.

"Mom, I don't get it. How is this supposed to stop the Nazis?"

"Well, if no one will cooperate with them, the occupation will be very expensive, hopefully more expensive than it's worth."

"That doesn't make any sense. Hitler doesn't care about expense. Can't he just print more money?"

"It's not just money. Look at all the troops he has here. He's fighting several nations and now he has lots of troops tied up here. Look at all the equipment the army brought with them. It's expensive in lots of ways."

'I think we ought to be shooting back. This is not the way of Vikings."

Father rushed into the room. "Is there some food ready. I really have to run."

"Sit. Eat." Mother pointed at the plate of eggs and toast on the table waiting for them. Arne and Mother sat down as well and for a few minutes everyone was too busy eating to deal with questions about Denmark's war strategy. After breakfast, both adults had to rush off.

Arne Sejr, as a 17-year-old, had not been involved in any of the preparations to resist an invasion. His parents seemed to have lost their minds. The King's radio address that morning talked about being "a good Dane." A good Dane should have a rifle and be lying in wait for a Nazi patrol. But that wasn't going to happen. The adults had already decided "no rifles" and he would abide by that even if it made no sense.

Arne spent all morning thinking. Finally he typed Danskerens 10 Bud (Ten Commandments for Danes):

1. You must not go to work in Germany and Norway.
2. You shall do a bad job for the Germans.
3. You shall work slowly for the Germans.
4. You shall destroy important machines and tools.
5. You shall destroy everything which may be of benefit to the Germans.
6. You shall delay all transport.
7. You shall boycott German and Italian films and papers.
8. You must not shop at Nazi stores.
9. You shall treat traitors for what they are worth.
10. You shall protect anyone chased by the Germans.

Join the struggle for the freedom of Denmark.

Arne typed and re-typed until he had 25 copies of the Ten Commandments. He made a list of the most influential people in his suburb … the mayor, journalists, doctors, and business leaders. That night, dressed all in black, the reflectors on his bicycle covered, Arne rode out to deliver his missives. The German patrols didn't worry him.

Arne stopped first at the home of the mayor where he stuffed a copy of the ten commandments into the mailbox. As he left the mayor's, he wondered why the street sign was painted over. The next three intersections were the same … all the street signs obscured by fresh paint.

On the fourth block, two men stepped into the street in front of him. He swerved so quickly that the front wheel of his bicycle slid out from under him and he hit the pavement. He rolled to a stop right in front of the larger of the two men.

"Well, well. It's Arne Sejr," the man said as one massive hand pulled him to his feet. "What are you doing? Does your mother know you're out at 2:00 in the morning?"

Arne rubbed his sore elbow. It was a colleague of his father.

"Well, what are you doing?" Arne asked. "Why'd you step in front of me like that?"

"Ah, ah, Arne. We're on official business … we'll ask the questions. What are you doing?"

"You're painting the signs," Arne said. "The Nazis will be lost. You are, aren't you?" Without waiting for an answer, he pulled out his ten commandments and showed the men. "I'm delivering these … just came from the mayor's."

"Who wrote this?" the big man asked.

"I did."

The small man squinted at the paper for a moment and chuckled. The chuckle quickly swelled into a belly laugh, which he tried to keep quiet.

The big man looked at him gurgling and snorting and asked, "What's so blamed funny? I think these are great."

The little man finally subsided, "I've been worried … but when our teenagers … haven't even been part of the planning … and he comes up with this … the Nazis don't know what they've started."

The big man nodded. "Now listen," he said to Arne. "We're part of the lookouts for a team painting signs. There're teams like us all over town, all over the country for that matter. You're probably going to run into more of them. If you get stopped, tell them the Axe okayed you. If they know who the Axe is, show them the flyer. If they don't know who the Axe is, they're not part of our operation and you gotta play it by ear. Got that?"

"Sure."

The man grinned. "Be careful. There's a Nazi patrol out here somewhere … we saw them about a half hour ago."

"Okay. You too," Arne pedaled away.

* * * * * * * * *

The alarm clock sounded much too soon. Two consecutive nights of very little sleep had taken a toll. Arne figured he could always take a nap later … he just hoped his boss wouldn't be too upset at his missing two days in a row. At 6:00 a.m. he was on his bicycle and at seven he rode into the driveway of his fourth friend. The conversation with each of them was nearly identical.

"You need to come to my house," Arne told each of them. "Can you be there at 8:00 a.m.?"

If they protested, Arne simply repeated that they had to come. All four of them were Arne's teammates from the secondary school soccer team. Even though all of them had graduated the year before Arne, he had been the team captain for three years running and they were accustomed to following his lead. In the end, they all came. He showed them the ten commandments.

"I took copies of this to the mayor and 24 other key people last night. What do you think of it?"

"It's great," Soren said. "Where'd you get it?"

"I wrote it, dummy."

"Okay, okay, I didn't know."

"This is good," Rok said. "I like it."

"Okay, we need to type up and distribute more of these," Arne said.

"What happens if the Germans see us?" Ib asked.

"At night," Arne said. "We take them around at night."

"Oh great, that's supposed to keep us from getting caught?" Ib said.

"Look, it's no big deal," Arne said. "Wear black. Cover the bike reflectors. No problem."

"Man, you can count me out. I'm not getting shot." Ib shook his head.

"What?" Arne said. "You're too chicken to deliver a few fliers? I don't believe this."

"My mother would shoot me herself if I got involved with this," Frej spoke for the first time. "I'm going home."

"A guy got shot by the Nazis last night, two streets over from our house," Ib said. "It's dangerous."

Ib and Frej were both on their feet.

"Sorry, Arne, can't help," Ib said. He and Frej started for the door.

"Go on home to mommy," Arne shouted. "We don't need cowards to kick the Germans out."

The door closed behind Ib and Frej and the remaining three looked at each other.

"Those two are so chicken," Arne said. He noticed Rok and Soren exchanging glances.

"You guys aren't afraid, are you?" Arne asked.

"Naw," Rok said. "We need to be careful ... "

Arne and his two remaining friends typed up and distributed sixty-five copies of the Ten Commandments the following night. Arne got home at 3:44 a.m. and eased in the front door only to find his mother waiting for him.

"Where have you been?" her tone frightened him. Now his father was there too.

Arne showed them the flyer. Explained what they had done. For just a minute, a smile crossed Father's face and then it was stone again.

"Arne, you will not leave this house at all, not for any reason, until further notice," Her voice still had that icy quality that frightened Arne. "Is that clear?"

"Yes, Mum. Sorry, Mum."

"Go to bed," she said.

Arne went.

Chapter 7. The German Soldier

Gerhard was in the first group of German soldiers to storm ashore in Copenhagen and he was sure he was going to die. His draft notice forced him to leave a good job and a fiancé in Stuttgart. All he wanted was to return to his job, marry his fiancé and raise three or four kids. Was that too much too ask? Instead, here he was, invading Denmark. Totally exposed, one machine gun in the Citadel could get us all. Nobody shooting yet, dear God let them all be asleep. There, just ahead, Danish soldiers waiting for us. His rifle came up and his sights found a Danish soldier.

"Hold your fire," the sergeant yelled.

Gerhard complied but kept his sights aligned on the soldier. A German officer walked up to the Danish soldiers and, after a short exchange that Gerhard couldn't hear, came back with the Danish soldiers following.

"Sergeant, guard these men," the officer ordered Gerhard' sergeant.

Maybe he wouldn't die today after all.

* * * * * * * * *

By the next morning, Gerhard was euphoric. The Danes didn't resist. They were too cowardly to defend their country. One of his uncles and a friend had already been killed in Poland. Being away from his fiancé was bad, but he could survive a couple of years where the enemy was afraid to fight back.

Gerhard' euphoria turned to outrage when he saw the morning newspaper. German officers don't murder people. The Danes are lying and should be punished. These pictures … they really make the General look guilty.

That afternoon, the rumor reached Gerhard that Himer was being replaced. He asked Jacob, the career soldier about it.

Jacob didn't give him a straight answer, he just said, "Pictures don't lie, my boy."

"Do you really believe General Himer shot him in the back? While he was kneeling on the floor? That's cowardly."

"Himer is a general. That doesn't make him a saint or even a good man or an honorable German. It just means he managed to work the politics well enough to keep getting promoted."

"What are you saying?"

"My young friend … do you think all officers are exemplary Germans? Do you think only good men get promoted?"

"Well, yeah. I think we have the best army and the best officers in the world."

"We probably do. Doesn't mean all of them are good people … or even competent officers. There are always some who get promoted because they're good at the politics instead of being good officers."

"That's not right, not the way it's supposed to work."

"You're right Gerhard, but that's the way it is … always has been and always will be."

* * * * * * * * *

Gerhard's squad was on patrol the next day.

"You got no right to be here," the Dane was young and loud. "Take your filthy asses back home. Let us alone."

The sergeant's reply was too soft for Gerhard to hear, but several men in his squad lifted their rifles to their shoulders.

""Cowards! Bastards! Your mothers mated with hyenas."

Two policemen came out of a café right beside the sergeant.

"That's Willie. Get him." One of the policemen called loudly. He tackled the man from behind and in an instant had him in handcuffs.

The two policemen hustled their captive down the street and around a corner.

* * * * * * * *

The older policeman, the one who tackled the young man, suddenly stopped and shoved their captive up against the wall.

"What was that all about? You got a death wish, shouting insults at the Germans?"

"Let me alone. I can't stand the cocky bastards. They come in here and think they're Gods! I had to tell them … had to show them we're not afraid."

"Yeah, well none of us are too happy with the Germans, but what good do you think it will do to get yourself killed? You know they will kill you?"

The young man looked at his feet. "Okay, you're right. I lost it … it was stupid."

"Look, get active with the resistance. We have plenty of ways of making life miserable for them, but be smart about it."

"How do I get with the resistance … I don't know nothing about it."

"That should be easy. Start with the newspapers. They're running the basic guidelines every couple of days. Listen to Moellar's broadcasts. Talk to your friends. If that's not enough, talk to a policeman."

"Okay, okay. Thanks for rescuing me."

"You alright now? If I take the cuffs off, you're going to be smart? Not going to get yourself killed?"

"Naw, I'm over it. I'm going to do what you said. And thanks."

The younger policeman spoke for the first time since they cuffed the young man.

"That was some fast thinking. I was still trying to figure out what was happening and you had already yelled about him being wanted and tackled him. That was something."

"Ah, I understood right away because I almost screamed at the Germans myself earlier today. I didn't have to think about it, I just reacted."

"I wonder how long we can play our double game," the young policeman said.

"We'll play it as long as we can," the older man said. "Then we'll move on to plan B."

Chapter 8. Meet the Resistance

Arne Sejr's parents weren't sure what to do with their adventurous and headstrong son but they wanted somebody to keep an eye on him. After some discussion, Arne's mother called her old university mentor, Professor Hal Koch, the famous theology professor at the Kobenhavns Universitet. Professor Koch suggested that Arne come and work with him.

Arne was no stranger to the university area, his home was only an hour's bicycle ride away, but this was his first time to live there. Professor Koch arranged a place for him to stay and a part-time job as a research assistant. It was unusual for a freshman to be a research assistant but not totally unheard of ... and the university allowed eminent Professor Hal Koch to do pretty much as he wished. The job was fake anyway; Arne's real duties were to help with the resistance.

Arne's duties hadn't started yet, and he had the afternoon free. He was strolling around the campus, mainly watching the pretty girls. He bought a snack and sat on the steps of the student union, looking out over the grassy commons, idly watching as students and the occasional professor passed up and down the sidewalk.

A tall blonde came out of the library, walking toward Arne. Her windblown hair stuck up at odd angles with one stray lock hanging in front of her face. She had a large generous mouth, high cheekbones, deep blue eyes, was wearing no lipstick or makeup ... and was absolutely gorgeous. Arne thought this had to be Freya, the Norse goddess of love. The girl noticed him staring. Freya-Goddess stopped, head cocked to one side, she blew out of the corner of her mouth at the wayward lock of hair.

"Do I know you?"

"No, 'fraid not." Arne, blushing, shook his head.

She shrugged and continued. Arne had never seen anything to compare with her ... he could have watched her forever. Then, as if she felt his eyes, thirty feet away, she turned and met his eyes again. She waved, turned onto a side path and was gone.

Sitting there in the afternoon sun, Arne fantasized about Freya-Goddess. What would it be like to kiss her or run his hands over her body?

Arne was roused by the increasing chill in the air. The sun was low in the sky and he sat in shadow. He glanced at his watch. Just in time to get to the meeting with Professor Koch.

The first one there, Arne took a seat at the long table just before Professor Koch came out of his inner office and three other young people came in. Arne nodded to the newcomers, they mumbled "hello," and sat down.

"We're expecting four more, we'll wait a minute more," Koch said. He went back into his inner office.

The other three seemed to know each other and chatted among themselves. A few minutes later, the outer door opened and a couple walked in followed by Freya-Goddess, hair still awry, one hank of hair hanging over her face.

The young couple immediately sat down. Freya-Goddess studied the room a minute and recognized Arne.

"Hello again." Arne said.

She blew at the lock of hair without any noticeable effect. "I think I do know you ... from somewhere."

"No. I'd remember if we'd met."

She shrugged and sat down across the table from him.

Professor Koch entered and went to the head of the table. He peered at them over the top of his reading glasses, then laid the glasses on the bookcase.

"I need to explain why you were invited to this meeting. Each of you has demonstrated a commitment to resist the Nazis. Each of you has been recommended to me by people that I trust."

"If you agree, you will become a team within the resistance. Before any of you say anything, I need to explain the procedure for making that decision. I will provide a thumbnail sketch of each of you, without identifying anyone. In that way you can see what each of you have already been doing. If you decide to become a team, you will learn each other's identities. However, if some or all of you want out, you can leave and no one will know who you are.

Koch paused and looked at each of them. "Any Questions?"

No one had any.

Koch looked around for his glasses and couldn't find them. A short, slightly plump girl pointed and said, "On the bookcase."

Koch retrieved his glasses and plunged into their histories.

When Koch finished, the big young man on Arne's right cleared his throat and said, "Very impressive group ... I'm ready to join."

This elicited a chorus of "Me too," "I'm ready," and "Yes".

Koch, looking right at Arne said, "And what about you my young friend? You haven't said anything." Once again he set his glasses on the bookcase.

"What exactly will we be doing?" Arne said.

"Oh, very good. Your duties will be quite varied, ranging from distributing newspapers to publicizing folk festivals, to demonstrations ... we may do a whole range of things depending upon what the Germans do. I won't know the particulars very much ahead of time."

"How will we operate?" Arne asked. "Who will we report to?"

"I will supervise you and provide your orders. I get my orders, ultimately, from the Freedom Council. While I will provide you with your missions, you will frequently need to improvise to carry out the assignments."

"I assume that means you will give us a general assignment or an objective and that we will then have to figure out the operational details?" Arne said.

"Precisely. Very good."

"Are all of us students here at the university? Is that our cover?" Arne asked.

"Yes. Two of you also work for me. The rest are in my classes, so all of you have good reasons to see me frequently. Any other questions?"

The big man leaned forward. "Why are we restricted to nonviolence?"

"Hmm. Here's the short answer. We, as a nation, decided that would be the best strategy. Your duty as a citizen is to help implement that strategy."

"I don't get it," the big man persisted. "How will nonviolence ever stop an army?"

"Hitler has all the guns," Koch said. He looked around for his glasses and again the short, plump girl pointed at the bookcase. Koch picked up the glasses, but instead of putting them on, he used them as a pointer for emphasis.

"Our strategy is based on the entire population resisting all forms of cooperation with the German occupying forces. I think you will discover that is a very powerful strategy. For details, you need to study the document I am about to give you. Other questions?" This time the reading glasses ended up on the table.

"Um. Just one," Arne said. "Who will be the team leader?"

Professor Koch laughed. "That depends ... I had thought I would ask you, but you haven't agreed to be part of the team?"

Arne shrugged. "Sorry. I definitely want in. I just had questions."

"Excellent. Now, everyone, this talkative young man is Arne Sejr of the Ten Commandments fame. I selected him as the team leader for a number of reasons, including commitment, daring and intelligence. In addition, his championship soccer team selected him as their captain in only his second year on the squad ... and kept him as captain for three years. Unprecedented." Koch picked up a pad of paper and a pen and once more searched for his glasses, this time finding them quickly.

Professor Koch had each of them introduce themselves and Arne learned that Freya-Goddess was named Brigitte Clausdatter. The name fit her perfectly. The big handsome man was Asger and Arne realized that he was a star, a very popular soccer player for the university.

The meeting ended with a study assignment. Koch gave each of them a fifty-four-page overview of Operation Total Resistance and told them to study it carefully. They would meet again tomorrow and he expected them to be thoroughly familiar with the document. Their resistance work would start as soon as they finished their orientation.

Chapter 9. SS General Dr. Werner Best

General Best secured his position as a general in Hitler's elite SS, not with his skills as a warrior, but rather as an astute politician. He prided himself on his understanding of people and, better than most, he understood the neuroses and demons driving Hitler and his inner circle ... and the political realities that propelled them to the unchallenged leadership of the German nation.

As Hitler's newly appointed Plenipotentiary for Denmark, General Best was determined that Denmark's resources would rapidly flow to Germany. Hitler personally instructed him to rule with an iron hand. It should be easy.

Himer was a puzzle, though. He had always been politically sophisticated ... how did he get himself into such a nightmare?

The whole situation seemed strange. The Norwegians were still resisting, although their army had been crushed. Why were the Danes being so passive? Nothing added up. Well, he would move cautiously until he had the whole picture.

Immediately upon arriving at his Copenhagen headquarters, Best summoned General Himer. Himer arrived impeccably dressed but with a faint stink of old whiskey. Best had a momentary feeling of sympathy which he quickly suppressed ... Himer had done himself in and he was not about to jeopardize his own career for the poor fool.

Best spent an hour questioning Himer but the answers didn't make much sense. Somehow the Danes had managed to make a normally sensible and clear-headed general lose control and disgrace himself.

Best moved on from Himer to the aide and the officers who had accompanied Himer to the palace. By noon Best felt he had a pretty good understanding of what had happened and was developing a grudging admiration for the Danish leadership. That admiration would in no way keep him from crushing them. He was not a man of principle except insofar as his own ambition was concerned.

The Danish strategy made no sense. They apparently intended to resist the occupation, even though they did not initially fight back. Well, that meant guerilla war. Fortunately he had been involved with crushing the Polish resistance. He knew how to deal with resistance fighters. They would be no more than a minor nuisance. Public display of their dead bodies was a useful tactic in keeping the general population docile and productive.

Best took a leisurely lunch by himself. When and where would the resistance strike? He was not overly worried about his personal safety, and he had lots of troops for guarding the major factories.

After lunch, Best dictated a short letter to Foreign Minister Joachim von Ribbentrop saying that the newspaper stories on Himer were accurate and that he found no extenuating circumstances to account for Himer's bad behavior. He then ordered Himer back to Germany and the tender mercies of von Ribbentrop. Only then did he turn his attention to the Danes.

Best's letter to Prime Minister Stauning was short and to the point.

> I will receive you in my office at 8:30 a.m. tomorrow. My
> aide will be at your office at 8:00 a.m. to escort you here.
> SS General Dr. Werner Best, Plenipotentiary.

"Sir, Fritz Clausen wants to see you," his aide said. "He's head of the Danish Nazi Party and he's been here every day, wanting to see someone."

Hmm. The man might be useful. "Show him in."

Fritz took two steps into the office, clicked his heels together and gave the Nazi salute. "Heil Hitler."

"Heil Hitler. I'm glad to meet you, party leader Clausen. Please, have a seat."

"Thank you, General Dr. Best. I'm anxious to offer my services and those of the Danish National Socialist Workers' Party."

"Thank you, Mr. Clausen. Your knowledge of the local situation will be most helpful."

"We will do whatever we can. However, most Danes are total fools when it comes to politics. Hardly any of them appreciate the genius of the Fuhrer. They keep prattling about individual rights and religious tolerance and equality for all. 'Religious tolerance' means nothing more than Jew-loving. Makes me sick. We get nothing but insults from most Danes, no respect at all. That should change now … "

Clausen continued for several more minutes but Best had already heard enough to form an opinion of the Danish Nazi.

Best thought, the man is filled with self-pity. He's as incompetent as the briefing papers suggested. Too stupid to realize the Danes aren't going to respect anyone whose allegiance is to a foreign ruler. Well, I can hand him off to the Gestapo and maybe they'll get some useful information out of him.

Best ended the interview after a few more pleasantries and assurances to Clausen that his help was definitely needed.

An hour later Best got a note from Prime Minister Stauning.

You and your army are in Denmark illegally, in violation of the non-aggression pact signed by your government. I therefore have no reason to meet with you unless it is to discuss the logistics of your withdrawal from Denmark.

Thorvald Stauning, Prime Minister.

* * * * * * * *

General Best thought the Prime Minister and King could be safely ignored for a bit. Getting food and materiel flowing to Germany is critical. Himer did a good job of organizing this effort. Just give the order and the entire operation begins.

Colonel Lochner arrived with a preliminary report on the media.

"Colonel, are the media secured?"

"No, sir, we're having some trouble, sir."

"What kind of trouble?"

"Several kinds, sir. There are no street signs, no street numbers. The newspapers have taken down their own signs. It took us a long time to find the newspapers. We found the radio stations by looking for their towers."

"Okay. So you've arrested the managers?

"No, sir," Lochner was sweating. "We haven't been able to arrest any of the managers."

"What? Why?"

"We can't find them, sir. None of them are at their offices. None of the offices have their addresses ... no personnel records, not anywhere. No one will admit to knowing where they live."

Best leaned back, elbows on the armrests, flexing the ivory swagger stick. Apparently the Danes anticipated the attempt to arrest the managers.

"Well Colonel," Best said softly. "You have quite a list of failures ... what have you accomplished today?"

"Yes, sir, we installed censors with the national radio station and most of the newspapers, sir. The process is continuing, sir. By tomorrow morning we will have censors with the rest."

"Someone must suffer for the reporting they did on General Himer. You will arrest the highest-ranking manager or official at each of these establishments. Report again tomorrow."

"Yes, sir," Lochner's salute was very sharp, the relief plain in his face.

Hmmm. Lochner practically ran out of here. He's not giving me the full story.

* * * * * * * * *

Colonel Lochner was worried about his career. Who the hell am I supposed to arrest? Most of the newspapers are all but deserted. Several of them look as if all the heavy equipment was removed in the last day or so. The streets and restaurants are full of papers nobody ever heard of before … Free Danish Press and The Resistance were the worst of them.

Well, by God, somebody will be arrested. Best isn't going to know a newspaper editor from a business man or a lawyer.

Chapter 10. The Checkpoint

A large radio provided a primary form of evening entertainment for most Danish families. Christian Moellar's broadcasts for the resistance had an audience consisting of upwards of ninety percent of Danish adults. Many German soldiers also tuned in.

The Nazis outlawed all radios and the large family radios were hidden away. The underground press printed instructions for tiny radios tuned to Moellar's frequency, radios that anyone could build at home. Within a few days, almost all Danes had such a radio.

Arne chalked another "V" on the wall, about his tenth for the last fifteen minutes, just before he and Morten came around the corner onto the main street and saw the checkpoint at the end of the block.

"Damn, damn, damn," Arne said. "Where are the cops? No damn warning at all."

Nobody between us and the damn checkpoint, no one to hand off the camera. If we turn and go back, they'll probably chase us. It's the SS, they might shoot Morten.

"You got to drop the camera," Arne said. "Maybe they won't notice."

"They're looking right at me. They'll see it."

A hundred feet, a lousy hundred feet to the SS checkpoint. Wait, there!

"Move over so that trash can blocks their view. Drop the camera there."

Morten was already angling over to the edge of the sidewalk. He lowered the camera on its tether until it gently touched the ground, let go of it, and kept walking, all without bending over.

"Good, good," Arne whispered. "They didn't notice."

"Yes. Have you ditched the chalk?"

"Crap, no," Arne said. "Forgot all about it. It's in my pocket. They probably won't search us."

We're there. Nothing to worry about … look nonchalant.

"Papers," The checkpoint soldiers barked.

They handed over their IDs.

One soldier studied the papers. The others studied Arne and Morten.

Arne willed his hands to be still and smiled at Morten. Just two innocent college students, we wouldn't dream of doing anything to resist the Germans. We never even heard of the resistance.

At last the soldier gave them their IDs and waved them on.

Arne resisted the urge to look back until they were at the end of the next block.

"They must have just set up that checkpoint," Morten said.

"We've got some free time," Arne said. "Let's wait down here so we can warn people. Maybe the cops will arrive before we have to leave. In the meantime, we can get someone to retrieve your camera."

Chapter 11. Food for the Fatherland

General Best saw no reason to change his predecessor's assignment of Colonel Klauer to purchasing foodstuffs for Germany. When Best met with Klauer on April 17, he already had a list of the major food wholesalers throughout the country and had, despite the lack of street signs and street numbers, located all of the ones in Copenhagen.

"I want at least fifty boxcars of food on the way to Germany within one week," Best ordered.

"Yes, sir," Klauer said. "It will be done."

Klauer dispatched his agents immediately.

Several hours later, eight of Colonel Klauer's agents returned, empty-handed. Each man reported the same thing … the wholesalers claimed to be out of stock.

"Tomorrow, early," Klauer said. "Take a squad of soldiers with you and go to the same wholesalers. Inspect the premises. If their warehouses are not on the premises, find them. Requisition all foodstuffs. If they claim the food is sold, tell them to refund the money, we take precedence. Don't take no for an answer and don't believe anything they tell you. Is that clear?

"One more thing," Klauer continued. "Take the manager aside. Tell him any foul-ups, if for any reason he doesn't deliver the food on time, we will shoot him. Make sure he is crapping his trousers before you leave."

* * * * * * * * * *

Lars Lagerberg, owner and manager of Fodevarer Vekselerer, Copenhagen's largest food wholesaler, was a very busy man after

Lieutenant Gryneus tried to buy food from him. The warehouse was bursting with meats, vegetables, flour, and canned goods.

Lars put every employee to work getting rid of the food. Took them all day and most of the night. Everything safely hidden away by 5:40 a.m. A little too close for comfort, but we made it.

Breakfast for the entire staff was costly, but the guys earned it. Glad I had time for a shower and a shave. It's 7:30 a.m. already, hope this paperwork is convincing. Nothing to do but wait, they'll probably be here soon.

Lars went for another cup of coffee and tried not to worry.

Lieutenant Gryneus and his squad of soldiers arrived at Fodevarer Vekselerer at 8:00 a.m. sharp and Gryneus and the squad's master sergeant shouldered their way into the manager's office. Lars was seated at his desk when they came in.

"Ah, Lieutenant Gryneus. What can I do for you today?"

"We will inspect your premises, just in case there might be some supplies that slipped your mind yesterday."

"I don't suppose I have any choice in this matter, do I Lieutenant?"

"No, you do not."

"I see. Well can you be about your business then? I have lots of work I have to do."

"We require someone to take us around and unlock doors … unless you prefer that we break them down?"

"Lieutenant, most of our doors are already unlocked. The only things that may be locked are a tool shed and that sort of thing. I'll send someone with you."

Gryneus went out and Lars imagination took over, anticipating the Nazis return. He's going to be furious. Will he even allow me to show him my paperwork? God, I hope he doesn't just shoot me. I need a drink. Nothing here … maybe coffee will help.

Lars drank a cup of coffee and then another and another, scalding his lip and tongue in the process. God, I'm sweating like crazy. Hands are trembling ...

When Greyneus slammed into his office, Lars put his hands in his lap so as to not reveal how badly they were shaking.

"Where is all the food? Why are all your storerooms empty? What did you do with the food?"

"Lieutenant, Lieutenant," he raised both hands, palms out in supplication. "I told you yesterday. We're a brokerage. We don't keep food on hand except in special situations. We don't buy unless we have a buyer … and then we almost always ship directly from our supplier to our buyer. Most of the food never comes through here. We don't have any food."

"Lagerberg, you're trying my patience. This place is set up as a warehouse. These warehouses had food in them. I can have you shot. I will shoot you unless you tell me where the food is. No more crap about being a brokerage."

Lars' managed to open his desk drawer and retrieve a file folder.

"Look, Lieutenant. This is a typical order for us. See. Here is our supplier and this, the customer. See here? These are the shipping arrangements ... the food goes straight from the supplier to our customer. We don't handle it at all ... we just broker the deals."

For the next few minutes, Lars pulled out folder after folder, all showing brokered deals. Gryneus studied them and Lars started to hope ... perhaps this Nazi wouldn't shoot him after all.

"Enough." Gryneus growled and shoved the folders away.

"All right. You have nothing on hand. I want a boxcar load of beef. How soon can you get it for me?"

"Oh, Lieutenant, that will be difficult. There's a shortage of meat. I don't know."

"You misbegotten jackass! What can you get for me?"

"Radishes ... radishes and turnips. Perhaps cabbage. Probably."

"Lagerberg, I'm coming back tomorrow ... and if you don't have at least one box car of some foodstuff," here Gryneus leaned in very close to Lars and spoke very softly. "I will personally blow your brains all over this office. Do you understand?"

Lars nodded mutely, unwilling to trust his voice to speak.

"Good. I'm glad we understand each other, Lars," Gryneus walked out without a backward glance.

Lars almost cried with relief. Not so brave, but I didn't crack. The bastard got no food from my company. Hands are shaking again.

Oh, Christ, not supposed to meet with them alone. It's done now, worked out okay.

Lars called his workers to a meeting. His speech to them was very short.

"Go home. Everybody. Don't come in tomorrow. Don't come back to work until you hear from me.

"The Nazis will be here tomorrow expecting to get a boxcar of food. They won't get anything and they'll be mad. Make sure no one is here."

He thought ... he prayed ... that the Nazis wouldn't be able to find him.

* * * * * * * *

Lieutenant Gryneus reported to Colonel Klauer that he was unable to get any food from Lagerberg's Fodevarer Vekselerer or from the other three other wholesalers on his list. Klauer's other agents reported essentially the same results. Three days of attempting to buy had so far netted less than one-third of a boxcar. Klauer saw no other option than to go directly to the farmers ... but that would take vastly more manpower than the ten buyers he had. He decided he had no choice but to report the bad news to General Dr. Best. He planned his report to General Best very carefully.

Colonel Klauer barely finished his salute before General Best started talking.

"Colonel, I have a note from Prime Minister Stauning ...our purchasing agents are apparently threatening the food wholesalers with being shot. The Prime Minister tells me that they have all gone home and won't return to work without assurances of their safety. Is there anything about this that you want to tell me? Colonel Klauer, how much food have you secured for the Fatherland?"

"General, sir, they wouldn't sell anything to us. I sent the agents with troops to search the warehouses and they were empty. We think they emptied them immediately after our first visit. We told them they had to find foodstuffs for us and that we would be back to verify the orders. When we returned, the places were all deserted."

"Did your agents threaten to shoot them?"

"When they stonewalled us, yes sir, at least some of the agents threatened them."

"I see. And how much food have you purchased?"

Klauer's vocal cords didn't seem to want to work. "Sir, one third box car, sir."

"Do you have a suggested course of action, Colonel Klauer?" Best's voice was very quiet.

"Given that none of the wholesalers will deal with us, I see only one option. We have to go directly to the farmers."

"What makes you think the farmers will be any more helpful than the wholesalers?"

"That's easy, sir. With a farmer, you can see what he has and he can't lie to you. He has so many head of cattle and so many acres planted in wheat and so on and anyone with a little farming experience can inventory it immediately. We can go to a farm, look around, and tell him what he has to deliver to us. A farmer won't walk away from his land. So we've got the farmer, sir."

"Okay. You have done badly so far, but I'm giving you another chance. I'll give you the orders to get men with farm backgrounds from the troops. Fifty enough? No? Seventy-five is all you get. Keep me posted, I want that food shipped. Soon. Dismissed."

Chapter 12. The Odense Steel Shipyard

Colonel Warner came straight to the point. "How long," he said. "Would it take to begin building submarines?"

"I don't think you understand," Per Nielsen, superintendent of the shipyard said. "We're not set up to build submarines. It would be highly inefficient."

Per rather admired Hitler and the Nazi emphasis on efficiency. Per thought it'll be okay if this guy has some technical background. He'll see that our strength is in building surface ships, not subs.

"Submarines are what we need. You will build submarines."

"Submarines require processes and machinery that we don't even have. It won't work."

Per had a sinking feeling that maybe this officer didn't understand engineering. Engineering issues were easy. Nineteen years. It took only nineteen years to rise through the ranks from laborer to superintendent. Quite a few of those years involved full-time work and full-time university programs at the same time. Nobody, but nobody understands this shipyard the way I do. Now this idiot officer tells me to make submarines?

It was the people issues that cause trouble. Always the people. This guy doesn't understand.

"You will get the machinery," Warner said. "You will train your people on the new processes. Our engineers are familiar with all of it. I will detail the necessary staff to assist you."

Per's mind suddenly went off on an entirely different track. Superintendent for almost three years now. Technically unchallenged and unrivalled, yet the workforce was increasingly restive. Every time he tried to increase efficiency, the workers, especially the machinists and welders, sabotaged the new initiatives. It was incomprehensible, yet the workers always won. The new, more efficient initiatives always failed. And this Nazi blithely talks about changing over to make submarines!

"The workers won't do it," Per said. "The workers resist all attempts to change the work processes."

"You will convince them," Warner said. "They have no choice."

No choice? That's going to go over well with the machinists.

"The workers are going to say they are forbidden to cooperate." Per said. "Government policy."

Colonel Warner just smiled, but something about that smile frightened Per.

"Personally, I don't mind," Per said. "But the workers will sabotage it."

"Per," Colonel Warner was still smiling but his eyes frightened Per. "Quit stalling. Your job is to ensure that the workers cooperate. Can you do that, Per?"

"I don't know," Per blurted. "I'm the best engineer there is, but I'm not good with people. The workers won't follow me on this. It won't work."

"Well, then, Per," Warner said. "I don't need you, do I?"

"I know this shipyard better than anybody. You need me to run the shipyard."

Colonel Warner lost his ghastly smile and seemed lost in thought. After a time he opened the door and looked up and down the hallway.

"Per, you have become a problem," he said. "I need the shipyard to build submarines. You tell me you can't do that. You say you can't get the workers to assist Germany, that they will refuse. Perhaps you can serve as an example to the others. Perhaps then they will be more reasonable."

Warner pulled his pistol and Per had time to become very frightened before a sledgehammer hit him in the forehead.

* * * * * * * * *

Warner's aide rushed into the room.

"Bring four of the troops. Carry the body to the nearest shop and drop him in the middle of the floor where everyone can see him."

Warner followed the troops carrying Per's body until they dropped it in the middle of a machine shop. He had to walk carefully to avoid stepping in blood pouring from the back of Per's head.

Warner stood there, waiting.

The shop grew quiet as the men noticed the body and turned off their machines.

"Your superintendent attacked me," Warner said. "I killed him in self-defense. Violence against our troops will not be tolerated. IS THAT CLEAR?"

Silence. More silence. No reaction whatsoever from anyone. Warner's skin began to crawl. Their boss dead on the floor, the smell of his feces thick in the air, and everyone just stood there.

"Where is the deputy superintendent?"

More silence.

"WHO IS THE DEPUTY SUPERINTENDENT?" Warner screamed at the nearest machinist.

The worker, a burly, middle aged man with thinning blonde hair and a pot gut, backed up. He seemed frightened but also at a loss.

"Nie sprech Deutsch," he said in fractured German.

Warner glared at everyone.

"Sprechen sie Deutsch?" he pointed at a man.

"Nien. Nein, no Deutsch."

Everyone Warner looked at blurted out variations of "Nein, no Deutsch." Warner didn't believe it. Denmark had a large border with Germany, most Danes spoke fluent German.

The room was hot and dusty and smelled of oil and burned metal and overwhelmingly of the dead man's voided bowels. Half a dozen flies had already found the corpse. He'd be full of maggots soon.

The men were frightened, standing in awkward poses, afraid to draw attention to themselves by moving. Good. They need to be afraid.

I wonder if these mulish Danes need a further lesson? Perhaps they would suddenly remember how to speak German.

No, let them have their little charade. Much good it will do them.

"I will be here at 8:00 a.m. tomorrow morning," he said. "I will meet with the deputy superintendent. Make sure he knows I'm coming."

Warner took another minute to look around the room, meeting hostile gazes with an icy stare of his own. The deputy superintendent would get the message.

He stalked out.

* * * * * * * * *

General Best was uneasy over Colonel Warner's report, but decided to let it go and see how things went at the shipyard tomorrow. In the meantime, Colonel Warner's counterparts were reporting on their initial contacts with other key Danish industries and mines. All were reporting stubborn refusal to acknowledge the legitimacy of the German occupying force and the use of delaying tactics.

The situation was decidedly strange. What could the Danes hope to accomplish by their obstructionist tactics? A few days delay at most, nothing more than a minor irritation.

Where was the real resistance, the bombs and attacks, the guerilla warfare? Perhaps these delaying tactics were a diversion. Perhaps the Danes want us focused on the wrong things. Perhaps this is a prelude to a series of attacks on our forces?

General Best drafted a memo to General Hanneken telling him to expect major guerilla attacks in the near future. The memo suggested that the targets of the attacks would likely include both German troops and key elements of the Danish industry and transportation infrastructure.

General Best was not seriously worried about the anticipated attacks. He knew how to deal with resistance fighters. For every German soldier killed by the resistance, kill five or ten Danes. It doesn't take long for the citizens to get the message. But why has the resistance so far been totally quiet … what are they up to?

* * * * * * * * * *

Colonel Warner was rather looking forward to his meeting with the deputy superintendent of the shipyard. After the little lesson with Per, the deputy should cooperate nicely.

The damned newspaper flat out called me a murderer. Thank God there were no pictures. The generals need to get the media under control ... how in hell are they managing to print this stuff?

Well, all will be forgiven when the shipyard is churning out subs.

Warner's reverie was interrupted by the realization that his little convoy of a truck and a staff car was turning around.

"Why are we turning around?" he asked.

"The streets are confusing with no signs," the driver said. "This is the wrong way."

Damn the Danes for painting over the signs. We should shoot a bunch of 'em on general principles.

They backtracked and hunted for fifteen minutes before finding the shipyard.

Funny, the front gates were closed.

His driver got out and discovered the gates were locked.

More games from the Danes. "Break the locks," he ordered.

Several minutes later the driver came back and reported.

"We don't have proper tools, sir."

"Shoot the damn thing."

A soldier fired at the padlock from a distance of five feet. The ricochet of the bullet was a high angry wine and Warner involuntarily ducked. The padlock was unscathed but the steel pipe just below it had a large dent. Of course. The rifle is sighted in for a hundred yards and at five feet will be shooting low.

The soldier tried again. This time the padlock broke.

"Arrest the first man we see," Warner said.

Warner motioned his driver forward. These bastards will learn not to screw with me.

The staff car rolled into the shipyard and drove the quarter mile to the headquarters building.

Where the hell is everyone? Place seems deserted.

The door to the headquarters building was also locked. No one was in the building. The bastards all stayed home.

What to do? Go to personnel and get names and addresses. He would force them to come back to work.

The personnel office was easy to find. A half hour of searching found nothing helpful. Another hour of searching convinced him there was nothing to be found.

This was incredible. How could a shipyard with several thousand workers have no records of its employees? Damn! The shipyard was prepared. They destroyed … or more likely, removed the employee records.

General Best was not going to be happy. The German High Command wanted submarines and they wanted them right away. How the hell do I report this to Best?

Chapter 13. Radio, Telephone, & Mail

"Did you catch Moellar's broadcast last evening?" Brigitte asked.

"He was really inspirational," Greta said. "Outdid himself on that one. I think the entire country listens to him … keeps the resistance on track."

"The Nazis are trying to jam his broadcasts, but mostly he gets through." Brigitte said. 'I guess we better study this manual Prof gave us."

Both girls were quiet for several minutes while they looked through the manual.

"This looks like fun," Greta said.

"Which part," Brigitte said.

"There's a section on how to keep the SS busy with fake phone emergencies," Greta said. "Look. Report a riot. Report a sighting of a British warship. British paratroopers landing at the municipal water reservoir. This is great."

"Show me the page."

The girls read for several minutes, breaking the silence only with occasional exclamations.

"Oh! Report a broken down German army truck."

"An anti-German sign."

"A big demonstration."

"Hey," Brigitte said. "The next section's on tying up the German communications. You call up one of the German offices and just engage them in any sort of conversation, just to keep the line tied up."

"Why wouldn't they just hang up."

"This says that the line stays tied up until the party that originated the call hangs up. Or until one of the intermediate switchboard operators disconnects the call."

"Can't they trace the call and come get you for that?" Greta asked.

"Well, yes, but the trace has to work back through all the manual switchboards, so it takes quite a while and is labor intensive. You want to make it seem that you really have something legitimate to talk about."

"Oh," Greta said. "You could call to get details about the regulations they promulgate. If you were a little dense, it might take quite a while."

"Exactly," Brigitte giggled. "The manual's full of other suggestions, too."

The girls studied the manuals while the train left Copenhagen behind and approached Gilleleje, their northernmost contact point. On the trip back they would stop at each of the intervening villages.

"What do you think of our team mates?" Greta asked.

"I'm real glad you're one of them!"

"Well, thank you. Me too … I mean I like you too."

"I had three older brothers but never had a sister. You're like the sister I always wanted." Brigitte gave Greta's hand a little hug and smiled at her, a smile that Greta returned.

"It does seem we can talk about everything. So, c'mon. What do you think about the others?"

"Asger spends most of his time flirting," Brigitte said. "He's sort of a pain, not a very serious person. Tyge is very quiet and seems sort of sad. Morten is a big puppy, all enthusiasm and ready to follow wherever the rest of us go. Arne is intense, all business."

"Arne is real cute," Greta sounded wistful.

Brigitte didn't respond right away. "Arne doesn't seem to notice girls at all … very focused."

"No," Greta said. "Arne notices. He looks at you all the time."

"At me?" Brigitte was dubious.

"He just tries to do it when you're not looking, but I see him."

"He never tries to talk to me," Brigitte said. "Wish he would, maybe it'd keep Asger away."

'I don't know about that," Greta said. "He likes to look. He's really smart, but he doesn't like it when people disagree with him, he thinks he has all the answers."

"Well, he usually does," Brigitte said. "He's usually right."

"Brigitte, why did you join up?"

"Humph. That's easy … I was pissed at the Germans and wanted to fight them.

Also, I wanted to feel good about myself. I needed to feel I was doing something worthwhile."

"You needed to feel good about yourself? You don't normally feel good about yourself?"

"Well, sometimes … I don't think I'm a very good person." Brigitte blew absent-mindedly at the hair that had fallen over her right eye.

"Why not?" Greta asked. "You're doing great for the resistance."

"The resistance makes me feel good."

"So how come you don't think you're a good person?"

Brigitte turned to the window, remembering her father. *He ignored me the whole last year of his life, never really forgave me.*

"C'mon," Greta said. "If we're going to be honorary sisters, we have to tell each other stuff."

"Honorary sisters, huh? Okay." Brigitte glanced out the window again, stuffing the hurt down.

"When I was thirteen my uncle, my father's favorite brother, came into my room and tried to have sex with me. Father came in before he could really do anything, but he saw Uncle with his pants down and on top of me … I was just waking up … trying to figure out what was going on. But Father never got over it, he never seemed to like me after that."

Greta waited as Brigitte relived her nightmare.

"I don't know what I did to cause Uncle to do that … I just don't understand. It was never the same, never right after that." Brigitte scrubbed at eyes that suddenly were full of tears.

"So … I'm really not a good person … but I think I can be a good resistance worker."

"You didn't do anything!" Greta was indignant. "Your uncle tried to rape you. It's not your fault."

Brigitte shook her head. "You don't understand, Uncle was a gentle man, my Father's favorite brother. I must have encouraged him somehow. Father never forgave me."

Brigitte turned back to the window. A moment later Greta squeezed her hand and then just held it. *At least Greta likes me.*

A few minutes later both girls went back to studying the manual.

"Hey," Brigitte said. "Codes to keep the Germans busy. Neat."

"What do we need codes for?" Greta asked.

"It's just to overwhelm the Germans with useless work. Here, look at this suggestion."

Greta skimmed the indicated paragraph and laughed.

"Nice. Make up some code and send a perfectly innocuous letter to a non-existent person. The Germans will work at it until they solve the code … and then won't have anything."

Brigitte was reading ahead and replied. "This says that if we are clever, they might even think the innocuous message itself is a code and keep trying to break it."

"Wouldn't they catch on?" Greta asked. "After a while they would surely realize we were fooling them."

"This says it doesn't matter. They'll feel compelled to solve the codes to make sure that none of them are serious."

"Oh, I like this," Greta said. "With very little effort, we can invent coded messages, but solving them takes lots of time. So this ties them up and doesn't cost us much at all."

"Of course," Brigitte said. "This only works if they take over the postal system and start monitoring our letters."

"Hah," Greta snorted. "In the meantime we could make sure Clausen and his fellow stikkers 'find' a bunch of coded messages."

Chapter 14. The Shipyard Strikes

Prime Minister Thorvald Stauning sent a note to General Dr. Werner Best.

> Colonel Warner of the German army murdered, in cold blood and without provocation, Mr. Per Nielson, superintendent of the Odense Steel Shipyard. We intend to put Colonel Warner on trial for murder. We require that you surrender him to our police.

The note would enrage General Best and he wouldn't consider handing over the murderer. No matter … the note was part of their negotiating strategy.

Vald wished that he were a braver person. He was terrified all the time since the Nazis' arrival. He got up and looked at himself in the mirror in his private bath … his beard was as long as ever, but it seemed sparser. Stroking it all the time is probably breaking it.

While Vald's note was in transit, Best's aide was telephoning Vald's office for an appointment. Vald's secretary claimed he was out of the office for the day and made an appointment for 1:30 p.m. the following day. She told Best's aide that Vald would not go to Best's office … if Best wanted to see the Prime Minister, he would have to come to Amalienborg Castle.

General Best, two aides, and a full squad of SS troops arrived at the Prime Minister's office at precisely two minutes before the appointed time. Best stationed the troops outside the meeting room and he and his aides entered and found both Prime Minister Stauning and King Christian waiting.

King Christian was seated at the head of the table, with Vald on his right and four others behind the king. Best seated himself at the far end of the table. He placed his ivory-topped rosewood swagger stick very precisely on the table, pointing directly at King Christian. His aides sat on either side of him.

For a moment no one spoke. Then Vald leaned forward, rested his elbows on the table and began, in Danish.

"General Best, what arrangements have you made for delivering Colonel Warner to our police?"

Best's countenance reddened slightly, but his voice was carefully controlled and he replied in Danish.

"Colonel Warner was performing his assigned duties, but we are not here to discuss Colonel Warner. My concerns involve your merchant marine fleet and the Odense Shipyard. We require the services of the fleet. The shipyard must be re-opened immediately."

"General, the fleet's orders are to stay away from Danish waters. So long as you and your army treat us well, our fleet will maintain neutrality in the war. If you treat us badly, the fleet will offer its services to the Allies."

"You dare? You dare to threaten me?"

"No threat, General," Christian said. "Prime Minister Stauning simply explained the situation to you. The fleet has its orders, orders which cannot be countermanded so long as we are occupied by a foreign power. So, you see General, we cannot help you with the fleet. Even if we wished to help, the fleet would ignore any order we issued while your army continued to occupy Denmark."

Vald studied Best. He can't quite hide his dismay. Score one for us.

Vald stroked his beard, vainly trying to smooth it. Wonder where the general will go next?

"Prime Minister, the Odense shipyard must re-open immediately."

"The workers are afraid to go to work," Christian answered. "They witnessed a murder and fear for their lives. Until that murderer is brought to justice and the workers have assurances that there will be no more killing, I'm afraid we won't be able to get them to return to work."

Best didn't say anything. Vald thought the general was a cautious man and would not be rushed into anything hasty the way General Himer had been. Wonder if he even realizes he's flexing his swagger stick almost to breaking?

"My Fuhrer has charged me with securing certain kinds of cooperation from you, from Danish industry. He has given me full authority to take whatever actions are necessary to secure that cooperation."

Vald waited. The mention of Hitler is supposed to impress us?

Best paused for a moment.

"For instance, I could have the six of you shot," Best's voice was pleasant, as if he were discussing the local ballet. "I could randomly select a hundred or a thousand citizens and have them shot. I can do whatever I feel is required. In fact, I have been ordered to do whatever may be necessary. Now, I personally am a peaceful man, I don't want to use violence."

Now it comes, thought Vald. Now he is trying to scare us ... and he's succeeding.

"I abhor violence," Best continued in that same pleasant voice. "However, I am ordered to secure cooperation in building submarines and in certain other industrial and agricultural production. I will do whatever is necessary to secure that cooperation. IS THAT CLEAR?"

He extended the swagger stick like a sword straight at King Christian.

Vald started to speak but King Christian laid a hand on his arm and he was silent.

"General Best, we are delighted with your personal dislike of violence. However, we are disappointed that you are so ready to abandon your deeply held principles and resort to violence simply because you are ordered to do so. In Denmark, an officer has a duty to disobey an unlawful order. Is that not the case in Germany?"

"I have been given no unlawful order."

King Christian raised one eyebrow and said, "Really?" and then turning to Vald said in a loud stage whisper clearly audible to everyone.

"Strange laws that allow for random killing of the innocent."

"Germany is at war and war has a certain logic of its own," Best said. "In particular, war requires machines and materiel. Denmark must contribute its share to the war. I will do whatever is necessary to secure Denmark's contribution. Now, the shipyard will re-open tomorrow."

"The shipyard will re-open after Colonel Warner is brought to justice," Christian said.

"I will execute both of you." He flexed the swagger stick. Some distant part of Vald's mind wondered how far it would bend before breaking.

"You could do that," Vald said. To his surprise, anger supplanted his fear. "You might want to consider General Himer's fate. King Christian enjoys considerable popularity with our citizens. Harming him will provide us with a much loved martyr and will harden the resistance immeasurably."

Vald sat erect, rigid with anger. King Christian sat back in his chair, arms resting comfortably in his lap, and it seemed to Vald that his eyes were alive with the joy of combat.

Best sat back in his chair, eyes darting from Christian to Vald and back again. Vald felt it ... Best didn't know what to make of them. A savage, Viking's glee rose in Vald's heart. Best can't understand us, he keeps expecting us to behave like beaten curs.

A moment later Best left without saying anything.

Vald's anger ebbed away and fear crept back in.

"That man frightens me more than Himer," Vald said. "He's cautious and won't do anything foolish ... I'm not sure how much of this I can take."

"Courage, my friend," Christian replied. "Courage. The situation is still what we thought it might be. Our planning scenarios still hold."

"It is not the scenarios I worry about," Vald said. "It is my own fortitude ..."

"Vald, you have dedicated your life to public service. You will not fail now."

"Well, they probably won't kill us ... and I keep reminding myself there are worse things than dying."

For a long moment there was silence, with both of them lost in thought. Finally Vald spoke.

"We need to up the pressure ... should we close the rest of the shipyards?"

"Best still thinks threats are useful," Christian said. "He won't renounce the threat of killing us ... and he certainly isn't ready to punish one of his officers for killing a Dane ... yes, let's close all of our shipyards. Contact Moellar in London and get it on the 6:00 p.m. broadcast."

The door burst open and a clerk rushed in.

"Sorry, sir," the man cried. "The general took a whole group of our people."

"What? Took a group?" Christian asked.

"Yes, sir, six or seven of our people, just dragged away."

"He's striking back," Vald said. "Punishing us for resisting him."

"We'll make a formal protest," Christian said. "I doubt it will do any good ... he'll kill them."

"We need to try to keep our people out of the way when he comes," Vald said. "At least we can make it hard for him to take them."

There seemed nothing further they could do.

* * * * * * * * * *

Moellar's broadcast informed the Danes and Germans alike about the meeting and the strike of the shipyards.

Best received a telegram from the German High Command demanding that he arrange an end to the strike and get the shipyards to work on submarines. The High Command would tolerate no delay ... submarines were needed as soon as possible.

Best considered his options while waiting for reports from the field. By noon he had all the information. His troops had visited most of the shipyards in the country. All of them were totally deserted. None of them had anything in the way of personnel records. How long could the Danes maintain a strike? So far they had been damnably efficient. They'd probably arranged for a lengthy strike.

Chapter 15. The Danish Nazi Party

Fritz Clausen called the meeting of the Danish Nazi Party to order at 8:00 a.m. on April 22. All twenty-seven of the key party leaders, all of them men, were present. Getting these busy men to the meeting on a workday was a powerful demonstration of their commitment and discipline. Their SS liaison officer, Captain Eschmann, should be very impressed.

Fritz was so inspired that he began an impromptu speech about their glorious future now that Denmark was ruled by "Our Fuhrer".

Clausen was both surprised and hurt when, barely five minutes later, Captain Eschmann interrupted him. It was bad enough that General Best had seen fit to send him a mere Captain … certainly the head of the Party deserved at least a Colonel … and now this pipsqueak dared to interrupt.

"General Best has asked for your help," Captain Eschman said. "As you know, many of your industries are resisting our orders. Further complicating matters, the large companies such as the shipyards, factories, and newspapers have hidden or destroyed their personnel records. We are unable to locate most of the leaders of these companies.

"What information do you have about any manager or executive in either a government or a private enterprise? We need names, position, and home addresses.

"What other Party members do you know who might have additional information regarding these managers? Again, we need names and contact information. To begin, please fill out this form with your name, address and contact information. We will begin interviewing you within the next day or so. Thank you."

Captain Eschmann waited until all the forms were filled out, collected the forms and, to Fritz's immense chagrin, left. A lowly SS private remained behind as their only liaison.

Fritz almost gave vent to his frustrations. No. Can't admit that Best and his staff are basically ignoring me. Put a good face on it.

He launched into a little pep talk.

"Our obstinate and stupid countrymen cause a great deal of trouble. We have a chance to provide some much needed assistance to the Fatherland and our Fuhrer. If we can locate these treasonous men who are leading the country astray, we will demonstrate our value to General Best and take our rightful place as leaders of the country."

Fritz paused to savor the applause that followed this pronouncement.

"I'm sure there's a great deal more we can do to help the cause. For instance, we should be able to identify leaders of the resistance and get that information to Captain Eschmann."

"Look, I don't know about the rest of you, but I drive a truck," a man in the back row said. "I don't know beans about managers and executives. How the hell am I supposed to provide information on these guys?"

"Do you know the name of your supervisor?" another man said. "The name of the head of your company? What about the address for any of 'em? Every little bit like that will help."

"We can be helpful if we just keep our eyes open," a third man said. "Notice those outspoken against us. Notice people actively working for the resistance. Make note of the Jewish dogs among us."

"Each of you should get a little notebook you can carry with you," Fritz reasserted control. "Begin taking notes on anything that might help the cause. Note people breaking the rules ... radios, cameras, illegal newspapers. Talk to your local Party members about doing the same."

The meeting went on the rest of the morning with the men sharing names of those they thought needed to be turned in to Captain Eschmann.

Chapter 16. The Folk Festival

After a week of around the clock preparations, Arne was ready for the folk festival. The schedule had many big names, including several of Arne's favorites. It's going to be great. Except we don't know how the Nazis will react. Could get bloody.

Getting ready has been a bummer. Asger is practically in open revolt about the work load ... and all of us are worn out.

Everybody knows there'll be a festival ... both the underground media and the remnants of the established media ran extensive announcements. We practically killed ourselves getting out the where and the why of the festival. Faelledparken, a little over a kilometer and a half from Amalienborg Castle was an ideal site. A kilometer long park, with a lake along one side and tree lined along its edges, it's ideal for large crowds.

Arne was impatient, he wanted to get there early, be able to be up close to the performers. Relax. Relax, plenty of time and the steps of the student union are pleasant in the sunshine.

Ah, here comes Poul ... he really is small, his name fits him well. Everybody likes Poul.

Damn! Asger and Brigitte together, and she's laughing at his stupid jokes. Well, they don't have to work together, I can assign them to different areas.

Where are the rest? Festival starts at six and the German curfew is at 8:00 p.m. ... only the police, firemen, and ambulance services are exempt.

Ah, there's Tyge and Morten. And coming from the other direction, Carin and Greta.

"What if the Germans shoot after curfew?" Poul looked worried.

Everyone is too quiet … Poul is voicing the concern of all of them. What is this timidity? They're Vikings, for God's sake.

"Well, what's the worst that could happen?" Arne said. "You didn't think this was going to be easy, did you?"

Poul looked at the ground, then up to meet Arne's eyes.

"Look, Arne, I know that nothing scares you, but some of the rest of us worry about getting killed. I just want to know what we do if they start shooting."

"Me too. Arne, we need to talk about this." Greta said.

"Okay, you're right. I'm sorry, your concern is legitimate. Now look, there will be thousands and thousands of us … they can't shoot us all. They're trying to avoid bad publicity. It will look pretty bad if they start shooting unarmed civilians. I don't think they'll shoot."

"Asger," Carin said. "What do you think?"

Why in hell would Carin solicit Asger's opinion? Of all of them, Asger seemed least committed.

"I'm not worried," Asger shrugged. "The Nazis don't scare me."

"Well, I think they should scare all of us," Tyge said. "But Arne's right, they can't shoot everyone."

"Here's our plan," Arne said. "We stay together, we watch out for each other. If we run from a patrol, we run in a controlled manner, watching each other. In the short distance we have to go, there are going to be lots of other groups around us. The ones who might have trouble are the ones who're a long way from home."

"I think we'll be okay if we stay alert," Brigitte said. "The key is to stay alert afterwards, as we're going home. That's when it will be dangerous."

They're worried … but also ready to do it. They'll come through.

The festival turned out to be dozens of singers, some groups and some solo, scattered throughout the spacious park. Hordes of people … Arne had never seen so many people in one place. Every inch of the park was crammed with people.

It's good to be a Dane. It's good to have Viking ancestors. We didn't always win, but we put up a good fight. Eventually the Nazis will see that Denmark is too stubborn … more trouble than she's worth and the Nazis will slink home and leave us alone.

They wandered from singer to singer throughout the evening.

"That's Kaj Munk," Poul said. "He's doing a poetry reading."

"Who is Kaj Munk?" Carin asked.

"You don't know Munk?" Poul said. "Everybody knows him. He's my favorite poet. Also a minister and a playwright. Way back he admired Hitler as a strong man, then denounced him and Mussolini as racists. Very outspoken."

"He gives very strong sermons against the Nazis," Tyge said. "He seems fearless."

All too soon it was ten p.m. and time to head for home. The crowd drifted out of the park as if they were reluctant to leave … and Arne at least was sorry it was ending. The songs had moved him.

"There's King Christian," Morten exclaimed. The King rode his horse perhaps fifty meters away. They stopped and watched. A squad of the Royal Guard attended Christian and all of them were surrounded by a large crowd of people. The king would be well guarded on the six-block ride to his castle.

Asger and Brigitte walked side by side with the rest of the group behind them. Halfway to Asger's flat, a cop sent them down a side street with a low voiced, "Patrol's down that way." For several more blocks policemen stood at every corner, directing the foot traffic away from the German patrols.

They were nearly to Asger's flat when gunshots sounded. Bang. Bang. Bang. All of them jumped and Asger broke into a run at the same instant Brigitte grabbed his arm. Arne couldn't tell if she was restraining Asger or re-assuring herself. Greta bumped into Arne and then stood so close that they were touching from hip to shoulder.

"Keep walking," Arne said. "Stay alert."

Nobody said anything, but they remained bunched up the rest of the way home, as if the physical proximity would keep them safe.

Chapter 17. The Curfew

The Sunday April 21 editions of the underground newspapers, *Free Danish Press* and *The Resistance* both carried large stories on the festival and reported that five people had been killed by Nazi patrols on their way home after the festival. Arne ate a hasty dinner and met the other members of his team.

"Why are we doing this?" Asger said without greeting anyone. "The Nazis are going to shoot to kill."

"We can't let them intimidate us," Arne replied.

"This is stupid," Asger leapt up. "Get yourself killed. I'm not."

"We've got our orders," Arne stood, face to face with Asger. "We need to do our part."

"Goody Two Shoes Sejr. I'm sick of your holier-than-thou attitude. Arne the great hero of the resistance. Ten Commandments Sejr. Ooh, great man Arne. All I hear is how wonderful it must be to work with the great Arne Sejr. If people only knew what a self-righteous, pompous little ass you really are. Tell me, Arne, when's the last time you had any fun? When's the last time you got laid? How come you don't have a girlfriend, Arne? There's more to life than work, you know. I'm sick of you and your moralizing attitude. I'm going home."

Arne took a step back, stunned, unable to reply. Self-righteous? Pompous? Both Brigitte and Poul started talking, none of it comprehensible to Arne. Poul stopped and Brigitte continued.

"Asger, you're being unfair. Arne does what Professor Koch says. Arne can't help it if others idolize him for the Ten Commandments. He does a good job as our leader."

Brigitte continued to talk, with Poul occasionally chiming in, but Arne was thinking about Asger's accusations.

Was this how others see me? Do they think I see myself as a great hero? No, this was crap-for-brains Asger. Nothing-but-sex-on-his-mind Asger was the one complaining.

Nobody saying anything. Asger sitting there looking at the ground. Nobody looking at me.

"Look, I don't have to be the leader of this team," Arne said. "If the rest of you feel the way Asger does, we can ask Professor Koch to appoint someone else as leader."

"You're our leader," Brigitte spoke quickly.

"I agree," Poul chimed in.

"Look," Tyge said. "Sometimes the pressure gets to us, but all of us want you to continue. Right guys?"

Morten, Carin, and Greta all nodded their heads yes. Asger continued to look at the ground and didn't say anything. Poul gave him a dig in the ribs and he grimaced.

"I'm sorry Arne, I'm just tired," Asger said.

"I can't help what others say about me. All of you know I'm no great hero, I'm just trying to give the Germans as much trouble as I can. Asger's right that I get too intense. I've got a one track mind and forget to relax. Maybe you could remind me that we need to take some R and R occasionally. Preferably before we blow up at each other."

Arne's smile took enormous effort, but most of them smiled back. Asger was a lazy, womanizer who seemed to have Brigitte under his spell. Did he really add anything to the group? Maybe I can find some excuse to send him away. No, that's jealousy. A real Viking wouldn't think such things.

They went outside at 7:00 p.m. and it seemed that all of Copenhagen was in the street. Arne strolled along, trying to overcome his jealousy and anger with Asger … and his shame at his own pettiness.

The Danes were enraged and had no intention of going in when the curfew arrived. The general plan for dealing with the patrols, which everyone seemed to have hit upon independently, was to simply bolt for the nearest house at first sight of a patrol and then to come right back out as soon as the patrol was a hundred meters down the street. The patrols would be faced with a street that emptied in front of them and filled up again behind them.

Arne was deep in thought, obsessively going over the incident with Asger, and didn't notice the patrol coming around the corner behind them. Brigitte grabbed his arm as she raced by. Arne pulled even with her as they raced for the nearest front door.

Everyone else was already inside when they reached the porch. Arne darted a fast glance at the soldiers as he leapt across the front porch. He and Brigitte collided as they reached the door simultaneously.

Arne tried to shove Brigitte through the door and succeeded only in putting his arm around her waist. The two of them jammed into the doorway, arms and legs entangled, face to face.

Arne had never been this close to Brigitte. He was falling but it didn't matter. Brigitte's smell filled his soul and he was drowning in her eyes.

An electric shock passed through him as they hit the floor. Brigitte lay half on top of him, hair spilling into his face. Somehow the door slammed shut and Arne didn't want to move, didn't want Brigitte to stop lying on his chest. He was acutely conscious that his legs were intertwined with Brigitte's and that her pelvis pressed against his thigh.

Brigitte lifted her head, blew at the hair falling over her face, met his eyes and started to giggle. The giggle progressed to a belly laugh and Brigitte dropped her head onto Arne's chest and roared. Arne joined her and they laughed until they were weak and helpless with it. All the while Arne reveled in the feel and smell and look of her. He would be happy to stay this way forever.

Eventually Brigitte rolled over, and someone reached out and pulled her to her feet. Arne climbed slowly to his feet and was thankful that everyone was laughing and talking and he didn't have to say anything.

Three different times patrols came down streets near them and each time they went into some stranger's house. Arne decided it was great fun and even managed to forgive Asger. Around 12:30 a.m. the crowds started to thin out and Arne and his colleagues hurried back to their rooms near the university.

For three days this strange game of hide and seek went on. The Nazis killed twelve more people, wounded perhaps three times that many and then gave up on the unenforceable curfew. They didn't have enough troops to keep the people off the streets.

Arne and his team celebrated their victory with several cases of beer and much singing. Poul played his guitar and led them, in a sweet tenor voice, in folk song after folk song.

"My cousin, Alvilda, telephones the Germans every day," Greta said when Poul took a break. "She likes to report sighting a British submarine or battleship just off the coast."

"Do they fall for that?" Tyge asked.

"They seem to," Greta said. "Alvilda says they usually claim that they were on a fishing boat and just got a glimpse of the British ship and they always give the sort of location that a fisherman would ... they talk about landmarks and such."

"I really wonder how much good those calls do?" Tyge sounded skeptical.

"They wondered too," Greta said. "Last week they put some of their people to watching the nearby harbors and then reported sighting another British warship. About twenty minutes after making their report, the two nearest harbors began boiling with activity. Three German ships left the harbors and raced for the reported location."

"Wow," Tyge said. "Sounds like they're taking the bait."

"My calls are small by comparison," Morten shrugged. "I usually can't think of anything better than a stalled German army truck on a lonely stretch of road."

"I called about one of the new rules yesterday," Carin said. "I kept some German soldier on the phone for almost half an hour while I tried my stupid best to understand the new rule."

Poul laughed and replied. "Carin, you always were devious. By the time you got through, the soldier explaining the rule probably didn't even understand it any more."

"I talked to Prof about false reports," Brigitte said. "He thought the Germans would check out all such reports, even if they doubted them. Prof said the Germans are obsessively thorough and will carefully check any report that might be true. We can use that against them. Same deal with the fake letters we send in code. We keep them busy doing nothing."

Poul finished his beer and started a new song about a glorious Viking victory. When the song ended, Arne noticed Brigitte and Greta, giggling over some private joke.

Arne went over to chat with Poul. Asger wedged himself between Brigitte and Greta, half turning away from Greta so that she was excluded from the conversation. A minute later Greta went to talk to Tyge. Asger had Brigitte to himself ... again.

"What the hell does she see in him?" Arne said.

"Who?" Poul said.

"Brigitte," Arne said. "She's always with Asger."

"Maybe Asger is the one initiating it," Poul said.

"She doesn't seem to mind."

"Arne," Poul seemed surprised. "Are you jealous? Of Asger?"

"Poul … I guess I am. Brigitte seems way too good for such a dipstick."

"Well go get her. You're our leader, show some initiative."

"I don't know … I don't think she's interested."

"Well then, send him on a long dangerous mission," Poul laughed. "Skoal." Poul drained his beer and started singing but Arne wasn't listening.

After several more beers, Arne thought of the perfect mission for Asger … it wasn't too dangerous, but it would take a long time.

Arne's headache the next morning was terrible. After three cups of coffee he walked to Poul's apartment. There was no answer when he knocked. He knocked again, harder and finally after the third time Poul appeared at the door.

"You look like hell," Arne said.

"Feel like it," Poul said. Poul turned away and Arne followed him inside.

"What do you want? I thought we had today off."

"We do. I just need to talk to you."

"Oh."

"I think I made an ass of myself last night." Arne said.

"No. You didn't say anything to Brigitte. I was with you all evening."

"Not to Brigitte. What I said about Asger."

"About getting Asger killed on some mission?"

"Yeah. I didn't mean that."

"Oh crap, Arne. I know that. You were just blowing off steam."

"Did I say it to anyone else. The last part of the evening is sort of a blur."

"No. It was just you and me commiserating against the celebrities who get all the pretty girls."

"Poul … I was actually thinking of ways to get rid of him."

"You were stinking drunk. Doesn't mean anything. Forget it."

Stinking drunk. First time drunk and I disgrace myself. Never again!

Chapter 18. The Shipyard Stalemate

The shipyard strike dragged on through its fifth day. General Best didn't know what to do about Colonel Warner. Turning him over to the Danish police was unthinkable. Perhaps we could punish Warner in a way that would be acceptable to the Danes? This was tricky … it might destroy morale in the rest of the troops.

The stalemate continued through two more days. Best hinted to Prime Minister Stauning that an administrative punishment such as reduction in rank and a fine might be imposed on Colonel Warner. Vald demanded that Warner be turned over to the Danish civil authorities.

Ten days after the shipyard strikes began, the High Command threatened to send Best to the front and to replace him with someone who would end the strike. General Best made an appointment with Prime Minister Stauning for the following day.

There were no opening pleasantries when Best came into the meeting with Vald and Christian.

"Colonel Warner sold military equipment to civilians," Best said. "He will be court-martialed and discharged. What happens to him after that is none of my concern."

Best watched Vald and Christian exchange glances. That caught them by surprise.

'When will this court-martial occur?" Vald asked.

"Immediately. We do not tolerate such behavior."

Best waited while Vald and Christian seemed to consider this news.

"Why are you telling us this?' Vald asked.

"Colonel Warner is a thief and a rogue. He does not represent the German officers. He is being punished for his crimes. Now you can get the shipyard back to work."

"I see," Vald said. "The shipyard will begin work on the day after we have Colonel Warner in custody."

"Do I have your word on that?" Best asked.

"Prime Minister Stauning has already given you his word, General," Christian said. "you can count on it."

* * * * * * * *

Christian Moeller's broadcasts from London reported on the cashiering of Colonel Warner and his subsequent Danish trial and long prison sentence. Since Moellar's broadcasts were received all over Denmark and much of Germany, all of Best's army, the German High Command, and everyone else with any interest soon knew the full story. The German High Command issued a severe verbal rebuke to General Best, but since the shipyards were back to work and apparently busily producing submarines, they did not enter it into his permanent record. Best was embarrassed by the verbal rebuke but also vastly relieved. He had survived with his career intact.

The lesson learned by Best's army was subtle … killing Danes openly could end your career. If you were going to kill Danes, it had best be done surreptitiously or with ironclad justification.

Chapter 19. The Wehrmacht Soldier

Gerhard spent his first week in Denmark patrolling the streets of Copenhagen in a jeep. The Danes ignored him and his squad mates and went about their business. The patrol's job seemed to consist in driving around, wasting petrol. Several of his squad mates tried to talk to some of the young women, but got nowhere.

Gerhard started to wonder why they were even in Denmark. Jacob said they wanted materiel and food from the Danes for the war effort, but Gerhard couldn't see that they were doing anything to get either food or materiel. Gerhard was relieved when General Dr. Best arrived to take charge of the situation.

On April 18th the newspapers reported that Colonel Warner had murdered the superintendent of the Odense Shipyard. Again, Gerhard asked Jacob what he thought of this. Jacob replied, "I don't know, Gerhard. It could be. Maybe the guy provoked him."

The shipyard strike surprised Gerhard and Jacob. Up to this point they believed the Danes were complying with whatever they were ordered to do. They fully expected the strike to end within a few days. And the newspaper stories that the Danes wanted to arrest Colonel Warner simply mystified them … how could the Danes expect to arrest an officer of the German army that conquered them? As the strike dragged on, their conversations kept coming back to the question of what the Danes hoped to accomplish. Most of them agreed that the Danes had to be crazy.

Gerhard's squad was assigned to patrol on the evening of the first folk festival, with orders to shoot anyone on the streets past the official curfew of 8:00 p.m. Gerhard was bothered by the idea of shooting people simply because they were out too late. Jacob dryly observed that he, personally, was a very bad shot and probably wouldn't be able to hit anyone.

Gerhard knew that Jacob was an excellent marksman. Jacob smiled and Gerhard understood: a soldier doesn't always have to hit a target.

Gerhard's patrol shot at several groups of people returning from the folk festival that night. As far as Gerhard could tell, his squad didn't actually hit anyone. In the three days that followed, before the Generals gave up and rescinded the curfew, Gerhard's squad shot at several more people, again without hitting anyone. According to the newspapers, however, 23 Danes were killed and 54 wounded during those four days.

Gerhard said to Jacob, "These Danes have no sense … why don't they just stay home?"

"If the situation were reversed, and the Danes invaded us, would you stay home?"

"I don't know … what are they trying to gain by breaking a curfew?"

"I'm not sure, maybe just trying to assert themselves, maybe just trying to show we can't order them around."

Chapter 20. Knud Einstad

Knud Einstad, master machinist, all six foot three inches and a hundred seventy-five pounds of him, was one of the first to arrive at the Odense Steel Shipyard the day it re-opened. Knud was ninety minutes early for his shift and he didn't go to his workstation. Instead he made a stop at central supplies and picked up a box. With the box on a two-wheeled cart, he made the four hundred meter hike to his own shop. Once there he opened the box and took out the manuals.

Knud visited each workstation in the shop, replacing the old manuals with the new ones. He packed all the old manuals and dumped them into a nearby furnace. When he returned, most of his fellows were at their stations.

Knud waved the other men over to his workstation.

"Now, I reckon everyone knows we're going to be building submarines for the Nazis?"

"What gives?" one of the young men said. "I thought we weren't helping these bastards?"

"We help them as little as possible," Knud said. "The only way we could avoid helping is to go home and stay there for the duration … and then they would replace us.

"Our first way of not helping begins with the new shop rules … safety rules, maintenance protocols, routing forms, machine procedures … the works. It's in the new manuals at your stations."

One of the men said, "Quite a bit thicker than the old one."

"Quite a bit," Knud smiled. "There are probably ten times more rules than there used to be. Not only that, but we will follow each and every one … to the letter."

"We'll never get nothin' done," one of the older men said.

"Idiot," The man next to him said. "That's the whole idea."

Knud lost his smile. "Okay, maybe we better review what we're about here."

A man on the far edge of the group said, "We made the rules as complicated and burdensome as possible ... we expect our productivity to be about one-tenth of what it was before."

Another man spoke up, "We'll be working away like beavers, the Nazis won't be able to complain about our work habits. It's just that nothing will be getting finished ... they'll all die of old age by the time they get a submarine out of us."

A third man added, "When you work on a part, make sure you don't finish your piece of it. Send it on to another workstation as soon as you finish one little aspect of it. That way it has to come back to you and maybe you'll have a backlog by that time so it has to wait for a few days."

Now several people were trying to speak, "Don't forget set up time. If you can arrange for the same part to come through your workstation several times, then you got to set up for it each time."

"For sure don't do a run of identical pieces. Do one piece, then set up for a different piece."

"Lose the finished parts ... mis-route them to the farthest corner of Hades."

Knud's grin got wider as the men talked about how to slow the work as much as possible. He let it go on for a few minutes, then held up a hand for silence.

"Okay guys. I don't know how long it will be until we actually get some submarine parts coming through here, probably at least a couple of days. I want you to use the time learning the new rules ... the more expert we are in the rules, the better we will be at slowing things down.

"I know, learning these rules is a pain. You gotta know the rules and you gotta know 'em well. The Nazis will be breathing down our necks before long and the rules will be our protection. Get some grease on those manuals, dog-ear them ... they must not look new. Our story is that we always operated like this. Quit bitching and get to studying.

"I need a few minutes with the master machinists ... the rest of you go get started studying."

All but three of the men drifted back to their own workstations. The youngest of the group waited until the four of them were alone.

"You sure we don't have any stooges in here? That idiot was actually worried that we wouldn't be able to get anything accomplished."

The oldest machinist shook his head. "I've known him thirty some years. He's just set in his ways and a little dense ... we'll have to work with him to slow him down, but he hates the Nazis."

"The four of us have a special role to play," Knud said. "For every part that comes through this shop, we'll decide whether and how to gimmick it."

Chapter 21. The Sub-killers

Knud and his shop mates had no real work on their first day back to work after the strike. Several squads of German soldiers arrived around mid-morning and recorded the name and address for every worker in the yard. The Germans didn't yet know that all of their IDs were fake. Knud wondered what would happen when the deception was discovered.

For the next week, Knud had little to do other than learning the new rules. The normal work of his shop had been suspended. Knud spent most of his time perfecting the design for what he called his "sub-killer."

When a submarine dives, its stability depends upon the relationship between its center of gravity and its center of buoyancy. The center of buoyancy must be higher than the center of gravity, or the sub flips upside down, the crew loses control, and it sinks to the bottom.

Knud's sub-killer changed the center of gravity by keeping a ballast tank in the bottom of the sub empty and filling one near the top of the ship. The second tank, the one near the top of the ship did not show up on the blueprints.

The real genius of Knud's idea was that the submarine did not sink the first time it dived. The valve that filled the bottom ballast tank also operated a small gear. This gear operated a mechanism that kept track of the number of times the valve was operated. After this valve was opened a predetermined number of times, the water that should fill the bottom tank was diverted into the top tank, dooming the sub.

The mechanisms that operated Knud's sub-killer were partially inside one of the pipes and the rest was hidden behind a bulkhead. The mechanism would be impossible to find without removing a welded steel plate.

Knud had very mixed feelings about his sub-killer. He would do almost anything to keep from building a submarine for the Nazis, but the idea of killing the entire crew nauseated him.

Once the critical, upper ballast tank was filled and the sub started its final dive, there would be no hope for any one on board. The sub would sink to the bottom with no possibility of rescue.

A second type of sub-killer utilized a noisemaker designed to fit inside a pipe. The liquid rushing through the pipe wound a spring and the device then made a loud banging noise for several minutes, loud enough and long enough for a destroyer's sonar to locate a sub that was trying to hide. This device also used Knud's idea of a counter that delayed operation of the device until after the sub's training runs were complete. By putting it in a pipe used in diving, it could be set to go off at the worst possible time for the sub and its crew.

The third and final sub-killer was a simple radio transmitter. It was designed to broadcast only in one low frequency, one not normally used by radio stations, but which could easily be triangulated if one knew what to look for. If the Allies had that frequency, their destroyers would be able to home in on the sub with pinpoint accuracy.

Chapter 22. Subverting the Enemy

Arne's team went through two days of training, including role-playing, on how to subvert the Wehrmacht, the ordinary German soldier.

To Arne's great delight, Brigitte and he were assigned to work together. On April 22 they went out for their first attempt to talk to the German soldiers. They walked into a small café and saw a group of three sitting at a table, just starting their meal. Brigitte took a deep breath, looked at Arne and at his nod, walked to their table.

Brigitte said, in German, "Hello. May we talk with you a minute?"

The oldest of the three soldiers pointed at two empty chairs.

"Please join us," he said. "My name is Jacob. This is Gerhard and that is Hermann."

"Hi. I'm Brigitte. This is Arne."

"Will you eat?" Jacob said.

"No, just a little talk," Arne replied.

"We're trying to understand something," Brigitte said. "We thought you might be able to help us?"

"What is it?" Gerhard said.

"You're Christians, right? So are we," Brigitte said.

"And we're the same racial stock," Arne added. "We look just like you."

"Yes, it is so," Gerhard said.

"You have families," Brigitte said. "Parents, brothers, sisters, girlfriends, wives, even children?"

'Yes, yes," Gerhard agreed. "But no wives or children yet. That will come later."

Arne laughed and said, "Yes, the same with us. All of us love the same great composers and read much the same literature."

Brigitte added, "You Germans and we Danes are very much alike, I think."

"Yes, I agree," Gerhard said.

"Why are you telling us these obvious things?" Jacob asked.

"Here's what I don't understand," Brigitte spoke very softly. "The Germans and the Danes are like brothers … why is Germany oppressing us? We should be friends rather than enemies."

"I'm not your enemy," Hermann said. "I would like to get very friendly with you."

Brigitte met his eyes for a long moment.

"You are my enemy," Brigitte said. "I don't hate you, but as long as your country occupies mine and you wear that uniform, we have no choice. You have decided to be my enemy."

"No, no, I never decided to be your enemy," Hermann protested. "I'm just following orders."

"We are ordered by our government to resist your occupation in all ways possible," Arne said. "To resist totally, everything short of violence. Our duty as Danes is to resist you."

"Ordered to resist us?" Jacob said.

"In all ways possible, except with violence," Arne replied.

"You resist us but can't use violence?" Jacob said. "Then how do you resist?"

"Well, for example, we refuse to obey orders," Brigitte said. "You remember the curfew? We refused to obey it and after a few days your leaders saw that it was unenforceable."

"I don't think much of a resistance that can't use guns," Hermann said. "You're not going to get anywhere that way."

"So you think the resistance should take up guns," Arne said.

Hermann looked momentarily confused and then seemed to realized Arne was playing with him.

"You haven't answered my question," Brigitte said. "Why do you oppress us?"

"Hell, I don't want to oppress anybody," Gerhard said. "I'd rather be back home with my fiancée."

"But you are oppressing us." Brigitte was unyielding.

"Hey, little lady, I'm sorry," Gerhard said. "I'm just following orders. I don't even know why we're here."

"Well, I know why," Hermann said. "Denmark needs to help in the war, needs to help Germany."

"Why would we do that?" Arne asked. "We don't want this war."

"Well, I can see your point," Jacob said. "I mean, look, we wouldn't be too happy if someone occupied us and started giving orders."

"That's not for us to decide," Hermann said. "We follow orders, the Danes are required to help, and we will see to it that they do."

"There, you see," Brigitte said. "You decided to be our enemy. We refuse to cooperate with your orders and you intend to persecute us."

Arne stood up.

"We're sorry that you decided to be our enemies. We will resist you but we won't use violence."

"Well thank you," Brigitte said. "Maybe when you're ordered to shoot some Dane, maybe you'll miss."

Arne and Brigitte left the three soldiers in the café and went out into the street.

"I need a minute to think about that," Arne said. "Let's get coffee."

They walked half a block to another café and ordered coffee. Afterwards they sought out another small group of German soldiers. By the end of the evening they had talked with a total of sixteen German soldiers about sports, favorite composers, the best beers, and religion. And always the resistance and nonviolence.

Arne and Brigitte left the last group of German soldiers and stepped into the street. Three young Danes stood nearby and followed them as they walked down the street.

Arne thought nothing of the young men until a hand grabbed his shoulder from behind, spun him around, and shoved him up against the wall. One of the men grabbed Brigitte and two of them held Arne.

"German lovers! We should shave both your heads."

"We're not." Arne said. "We … "

"We saw you. Three different groups of soldiers. Traitors."

He punched Arne in the stomach, knocking the wind from him and doubling him over.

"Idiots!" Brigitte's fear turned to fury. "That's Arne Sejr, you morons!"

Brigitte gave her captor a violent shove, knocking him backwards, sprawling on the sidewalk.

"Arne Sejr? Ten Commandments Sejr?"

Brigitte rushed to Arne, shouldering past the two men who still held him. She caught him around the shoulders and held him.

"Arne. Arne, are you okay?"

Arne could only nod. A moment later he drew in a long shuddering breath as his diaphragm began to work again.

"Can you walk?" Brigitte asked.

Arne nodded.

"We need to move," Brigitte said. "Those soldiers might come out any minute."

Brigitte, still with her arm around Arne, started off down the street, with three shamefaced young men following. She turned the corner and stopped. She looked into Arne's eyes and held both his hands.

"Are you really okay?"

Arne was recovered from the punch to the stomach, but Brigitte's concern and her nearness were exciting.

"I'm fine," he was immensely grateful that his voice sounded normal. He turned to his three assailants.

"Okay, what was that all about?"

"Mr. Sejr, we're really sorry. We thought you were sucking up to the Germans. I hope I didn't hurt you."

Arne laughed. "Well, getting the wind knocked out is unpleasant, but it passes. Actually, we *were*, sort of, sucking up to the Germans. We, and a whole lot of other people, talk to them, trying to make them question what they're doing. We're trying to destroy their morale."

Brigitte, still angry, asked, "What are you doing to help the resistance?"

The three men looked at each other and shrugged. The tall thin one finally said, "We don't know what to do."

Arne and Brigitte looked at each other and Brigitte asked, "Have you tried to find the resistance?"

The young man who punched Arne said, "We didn't know how."

Brigitte's scorn showed on her face for a minute before she replied.

"Listen to Moellar's broadcasts. Read the newspapers. Talk to a cop. Ask your friends. Show a little initiative, practically everyone's involved."

The three just stared at her. Finally one said, "Okay. Okay, we can do that. Sorry we punched you."

"Don't worry about it. Just get involved," Arne said.

The three young men walked away and Brigitte and Arne started toward her flat.

"Can we really trust them?" Brigitte asked. "Could they be snitches for the Germans?"

Arne chalked a "V" on the wall they were passing before answering.

"Probably something like seventy or eighty percent of Danes are involved in resistance of one sort or another. I think the Germans probably realize that by now ... it hardly seems worth while to search for resistance members when they're all around."

"I told them who you are. You're not just any resistance member."

"Brigitte, it's all right. If they arrest me now, they just create a martyr. They're not going to do that."

Brigitte slipped her arm into Arne's.

"I hope you're right. I couldn't forgive myself if I caused you to be arrested.

"We did so well this evening." She squeezed his arm and released it.

Arne was sublimely happy to be admired by Brigitte and exhausted from the effort it took to interact with the Germans and the three overzealous young men.

The next morning Arne overslept and was 20 minutes late for their debriefing with Professor Koch. Tyge and Greta had just finished and Morten was starting to report.

"We talked with three different groups of soldiers. Several of the soldiers had a background in scouting so we had something in common right away."

"Morten blew them away," Carin interrupted. "They peppered him with questions and found that he had more merit badges than anybody they knew. The one group was ready to give him honorary German citizenship until he pointed out that they were officially our enemy."

"They asked Carin about her background," Morten said. "They didn't believe her when she told them she worked on a fishing boat. She took out a piece of rope and challenged them to name a fisherman's knot. They named half a dozen knots and she tied them all. After that we got down to talking about what they thought they were doing here."

"I asked them what they would do if they were ordered to shoot demonstrators," Carin said. "One of them said that it wasn't a problem because he couldn't hit anything anyway."

"They all laughed at that, but it was clearly an uncomfortable topic for them," Morten finished.

Prof. Koch very gravely inquired of Arne if he had slept well and if he was now ready to join them. Arne blushed, embarrassed that he had been late. After Arne and Brigitte filled the others in on their experience, Prof asked "Well, what do you think? Is this working?"

"It's working," Brigitte said. "The problem is avoiding getting our heads shaved from our countrymen who think we're collaborators."

Chapter 23. Food for the Fatherland – Again

It took Colonel Klauer two days to pull together the seventy-five men with farming backgrounds and another two days to train them in the rudiments of requisitioning food from the farmers. On April 24th, the new agents were disseminated across Denmark, with the original ten agents designated as supervisors. The farmers resisted, but as Klauer had explained to General Best, it was hard to lie about how much stock you have in the field. The food was purchased, trucked to the nearest railroad and loaded into boxcars.

On April 29 three box cars departed from the far northern city of Hjerring. On the same day four cars left Frederikshavn. In all, fifty-two boxcars of food left various Danish cities between April 29 and April 31, all scheduled to arrive in Tinglev, the staging area for the train to Berlin, no later than May 2 .

None of these fifty-two boxcars arrived in Tinglev. German inquiries revealed that all of the boxcars started their journey as scheduled. According to the railroad's official records, none of these boxcars ever arrived anywhere.

Colonel Klauer had the unenviable task of explaining what had happened to General Best.

"Do I understand correctly, Colonel?" Best said. "Fifty-two box cars of food disappeared and can't be found?"

"According to the railroad records, yes sir. We don't know where any of them are, sir."

"The High Command expects a train load of food in two days time. If it does not arrive, they will be very unhappy. That will make me unhappy.

"If I am unhappy, Colonel, you will suffer."

Colonel Klauer drew himself up to his full six feet one inches.

"Sir. The resistance stole the train. I was remiss in not putting a large enough guard on it. With your permission, sir, we will redouble our efforts and have another train in Berlin within ten days, sir."

"Very well, Colonel. I expect a written report about this stolen train … right after you finish organizing the effort to get the next trainload. I also want to see a written plan for ensuring the safety of the next one. Dismissed."

General Best spent almost an hour composing a telegram to his boss. He finally sent the third draft, explaining that the resistance managed to steal the trainload of food due to the negligence of Colonel Klauer.

* * * * * * * * *

Colonel Klauer issued orders that put his purchasing agents into a frenzy of buying. In the next three days they purchased enough food to fill forty-eight boxcars and in one more day it was all loaded into railway cars. Colonel Klauer would take no chances this time … each car had its own escort of soldiers with strict orders to baby-sit it until they were relieved.

Once again three boxcars were coming from the region around Hjerring. Sergeant Topf and eight soldiers were assigned to make sure nothing happened to these cars until they arrived in Tinglev. The soldiers were picked up in Hjerring at 9:22 a.m., rode in the boxcars to a siding a few kilometers north of town, and waited while trucks were unloaded into the railway cars. Trains passed every half hour or so, most of them freight trains. By 4:00 p.m. the railway cars were finally loaded and the last truck prepared to leave.

"When will the cars be picked up?" Sergeant Topf asked the truck driver.

He shrugged. "Don't know. Probably soon … the trains go by all the time."

Sergeant Topf settled down to wait. No buildings or any sign of civilization, just a railroad siding and a narrow country road. Stomach's growling. Nothing to eat or drink since breakfast. Who knew we'd end up in the middle of nowhere.

Four trains passed their siding in the next eight hours. None even slowed down. At midnight Topf sent two of his men down the narrow country road, in the direction the trucks had gone, with instructions to find a vehicle, commandeer it, and return with food and water. They were also instructed to report that the Danes had stranded them.

A few minutes past 1:00 a.m. a freight train pulled into their siding and proceeded to hook their boxcars to itself. Sergeant Topf's men had not yet returned from their mission to find food and water. Despite his misgivings, Sergeant Topf decided to go with the train rather than wait an uncertain time for his men. Topf and his remaining six soldiers crowded into the caboose.

The train moved smoothly through the night and very soon pulled into the large railroad yards in Hjerring. Sergeant Topf sent two more of his men for food and water. They returned promptly, laden with supplies. Topf personally took food to the three men assigned to watch their boxcars. The rest of them got what sleep they could in the cramped caboose.

Shortly after 7:00 a.m. Topf checked on the boxcars and discovered that they were on three different sidings.

"What's going on?" Topf demanded. "Why are the cars separated?"

"The workers said they have to shift one car at a time because the sidings aren't long enough," the soldier explained.

"Bull," Topf said. "They're playing games again."

Topf headed for the yard superintendent's office. The railway official assured Topf that his cars would be headed south within the hour.

Sergeant Topf was having trouble staying awake when his boxcars finally left Hjerring. It was 10:22 in the morning and he had managed to snatch only a few little naps the previous night. They were again in the caboose, with their boxcars just ahead of them, as the train moved out of the Hjerring yards. The train moved smoothly for a time and Sergeant Topf was awakened by the train stopping on a siding. He looked at his watch and discovered they had been traveling only 25 minutes. He had just decided to climb down and ask the engineer what was going on when a passenger train passed them going south.

A few minutes later the train started up again ... but wait. Our cars aren't moving.

Catch the damn train. Too late, it's gone. Shit shit shit.

Sergeant Topf looked around ... trees and more trees. The tracks stretched away to the south and to the north and other than the tracks there was nothing but trees.

This time Sergeant Topf didn't hesitate. Two men started hiking north along the tracks and two men started hiking south. Sergeant Topf and his two remaining men stayed with their railway cars.

* * * * * * * * *

Sergeant Topf didn't know it of course, but all of the railway cars of food for Germany were having similar experiences. The logistics of moving railway cars is complicated at best, and with a little creative incompetence, the Danes could ensure that the German cars moved at a glacial pace or, as Sergeant Topf was experiencing, didn't move at all for long periods of time.

The reports of delays and lost cars started coming in to German HQ shortly after Sergeant Topf was abandoned on the siding in the trees. Six such reports arrived on Colonel Klauer's desk at 4:06 p.m. on May 10. At 4:38 p.m. Klauer stormed into the office of Peter Knutsen, the President of the Danish State Railroad, only to find that President Knutsen had gone for the day. Klauer left a message to the effect that any further delays would be met with summary executions, starting with President Knutsen and the various station masters and continuing on down through the ranks of the railway workers until cooperation was ensured.

The following day, May 11, all railway managers above the level of foreman stayed home.

Vald sent General Dr. Best a strongly worded note protesting the death threats to the railway workers. The note pointed out that these officials were afraid to come to work and, as a consequence, the railway logistics were badly tangled and traffic wasn't moving. Vald concluded that these officials would return to work as soon as they had assurances that they wouldn't be harmed.

General Best called Klauer into his office and showed him Vald's note.

"Colonel Klauer, do you see the game they play? They find a way to interfere with our mission. We threaten them. Christian Moellar then publicizes our threat throughout the civilized world. Meanwhile the ones we threatened disappear and work stops. We then get trouble from the High Command because work has stopped."

"Yes, sir. But sir, why don't we round them up and shoot some of them?"

"They have been very clever, Colonel. No personnel records are available. The President of the Railroad is a prominent man ... we might find him. The lower level managers? We can't even find their names much less where they live. So we can't round up the guilty parties.

"We could randomly select people off the streets and execute them in the town square ... but, when Wagner killed the Superintendent of the Shipyard, every shipyard in the country went on strike ... and stayed out until we cashiered Wagner for selling materiel. I suspect that executing a randomly chosen group would lead to a general strike ... and that might get all of us replaced. The High Command wants food and materiel from

Denmark, and we have to figure out how to get them, in spite of these sniveling Danes and their resistance.

"So you see, Colonel, we have to use finesse. Much as I'd like to, we can't go around killing Danes and we can't make public death threats to them."

General Best gritted his teeth and composed a conciliatory note to Prime Minister Stauning. He asserted that Colonel Klauer was merely carried away with zeal for his job and didn't really mean to kill anyone. General Best gave his personal assurances that no railway officials were in any danger from the occupying forces.

On May 15 the railway officials came back to work.

On May 18 the German army began to take over key positions within the railway system. On May 22 the Danes decided that their delaying tactics would no longer be effective and the entire railroad workforce, except for the track maintenance crews, quit and went home. They took with them all manuals and operational procedures and all records of where the rolling stock was located. The steam engines lost their pressure relief valves and pressure gauges. The diesel locomotives were missing their ignition systems and fuel pumps.

The Germans had wrested control of the railroads from the Danes. Before the railroad could transport anything, the Germans had a difficult task of rebuilding.

Chapter 24. The Bridges South

The morning of May 23 dawned bright and sunny with temperatures forecast to reach the mid seventies … a perfect spring day. Arne and his team were assigned as temporary workers for a road construction crew in Tunde, about fifteen kilometers from the German border. They speculated endlessly on the bus ride south, but none of them knew why they had been sent on this mission. They arrived in Tunde, a city near the border with Germany, the evening before they were to start work and found the slightly run down rooming house where they were to stay.

Their landlady was a grandmotherly sort who provided a large breakfast of eggs, potato pancakes, and toast with wonderful home made strawberry jam. Arne ate so much that the girls began to tease him about it. He gave them a mock glare and kept on eating.

At 7:32 a.m. a small lorry pulled up in front of the rooming house. The driver, a middle aged man came in, greeted the landlady with a big hug and turned to them.

"Hi, I'm the foreman for the road crew and I'll take you to the job. You ready?"

"Couple more bites," Arne mumbled.

"I think you're going to explode," Carin said and poked him in the side.

"Nope," Arne patted his bulging stomach. "Just getting fueled up for a long day."

They made the ten-minute ride to the job in the back of the truck, except for Carin and Greta who rode up front. A crew of about a dozen men was already at the job site, the bridge over the river Gammela on the main highway route 11 between Denmark and Germany. The foreman wasted no time in getting them started.

"This here bridge is unsafe and has to be replaced. Today we start taking it down. Most of you already know your assignments. Arne, I need two flagmen and a couple of lookouts on the tops of those hills just north and south of us … if an army patrol comes this way, I want to make sure we're ready for them. Detail somebody as the lookouts and my guys will show them how to signal us. The rest of you will work as assistants … you fetch things and do whatever my guys tell you. Danny is putting up detour signs, so there shouldn't be much traffic, but there may be some … you gotta make sure they don't crash."

"Tyge and Poul take the lookouts," Arne said. "Carin and Greta as the flagmen. The rest of us work as the assistants."

"Crap," Carin said to Greta. "Standing around all day with nothing to do. Rather be carrying things."

"Let's see if Arne will let us trade off at noon," Greta said.

Throughout the morning Arne helped, mostly carrying things or fetching tools, and wondered why they were there. It makes no sense. Why assign a resistance team to road construction? And lookouts for routine road-work?

About mid-morning the foreman suddenly blew a whistle.

"Company coming. German patrol. Make sure everything looks proper. Keep working normally."

Six of the men who had been working under the bridge ran from underneath and joined those working on the bridge roadway. Arne continued carrying the planks he'd been assigned to move.

A minute later two trucks full of German troops arrived.

The Lieutenant in charge jumped down.

"Who's in charge here?"

"Me," the foreman grunted.

The Lieutenant looked him up and down. "What's going on? What are you doing to this bridge?"

"We're preparing to replace it," the foreman said

"Replace it? Why? On whose orders?"

"Government's orders. I don't know why … I do as I'm told."

"Let me see those orders."

The foreman meandered to his truck and rummaged through a small mountain of paper. After several minutes, he strolled back, smoothing a paper as he came.

"Here it is … says right here, bridge to be replaced. Gives us our orders for the day … get bridge ready for removal."

The lieutenant read the document, then studied the construction site. There were several large piles of heavy planks, a line of orange traffic cones down the middle of the bridge, men using heavy jackhammers on a section of the bridge, and numerous other workers busily attacking one lane of the bridge.

The Lieutenant handed the paper to the foremen. "Carry on."

The entire crew stood and watched as the Germans roared across their bridge and out of sight around the corner.

A half hour later Morten rushed up to Arne.

"They're rigging explosives below the bridge. They're going to blow the bridge."

"Oh!" Arne said. Suddenly it all made sense. "This bridge is practically on the border with Germany. We're blowing all the bridges today. We're cutting the highways with Germany. All we're doing on top of the bridge is just camouflage."

The foreman glared at Arne.

"Arne, you're a smart kid. If that was what we're doing, it would be sabotage. We're just following this official work order. In the meantime, keep your mouth shut. Just in case that patrol comes back."

At 11:08 a.m. the charges were all set, the detour signs and barricades were in place, and they all moved up the road about four hundred meters.

The bridge was a concrete span with three sets of concrete pillars and the charges knocked down all of the pillars and broke the roadway into numerous pieces.

The foreman announced a change of plans.

"Don't nobody come to work the next few days until you get the all clear signal … the Nazis might be a little unhappy when they discover they got no railroad bridges and no highway bridges crossing the border."

Chapter 25. Nazi Reaction to the Bridges

General Dr. Best was still on his first cup of coffee when General Hermann von Hanneken slammed open his door with such force that it banged off the wall.

"You're coddling these bastard Danes. We need to execute a few thousand. If you're too chicken to do it, I will."

What had set off his colleague? Hanneken was a competent but unimaginative field officer, hopelessly inept in political matters. Nevertheless, as head of the occupying army, Hanneken held rank equal to his own. He had to be dealt with diplomatically.

"Personally I would like nothing better than to execute a few thousand of these Danes. They've caused nothing but trouble. But what exactly has you so upset?"

"Upset!" Hanneken yelled. "I'm damned furious. Aren't you?"

"Well, yes … ," Best spun the swagger stick like a propeller.

"Every bridge is out. Sabotage. Treason. How are we going to …?"

"What are you talking about?" Best found himself on his feet. "The bridges?"

"You don't know? All the bridges at the border, roads and railroads, all the bridges are blown. There isn't a single way for a truck or a train to cross into Germany."

Best sat down again.

"You didn't know!" Hanneken snorted.

"You can't let them get away with this. Round up a bunch of them and execute them in the public square. We should shoot at least a thousand of them."

Best sat there, ignoring Hanneken while he thought. At last, the true resistance begins. This is just the opening move. If Hanneken has gone soft on security we could be in real trouble. The bridges require immediate punishment.

Hanneken has been lobbying the High Command for drastic action. High Command is losing patience with the situation, they want results now.

The cursed Danes might be cowed by public executions. They might also react strongly. The merchant marine fleet might volunteer assistance to the Allies. Nevertheless, he didn't see that he had much choice.

"They need to be taught a lesson," Best said. "We need to do this carefully. First, I want all the information you have on the bridges. Then, we will plan out how we're going to do this."

"Plan it out?" Hanneken said. "It's simple … grab a couple hundred, announce why they're being shot, and do it in the public square. This afternoon."

"General," Best demurred. "We need to make this all nice and legal and have our press campaign all together when we do it. You don't want to end up like General Himer do you?"

"A thousand, right?" Hanneken sighed.

Best nodded and waited for Hanneken to leave so he could think this through. He needed a little time. His first act was a telegram to the High Command stating that the guilty parties were being arrested and that there would be public executions. He added that General Hanneken was already repairing the bridges and that Danish truck convoys would be assembled and used until the railroad bridges could be repaired.

The big question was who to arrest, since the railroad personnel had already disappeared. He called his Gestapo chief and told him to see if the local Nazi party could give them any names and addresses for railroad personnel or appropriate government officials.

By the next day one railroad vice president, fourteen mid-level railroad managers, and eleven officials from highways were in custody. Best also ordered the arrest of three members of parliament who sat on committees concerning transportation. Then they set up checkpoints on the road and arrested business owners and professional people until they had twelve hundred Danes in custody.

General Dr. Best's press release May 27 announced the arrest of those responsible for blowing up the bridges. The detainees were to be tried for treason and would be executed if found guilty. Military trials were scheduled to begin immediately. Those convicted would be executed upon completion of the trials.

A veneer of legality and due process would blunt the media coverage of a slaughter of a thousand innocent Danes. The Danish people would get the message that resisters would be shot. The "guilt" of the railroad and government officials was determined before their trials ever started ... all of them would be executed.

Of the twelve hundred Danes arrested, roughly one in six was to be freed to keep up the pretense that actual trials were being conducted. The other one thousand would be convicted and executed.

Best smiled as he caressed his swagger stick and dreamed of a cowed and beaten Denmark. The situation looked good. The High Command wanted drastic action and the Danes gave us a perfect excuse. A thousand corpses should whip the Danes into line.

Part Two: A Test of Wills

June through August 1940

Chapter 26. The Churchill Group

Knud Pedersen was 17 and filled with the self-righteous fury of a young man who not only knows he is right but is resentful at being told to be quiet by his timid elders. Denmark occupied by the Nazis, and the adults in charge doing nothing about it. The entire country quiet and peaceful. Everybody asleep. The cursed Germans go about their business without any opposition, doing whatever they damned well please.

On the second day of the occupation, Knud saw an SS trooper trying to flirt with a young Danish woman. Knud dashed across the street to confront the soldier.

"Leave her alone, you piece of dog crap," Knud shouted.

The trooper turned and smashed Knud in the face with the butt of his rifle. Knud fell to the ground, stunned.

Knud tried to sit up and realized blood was pouring out of his nose. A moment later the muzzle of the rifle against his cheek forced him down and held him there. It hurt! My cheek might tear ...

"Now you die, stupid Dane!" The trooper told him. "Think about it before I kill you ... not smart to attack the SS."

Knud lay there, mind frozen ...

"Hold!" The sergeant walked up. "What is this?"

"This Danish swine insulted me. He needs a lesson."

The sergeant kicked Knud in the ribs, twice, two sharp pains that doubled Knud into a fetal position and left him gasping in pain. The sergeant said something that Knud couldn't understand.

When his vision cleared he saw the Nazis strolling down the street already half a block away. When he tried to sit up, a sharp pain in his ribcage caused him to slump back to the ground. Two Danes who witnessed the incident helped him into a taxi and sent him off to the nearest hospital.

Knud had two broken ribs, a serious bruise on the side of his face, and a massive wound to his ego because he had been paralyzed by fear.

In the following weeks Knud talked to five different men about the need to resist the Germans. All of them told him the same thing: they were resisting, the entire country was resisting. Knud couldn't see that anybody was resisting, all this talk about non-violence was just cowardice.

By the end of May the bruise on Knud's head was gone and his ribs only hurt a little when he took a deep breath or exerted himself. The wound to his ego was festering instead of healing. He couldn't accept being afraid of the Nazis, he came from Viking stock, his ancestors were warriors and he wanted to be a warrior too.

Knud began to talk to some of his high school classmates about starting a resistance group to fight the Germans. He quickly gathered a group of eight boys, ranging from 14 to 17 and named them "The Churchill Club" after Winston Churchill. Knud argued that sabotage against the transportation of iron ore from Norway would seriously hurt the Nazis. His recruits enthusiastically agreed.

Knud's first step was to manufacture nitroglycerine in his high school chemistry lab. Knud worried they might blow themselves up, but the first batch would not explode no matter what they did to it. The second and third and fourth batches were equally inert. Knud gave up on manufacturing explosives and decided to steal bomb materiel from the Germans.

They needed guns. German officers, when eating in a restaurant, often left their pistols with their coats in the entryway. Knud and one of his friends walked boldly into a restaurant and approached a group of four German officers. They began asking, in a friendly way, about the soccer teams in Germany. Two of the officers were fans of rival teams and were soon in a spirited discussion about the relative merits of their teams. Knud asked a question each time the conversation started to flag. After fifteen minutes, Knud thanked them politely and hurried to the pre-arranged meeting place in a nearby park.

The other boys were there, giddy with excitement. They had four of the .32 automatics that the officers favored, along with an extra clip for each gun. The following day they repeated this process and got three more guns. Knud decreed that their youngest member, the 14 year old, should not have a gun, but should be restricted to less dangerous activities such as being a lookout or carrying messages.

Knud began to look for an opportunity to steal a truck with explosives. He learned how to hot wire a truck, but he quickly realized that there was no way to tell what a truck was carrying unless he could somehow observe its loading. A week of sneaking around trying to spy on the Germans almost got them caught but yielded no helpful information. The boys were getting impatient … they had joined Knud to fight Germans, not skulk around alleyways.

Knud decided it would be worthwhile to steal a truck so long as it had a load of some kind. Stealing the truck would at least deprive the Germans of it and might provide them with useful materiel. They spent another couple of days watching likely truck stops before an opportunity presented itself.

Their plan was simple. Knud and one other boy would steal the truck. Knud's job was to hot-wire it and drive it. The strongest member of their group had the job of cranking the truck to start it. All of the other boys, save the 14 year old, were assigned to protection. They were scattered around nearby and were to start shooting if the Germans discovered Knud before he could escape.

They stole the truck without any problems and drove it to a nearby garage. The truck was almost empty, but it did contain ten hand grenades, twelve rifles, and four large boxes of cartridges for the rifles. After some debate, they decided to take the rifle cartridges apart and to use the powder for bombs. That night they drove the truck to a vacant lot, stuffed a rag into the petrol tank, lit it and ran. The tank exploded ten seconds later. They all agreed the fireworks were quite satisfactory.

They had ten grenades and, after they emptied the thousands of rifle cartridges, seven gallons of gunpowder. Seven gallons of gunpowder would blow up half the city.

Their first major target was a railroad locomotive. They put two quarts of gunpowder in a paper bag, wrapped it tightly with tape, and made a fuse from a candle. Knud stuffed their paper-bag-bomb into a cavity just below the enormous diesel engine, and fumbled with his matches for a minute. The wind blew out the first one. The second match lit the fuse and they all ran.

Two blocks away they waited but there was no explosion. Finally they went back and saw that some of the paint had burned but otherwise there was no damage to the locomotive.

Finally one of the boys said, "Gunpowder burns pretty hot. Doesn't explode unless it's confined. I guess it just burned."

The next day, to keep the boys busy until they could make good bombs, Knud set them to sabotaging trucks.

"We can do a lot of damage by putting sugar in petrol tanks. We'll work in teams, with one guy putting the sugar in the tank and three others providing lookout and cover for him."

"Where do we get the sugar? My family hasn't had sugar for over a week."

"We'll steal it," Knud declared. "The market near my house."

Over the next ten days they put sugar in twelve trucks. Stealing the sugar was easy enough, but twice they were nearly caught while putting it in the gas tanks. At night they used the grenades and managed to destroy three trucks. When they ran out of grenades they burned the trucks with gunpowder.

Knud was surprised to learn how technically demanding bombs were. Knud rarely remembered how scared he had been when the SS trooper told him to prepare to die. His Viking warrior spirit flowered and gloried in the trouble they were causing the Nazis.

Chapter 27. The Freedom Council

Vald called the Freedom Council meeting to order an hour after receiving Best's press release announcing the arrests of those supposedly responsible for destroying the bridges. King Christian, five politicians, a general, an admiral, and Professor Koch were in attendance. All had been deeply involved in planning the strategy of nonviolent resistance and now constituted the secret planning council for the resistance. Vald began by passing around a copy of the press release.

"It seems that Best wants to do two things," Vald said. "He wants to appear legal and proper and to intimidate us by executing our people. We have to decide what to do."

"We anticipated that, at some point, they would decide to kill a whole group," the general said. "This is crunch time, we have to go all out in resisting it."

The youngest member of Parliament spoke, "I agree. General strike, nationwide."

Vald saw a general nodding of heads.

"I suspect that's right," Vald said. "One of our planning scenarios considered this situation, but I want to make sure we consider all angles. If we go all out, we better win, because we have nothing in reserve. So, I pose the question to you: Is this the time? Do we promise to send the merchant marine to help the allies and to have a lengthy general strike if they execute our people? How do we respond if they decide to execute only some of the detainees? Does our planning scenario still seem to provide the best guidance for this situation?"

The meeting went on for better than two hours while they carefully considered the mood of the country, what they knew of Germany's intentions for them, the temper of the German troops, and what their options were. A key issue was the extent to which the German troops would or would not use violence against the Danes and to what extent orders to use violence against the Danes would effect the morale of the troops and the morale of the Danish resisters.

Professor Koch, waving his eyeglasses like a club, summed it up for them.

"We have to make a stand here. If we lose now, we will truly be at their mercy. We can't let them execute our people. The German troops know we aren't using violence against them. At least some of them will be reluctant to use force against us. If we can maintain our nonviolent discipline, we can save our people and destroy the German morale at the same time. We should follow the planning scenario and hang tough. I think our only other choice is capitulation."

King Christian spoke for the first time that evening.

"I thank you for your wise counsel. It seems to me that the Viking spirit is very much alive and well in Denmark. I am very proud of all of you and of our people. I will be honored to work with Prime Minister Stauning to defy the German invaders."

* * * * * * * * * *

General Dr. Best was expecting the request for a meeting when Prime Minister Stauning's note arrived. He derived great satisfaction from being able to insist that Vald and the King come to him for the meeting.

General Dr. Best received Prime Minister Stauning, the King, and their four advisors at 2:00 p.m. on May 29th. Best sat behind a large desk, in a chair that was slightly elevated, flanked on either side by aides. The Danish officials were seated in chairs in a semicircle facing the desk. Best continued sitting while they filed into the room and found seats.

"What can I do for you?" Best said.

"You have arrested a large number of our citizens and, apparently, intend to make a public example of them," Vald said. "Is that correct?"

Best leaned forward, elbows on his desk. He toyed with the swagger stick.

"We intend to punish those responsible for destroying the bridges."

"General Best, we destroyed our own bridges, which we have every right to do. There has been no crime and therefore no one can be punished for it."

"You interfered with our plans. That is treason to the Fatherland, punishable by death."

"Denmark does not recognize the authority of the Fatherland," Christian said. "Germany has no legitimacy here. Furthermore, I was the one who gave the order to destroy the bridges. You arrested a group of innocents."

"The trials will determine guilt or innocence. The guilty will be executed."

"General, we all know that the men you arrested are innocent," Vald said. "We also understand that this is intended to frighten us.

"We will not be intimidated. All production has stopped. A nationwide general strike started this morning and will continue so long as the death threat hangs over our citizens. Germany will get no food or materiel from us. Furthermore, the fleet will offer its services to the Allies the instant you begin executing our people."

Best jumped up. He towered over the Danish delegation from his raised platform, swagger stick pointing at them.

"Insolent fools. I hold the power. Get out of here before I decide to arrest you."

Best stalked out of the room, swagger stick slapping his leg with each step.

"Let's go home," Christian said.

Vald wanted to emulate Christian, to appear calm, but his stomach was churning. Will Hitler insist on slaughtering large numbers? Will Best decide that mass executions are the best bet for his own career? Best will do anything, no matter how barbaric, to benefit himself. Does a civilized man actually stand a chance against such monsters?

Chapter 28. Fritz Clausen Again

The sun was shining and flowers were bursting forth but Fritz Clausen was oblivious to the spring beauty around him as he hurried out of his house and headed for the main thoroughfare to catch a cab. His assistant was waiting for him with numerous notebooks, notebooks full of incriminating information on resistance members.

Clausen's anticipation of the arrests of the Danes named in the notebooks was so strong he actually shivered with delight.

Clausen thought the notebooks would garner some respect from General Best. General Best ignores me. One brief meeting, then nothing. A lowly captain as our liaison.

How many years now? Dedicated to the Nazi cause since 1933. Nobody, not even my lieutenants appreciated the hard work. My work, my commitment … and all it earned me was ridicule from stupid Danes. Life is really unfair. Worst of all, General Best, Hitler's personal representative to Denmark, ignores me.

Five minutes later his cab stopped in front of the restaurant that was the meeting place. Fritz dabbed at his eyes … it wouldn't do to show weakness in front of his assistant … paid the cabby, squared his shoulders, and went inside.

The man had five notebooks with hundreds of names.

"This is magnificent," Clausen whispered. "I'll take this to Captain Eschmann right away. Tell the men this is critical and they need to continue. I'll see you in a week. Goodbye."

Clausen fairly ran outside and hailed another cab.

"Take me to the Shell House."

"Why you going to the SS?" the cabby said.

"I have a delivery to make."

"Well, I'm not helping the SS. You can walk."

Clausen was stunned and frightened by the cabby's strong reaction. He got out, and as his fright turned to rage, caught another cab and told it to take him to Pladhausen Square which was where the Shell House was located.

Captain Eschmann was not available when Fritz arrived at his destination. Fritz wrote him a note and left the notebooks.

Captain Eschmann arrived an hour later and began looking through the notebooks. "Got a minute?" Eschman asked a colleague. "Clausen, our local Fuhrer worshipper, dropped off a pile of notebooks full of names, hundreds of names. Says these are resistance members. I don't know if any of this is any good. Listen to the notations:

    expressed hatred for the Fuhrer
    said he strongly supported the resistance
    boasted about defying curfew
    always talking about Moellar's broadcasts
    shared food from his garden (to help defy the blockade)
    openly reads the illegal newspapers
    carries a camera

What'd you think?"

"Are those describing the same person?"

"No, each of them is about a different person."

"Hell, those things apply to nearly everyone in the whole damn country."

"Well, that's what I thought. I don't see that this helps much."

"Clausen and his lads couldn't find a hole in the ground. Get him to be much more selective. He might …maybe, maybe … identify a few leaders that would be worth our while to go after."

Captain Eschmann groaned and said, "Okay, I'll talk to him. By the way, we got some useful information from interviewing his bunch about corporate leaders. We've picked up a few executives and are putting the screws to them."

Chapter 29. The Mass Demonstrations

With the general strike in full swing, no one went to work. Arne's team was in the crowd gathered in the Radhuspladsen in front of Gestapo headquarters in the Shell building. They'd been there for more than an hour, along with thousands of other Danes.

Morten struck up a conversation with two young Jewish men, David Levine and Herbert Pundit. Arne looked over and heard the younger one talking.

"My mother was afraid I would get hurt, until David promised to keep an eye on me."

"Typical mother," David laughed. "She doesn't want her son in any danger."

"Mother thinks David has to take care of me. I'm sixteen, I can take care of myself."

"You should be glad you have a mother to worry about you," Tyge said. "My mother died years ago."

Arne noticed that Herbert kept looking at Carin. Young Herbert wants her to notice him. No surprise there, Carin is petite and strikingly pretty. Herbert has no idea how tough and resourceful she is. Much more woman than a sixteen year old could handle.

"Jews are apparently being arrested in some of the Nazi occupied countries," David said. "Do you know anything about that?"

'No, but it wouldn't surprise me," Morten said. "Hitler says everyone except the pure Aryans are trash and should be eliminated."

"What, have you read his book?" David asked.

"Most of it," Morten grimaced. "It's such nasty garbage it's hard to read … really poisonous stuff. Hitler is crazy."

A murmur swept over the crowd. A contingent of SS troops moved into the western end of the square and set up half a dozen machine guns. An officer with a bullhorn moved in front of the guns.

"Disperse now. Leave the square immediately." The officer's voice, amplified by the bullhorn, was easily heard throughout the square.

"Nobody move," Arne ordered.

"You have ten minutes to clear the square," the bullhorn roared. "In ten minutes we begin shooting."

Arne and his group kept their position.

People began moving out of the square, at first slowly and then more and more rapidly.

The people around Arne's little group moved away.

"I'm outa here," Asger said. He jogged away.

"Arne, I think we need to leave," Tyge said.

It was clear that most of the people in the square were leaving. In a few more minutes they would be alone.

"Okay," Arne relented. "Let's go."

They ran.

As they exited the square, Arne looked at his watch. The ten minutes was up. The Germans began shooting while a number of people were still in the square.

Arne glanced behind him as he ran down the street leading away from the square. He could still see one of the machine guns. Behind him people were falling down. He fled to the end of the block and ducked behind a fence, with his team and the two Jewish men, David and Herbert beside him. A number of injured people were struggling down the block toward them. Asger was waiting behind the fence.

Arne waited a few seconds to make sure the firing had stopped.

"Come on," he said. "These people need help."

Arne dashed back toward the square. Most of his group, including David and Herbert, followed closely. Morten and Poul followed a moment later and Asger came along well behind.

A minute later they had eleven injured people behind their fence. Brigitte tore strips from a petticoat. David and Herbert were bandaging arms and legs. Greta and Poul pressed wads of cloth on the chest and thigh of a man. As Arne looked the man's head sagged and his eyes closed.

"Tyge," Arne said. "You and Carin go find a city bus to come and pick up the wounded. Hurry."

With the transportation taken care of, Arne looked around to see what else he could do. Greta and Poul were still bending over the man with multiple wounds. Next to them a middle-aged man sat slumped against the fence, face ashen and blood running down his arm and chest.

Arne bent down and saw the bullet hole high in his shoulder, blood oozing slowly out of the golf ball size wound in the front of his chest. Shot in the back. He pressed a clean hankerchief into the wound.

"Can you hold this?" The man didn't react. Probably in shock already. Nothing I can do for him. The wound isn't bleeding much.

Arne went to the next victim. This man had a wound in the thigh. He was using his hands to press on the wound, but the blood welled up around and between his fingers.

Arne ripped off his shirt, balled it up and pressed it into the wound. Can't tell if it slowed or the shirt just soaked it up. Keep pressing. Seemed to slow.

A private car stopped and took three of their most seriously wounded, including the man Greta and Poul had been working on.

Some interminable time later Tyge and Carin arrived with a city bus and they hustled their victims on board, got on themselves, along with David and Herbert, and rode to the nearest hospital.

Greta and Poul's man was dead on arrival but it seemed that the rest would probably recover.

Arne looked at his people and despaired. Most of them had never seen anyone die, and none of them had ever been shot at. Greta sobbed with her head in her hands, while beside her Poul stared at nothing, and gently stroked her shoulder. The rest showed outrage, despair, and fear. Even Asger, who always seemed to have a swagger, stood numb and quiet.

Brigitte sat by herself, a little away from the rest who were clustered together as if for warmth. None of them seemed able to comprehend what had just happened.

He had to do something, but what? He started to talk, not really knowing what he was going to say.

"Is anybody hurt?"

No one responded. He tried again.

"I'm proud of you. We saved those people … without us more would have died."

"He died. We failed." Greta's voice was dead and toneless.

"Greta, you're not God," Arne said. "You did all anybody could have done. The chest wound alone was probably fatal. There was nothing you could have done."

Greta's only response was to sob louder. Tyge gathered her into his arms and held her.

Poul continued to sit and stare at nothing. Carin went over and, kneeling in front of him, whispered something.

Not knowing what else to do and feeling helpless, Arne waited.

The little courtyard where they sat next to the hospital entrance had one substantial tree in it. A little breeze stirred the leaves and the sun's rays peeked through them, making a dappled ever-changing display. Arne picked out patterns in the light, now an auto, there a face. Nazis and guns and death receded and he watched the patterns of light on the wall.

No more sobbing. Just silence. With a start, he looked around. Everyone was sitting quietly. Tyge and Carin were both looking at him. They expect me to do something.

It's past lunchtime. Eating is good.

"I'm going for food and beer. How about waiting in the park across the street? Morten, can you help?"

As Morten got up, Brigitte also stood. "I'll come," she said.

Arne and Morten and Brigitte walked very close together, with Brigitte in the middle. None of them spoke, but seemed content to draw strength and comfort from each other.

They returned with as much food and beer as the three of them could carry. Greta announced that she couldn't eat, that her appetite was spoiled. Tyge cajoled her into eating a bite and she discovered that she was actually ravenous. An hour later, full of food and beer, they began discussing what to do next.

"Are we going to continue demonstrating?" Brigitte asked.

'We'll probably get shot," Poul said, "but I'm too mad to care."

Arne saw their serious faces and realized that Poul spoke for the group.

They started walking toward the SS headquarters. There were swarms of people on the street, most headed the same direction they were going. Poul had spoken for much of the city.

Three blocks later the group in front of them turned and ran.

"A patrol, a patrol!" someone shouted.

They ran around the corner. A Wehrmacht patrol walked down the street they had just left.

Twice more they ran into Wehrmacht patrols. Both times they ducked into side streets and the patrols ignored them.

Two blocks from City Square they came face to face with an SS patrol at a distance of just over a block.

The SS started shooting. Greta, a few steps behind the rest, cried out just as Arne dashed into the side street. Glancing back, he saw she was on the ground.

Arne sprinted to her. He heaved Greta into a fireman's carry and began a lurching run toward safety. Bullets sang past him and one hit the pavement close by, stinging his leg with fragments of concrete or steel.

Most of the team was well down the block and safe.

What the hell? Tyge, Brigitte and David were all racing toward him. He tried to wave them off and almost dropped Greta.

He looked for a hiding place as soon as he gained the relative safety of the side street. Carrying Greta, they couldn't outrun the Nazis.

A German shouted something. No doubt urging the soldiers on to catch them.

Tyge was trying to help but was mostly getting in the way. David ran beside him, but wisely didn't try to help.

"Over here," Brigitte called. "This way."

Arne saw an elderly lady, on her front porch two houses away, gesturing for them to come. Arne staggered onto the porch, relinquished Greta to David and Tyge and they all spilled into the lady's parlor. The SS was nowhere in sight.

"Move inside, go farther back," the lady said.

They watched from the middle room. Moments later the SS went past the house and disappeared from view.

Tyge bent over Greta. "It's my leg, they shot my leg."

"It'll be okay," Tyge said. "Bullet missed the bone."

Their rescuer brought bandages while Brigitte washed the wound, a neat hole through the calf of her left leg. Brigitte wrapped it with gauze and bound it with tape.

Tyge asked, "What do we do now?"

The lady of the house replied firmly, "You have a little snack while we wait for the Germans to go away. Then, in a little while, I'll get my friend with the motorcar to come take her to the hospital."

"That would be wonderful," Arne said. "Thank you."

A half-hour later Arne and Brigitte left to rendezvous with their team. Tyge went with Greta to the hospital with plans to meet them that evening. David and Herbert said goodbye and started home.

Arne and Brigitte headed toward the little café designated as their rendezvous. Arne was jumpy. The damned SS could come around the corner at any moment. We need eyes in the back of our heads. I'm twisting my neck off … but Brigitte seems calm.

"Aren't you afraid?" Arne said.

"Yes, but I'm also determined ... I'm not going to let them win."

"I'm twisting my neck off trying to see in all directions at once ... but you're just walking along calmly. How do you do that?"

"Hmm ... I guess I'm relying on all these people to also be on the lookout." She gestured at the four or five other groups of people on the street ahead of and behind them.

Brigitte stopped walking.

"Arne, that was a good thing you did back there. You saved Greta."

"Oh, well. Any of us would have done it. I was just the one who heard her cry out."

"No. Several of us heard her." Brigitte met his eyes. "Asger was right beside me and never even slowed down. Tyge and I both stopped but we just stood there while you ran back."

"I was the closest ... there was no time to think about it, I just did it. You saved us ... if you hadn't found the old lady they would have caught us."

"Well, I just wanted to tell you I think you're very brave."

Brigitte dropped her eyes and started walking again. She seemed lost in her own thoughts while they covered the seven blocks to the rendezvous with their teammates. Arne chalked V for victory on a great many walls as they walked.

The newspapers the next day were full of stories of the nationwide general strike and of German troops firing on peaceful demonstrators. The newspapers reported various numbers of casualties but the Copenhagen hospitals claimed a total of twenty-three gunshot deaths and an additional one hundred and eight wounds. Moellar's broadcasts emphasized, over and over, the importance of maintaining nonviolent discipline and the impact that nonviolent actions could have on the morale of their opponents. He said that any use of violence by the Danes would enable the Germans to justify the use of violence against them. So long as they maintained their nonviolent discipline they would eat away at German morale and the German ability to use violence against them.

Chapter 30. Detective Work

Professor Koch seemed fidgety, hardly his usual composed self. He held his reading glasses, making slashing motions with them as he talked.

"Arne, there have been a rash of sabotage actions in recent weeks, all of them here in Copenhagen. It's mostly sugar in petrol tanks and burning of large trucks. So far there have been no fatalities, but the Freedom Council is worried. Someone is using violence against the Germans and it compromises our entire strategy. We suspect a group of young people and want you and your group to work with the police to find them."

"Um, I guess the police will tell us what to do?" Arne asked.

"Yes, Detective, um … " Koch looked for his glasses, remembered they were in his hand and put them on. "Detective Rorkark is expecting you. I would like you to begin immediately."

"Okay, Professor. What do we do when we find them?"

"Probably just talk to them, but Detective Rorkark will handle that. Hopefully we will get them involved in some productive resistance activities. You have to be careful … it could be that this is a group of provocateurs, people working with the Nazis to give them justification for using violence."

* * * * * * * * *

Detective Rorkark was an older man, heavyset but with an easy manner and Arne immediately liked him. The detective, his partner, and Arne's group were gathered around an old much-scratched wooden table in the police station. The group spent a few minutes with everyone getting coffee from the large coffee pot in the corner.

"We've got people all over the city looking for these guys,: Rorkark said. "I'm sure the Germans are looking too. We want to stop them, get 'em doing something productive instead of hurting the resistance. Also, we don't want the Germans catching them … and they are getting bolder which means they will get careless and will be caught unless we get to them first.

"We need more eyes and ears within the colleges and high schools, we think that's who these guys are."

Arne, Poul, and Carin were sent to enroll in different high schools under assumed names. The others were assigned to universities.

Arne went directly to his assigned school, the Royal Danish Veterinarian and Agricultural High School, and presented the identification papers the police prepared for him. A few minutes later he sat down with the guidance counselor. The counselor told him Detective Rorkark asked for her help.

"Your teachers know only that you are here on a resistance assignment," the counselor said. "They will understand if you fail to come to class and they can be trusted. They will answer any questions that may help you."

"Detective Rorkark suggested we look for good students or natural leaders whose behavior has changed recently," Arne said. "Especially things like unexcused absences or falling asleep in class or nervousness."

"Oh, good," the counselor said. "I'll talk to the teachers and see if we can generate a list of likely suspects. How will you proceed?"

"Well, mostly just try to meet as many people as possible and keep my ears open for the next few days. My instructions are to be very angry at the Germans and very anxious to 'do something'. The detective told us to be angry enough that the saboteurs might approach us, but not to encourage violence."

For the next three days Arne pretended to be a student at the Royal Danish Veterinarian and Agricultural High School. He spent time at everything except going to class. There were two lunch periods and he ate a light lunch at both. He spent hours in the library, chatting with anyone who happened to be there. Students began congregating outside at 6:45 a.m. and Arne was there. After school there were myriad activities and clubs and Arne sampled as many as he could.

On the fourth day the Guidance Counselor called him to her office.

"Arne, I have four names for you. Almost every teacher in the school helped. I compared lists from the different teachers and there are a few boys who are on two or more lists. These guys can't stay awake in class and it just started in the last few weeks."

"Wow, fantastic," Arne said. "I don't know any of them, but maybe I can meet them."

"Here are the class schedules for them. Oh, and three of them are in the chess club but haven't been to a meeting in three weeks."

They spent the next fifteen minutes without coming up with a good plan for Arne meeting any of the four suspects. They finally decided to try and find someone reliable who already was friends with at least one of them.

The following day the Counselor sent for Arne at 10:00 a.m. and introduced him to a gangly young man named Lauritz.

"Arne and Lauritz, this is resistance business, so the less you know about each other the better. I'm going to tell you just enough so that the two of you can do a job for us, okay?"

Both boys nodded.

"Good. Lauritz, Arne needs to meet Gregers and Olav … the resistance needs this connection. Here's how to do it. You two spend an hour or so getting to know each other – favorite sports, hobbies, family background … enough so that you can pretend to be old friends. Then the two of you hang out together until an opportunity comes up for you to introduce Arne to Gregers and Olav. It has to appear natural and casual. After that, Lauritz, you're done with your assignment. Okay?"

"Sure, I can do that." Lauritz said. "I sometimes eat lunch with them. If you can go with me to the 11:30 lunch we can probably eat with them. Oh, but I have class between now and then."

"This is important," the counselor said. "Skip class. I'll fix it with your teacher. Go talk to Arne, then take him to lunch."

Arne and his new "old friend" were a few minutes early for lunch and picked a table where Lauritz could easily wave over the ones Arne wanted to meet.

"Gregers, over here," Lauritz said ten minutes later.

Two boys came over and Gregers said, "How'd you get here so early? You're usually the last one here."

Lauritz laughed. "I think our teacher misread the clock and let us out early. Hey, I want you guys to meet my friend. Our families spent a couple summers together at the beach … he just transferred into the school so he doesn't know anybody yet."

The boys shook Arne's hand and introduced themselves as Gregers and Olav.

"Did you hear about the German trucks that were burned last night?" Gregers asked. "Three big trucks, all total losses. I bet that made some Nazi bastards pretty mad."

"Wow. Three trucks," Arne said. "Man, I'd like to do something to hurt the Nazis. How did they do it?"

"I heard they used gunpowder," Gregers said. "It burns real hot."

"Oh, man. Gunpowder," Arne said. "Why didn't they don't just blow it up?"

"Unless you got it tightly enclosed, gunpowder just burns, doesn't explode," Gregers said.

"Hey, Lauritz, you and Arne go back a ways?" Olav said. "You know each other well?"

"Oh, yeah, he's my buddy," Lauritz said. "Saved my life once when our dingy overturned and I hit my head … and he hates the Nazis."

"Okay, I guess he's no stikker, then," Olav said.

"A stikker!" Lauritz said. "Not my man, never."

The conversation took an abrupt turn when Olav said, "There's that girl you're trying to get to." The boys spent the remainder of the lunch time in what Arne thought was a very juvenile discussion of the attractiveness of various girls. Arne had little to say for the remainder of the time, feeling that he had said enough if these two were indeed part of the saboteur group.

Arne did not have long to wait. The following morning, before school, his two new acquaintances from lunch came up to him.

"Hey," Olav said.

"Hey, yourself. What's up?"

"You said you wanted to hurt the Nazis," Olav said. "Are you prepared to take some risks to do it?"

"With all my heart. I was ashamed they just rolled over us without a fight."

"How do we know you're not a stikker?"

"Didn't Lauritz vouch for me?"

"Yeah, but he's a little gullible."

Arne considered giving them his true identity, instead replied, "You know the counselor? She can vouch for me."

This seemed to satisfy them and they left after saying, "You'll be hearing from us."

Arne went into the building with the rest of the students, but instead of going to class stopped by the counselor's office and then went to see Detective Rorkark.

Arne reported both conversations with the boys and asked what he should do next. The detective thought for few seconds then said, "What's your assessment of them? Are they acting out of patriotism?"

"Definitely. These guys weren't putting on an act."

The detective agreed. "If they were provocateurs, they wouldn't have responded to your initial conversation. They would either have just ignored you or … and this is unlikely … if they decided you would make a good target, they wouldn't bother trying to verify your patriotism, they would just take it at face value."

He continued, "Play it cool. Try to meet the others, allow yourself to get recruited, but be a little timid. You know, 'I can't go on any missions until I get some training' or 'I really want to but my father insists that I help him this evening' … something that lets you get close but not actually carrying out sabotage. As soon as you have the names, we move in."

Arne went back to the school and tried to hide his elation as he went about his normal business. At lunch time the two boys approached him.

"Do you know the café just down the street? Where everybody hangs out after school?"

"Sure. Been there several times."

"Can you be there today right after school?"

"Okay. What am I doing there?"

"Somebody wants to talk to you. About fighting the Nazis. Can you be there?"

"Wow, yeah. How will I know him?"

"He knows you. You just get a table and wait."

When school ended, Arne went directly to the café. He selected a table in the back, against the wall. The time dragged by but Arne's watch said he waited only seven minutes.

The young man that came and sat down at Arne's table was Arne's twin in height and build. He didn't say anything and the two of them just sat there looking at each other. Despite his youth, the fellow had circles under his eyes and the fingers of his right hand drummed ceaselessly on the table. Finally the newcomer spoke, "Let's go for a walk."

Arne didn't say anything, just nodded and got up and headed for the door. They walked a block in silence, until they were well away from people. Finally the newcomer spoke.

"You hate the Nazis and want to fight them?"

"Who the hell are you and how do I know you're not a stikker?"

The newcomer stopped and fixed Arne with an icy glare. "I'm one of the few who are actually doing something about the Nazis. The question is whether or not you want to help."

Arne considered this, then began walking again and the other fell in at his side.

"You're friends of Gregers and Olav? Okay, so you checked me out … but I don't know you. You could be anything or anybody. So tell me why I should trust you."

They walked several paces before the other answered.

"Fair enough. I'm responsible for sugar in the petrol tanks for at least 15 German trucks and burning ten more of them. We stole a German truck with guns and ammunition. We stole nine pistols right from under their noses. That's who I am. What have you done?"

"Well, I've been in a lot of demonstrations. I helped blow up the bridges at the border."

"Demonstrations. What the hell good are they? Just gives the Germans an excuse to shoot at us. Blowing up the bridges, that's more like it." He stopped and faced Arne, eyes gleaming.

"Hey, what do you know about explosives? Do you know how to blow up bridges?"

"No, sorry, I was just part of the support team for the guys who actually blew the bridge. I don't know explosives."

"Oh, crap. I've been learning about bombs but it's pretty complicated and I don't have a place to make them."

They walked for another half hour. When they parted Arne knew the other was named Knud Pedersen and even knew where he lived.

* * * * * * * *

The following morning Arne and detective Rorkark, in plain clothes, waited in the detective's nondescript old car in front of Knud's house. When Knud came out the front door, Arne and the Detective got out of the car and Arne called to him.

For a second Rorkark thought Knud would run, but then he seemed to realize that they knew where he lived and there was no point in running.

"Knud, we just want to talk," Arne said. "We're both with the resistance and we need to talk."

"So. You are an informer. You're an informer for the so-called resistance that doesn't actually do anything."

"Knud, you need to talk to us," Arne said.

"Talk. That's crap. All the resistance ever does it talk. You're all a bunch of friggin cowards."

Rorkark told himself not to lose it, this guy is just young and foolish.

"Young man," Rorkark said. "You're talking to one of the heroes of the resistance, somebody whose real name is known all over Denmark, over much of the world actually. So a little less mouth and lots more respect is in order."

Knud met the Detectives angry glare for long seconds before looking away. When he finally spoke it was almost to himself.

"I hate talking. Oh, well, what do we do? Go for a walk?"

"Let's take my car," Rorkark said.

Knud got in the front and Arne rode in the back. They drove in silence for the few minutes it took to reach one of Copenhagen's large parks. There was nobody around so they parked and sat at a picnic table, screened from the street by large bushes.

"'Knud, you seem to think you're the only patriotic Dane?" Rorkark said.

"No Detective, just one of the few with the balls to actually fight the Germans."

"You don't think the resistance is fighting the Germans?"

'No, I can't see that this so-called strategic non-violence accomplishes anything at all. The Nazis do whatever they want."

"Well, it's true that the Nazis do what they want. However, they don't get what they want. They came here to get war materiel ... ships, submarines, guns, food. They manage to get some food but at a very high cost in manpower. They have so far gotten no guns or ships and it doesn't look like they will. The Nazis have more than 100,000 men here and what are they getting out of it? Damn little. Denmark has so far been a very expensive operation for them."

"Those are pretty words. We're Vikings ... warriors. We should be fighting them, not playing games with them."

Detective Rorkark realized he wasn't getting anywhere. Knud was committed to violence. Time to shift tactics.

"Knud, look, this really isn't open for debate. We spent years as a nation developing strategic nonviolence, more years training and preparing to implement it and we are committed as a nation. As a patriotic Dane, you are obligated to do your part and not to undermine our national strategy."

He paused to make sure Knud was listening before continuing.

"A fundamental part of the strategy is to take away from the Nazis any excuse for their soldiers to use violence against us. The normal soldier can be induced to kill only because his superiors demonize the opponent, usually by pointing to the violence they are committing. When we use violence against the Nazis we help them because then their soldiers can be induced to kill us. And they have most of the guns."

He paused again. Knud was glaring at him. The detective leaned forward and jabbed his finger into Knud's chest.

"Knud, you better hear me now. You and your group are aiding and abetting the enemy by using violence against them. We believe you acted out of good intentions ... misguided, but well intentioned. My instructions are to find you, explain the situation to you and to get you to cease and desist the violence.

"Now here is the kicker, Knud. If you do not stop the violence, I am to arrest you and everyone in your group. The charge will be treason. And treason carries the death penalty. Nobody wants that, Knud, but you are endangering us all."

Knud's face twisted and for a moment he seemed on the verge of crying. Rorkark waited.

Knud sat there for quite a while.

Finally Knud looked up at detective Rorkark and said very softly, "You know, this really sucks. You really would charge me with treason?"

"Your situation was covered in our contingency planning before the Nazis even came," Rorkark said. "Yes, if you didn't stop, we would charge you with treason. My orders come directly from the Freedom Council."

Knud's eyes got very big. "The Freedom Council. They discussed me?"

"Yes, Knud, they discussed you. Told me to deliver the message. Did you get the message?"

"Okay, okay, I got it ... no more violence, but I don't have to like it."

Detective Rorkark said, "Let me tell you a story. A friend of mine was a manager of a small machine shop up north. The Germans came to him, well, actually an SS officer came, and informed him that he would, beginning immediately, make a certain machine part for them, thousands of them. My friend told the officer that he was forbidden by his government to do so. The SS officer didn't argue with him, just pulled out his revolver and shot my friend through the heart. Actually, he shot him three times.

"The SS bastard then arrested the assistant manager and explained to the ten workers that if they didn't show up for work the next day, the assistant manager would die.

"The workers all came in the next day and seemed to be working very hard. However, at the end of the day very little had been accomplished. There were a lot of ruined parts and wasted material, but no finished products. This went on for a week. Now, all this week the assistant manager was on site during the day and in custody each night. There were three soldiers who took turns guarding him around the clock, 24 hours a day.

"At the end of the week the SS officer came to see how much they had accomplished. There were large piles of waste materials and quite a few 'finished products'. When the officer carefully measured the parts, none of them were satisfactory. All were misshapen or the wrong size. The Officer flew into a rage and ordered the assistant manager's guard to take him out back and shoot him.

"They tied his hands behind his back and the guard departed with the unfortunate manager. Five minutes passed and they heard two shots. Another five minutes passed and the officer sent one of his SS troopers to see what was taking so long.

"A minute later the trooper ran into the room and announced they were gone. The guard had deserted ... he and the assistant manager had fled.

"We later found out that the guard told the manager he didn't want to shoot him but was afraid to disobey orders. The manager promised to hide him and they quickly agreed to flee together.

"The SS officer shot the shop foreman and threatened to kill the entire staff if they didn't produce. The staff left that evening and didn't go back. The full story came out in the press a few days later and the murderous SS officer got transferred somewhere, probably to the front line.

"Now, Knud, I want to ask you. Do you think it was easy standing up to that SS butcher? Think about that, Knud. The resistance has been doing that and similar things, all over the country. And the Nazis aren't getting a damn thing from us. I think that is pretty effective fighting."

Knud looked from one to the other, then said to Arne, "So you're a big hero, huh?"

"I'm no hero, I just ... "

Detective Rorkark interrupted. "Arne's a hero several times over. Wrote the Ten Commandments. While you and I were still trying to figure out what hit us, Arne wrote and delivered the Ten Commandments. Carried his wounded friend to safety under fire from the SS. Has risked his life in many operations already. Oh yes, he's a hero all right."

Knud had no more to say.

Detective Rorkark had one parting comment. "I will expect you and all of your group to meet with me tomorrow at the police station at 4:30 p.m. ... and we'll figure out how best to put you to work for the resistance."

Knud nodded yes, several times, emphatically.

Chapter 31. Truck Convoys

Highway bridges were relatively easy to replace because temporary bridges could be built quickly. Truck traffic could negotiate narrow bridges with steep approaches or even go through several feet of water if there was a solid bottom.

Trains required a bridge that was level with the existing track … it was a long-term project to replace a railroad bridge. Thus the obvious response to destroying the bridges was to build temporary road bridges and organize truck convoys. The Danes understood this and did their best to hide their heavy trucks.

The same day the bridges were blown, the government's big lorries and those belonging to the big shipping companies all went into hiding. The Nazis set up checkpoints along the major highways, with orders to requisition all heavy lorries and their drivers. By the end of the second day they had hundreds of mid-size lorries but only twelve of the big articulated lorries. On the third day Best ordered a search for the big rigs and three days later they found twenty-seven additional articulated lorries hidden in several large warehouses. They shot the three men who were working in the warehouses with the lorries.

While they were gathering lorries, Best's troops had managed to get the railway cars of food to the southern city of Tinglev. On May 31st thirty-nine big lorries and one hundred eighty-seven medium sized lorries arrived at the railroad yards in Tinglev. Each lorry was driven by a Dane and each carried at least one German soldier. The articulated lorries each had two German soldiers. Gerhard, Jacob, and their squad was assigned to ride with the medium sized lorries. In addition, there were five hundred soldiers assigned to help transfer the food from the railway cars to the lorries.

They quickly discovered that most of the vegetables were spoiled and had to be thrown out. Seven refrigerated cars had lost their power and the meat had spoiled. They still had eleven boxcars of wheat and other non-perishables and fourteen refrigerated cars of meat. The non-perishables were immediately loaded into the mid-sized lorries and, while the SS was shooting at Arne and the other demonstrators in front of their headquarters, the convoy started toward Germany.

The convoy had been on the road for only a few minutes when one of the engines died. The entire convoy of one hundred twenty-six lorries stopped while they tried to re-start the engine. When it wouldn't start, the Captain asked for a mechanic. The sergeant fetched Jacob and Gerhard. They tinkered with the engine for a few minutes and Jacob announced, "The engine is frozen … seems like it lost all its oil and froze up."

They left the truck, still loaded with wheat, and continued. Five minutes later another lorry died. Again, Jacob and Gerhard examined the engine and Jacob again announced the engine was frozen. The Captain forced the Danish driver out of his truck, walked him a few feet into the field along side the road and shot him in the back of the head. Gerhard began making gurgling noises and Jacob slapped him in the back of the head and whispered "Steady, lad. Don't throw up."

The Captain announced, "Get all the drivers out here, now."

When all the drivers were gathered together, the Captain climbed onto the hood of a truck and addressed them.

"Your trucks are mysteriously breaking down. I'm not sure how you are arranging this, but it stops now. The driver of this truck is dead. If your truck stops, you will also die. You are responsible for maintaining your truck in proper working order. If your truck breaks down, you will be shot. Is that understood?"

The truck drivers exchanged nervous looks but didn't say anything. The Captain repeated, "Do you understand?"

"Yes Captain, we understand."

"But we can't help it," another said.

"Bring me that man," the captain said. When his troops dumped the man in front of him, he continued, "What do you mean, you can't help it?"

"Please Captain, don't shoot me. I have a wife and two small children. Don't shoot me … I didn't do it."

"Didn't do what? Speak up, fool."

"The sugar. There's sugar in the petrol tanks. But I didn't do it, Captain. I didn't do it."

Sugar in the petrol tanks! All the engines will freeze up and there's nothing to do about it.

"When? How did the sugar get in the tanks?"

The Captain's informant, still kneeling in front of him, looked over his shoulder at the other drivers and didn't answer. The Captain pulled his .32 automatic and put the muzzle against the man's forehead.

"I asked a question."

"Don't shoot. Please. It was last night, some of the guys put sugar in the petrol tanks."

"Who? Who did this?"

"I don't know, Captain, I swear I don't know. It wasn't me. I had nothing to do with it, didn't know about it 'til it was done."

"Now listen carefully. If you don't know who did it, I have no further use for you and will kill you. Are you sure you don't know?"

The man prostrated himself and sobbed loudly. Between sobs he gulped out, "I swear Captain, I don't know nothin, I wasn't any part of it. Don't, please … "

The sharp bang of the .32 firing into the back of his head cut off his pleading. The drivers stood in stunned silence while the Captain decided what to do next. Gerhard gulped audibly and Jacob gave him a vicious elbow in the ribs .

The Captain knew that failure to deliver the convoy of food was going to be a mark against his record. Sure as hell somebody will pay. That one, looks about to faint.

"Bring me that one in the blue shirt."

The unfortunate he had selected looked around wildly, apparently hoping the summons was for someone else. By the time they deposited him in front of the Captain, he was nearly hysterical with fear. When he too protested his ignorance, the Captain shot him and this time pointed at a man who seemed to have more self-control.

"Well, can you tell me who is responsible … or would you like to be shot?"

"If I tell you, will you let me go?"

The Captain studied him. The man was thin, almost emaciated, with a long narrow face. His eyes seemed to shift continually and never quite met the Captain's. Nevertheless, he didn't seem afraid.

"If you tell me, I won't shoot you."

"If I tell you, and you don't let me go, they'll kill me. Promise I can leave and I'll tell."

"Okay. Tell me."

"Promise on your honor as a German officer."

"I promise that if you tell me who put the sugar in the petrol tanks, I will release you, on my honor as an Officer and a German."

"Okay. That one in the grey cap." He proceeded to identify six men, all of whom the troops pulled to one side.

The Captain looked from the group of accused back to the informant. "How did you know?"

"Uuu … The guy in the cap told me. He was bragging about it."

The man in the cap spoke, "He's a bloody liar, just trying to save his own … "

A guard hit him in the head with a rifle butt and he fell down and didn't move.

The Captain spoke very softly, so that only his informant could hear, "You are a sniveling coward … I suspect the man in the cap spoke the truth. No matter. The Fatherland will have vengeance for destroying the trucks." More loudly he continued in a normal tone of voice.

"You have ten seconds to get out of my sight. After that I start shooting. One."

The informant leapt into a run and was out of sight behind the trucks before the captain got to four in his count.

"These six … line them up and shoot them."
The bodies were left in the field where they died.

* * * * * * * *

The Captain decided there was nothing that he could do except keep driving until the trucks all quit or they got to Berlin. Unfortunately for the Captain, one after another of the trucks quit over the next hour.

Unfortunately for the Danes, the Captain shot the drivers of the next three vehicles that quit running. After that he gave up on killing and simply ordered that the entire group of drivers be held captive. If he couldn't deliver the food, the drivers would at least suffer in captivity.

The Captain's next thought was to simply requisition all trucks, of whatever size, that came down the highway. After an hour in which only small trucks came down the road, it became clear that he didn't have enough troops to make this strategy work. Finally, reluctantly, he sent one of his sergeants to find a telephone to report their failure to his superior. Then he settled back to wait.

* * * * * * * *

Gerhard asked Jacob, "How can an officer shoot an unarmed man? Just execute ten men? Can he get away with that?"

Jacob just shook his head, "I don't know, Gerhard. Some officers are real bad apples. Who's going to do anything 'bout it? He's the commanding officer … there's nobody to do anything about it."

Jacob shifted topics.

"Now, Gerhard, you've got to protect yourself. I been in the army a long time and I know the score, so pay attention. When an officer is doing something he's not supposed to, you need to have a poker face. Suppose the Captain shoots that guy, looks up and sees that you disapprove. Guess what, first time he has a chance to get rid of you he will. He needs a volunteer for a suicide mission? You'll be it."

* * * * * * * *

The following day the Captain had a very unpleasant surprise. The underground newspaper *Free Denmark* carried a blow-by-blow description of the truck convoy and the Captain's executions, complete with several pictures.

Realization hit him like a blow to the face … his men had reported a motorcycle with two men on it that followed the convoy from the time it started. He, fool that he was, had told the soldiers to ignore it, that it couldn't hurt them.

The Captain's surprise and humiliation were complete a day later when General Dr. Best called him into his office, showed him pictures from English newspapers and told him the story had been carried worldwide.

"Not only did you fail, but they made a fool of you," Best said. "Then you give them a fantastic propaganda victory. Pictures of shooting prostate men in the back. You have disgraced the Fatherland and dishonored the officer's corps. You are not worthy of an officer's rank."

Best demoted him as far as regulations would permit and sent him away.

The Danes continued the general strike and kept the streets full of protestors. Best asked the King and Prime Minister for a meeting.

Chapter 32. Vald as Berserker

General Dr. Best arrived at Amalienborg Castle for the meeting on June 2, at 1:30 p.m. Most stores, factories and offices in Denmark were closed. It seemed that most of the population was in the streets, many of them massed around the Nazi offices.

With a general strike, nothing got done, no materiel moved to Germany, and the High Command got more and more impatient.

This assignment originally seemed easy. Organize shipments of war materiel to the Fatherland. A commendation and promotion in rank seemed likely. Fat chance. Nothing is going right and they've had us on the defensive the whole time. How the hell did the Danes manage this?

Best's dark thoughts were interrupted by his car stopping in front of Amalienborg Castle. He decided it was time for firmness and strode rapidly up the steps, trailed by four aides.

A member of the Royal Guard escorted Best and his aides into an ornate meeting room and seated them at one end of the large table in the center of the room. Best fidgeted with his swagger stick for the next ten minutes and grew increasingly angry as he realized that the King and Vald were deliberately making him wait. Just as he was considering leaving, the King and his party arrived.

* * * * * * * * * *

The King seated himself at the end of the table, facing Best. Vald sat on the King's right and five advisors arranged themselves behind the King.

The two parties were separated by several empty chairs in the middle of the table.

Vald wondered how long they could sit there before Best lost patience.

Finally, Vald spoke, "Well, General, you asked for this meeting?"

"It seems that all your people are in the streets and that no one is working," Best said. "Why is that?"

The King leaned forward, "You illegally killed at least ten of our people and arrested over a thousand more. Our people are protesting your illegal, barbaric actions."

"I have reprimanded and demoted, to private, the officer who did the killing. He exceeded his authority, he was not to kill anyone."

"We require justice, we require that this officer be tried by a Danish court."

"That is not possible," Best snapped. "He is ... was ... a German officer and was dealt with as an officer."

"The killer is in Denmark illegally, committed a crime against Danish citizens on Danish soil, and must be tried by a Danish court," Christian said.

Best half rose from his seat, "This is getting us nowhere. I am required by the German High Command to secure certain war materiel from Denmark. If you do not provide it, there will be very severe consequences."

The old King leaned back in his chair ... and then forward again, leaning both elbows on the table before replying.

"You can threaten us all you want. Nevertheless, we will not be cowed and we will not cooperate. We demand the murderer. In the meantime, the strike will continue and nothing will be produced for Germany."

Vald watched Best flexing and relaxing the swagger stick. He'd like to kill us. He's afraid of the bad publicity or he'd do it himself.

For a time no one said anything.

Finally Best said, "Wait for me at the cars."

After his aides obediently trooped out, Best said to the King, "Perhaps you and I could talk in private?"

"Vald stays," Christian said. "The rest of you leave."

When only the three of them were left, Best spoke. "Will you accompany me on a short walk in the park?"

"We can talk here," Christian said.

"The walls might have ears. I can not speak frankly here."

The King looked at Vald and Vald shrugged.

"Come," Christian said. "We will walk in my gardens."

No one spoke again until they were outside in the King's gardens and had walked a bit.

"My superiors require that I ship certain war materiel to Germany," Best stopped and faced the two Danes. "Your obstinacy is preventing that. You have two options: either you cooperate or your citizens will die. After a sufficient number of your citizens have died, the remainder will cooperate. You will have gained nothing except unnecessary deaths."

Vald was momentarily terribly frightened and tongue-tied. Then he remembered his Viking ancestry and an icy calm rage settled over him ... even as he began to speak, a distant part of his mind wondered if his mental state was similar to the famed berserker condition that his ancestors sometimes experienced in battle. Vald spoke almost as if he were lecturing in a university classroom.

"You truly do not understand your position, General. First, the world will know your every action and executions will bring shame on your precious Fatherland. Your Fuhrer will not be pleased by the media coverage of Germans slaughtering innocent civilians. The bad publicity may even bring the Americans into the war against you."

Vald paused to let that sink in while he stroked his beard.

"The second point, General, is that your troops and our people will be fully informed about any killings. You may have noticed that our underground press is remarkably efficient. There will almost certainly be damning pictures to go with the stories.

"Third, you and your SS officers may have forgotten your humanity, but the average German soldier has not. How long do you think your Wehrmacht soldiers will obey orders to kill nonviolent protestors? Especially since they know that no violence is being offered against them. Your Wehrmacht soldiers are patriotic, certainly, but they are also Christians with a highly developed sense of right and wrong. If you set them to killing innocent civilians, they will quickly become so demoralized as to be useless.

"Fourth, we consider this struggle a military campaign and as such we expect casualties. You will have to do a great deal of killing to produce more casualties than we would have with a campaign of violent resistance. So, you see, we are not intimidated by the threat of deaths.

"Finally, we will not be cowed and we will not cooperate. We will resist until you give up and go home."

Again Vald paused. General Dr. Best seemed to be swelling up with rage and Vald wondered if perhaps Best might shoot him. The berserker part of his mind didn't care, rather it was savagely gleeful at the effect on the Nazi general. Vald continued.

"We have only one option, because we refuse to consider any other ... and that option is to resist you. You, however, have several options.

"One, you can begin killing us, bring the Americans into the war, and get yourself cashiered.

"Two, you can temporize, stall, and try to mediate between your superiors and us. This course will allow you to survive for a bit longer but will probably fail before long.

"Three, you can explain the true situation to your superiors and then, if you convince them, we will coexist with minimal damage to each other until the High Command decides to withdraw German forces from Danish soil. This course, if successful, will allow you to survive and perhaps even to look good."

When Vald stopped talking, Best was making small, inarticulate noises deep in his throat. The swagger stick was beating out a loud rhythm, slamming into his leg over and over. Vald waited patiently but noticed that his Berserker calm was ebbing away and he began to worry that his fear might return.

"You're insane," Best shouted. "I'm the one with the power here. You are conquered. I'm in charge."

Vald shook his head, "You have no power over us because we are willing to die. You might kill us but you can not force us to do anything."

Best glared at Vald for long seconds. Vald met his gaze. Finally, Best stalked away.

Vald and the King watched him go. The King turned to Vald.

"My friend, that was magnificent. I didn't know you had that in you. I thought you were afraid of the Nazis?"

"I didn't know I had that in me either," Vald gave a short bark of laughter. "A cold rage took over and there was no room for fear. I will probably be afraid again later, but I wasn't just now."

"I hope all our people are out of the way," Christian said. "He's angry enough to personally execute anyone he meets."

The next day Vald was informed by the police that eleven Danes were shot dead on the streets of Copenhagen in the hour immediately after his meeting with General Best.

Chapter 33. General Hanneken the Butcher

The day after Prime Minister Stauning lectured him, General Best's Gestapo chief handed him a document.

"Herr General, this purports to be a summary of the Danish resistance strategy. It is a very strange strategy, one which I must admit I do not understand. However, it does fit with what they have done so far."

General Best thanked the man and immediately read the fifty-four page document. Strategic nonviolence. So this is what that idiot Vald was raving about. The idea is ridiculous!

The Danish strategy has been troublesome. They can't renounce violence, although they've used none to date. Well, now we can figure out how to take the proper countermeasures.

General Best set a meeting with General Hanneken for later that afternoon. He greeted General Hanneken, in his office, with a glass of his best whiskey. After the pleasantries, Best got down to business.

"General, I met with the King and Prime Minister Stauning. They told me that they had no intention of ever cooperating in any way. They claimed that we will never secure any materiel from them and that there is nothing we can do to force them. They called the Fuhrer 'a stupid little man' and said the Aryan race has been mongrelized."

Best played with the swagger stick while he gauged the effect he was having on Hanneken and was pleased to see the man was outraged.

"I hesitate to repeat what they said about you, but I think you probably should know the depth of their treason. They accused you of having Jewish and Gypsy blood, said you were not worthy of being a German officer."

Hanneken was on his feet "I'll kill them! I'll kill them all."

"We need to teach them a lesson," Best said.

"Yes. A big lesson. I'll shoot a thousand of them in the town square."

Best tried to rein him in just a little bit.

"We need to put a veneer of legality over the executions," Best said. "We want to execute leaders, professional people. Let's get about a hundred of them … perhaps with the checkpoints. We'll post a big notice explaining we caught them when they attacked a patrol. Then we shoot them in the town square and leave the bodies, with the notice. Perhaps we can do that several times a week for the next few weeks?"

Hanneken promised to begin the executions the next day. Good. Hanneken will do all the dirty work. If the killings succeed in cowing the Danes, I'll get credit. If the killings fail to cow the Danes or otherwise backfire, Hanneken will get the blame.

Best was determined to survive these obstinate Danes. Sacrificing Hanneken was a small price to pay.

The following day, June 3, at 12:00 noon, a convoy of ten army trucks pulled into Radhuspladsen (city square) and ninety-three Danish prisoners, all men, disembarked from the trucks. The men were lined up against the wall of the Kobenhavns Radhus (City Hall) and shot. A large poster on the wall proclaimed:

ATTACKS ON GERMANS
PUNISHED WITH DEATH!

The Nazis left the bodies where they fell to make sure the populace got the message.

* * * * * * * * * *

Professor Koch immediately put Arne and his team to work to ferret out the truth of the executed men. Professor Koch secured the dead men's names, addresses, and places of work. Arne was assigned to find people who had witnessed the men being arrested at checkpoints. They worked the routes these men took to go to work, seeking others who took the same or similar routes and found out where there were checkpoints on the fatal day. Then they searched for people who were there when these men were arrested. Within two days they had witnesses to the arrest of thirty-seven of the men. Thus, they could confidently state that the dead men had not been engaged in attacking a German patrol.

On June 6, Professor Koch decided they had enough evidence and wrote a detailed expose, including grisly photos, which they then dispatched both to the Danish underground media and to Moellar in England. The first international story on the "Execution of the Innocents" appeared on June 7 and the story was in all the major US papers on June 8.

Hanneken continued to execute Danes every other day in the City Square. By June 9, four hundred and seventy Danes had died in that bloody square.

On June 10, at 9:00 a.m. General Hanneken announced that two hundred and seventy-three Danes were innocent of blowing up the bridges and had been released. Further, nine hundred and twenty-seven Danes had been found guilty of treason against the German Fatherland in the matter of blowing up the bridges and had been sentenced to death. The executions were set for June 14 at 8:00 a.m.

Chapter 34. Gerhard vs. the Demonstrators

While Arne and his team were busy doing investigative work for Professor Koch, much of the rest of Denmark had been busy demonstrating against the ongoing executions. Gerhard and Jacob were repeatedly assigned to patrols whose standing orders were to shoot any and all demonstrators. Gerhard didn't want to shoot anybody, but he also was afraid to disobey an order.

Their first patrol they came upon a group of perhaps fifty Danes, men and women, some of whom were carrying placards. The patrol stopped and watched from a side street as the demonstrators passed by. Gerhard was very relieved they were given no orders to shoot. Similar incidents happened several more times and Gerhard started to relax.

Jacob told him to stop worrying, and added, "Remember, some of us are lousy shots anyway."

On their third day of patrolling since the mass demonstrations started, they were watching a group of Danes pass by when an SS squad came up behind them. Their sergeant saw the SS squad and leapt into action.

"Prepare to fire," the sergeant shouted.

"Aim to kill."

"Fire."

The range was point blank, perhaps twenty yards. Pandemonium erupted, with demonstrators screaming and running in all directions. Gerhard knew he wasn't hitting anyone, he was firing well over their heads.

None of the demonstrators were falling down. The entire squad was shooting in the air.

Gerhard continued to shoot until all the demonstrators managed to run out of sight. He looked at Jacob who grinned at him and Gerhard found himself grinning back.

Just then more gunfire erupted. Demonstrators who a moment before were fleeing up the street came running back down it. They watched as a man and a woman fell in the intersection ahead of them, then another man and a fourth person … none of them were moving.

An SS jeep with a machine gunner came down the street, with a squad of foot soldiers spread out around it, following the fleeing Danes, firing as they went. Gerhard listened to more shots, screams, and finally, Thank God! Silence.

A minute later their sergeant prodded them into action.

"Attend to the survivors. On the double."

Gerhard could see bodies all over the street in a three-block section. Eight dead and fifteen seriously wounded. We spooked the demonstrators right into the SS.

Gerhard's unease increased the next day with the beginning of Hanneken's executions.

Chapter 35. The World is Watching

"We get the Nazis to work against themselves," Professor Koch said. Arne and his team seemed attentive.

"The Nazis are obsessively thorough. They listen in on telephone calls and are reading much of the mail. We use that to tie up their people.

"As nearly as we can tell, the Gestapo code breaking unit keeps getting bigger and bigger. Here's a strategy to worry them. Rent a mail box under a bogus name. Send a series of coded letters to it. Keep most of the letters short and use a different code for each, so they will be impossible to decode. Occasionally send a longer letter with a code they can break. Make the longer letter very suggestive of a resistance plot, but without much detail.

"They will try and try to decode the short letters. They will detail someone to watch the rented mail box. Obviously, you will never return to that mailbox. After a month or two, start over with a new mailbox.

"Any questions?"

"How much text is enough for them to decode a message?" Arne asked.

"That depends entirely upon the coding method," Koch said. "We provide some guidance in this document." Koch passed around a stapled document.

"For the letters you don't want them to decode, keep them very short … just a line or two and make sure you never use the same code twice in the series. That will make it almost impossible to decode. They will go crazy, searching for a pattern where you have carefully made sure there is none."

"The telephones are a little different," Koch said. "We can't be calling other Danes with suggestive calls or we get them in trouble. There isn't any way for us to disguise the person receiving the call. We can provide the Germans with false alarms. And we can call the Germans with questions and keep them on the line as long as possible. Just don't stay on the line long enough for them to trace the call and come get you. Only make these calls from pay phones," Koch finished.

"The Germans outlawed radios," Brigitte said. "We need more of the instructions for making tiny radios."

"The underground newspapers are printing them later this week," Koch said. "Very soon everybody will know how to make a radio tuned to Moellar's frequency … and it will be about the size of a pack of cigarettes."

"What about the jamming?" Carin asked.

"There are some areas where the Nazi jamming is working and our people don't get Moellar at all," Koch said. "Mostly, people are getting his broadcasts. There's not much we can do about the jamming, though."

* * * * * * * * * *

"Vald," Hanne said. "Can't sleep again?"

"No, Love."

"How long have you been up?"

"Never got to sleep, gave up after a bit and came down to the porch. The porch is peaceful."

"Vald, come with me," Hanne ordered. Vald meekly obeyed and they climbed the stairs back to the bedroom.

"Come on, lie down with me," Hanne urged.

Vald lay down and she cuddled his head against her breasts and gently stroked his shoulder and back. Hanne was worried. Third night this week that Vald didn't sleep. His ribs stick out, he's barely eating. The strain is killing him.

After a bit Vald began to snore. Hanne planned to make him his favorite breakfast in hopes of getting him to eat more than two bites.

* * * * * * * * * *

The Freedom Council met and argued over what to do about Hanneken's mass executions. They decided they had to continue the general strike. Vald agreed with them, he just wasn't sure his body would survive the ordeal.

The Freedom Council also instructed Vald to seek diplomatic help from the rest of the world.

The Danes had a secret telephone cable between Copenhagen and Sweden, installed prior to the invasion, with branches to several locations, including Amalienborg Castle, and Vald's home. The US, Canada, several Latin American governments, and Australia, were not yet involved in the war. A major part of Vald's job was to lobby these sympathetic countries to garner what support they could.

Franklin Delano Roosevelt knew Hitler was a madman who had to be stopped. The US Congress, however, was controlled by men who were strongly isolationist and felt that the war was Europe's affair and these powerful congressmen were determined to keep the US out of "Europe's War".

Millions of tons of war materiel, under the legal fiction of Lend-Lease, flowed to England while the rest of Europe fell to the Nazi Blitzkrieg. Churchill and England stood virtually alone and they were reeling in their last extremity while Hitler sought to bomb them into submission. Hitler's preparations to invade across the English Channel continued.

The US media, with Roosevelt's urging, portrayed Denmark as a virtuous David valiantly opposing an evil Goliath.

On June 9th King Christian and Vald decided the time was right for formal diplomatic protests from some of their supporters. Calls to Canada, Australia, and the US quickly gained promises of support. All three countries sent formal notes protesting Hanneken's daily executions, the violence of the SS against peaceful demonstrators, and the planned execution of the 927 Danes arrested for the destruction of the bridges.

All three countries included informal notes, full of diplomatic jargon and niceties, but unmistakably suggesting that public opinion was turning sharply against Germany and that this might be a precursor to entering the war against Germany.

General Dr. Best got the phone call early on June 13 from Foreign Minister Ribbentrop. Ribbentrop wanted Best to understand that the executions were giving Germany a very bad image around the world. They had to stop. Best was ordered to find some way to pressure the Danes into compliance so that the necessary war materiel could be secured. But the bad press had to stop or Best would be replaced.

"Minister Ribbentrop," Best said. "I have been trying to dissuade General Hanneken, but as you know he has the same rank … I can't order him to do anything. I don't think he will stop the executions without a direct order to do so."

"General Best, what effect are the executions having on the Danes?"

"Prime Minister Stauning told me they look at the situation as a military campaign and are fully prepared for sizable casualties. The people are certainly not cowed … the streets are full of demonstrators from dawn until dusk. Our patrols run them off one street and they show up again on the next street. And if we fire upon them, they invariably manage to get pictures of the troops firing and of the dead bodies in the newspapers. My professional judgment is that the executions are not having the desired effect upon the Danish population."

"General Best, I will telegraph General Hanneken with two directives: stop the executions and defer to you in dealing with the Danish population. Hanneken's job is narrowly defined as managing our troops in Denmark. Your role, General Best, is to choose the strategies and policies for dealing with the Danes such that the necessary war materiel get to Germany in a timely fashion. And this has to be done without making Germany look bad to the rest of the world. Is that clear, General?"

"Yes, sir, very clear. You can count on me, Minister."

"General Best, I sincerely hope so. Your record so far does not inspire confidence. I suggest that you take a few days to review the situation and plan out a strategy. When you have done so, forward the plans to me."

"Yes, sir. Thank you, sir."

General Best offered a silent prayer of thanks that Hanneken's political naiveté made him the fall guy for the executions. Now, a strategy to crush the Danes without generating bad press. The *threat* of executions might still be useful … the Danes don't know we can't use mass executions.

Time for another meeting with the Danish leaders … haven't talked with them since that fool Vald's lecture in the King's garden … perhaps the executions softened them up.

General Best was three minutes early for the meeting with Christian and Vald in Amalienborg Castle later that morning. Vald has dark circles under his eyes and he's gaunt. The King looks tired. The pressure is getting to them!

"Gentlemen, I have prevailed upon General Hanneken to halt the executions scheduled for noon today and to postpone the executions of the bridge saboteurs. In return, can we get everybody back to work?"

Vald and the King looked at each other for a moment before the King spoke.

"General, your people have committed a large number of atrocities against peaceful people. We require justice, Danish justice, for those guilty of murder against Danish citizens."

"You're crazy," Best said. "Germany will not give you a General to prosecute for murder. Anyway, you say murder. I say legal execution of traitors. We can argue over this forever. I am offering you a way to end the killing and to move forward. Do you want to continue a pointless argument or do you want to save your citizens?"

"General, you say the executions of the bridge saboteurs have been postponed … for how long?" Vald asked.

"Indefinitely."

"Why is that?" Vald said.

General Best shrugged, "I dislike killing and convinced Hanneken to stop … for now."

"So, General, you have been ordered to stop the executions and decided to use the threat of renewing them as a bargaining chip," Vald said.

Best thought, how could he know? Damn, he was fishing and I just gave it away. Christian is smirking at me. Damn!

"General, we will not return to work while Germans can kill Danes with impunity," Vald said. "We return to work when it is established that Germans will be punished for killing Danes. We understand that General Hanneken is probably beyond our reach. However, you have a Wehrmacht captain … demoted to private according to you … who killed eleven of our people in cold blood. You also have an SS Captain Kodritz whose unit has killed at least thirty-two of our peaceful demonstrators in the last week. Other SS units have each killed a few demonstrators, but none with the barbarous enthusiasm of Captain Kodritz's unit. We require that these two captains be tried for murder in Danish courts. When we have these two in custody, then we will return to work."

Best thought, always the same, these two fools, always the same insane demands.

"You doom your people," Best said. He left, tap-tapping the swagger stick against his leg.

* * * * * * * *

General Hanneken stopped the executions and put his patrols to marking time. They still moved around, but none of them shot at any demonstrators.

Three days later, on June 16, General Dr. Best sent Foreign Minister Ribbentrop a summary of his plan for crushing the Danes, with a minimum of bad publicity. The paragraph that convinced Ribbentrop was:

> The Danish population and leadership have shown remarkable cohesion and unity of purpose. This unity has been instrumental in thwarting our plans to date. We must neutralize the leadership, destroy the Danish unity of purpose, and fragment and demoralize the population.

The rest of the document went into some detail on how to achieve these objectives. Two days later Ribbentrop congratulated Best on a well-conceived plan and told him to implement it immediately.

Prof. Hal Koch's Journal, June 15, 1940

Paris is gone. The Nazis have Paris. How can this be? France had military parity with Germany, France had the impregnable Maginot Line ... how can France be obliterated in thirty-four days? Belgium surrendered after eighteen days. The Netherlands barely slowed the Nazis down. What hope is left?

Britain, protected by the English Channel holds out, but for how long?

Germany seems invincible, able to crush any foe with ease. Can this really be our fate, to be subjected to a madman who preaches death to Jews and slavery for all non-Germans?

Despite all evidence to the contrary, I still hold fast to my faith in a merciful God. I shall pray and I shall not despair.

My countrymen make me proud. The resistance is frustrating our "conquerors" at every turn.

It took me two hours yesterday to convince a group of hot-headed students that bombing Nazi trucks and ships would be counterproductive to our cause. I think they finally understood that much of our power comes from the average German soldier understanding that we pose no physical threat to them ... and that they therefore become reluctant to use force against us, even when ordered to do so.

Chapter 36. Crushing the Danes

When Vald arrived at his office on June 22, he found two SS troopers waiting.

"What do you want?" Vald asked.

"We are to guard you," one said. "We are to see that you are unharmed. All day and all night."

Vald shuddered. The man's mouth curled up but the eyes were cold. Better to be guarded by sharks than these two.

Vald walked to King Christian's wing of the building, with the two SS troopers following. As he expected, there were SS troops in the King's office

Vald walked back to his office and arrived in time to see an SS squad leading six of his senior staff members out of his office suite.

"What's going on here? Release my people. You have no right to detain these people."

The officer faced him, pulled out a sheet of paper and read from it. "The following aides to Prime Minister Stauning are to be arrested immediately on charges of espionage and treason," he smiled. "I believe that explains everything, Prime Minister. Now … get out of the way or I'll knock you down."

The SS squad escorted his aides past him and out the door. Five of the King's aides, seven senior members of parliament, and twenty-five senior military officers were arrested.

Vald went to discuss the situation with the King, but the SS troops forced their way into the room with them. Vald shuddered. I won't be able to do a God-damned thing. These jackals won't let me do anything.

* * * * * * * * * *

At 3:04 a.m. on June 23 an SS officer, out of uniform and dressed all in black, carefully pried at a window in the residence of a leading Copenhagen business man. The latch broke with a loud "snick" and the window rose smoothly, allowing the officer to climb into the house.

Once inside he paused, waiting for his eyes to adjust to the darkness. After perhaps a minute, when he still couldn't see, he cautiously used his torch long enough to develop a mental map of the room.

He went to the front door and unlocked it. Going up the stairs caused no noise at all except for one step which squeaked loudly. He paused at the squeak, waiting to make sure it hadn't roused anyone. He was patient, secure in the knowledge that his two lookouts would alert him if there was any danger from outside.

He drew his knife as he reached the top of the stairs. Which door goes to the master bedroom? Door works with almost no noise. Oops, two beds with children. Yes. A bed with two adults in it. Easy, easy, no hurry. Long hair, it's the wife.

Easing around the bed, his foot hit something which made a small grating sound as it slid a few inches across the hardwood floor. Wait, don't move. Okay, nobody stirring. On his stomach, facing me.

Nice thick, long hair.

He grasped a handful of hair with his left hand, jerked the head up and back, and drew his knife across the exposed throat and carotid artery.

Damn! A geyser! My whole leg is drenched.

The man convulsed, arms and legs flailing and he released the head and stepped back. Almost instantly the convulsions stopped and his victim lay still, blood still pumping from his neck.

The wife sat up in bed.

Stupid woman doesn't even realize he's dead.

He didn't wait for her, simply walked out of the room. He was halfway down the stairs when the screams started. In another 15 seconds he was in the unmarked car with the driver and his lookouts and they were moving sedately away.

The SS assassin almost laughed aloud at how easy it had been. Hope the other teams were successful. These obstinate bastard Danes would learn to fear them now.

* * * * * * * *

When the citizens of Copenhagen started for work on June 23, they encountered checkpoints on all the major thoroughfares throughout the city. Well-dressed men were randomly arrested and taken to Gestapo headquarters. Their interrogations focused on finding the leadership for the resistance and involvement in the destruction of the bridges.

The interrogations used a sophisticated mix of psychological ploys and physical torture. After several days, most prisoners began naming their friends, anything to get the pain to stop. After the prisoner implicated most of his friends, the SS released him.

Those prisoners who held out for five full days were declared to have confessed to violence against the German army and were summarily executed. Those named by the prisoners were not even sought by the SS. The purpose behind the arrests and interrogations was not to get information on the resistance. The purpose was to spread fear and shame. Fear of being tortured and shame at having implicated one's friends.

* * * * * * * *

On June 26th when the Danish police arrived for their morning briefing
for the day, they were greeted by Nazi troops and arrested. Ten thousand
Danish policemen were arrested that day and shipped to the Theresienstadt
concentration camp.

After arresting the policemen, the Nazis released all the inmates of every
Danish prison and psychiatric hospital. The mass murderer and the petty
thief, the homicidal psychopath and the hopelessly depressed … all were
turned out into the streets to fend for themselves. In addition, they shut
down every addiction treatment program they could find.

By the end of the day on June 26 Denmark had no policemen anywhere
in the nation and every incarcerated criminal and psychotic in the entire
country had been released.

* * * * * * * *

June 27th the Germans barricaded every main road and railway line
leading into Copenhagen. People were allowed to move into the city but no
one was permitted to leave. The electricity and the municipal water supply
were shut down. No food or fuel was allowed in.

A formal note from General Best to Prime Minister Stauning informed
him that Copenhagen would be denied all electricity, water, food and fuel
until such time as the Danes agreed to cooperate in the war effort.

As a final measure, all meetings of any kind with more than four people
were banned. Church services with more than four people were prohibited.

Chapter 37. Vald's Despair

Vald's staff rallied and adjusted to compensate for those who had been
arrested. None of them knew how to deal with Vald while two SS soldiers
were constantly present. They couldn't even brief him properly. The SS
read much of the paperwork that came across his desk.

Vald felt useless. Don't know what's going on. Can't help make
decisions.

Don't even get my time with Hanne. She's been my rock, keeps me
sane. I need her more than ever.

The general strike is still on, we never figured on keeping it going this
long. People are worn out … when they get too tired, they'll start giving up.

The bastards are about to win … the resistance is collapsing. We'll become drones for the German war effort.

* * * * * * * *

Every night there were four or five or six seemingly random murders of well-to-do citizens in Copenhagen. Street crimes and burglaries were suddenly endemic all over the country and there were no policemen to deal with them. The SS was torturing scores of people and executing one or two each day. No food or fuel was coming into Copenhagen. There was no water to bathe and no electricity.

Vald went to his office every day and went through the motions of his job, but walked and talked from within an impenetrable dark fog of despair, followed everywhere by two members of the SS that seemed to Vald to be demons from the deepest levels of Hell.

* * * * * * * *

On July 2, at breakfast, Hanne had all she could stand. Ignoring the two SS soldiers, she thumped her tea cup on the table, slopping tea over her eggs.

"Vald, what are you going to do?" she demanded. "You've been walking around like a zombie. It's time to fight back."

Vald just looked at her and didn't say anything, just slowly shook his head once and then dropped his eyes to the table, staring at nothing.

"I know you can't play your usual role, but there are other things you could do."

"Like what?"

"Why don't you do something to boost morale?"

Hanne reached across the table and took his hands, studying Vald. He's the most important politician in the country. His suit always looks rumpled, shirt-tail is usually out … and his beard stays neat for maybe ten minutes. And I wouldn't change a bit of it.

"My love," Hanne said. "Talk with King Christian. You can play an important symbolic role … find some symbolic things to do that will lift people's spirits."

* * * * * * * *

An hour later Vald was talking with King Christian.

He was astonished to find that they could discuss strategy in front of the SS, by using shorthand reference to sections of their planning scenarios, without revealing more than general theoretical notions. After an hour with Christian, Vald's despair had been replaced with a savage glee, although a part of him worried that the SS might decide to kill him.

Vald composed a note and managed to pass it unnoticed, under the nose of the bored SS soldiers, to one of his staff members. The aide was instructed to ask about Hanne's health when everything was in readiness.

Copenhagen was in its sixth day under the German blockade. The city included a large sprawling area and the Germans did not have enough troops to effectively block all the small roads, much less the footpaths. The people were still eating because many residents had private vegetable gardens and there was a huge smuggling operation underway.

Vald's aide inquired about Hanne's health four hours after receiving Vald's note. The following day Vald put a potted plant on his patio before leaving the house.

Vald got on his bicycle and rode off down the street, with the SS soldiers following in a car. Vald hummed to himself as he pedaled along. It's good to be alive.

A half hour leisurely ride brought Vald to the outskirts of the city and a country lane with a stone wall along one side. Vald slowed down as he spotted the narrow gate in the wall. He turned through the gate and laughed out loud as he sped off down the footpath on the other side. He waved to the "workman" standing off to the side and noted his camera as he took pictures of the SS running down the path after him. Within seconds he had turned a corner and was out of sight. In a few minutes he slowed and resumed his relaxed pace, confident that the SS couldn't catch him on foot.

Vald pedaled to a little country store and purchased twenty pounds of flour which he carefully poured into forty small paper bags. Each bag also got a small typewritten note. The forty small bags of flour completely filled the basket behind his seat.

He took a different route back into the city and managed to avoid all German patrols. He rode for a little more than an hour and was beginning to tire and was hurting from blisters on his inner thighs.

Just as the blisters were really beginning to bother him, he arrived at Radhauspladen, the city center square.

Vald rode right up to the SS headquarters and started handing out the bags of flour to passersby. He attracted a substantial crowd and had only a few bags left when an SS officer came over to him and demanded to know what he was doing.

"I'm helping break the blockade," Vald said.

Vald offered a bag to a man walking by but the SS officer grabbed it and looked inside. Spotting the piece of paper inside the bag, the officer pulled it out and read:

This flour is being handed out in front of the SS offices, by the Danish government, to show how silly the Nazi blockade is. We will win soon and the German occupiers will slink home in disgrace. Have a nice day and remember to be proud to be a Dane."

The SS officer threw the bag of flour at Vald, striking him in the chest and the flour exploded all over his clothes.

A moment later all of Vald's being was concentrated on the pistol the SS officer was pointing at his head. The officer was fairly spluttering with rage and Vald couldn't understand any of what he was saying.

Vald managed to say, "I am Prime Minister Thorvald Stauning and I am here following orders from my Government. There are cameras recording us … see there?" and Vald pointed to a camera crew on a nearby roof.

The officer stopped talking, looked at the camera crew, seemed to notice the crowd which now numbered perhaps seventy people, and slowly lowered his pistol. A moment later he strode away, with the pistol still in his hand. He disappeared into the building.

"Show's over, time to leave," Vald announced in a loud voice.

A loud cheer erupted from the crowd. Vald saluted them and swung onto his bicycle. As he rode away, he saw that the camera crew on the roof were already leaving and the crowd in the square was starting to disperse. Vald rode only far enough to get out of sight from the SS headquarters and then got off his bike, wincing from the blisters on his thighs.

He strolled along, pushing the bike until he met a teenager coming the other way. A short conversation elicited the boy's assistance … he happily agreed to take the Prime Minister's bike to Vald's home. Vald got on the next bus and rode it to his office.

The underground newspapers had extensive coverage of Vald defying the blockade. There were pictures of the SS trying to catch Vald's bicycle on foot. There were pictures of Vald handing out flour in front of the SS building, of Vald talking to the SS officer, of the SS officer brandishing his pistol in Vald's face, and of the officer stalking back into the headquarters building.

The general tenor of the stories was that of an amusing incident, that Vald hadn't done anything very extraordinary, and that the Nazis were bumbling fools. King Christian, when he saw the stories, laughed with delight and congratulated Vald profusely. Vald slept better that night than he had in a very long time.

Chapter 38. Poul's Song

Arne and his colleagues knew that the Nazis weren't as bumbling as the story on Vald portrayed them. Seven of their colleagues were killed while smuggling food during the first week of the blockade.

Food was coming into Copenhagen by boat, by small truck along back roads, on bicycles and motorbikes, and via people carrying it on their backs. The Nazis didn't have enough troops to stop the smuggling, but they certainly had enough to make it dangerous. When a Wehrmacht patrol caught smugglers, they were arrested and incarcerated and no one knew for how long or whether they would be turned over to the SS for "interrogation". The SS executed smugglers on the spot.

Eight days into the blockade, Arne and his group were asked to assist with the distribution of four small trucks of flour. In addition to Arne's group, there were a dozen men with hand carts to carry the flour away and the leader of that group was David Levine, the man they met at the demonstration in front of the Gestapo HQs.

"Arne, so good to see you again," David said. "You doing the lookouts?"

"We'll provide plenty of warning if the Nazis show up," Arne said. "You don't have to worry."

"Okay then," David said. "You heard the man, let's get to it."

The moon was nearly full but clouds pushed by a strong wind partially obscured the sky. Visibility changed rapidly from next to nothing to suddenly being quite good when the moon peeked through the clouds.

There were five roads that came into the little area where the transfer was to take place in a parking lot behind a small warehouse. Arne had scouted the area earlier and had chosen spots for the lookouts.

Tyge was assigned to the top of the warehouse where he could see the signal from any of the others if they had to use their torch

Three of the roads had good spots, where the lookout could see down the road, could signal them if a patrol came, and had a good escape route. Arne assigned Asger, Greta, and Carin to these spots.

The other two roads worried Arne. The only places where a lookout could see a patrol coming had neither a good escape route nor a good way to signal the danger. Arne solved the problem with the first road by putting Brigitte on the ridge above the road with a hundred meter long string that she could yank if she saw a patrol. Morten, at the other end of the string, would then shine his torch to alert the group. Both Morten and Brigitte should be able to simply sit still and be safe until the patrol left.

The final road Arne took for himself. There was no reasonable place to hide and watch the road except the ditch. Arne put Poul where he could shine a torch to warn the others and still be shielded by a slight bend in the road. Arne had three hundred meters of string stretching to where Poul would wait.

Arne described the arrangement for himself and Poul. Tyge objected.

"Arne, this arrangement is too dangerous. We could put someone in a tree on top of the ridge and they should be able to see the road."

"No, I already thought of that. The ridge is too far away and you can't see well enough."

"This isn't workable. It's too dangerous. The patrol will be on top of you before you see it."

"Listen Tyge, I thought about all this. We're out of time for talking. Now let's go. Everybody to your positions."

Tyge stood there … for a moment Arne thought he would continue his objections. Finally Tyge shrugged and walked off toward the warehouse and his assignment.

* * * * * * * *

Poul sat behind a small hedge on the side of the road, with a string looped around his finger and connecting him to Arne three hundred meters away.

The moon came out and Poul looked around. Wonder if that little dark bump on top of the warehouse is Tyge? Dark again, can't see a thing.

Lots of little noises. Nobody there, probably a squirrel. Or a cat.

This is a lousy arrangement, Tyge is right. Arne is in the worst spot, but this is pretty bad too.

Damn, only 12 minutes gone. This night is never gonna end.

Ahh, moon's out. Good, nothing around.

The moon stayed out and Poul relaxed and his mind wandered. He remembered his girlfriend and the sweetness of her lips. Before long he was lost in a fantasy involving much more than just kissing. Eventually the clouds covered the moon again and he vainly tried to see around himself in the dark.

He turned to the right but could see nothing but the hedge shielding him from the road. He turned to the left … same thing, nothing but darkness. As he faced forward, he felt a small tug on the string. He aimed the torch at the warehouse and waited, tense and nervous.

Nothing happened, no more tugs. Was there really a tug? Maybe just my own movements? Arne was supposed to tug three times. There was one tug. What was happening? Can't hear anything.

The moon came out again and Poul almost dropped his torch. A patrol was already at the bend, within line of sight. They'll see the signal. Worse, they'll catch on and race to the warehouse, catching the others and Tyge.

What the hell do I do?

Aw shit.

Poul put the torch down, sang loudly, and stepped out into the street facing away from the patrol.

> "Og dette skal være
> vor Peter til ære, hurra!
> Og dette skal være
> vor Peter til ære, hurra!

What's the patrol doing? Don't turn, don't look, keep singing. Stagger, stumble!

> Og skam få den der ikke
> vor Peters skål vil drikke
> hurra, den skål var bra, den skål var bra.
> Bravo, bravo, bravo, bravissimo
> Bravo, bravo, bravissimo"

Can hear the damned jeep. Almost across the road. Maybe I can run …

Poul glanced over his shoulder. Patrol's right on top of me. Shit! Shit! Shit!

Two soldiers jumped out of a jeep before it even stopped and, rifles leveled at him, ordered him to stop.

"Good evening." He tried to slur his words, "What'd you say?"

The soldiers collected him and took him back to the jeep. An SS lieutenant came up and sniffed Poul.

"No smell of liquor." He said. "Tell me what you're doing here and I won't shoot you."

"Going to see my girlfriend. I thought maybe you wouldn't bother me if you thought I was drunk."

"And where does this girlfriend live? There don't seem to be many homes in this area."

Poul pointed and said, "Over there about a half-mile."

"Are you on resistance business? What are you really doing?"

"I told you … trying to see my girlfriend."

"You realize I can just shoot you for violating the curfew?"

"Lieutenant, please, haven't you ever done anything foolish for a girl?"

"You're not dressed for seeing a woman. Singing so loud … was that to warn somebody?"

Poul was afraid. This bastard is going to shoot me. So many things I'm never going to get to do.

It's totally unfair. These sons of bitches!

"I'm just an ordinary Dane," Poul said. "Going about my business, and it's none of your affair."

"Okay," The Lieutenant said. "So … you're not going to tell me anything."

The Lieutenant studied Poul for a minute.

"Shoot him. Leave him right here in the middle of the street as a lesson to his colleagues."

Poul's heart lurched and his vision dimmed.

No, damnit! I'm a Viking and they will sing songs for me.

Poul lifted his eyes and stared the Lieutenant straight in the eye. I won, you chicken shit bastard! You won't catch any of the others …

* * * * * * * *

Arne had no clue that anything had gone wrong until he heard Poul singing. The patrol was driving without lights and it got fairly close to him in the darkness before he saw it. Nevertheless he gave the string three sharp tugs in plenty of time. Then he lay quietly in the ditch while the patrol drove past him.

Poul's singing startled him badly … had Poul lost his mind?

Arne started toward Poul, keeping to the grassy shoulder of the road. He was perhaps halfway to Poul's position when he heard the shots.

Arne froze, then sank to his knees and doubled over, arms folded across his stomach, head bent to the grass, a terrible fear immobilizing him. It's my fault. Tyge told me. Said this was no good. I didn't listen.

Arne's breath came in ragged gasps and he rocked back and forth where he crouched. Finally he pushed himself to his feet and continued … Poul might still be alive.

Poul was in the middle of the street, in a large pool of blood. So much blood. God almighty, nobody has that much blood.

Kind, gentle Poul. Everybody loved Poul. Tyge told me. I ignored Tyge and now Poul's dead.

* * * * * * * *

Arne was standing there in the middle of the street when Brigitte and Tyge came sneaking up. Brigitte saw Arne in the middle of the street and ran to him, not seeing Poul until she was almost there.

She stopped, transfixed by the body of her friend. Then she shook herself. The patrol might come back … we've got to get out of here.

She ran the last few steps to Arne and grasped his shoulders, swinging him around to face her.

"Arne, are you alright? Are you wounded?"

Arne didn't say anything, just shook his head.

"Come on, the patrol may come back, we gotta get out of here."

"Poul's dead. It's my fault."

"Not your fault. Come on."

"My fault. I wouldn't listen. We can't leave him like this."

"Arne, there's nothing we can do for him. Come on."

"No! I can't leave him in the middle of the street … it's like nobody cares."

"Okay, okay," Brigitte gave up. "Tyge. Help. Let's carry him over to the grass."

They carried Poul to a patch of nice grass and laid him out there. Arne arranged his hands on his chest.

Brigitte took Arne's hand and he followed her like a little child, stopped when she stopped and walked when she walked. When she ducked to hide, Arne stayed upright until she tugged him down.

Brigitte took Arne to Tyge's flat that night and put him into Tyge's bed. The last thing she saw before turning off the light was Arne, on his back, staring blindly at the ceiling. She made Tyge promise to stay with him through the rest of the night and to take him to see Professor Koch in the morning.

* * * * * * * *

Tyge woke up stiff from sleeping on the floor. Arne was asleep, tossing and turning and occasionally moaning. Tyge wasn't sure what to do, but eventually decided to leave him alone until he woke up on his own.

Tyge bathed, looked for coffee and found only the substitute, zichory, which he drank in spite of not liking it. Arne finally woke up at 10:22 a.m.

Tyge said, "Arne, get up, you're supposed to go see Professor Koch."

Arne just grunted, but he did get up and got dressed. Tyge waited for him and they left the flat together. Arne turned left at the sidewalk, away from the university and Professor Koch's office.

"Arne, where are you going?"

"Home."

"Uh … Arne … Professor Koch wants to see you." Tyge hadn't heard from the professor but he was pretty sure Brigitte would have reported Poul's death by now and that the professor would want to see Arne.

"I got Poul killed. I quit. I'm going home."

"Arne. Arne, it's not your fault. The Nazis did it … you didn't do anything wrong."

"I put him there … he's dead. You told me not to do it. I messed up and Poul's dead. I can't do it … I'm going home."

Tyge stood there on the sidewalk and watched Arne shuffle away, shoulders slumped forward and seemingly staring at the sidewalk. Instead of his usual graceful rapid strides, Arne walked down the sidewalk like an old man whose knees and back hurt.

Tyge knew he was going to miss Poul terribly, but he was suddenly afraid he was going to lose Arne too. When Arne turned the corner and was lost to sight, Tyge came to a decision and turned and ran to Professor Koch's office.

* * * * * * * * *

Professor Koch listened to Tyge and then walked to Arne's flat. Arne listened to him but all he would say was, "Poul's dead because of me." After 45 minutes Professor Koch left and sent for Brigitte. He told Brigitte to watch over Arne for the next few days. He told her to be with him, make sure he eats, and to talk with him when he wanted to talk.

Brigitte went from Professor Koch's office directly to Arne's flat. Arne didn't answer when she knocked on the door. She tried calling and after several calls and more knocking he came to the door and asked what she wanted.

"Professor Koch asked me to keep you company."

"Oh." Arne stepped aside, waved at the inside of the flat and mumbled, "Make yourself at home."

Arne went into his bedroom and closed the door.

Brigitte looked around for a minute, studied the bookcase, and selected a novel. Two hours later she was halfway through the novel and Arne was still in his room. She got up and searched the tiny kitchen. She found some ham and a loaf of bread and prepared two sarnies. She took a sarny and knocked on Arne's bedroom door.

"Arne. I made you a sarny."

Arne's mumbled reply was incomprehensible.

"Arne, I couldn't hear you. When did you last eat?"

"I'm not hungry."

"Hey, I went to the trouble of making you food … you could at least eat it."

After a moment of silence, the door opened but Arne just stood there looking at her. He looks a wreck … bloodshot eyes, clothes askew and rumpled from sleeping in them. Hair sticking up all over his head.

She took him by the hand and said, "Come sit with me while we eat."

Arne followed her over to the table and sat down across from her. Brigitte chatted about little nothings, occasionally urging him to eat because he seemed to forget.

Arne finished eating about the same time that Brigitte ran out of small talk. They sat there in silence for a while and then Arne got up without a word and went back into his room and closed the door. Brigitte went back to her novel.

At 6:30 p.m. Brigitte knocked on the bedroom door again.

"Arne?"

His reply was muffled but she thought he said, "Yes?"

"Arne, I'm going home now. I'll stop in to see you tomorrow."

"Good night," he said. After a second he added, "Thank you."

Brigitte thought about Poul while she walked to her flat. He was easy to talk to, selfless, and wise. She admired Arne but she loved Poul like a brother. Tears were running down her cheeks when she climbed the stairs to her flat.

Brigitte woke up the next morning at 6:30 a.m., her usual time, thinking about Poul and Arne again. There was nothing she could do for Poul, but she resolved to help Arne. She bathed, dressed, and was on her way to Arne's flat by 7:05 a.m.

Brigitte knocked and called repeatedly. She finally tried the doorknob. Unlocked. Bedroom door is closed.

She knocked on the bedroom door and it swung halfway open. Arne's sleeping, still in his clothes. Covers all in a tangle.

Maybe I should leave. Staring at him in his bedroom while he sleeps … feels pretty weird … I better just go home.

Brigitte turned away … and remembered Professor Koch's words. "Arne needs our help. He's lost in guilt and sorrow and pain and doesn't know how to get back. Brigitte, you have the best chance of helping him."

Why the hell does Prof think I can help him? I don't know how to help.

Growing up on the farm, Mother always said, when you don't know what to do for a sick animal, just do the normal stuff. The normal stuff is always important.

Brigitte turned the light on, marched to the window and opened it to get some fresh air.

"Wake up, Arne. Breakfast in 20 minutes. Get bathed," Brigitte made her voice as cheerful as she could.

By the time Arne emerged, freshly bathed and in clean clothes, she had buttered bread, squarest (sliced cheese), strawberry jam, and a large pot of zichory.

Arne just stood there looking at her, at the breakfast, and then back at her.

"Why …? What … ?" He stopped.

"Well, Professor Koch asked me to keep an eye on you." She shrugged.

"Um. Okay."

They stood there while a silence stretched out around them. Finally Arne said, "Smells good. Looks good."

"Hope you like it."

"I do. I will."

They ate in silence, but Brigitte thought this silence felt a little more comfortable.

Halfway through his second cup of zichory, Arne asked, "How long are you going to 'keep an eye on me'?"

"Well sir," Brigitte smiled. "As long as necessary."

Arne drank the rest of his zichory and pushed back his chair.

"Thank you, Brigitte," floated back over his shoulder as he headed for his bedroom.

Brigitte was struck by inspiration.

"Hey. Where do you think you're going? Your orders are to go for a walk this morning."

Arne stopped and asked. "Whose orders? Where to?"

"The Professor's," Brigitte lied cheerfully. "It doesn't matter where, as long as it's outside."

Arne grumbled but he went with her.

They walked all morning, mostly in silence. It was a nice summer day and Brigitte was sure that getting some exercise was better for Arne than hiding in his bed asleep all day. At lunchtime, Brigitte bought two rolls stuffed with meat and Arne bought beer for both of them. Over the second beer, Arne started talking about Poul and wondering why he started singing, why had he revealed himself to the patrol.

Brigitte listened, occasionally making encouraging noises, but really just letting Arne talk. Arne continued talking as they walked back to his flat . Gradually he shifted from the night of the raid to how much Poul meant to him as a person and a friend. As they entered the flat, Brigitte said, "He was like a brother to me. I loved him."

Arne sat down, looked at Brigitte and saw tears running down her cheeks, and started to cry himself. He sat there crying quietly until Brigitte gathered him in her arms, cradled his head on her bosom, and held him while his crying turned into convulsive, racking sobs.

Arne cried for a long time. Finally his tears dried up. He straightened up and went to blow his nose and wash his face. When he came back he was embarrassed.

"I'm sorry … I cried all over your blouse, it's all wet. I'm sorry."

'It's okay to cry for our friend. I can wash the blouse … it doesn't matter."

They talked for a few more minutes and Brigitte left to go see Professor Koch.

* * * * * * * * *

Arne tried, without much success, to read a novel. When he wasn't thinking about Poul, he was ashamed that he had completely broken down in front of Brigitte.

The next day Professor Koch knocked on Arne's door at 8:32 a.m.

"Hello, Arne. May I come in?"

"Sure. Have a seat."

"Arne, we need to talk. I know you're suffering from Poul's death."

Arne didn't respond right away.

"Prof," Arne stopped.

"Prof, it's my fault."

"Nonsense." Koch said. "You did nothing wrong, it's nobody's fault."

"Prof, you don't understand. Tyge told me beforehand. He told me the placement of lookouts was wrong. I wouldn't listen, didn't even consider what he was trying to tell me."

Professor Koch took a deep breath and thought for a minute before responding.

"Arne, let me tell you a story. You know who Olaf Haraldsson was? Olaf the Saint?"

"Of course. The great Viking warrior who became the King of Norway at age 22."

"Well, Olaf sailed as a Viking starting at age 12. At age 16 he was leading raids against villages along the Baltic Sea. When Olaf was 19 he misjudged a village, the raid was repulsed, Olaf lost a lot of men and narrowly avoided losing his ship."

Koch paused to let the Arne consider the story.

"Arne, the point is that everybody loses sometimes. God gave us free will and that means that there is uncertainty and chance in life. We can have the best plan, a perfect plan, and still have things go wrong."

"I got that part … my plan certainly went wrong."

"Yes, Arne, your plan went wrong but that isn't your fault."

"Sure feels like it is my fault."

"Of course it feels like your fault. But, Arne, it's not your fault, you are not in charge of the outcomes, the outcomes are God's business. All we can do is to try our very best and then leave the results in God's hands."

"In God's hands? We aren't supposed to worry about the results? We just let God worry about the results?"

"Yes, Arne, the results of our actions are in God's hands. I'm not saying we shouldn't care about the results, I'm just saying the results are out of our control. What we have to do is try our very best to do the right thing and then recognize that only God controls the outcome."

Arne sat in silence and Koch patiently waited.

"Okay, Prof, but I should have at least considered what Tyge was saying. Maybe if I had listened things might have gone better, Poul might still be alive."

"Things might also have gone a lot worse. The patrol might have caught several of you or even the entire group unloading the lorries." Professor Koch paused before continuing.

"Look Arne, you should have listened to Tyge, but for entirely different reasons. A good leader listens to his people. You are very smart, but you won't always think of everything ... and even when you do, your people need to know that you listen to their ideas and concerns.

"Arne, because you are smarter than most, you are able to ride roughshod over others. You get impatient, refuse to consider anyone else's ideas, and order everybody around. They go along with you because you are a good leader. They also resent that you don't listen to their ideas."

Arne sat, gazing out the window. Koch hoped that focusing on a real shortcoming would help Arne get past blaming himself for Poul's death. After several minutes Arne spoke.

"You're right. I get impatient with them. Much as I loved Poul, he was very cautious ... and so is Greta. Asger is foolish and lazy. Tyge is serious and smart but he takes so long thinking about things it drives me crazy. Carin is fearless and willing to try anything. Morten just goes along with whatever the rest want to do. Brigitte almost always backs me up ... and will jump in and take charge when necessary."

"So, Arne, what do you need to do?"

"Well, Prof, all of them have things they're good at. I need to encourage them to speak up and I need to have the patience to listen. Most times we can afford to do more talking before we swing into action."

"Good, Arne you have the makings of a great leader ... and understanding your own shortcomings is a key strength." Koch patted him on the knee and said, "Are you ready to come back to work? The food situation is pretty desperate. Some people are on the verge of starvation, we need you and your team."

Arne sighed and nodded yes, he would continue smuggling food past the German blockade.

* * * * * * * *

Asger was gone. The only thing they could find out was that he had moved back to his home-town.

On the next two missions, Arne assigned Brigitte roles that kept the two of them entirely separate. At the end of the week, Brigitte approached him. "Arne, join me for a cup of zichory?"

"Can't ... uh ... can't," Arne stammered. "Maybe some other time."

Arne berated himself as he walked away. *A week ago I was fantasizing about getting together with her. Then I break down and cry all over her. She thinks I need a nursemaid.*

Chapter 39. Enthusiastic Collaborators

SS Captain Eschmann finished scanning through the notebook provided by Clausen's informers and threw the book down in disgust. The pages were filled with trivial details on ordinary citizens and none of it seemed useful in identifying leaders whose removal might actually be helpful. His orders were to find ways to use the local Nazis. So far, all he had gotten out of them was the names and addresses of a handful of corporate executives.

Captain Eschmann went for his third cup of zichory while he thought about the issue. While stirring the zichory, the idea came to him. *These morons might be manipulated into helping with Best's plan to destroy the fabric of the Danish culture.*

He walked rapidly back to his office and sent his aide to set up a meeting with Clausen and his top associates.

Two days later Captain Eschmann greeted six of the Danish Nazi officials with a warmth he did not feel. Despite their eagerness to help the Nazi cause, he felt contempt for anyone who would so betray their own country. Pushing his revulsion down deep inside, he launched into his spiel.

"Colleagues, we face a difficult situation. As you well know, Danes are a stubborn and obstinate people. So far, your government and corporations have interfered with and prevented almost all of the assistance requested by the legally appointed representatives of the Fuhrer. I asked you here today to consider what further assistance you and the Danish Nazi Party might be able to offer.

"I should tell you that General Best has personally asked me to offer his congratulations for the exemplary work you have done so far. The information you and your people provided has been invaluable. Based on this work, General Best encourages you to take the next step in achieving our Fuhrer's glorious vision for a united and efficient Europe.

"When we take a young man into the army, he is immature, soft and full of silly ideas. Army training takes this soft, immature young man and makes a man of him. He becomes properly trained to follow orders efficiently and thereby be an important part of something greater than himself.

"Now, we face a similar problem with Denmark. Your country is soft and immature. Before Denmark can take its proper place alongside

Germany, it must be rebuilt so that it can be part of our Fuhrer's glorious vision.

"General Best has put into action a number of tactics designed to achieve this end. However, we are short-handed. After all, we are still fighting a war with Britain and we have several other countries where this same process of rebuilding is going on. You and the Danish Nazi Party could be a big help here."

Clausen was leaning forward in his chair and spoke eagerly.

"Captain, this is exciting. Your reasoning follows ours exactly. Our countrymen must be brought down and re-educated to understand the Fuhrer's genius. What exactly can we do to help?"

"We must crush the Danish national spirit," Eschman said. "We must destroy the sense of national unity. As soon as people feel they are isolated, they will be amenable to our program."

Captain Eschmann did not say that the immediate program for the Danes was that of docile slaves churning out war materiel for Germany.

"How will we do this?" Clausen asked.

"We need to attack the sense of national identity and feeling of unity. There are several ways of doing this. We can destroy important cultural symbols. We make people fearful and distrustful of each other. We use propaganda, for example an underground newspaper, providing our point of view."

In the next three days, Captain Eschman and Fritz Clausen organized a group committed to the destruction of important cultural landmarks. Clausen led this group.

Another group planned a program of violent crimes, both in the streets and in homes.

A third, much smaller group was assigned to begin an "underground" newspaper that would actually be a Nazi propaganda organ.

Captain Eschmann assured all three groups that funding and materiel would be provided as needed.

Chapter 40. Nightmares

Arne was brave and a little reckless and blessed … or cursed? … with a feeling of personal invincibility. Before Poul's death, Arne never suffered any real tragedy and he had this foolish assumption that he was smart enough and quick enough to stay one step ahead of the world, that he could always figure a way out of trouble.

Poul's death shattered this facile belief. Not only did he fail to stay out of trouble, it was his own foolishness that killed Poul. Tyge tried to tell him and he refused to listen.

His self-confidence was badly shaken and he worried incessantly about the rest of his group. They were smuggling food into Copenhagen day after dangerous day after weary day. The night before any operation that seemed at all dangerous, Arne would go to bed and then lie there, obsessively worrying about all the things that might go wrong. Eventually he would fall into an exhausted stupor.

The first of the nightmares began innocuously. Tyge was explaining something in that earnest way of his but Arne impatiently walked away in the middle of a long-winded sentence. A moment later an SS officer walked up and shot Poul. The Nazi kept shooting until there was blood everywhere, gallons and gallons of blood and Poul was shot to pieces. The Officer smiled at Arne, holstered his sidearm with a flourish, and turned and walked away. Arne turned to Tyge for support and suddenly realized that Tyge had been trying to explain how to save Poul. By refusing to listen, he killed Poul.

Arne woke up, drenched in sweat and in the grip of despair. Poul's death was his own stupid, arrogant fault.

Arne staggered out of bed and paced until dawn, gripped by a bottomless pit of guilt and sorrow.

The nightmares thereafter came frequently and in many variations. One particularly troubling dream had Poul pleading with Arne, "Why did you let me die?" Another had Brigitte getting shot. All of them left Arne devastated.

Arne had almost stopped sleeping. He was losing weight, had huge dark circles under his eyes and was increasingly irritable with everyone.

* * * * * * * *

One evening a fortnight after Poul's death, Brigitte protested, "Arne, the lookouts aren't far enough out. Except for you and you are too isolated, too far from the rest."

'If they go farther out, they don't have good escape routes," Arne retorted.

"They can hide," Tyge said. "When they're too close, the work group won't have time to escape."

Arne looked at Tyge for a minute, then said, "Fine. You make the assignments."

"You want me to make the assignments?"

"Yes," Arne swallowed. "Please."

Tyge made the assignments. As they all walked off, Tyge turned to Brigitte and spoke.

"Is he okay?"

"He hasn't been right since Poul died, " Brigitte said. "He takes crazy chances and tries to keep the rest of us from taking any chances at all."

"I think we need to talk to Professor Koch about this," Tyge said. "This isn't working."

Brigitte thought a minute, then said, "Let's take tomorrow off and try to get this straightened out … before someone else gets killed."

* * * * * * * * *

Brigitte, Tyge, and Greta were at Professor Koch's office when he got there the next morning at 9:00 a.m. They spent 45 minutes talking about Arne and the way the unit was working … or not working … since Poul's death.

Finally Professor Koch summed up their discussion.

"The main problem seems to be that Arne is not making the best decisions about how to keep the group safe." Professor Koch sighed deeply, looked around for his glasses and then gave up on them. He continued. "Arne has been carrying the burden of being in charge … and in a situation where the leader can't possibly control the dangers threatening the group. With Poul's death, the burden is more than he can stand."

Koch continued, "We can replace Arne with someone else. Or, we shift to a more collegial decision making structure, one in which several or all of you share in the burden of the decision making." He looked at each of them in turn. "Is there anyone else that might make a good leader for the group?"

Greta pointed at Brigitte and Tyge and said, "Our best bet would be one of these two. They're the ones everybody looks to if Arne isn't handy."

Brigitte and Tyge simultaneously shook their heads and both said, "Not me."

Professor Koch smiled and said, "Well, that's a good sign … not wanting the job is almost a requirement."

"What about this collegial structure you mentioned?" Brigitte said.

"I think you are already doing this informally," Koch said. "The general idea is to use everyone's insights to the extent possible. For instance, in planning an operation, the ideal is to make sure that everyone's expertise and insights are included rather than one person going off in a corner and planning it by himself. I think it would help Arne if it was clear that a group of you decided on the plans rather than it being entirely up to him."

"Yes, we talk things over ahead of time," Greta said. "Then we rely on Arne to make the final decision."

"That puts the pressure on Arne," Tyge said. "It's easier than taking responsibility ourselves."

Finally Brigitte said, "Okay, we have to step up and take responsibility." Greta and Tyge simply nodded in agreement.

"This is good, this should help a lot," Koch said. "One other thought. You're doing a lot of lookout work. Are any of you especially good at arranging the lookouts? Or, you are transporting food yourselves … how about picking the routes for bringing in the shipments? It might make sense to develop specialists who would routinely take charge in some of these special situations?"

Greta spoke quickly, "Tyge is real good at arranging lookouts."

"Morten is a genius with maps," Brigitte added. "He can find routes to avoid patrols better than anybody."

"Carin is very devious and very quick," Greta said. "If a situation calls for confusing or fooling the Germans, she can always come up with something."

They talked for a few more minutes but quickly came to the conclusion that formalizing a more collegial decision making structure was probably their best solution. The three young people left and Brigitte told Arne that Professor Koch wanted to see him right away.

* * * * * * * * *

"Arne, you look terrible," Koch looked at Arne over his glasses. "When is the last time you got a reasonable nights sleep?"

"I don't know, Prof. It seems a long time ago."

"Tyge, Brigitte, and Greta are worried about you. They say you're not sleeping and are so worried about them that you're not making good decisions."

"They're right. I'm a mess. I don't think I can do this anymore."

"Arne, you've been carrying the burden for the entire group. They realize they've been looking to you to make all the hard decisions and I talked with them about taking some of the weight. They're ready. We just need to clarify exactly how it's gong to work."

Koch had the ever-present reading glasses in his hand and was waving them around as he talked. He outlined their discussion of the collegial decision making structure and emphasized that actually making it work depended upon Arne and the group coming to a clear understanding of where and how to employ it and under what circumstances they would revert to a more traditional command structure.

Arne agreed to work out the details with his group.

"One more thing," Koch said. "You have to get some sleep." He handed Arne three pills.

"Use these the next three nights. I'm not giving you more because these things are addictive if you use them for too long."

Arne accepted the pills. He didn't mention the nightmares.

Chapter 41: Crushing the Danes #2

Captain Eschmann was astonished at the men Clausen brought him for the campaign to crush the Danish spirit. Some of them were true believers in the Nazi cause, but most of them were degenerates with a grudge against the world or, even worse, simply eager for an opportunity to enrich themselves.

Eschmann described these men to his colleagues as "Clausen's scum." Despite his contempt for them, he knew that he could not only use them, but that with a little care he could win accolades from General Best.

Captain Eschmann divided the men into three groups. The few ... very few ... with intelligence and education were assigned to the propaganda group. Their job was to create a favorable impression of the German occupation. They were promised whatever resources they needed for radio broadcasts, newspaper stories, or whatever other forms of propaganda seemed useful.

Eschmann was even more selective about the second group. These men were the elite saboteurs, those who would destroy important cultural symbols. As saboteurs, they needed considerable training with small arms and explosives, as well as teamwork and reconnaissance.

The last of the men were assigned to the street crime unit. They were trained in picking victims, in how to rob someone in public in broad daylight, and how to escape. They were shown the rudiments of using a knife in both attack and defense.

Most of the men were organized into groups of three or four so that, in case of trouble, there was backup for the point man. A few of the men were such loners that they flatly refused to work with anyone else. All of them were instructed to blend in with their intended victims in every way possible and to then engage in as much street crime as they could.

Captain Eschmann assured them that the German army would protect them, although he knew that this promise was an empty one. The German army had no way of knowing who these men were and Eschmann wasn't about to create a paper trail tying the army ... or himself ... to street crime.

With the promise of army protection and the lure of easy money, the street crime men went to work with enthusiasm. Copenhagen saw an immediate, dramatic increase in daring robberies, many of them occurring in very public places where the victim was surrounded by other citizens.

In those cases where anyone pursued the mugger, he was often slashed and sometimes seriously wounded by one of the mugger's accomplices.

Eminent Professor Koch, lifelong resident of Copenhagen, began to fear not only for his personal safety but for the very soul of his beloved city. He could almost feel the residents withdrawing into themselves, looking at each other with suspicion and distrust. As the muggings went on, the fear became palpable.

* * * * * * * *

General Dr. Best was not happy, not happy at all. He was having trouble sleeping and his stomach bothered him almost continuously. Losing weight. Might have an ulcer. Leg's getting sore, gotta stop with the swagger stick.

They had finally managed to secure, after months of unbelievable delays and obstacles, five hundred rifles from the local factory of Dansk Industri Syndikat A. S.. And every damned one was unusable. Some had a crooked bore. Others with oversize firing pins jammed after the first shot. The list of defects went on and on.

The work on the submarines proceeded at a glacial crawl. Our engineers can't seem to speed it up. The first artillery pieces, from another subsidiary of Dansk Industri Syndikat A. S., were made of the wrong steel and were in imminent danger of bursting.

The German High Command stubbornly refused to understand the dilemma. They insisted Denmark deliver war materiel and yet prevented any actions that would create unfavorable publicity for the Fatherland. And the Danes were crazy, they continually resisted any and all orders.

Moreover, the troops were stretched thin, way too thin. We didn't count on having to run the railroads or rebuilding bridges. We didn't plan on running the post office and telephone companies. Nor on having to drive huge truck convoys. We didn't expect to look over the shoulder of every machinist and welder in the shipyards and arms factories.

There's only one area in which we meet the expectations of the High Command. Huge numbers of troops scour the country for food stuffs. When we find a herd of steers, we guard it, send for trucks, butcher the steers and ship them to Germany.

When we find a field of cabbages, we watch it until it's ready for harvest, load it on trucks and drive it to Germany. When we find a herd of dairy cows, we watch the herd. We watch while the cows are milked, confiscate it and drive it to Germany. Vast quantities of food are moving to Germany … but the cost in manpower is huge.

The High Command is pleased with the food shipments. A lot of Danes must be going hungry. Or soon will be. Serve them right if half of them starve.

Three weeks of night-time assassinations ... seventy-three so far. Street crime also dramatically up ... with all the criminals and psychotics released, the Danes are being terrorized.

The Gestapo has tortured hundreds of Danes ... I'll bet every Danish man is afraid by now.

Surely the Danes will break soon. Please, let them break before the High Command loses patience and breaks me.

Chapter 42. The Freedom Council

King Christian left his office with his omnipresent Nazi guards a step behind. He climbed the stairs to the second floor and entered the toilet half way down the hall. His guards followed him into the toilet. He went up to the urinal and pretended to use it. He leisurely washed and dried his hands and, barely opening the door, slipped sideways out of the door into the hallway.

The instant Christian was clear of the door, two of his Royal Guards slammed into it and engaged several heavy bolts to secure it. Angry shouts rose from inside, followed almost immediately by pistol shots.

The bullets did not penetrate the specially prepared door. One of Christian's helpers spoke.

"That'll hold the bastards."

"Good work, men. I'm off to a meeting."

Christian hurried out a side door, got into a waiting car and found to his delight that Vald had arrived moments earlier. They embraced, both a little giddy and feeling like adventurous ten year olds.

"How are we going to avoid the checkpoints?" Vald asked.

The driver pointed to a man on the corner wearing a blue cap. The man raised his hand over his head and then pointed down the street in the direction they were already going.

"We're not taking any chances," the driver said. "We've got watchers all along our route and on two alternate routes. Oops, see there. That one is telling me there's a checkpoint. We go around this one."

The driver made a right turn and then a left and passed one block over from the checkpoint.

* * * * * * * *

The other members of the Freedom Council were waiting when Christian and Vald arrived. They had missed several meetings because of the SS guards, so there was a period of greetings, hugs, and "Are you okay?" before the meeting was called to order.

"Are the people holding up?" Vald asked as soon as they were all seated. "I'm feeling cut off from everything … it seems Best is on the verge of winning."

For a long moment no one responded. Finally a General spoke.

"Everyone is hungry, tired, terrified … the assassinations, tortures, muggings. There isn't enough food to go around, everybody has enough to drink but most of us don't have water to bathe, no electricity, no petrol for vehicles … In the last three weeks seventy-three men were killed in their beds in Copenhagen alone … all of them had their throats slit."

"How are we doing with the Watch Groups?" Vald asked.

"The murder victims have all been prosperous men, so we're focusing on those neighborhoods. We have close to full coverage for those neighborhoods. If you look at the newspapers today you will have a very pleasant surprise. We actually caught one of the bastards last night, caught the knife man and his driver. There were four men in the team, two lookouts, the knife man, and a driver. The lookouts both got away, but we got the other two."

There was a stir of excitement all around the room and King Christian exclaimed, "How did we catch them? Do you have details?"

The General looked very pleased as he told them.

"One of our guys spotted the car coming down the street with no lights. By the time their lookouts were in place in the front and back of the house, we had six guys assembled and more on the way. The knife man had just slipped inside a window when we moved in. The lookout on the front porch spotted our guys and blew his whistle and ran away. We chased him but he got away. Before the driver could react, two of our guys had him out of the car and on the ground. Our guys ran to both the front and back doors and started beating on the doors and yelling. The knife man came out the window he used to enter the house and ran into a club. He's in the hospital with a broken arm and a serious bruise on his head."

"Did either of them have any ID?" Vald asked.

"No. They were completely clean. The knife and the car are both German military, as were their clothes. They had removed all insignia, but the clothes are clearly German military. Also, both of them were carrying German pistols. Both of them had the little .32 automatic that the officers like."

"Why didn't they use the pistols?" Vald said.

"The knife man tried to use his, but he stuck the pistol out the window and one of our guys smashed his arm with the bat. We surprised the driver. The first thing he knew was when his window shattered and he was being dragged out of the car. The lookouts just ran."

"So we got lucky," Vald said.

"I'm not so sure it was so much luck," Koch said. "These assassins are sneaking around in the dark, cutting men's throats. They've been doing it every night now for the last three weeks. They might start to enjoy the whole thing, become arrogant and over-confident. In this case they will be easy to surprise and may well react stupidly when they are."

Koch paused a moment to see if there would be any disagreements with his analysis. When there was none, he continued.

"Second possibility, if the man has a shred of conscience left, he will be increasingly bothered by what he is doing and will be more and more stressed out by it. In this case he will make stupid mistakes from fatigue. In either case, our guys should have a very good chance of capturing them, if … and this is the key … if we have them significantly outnumbered and we take them by surprise."

"General, do our guys know the assassins have pistols?" Vald asked. "What sort of guidelines have we given the Watch for this situation?"

"Well, we didn't know, but we assumed the assassins were armed. The guidelines are pretty basic, really. The Watch captain decides on one of two tactics. If he thinks they can, they try to capture the Nazis. If he doesn't have enough men or thinks he can't surprise them, he tries to scare them off."

"These men are cold-blooded killers," Christian said. "We should give them a trial and when they are found guilty, we execute them. Then deliver the bodies to General Best. Executing these two won't stop the killings, but it will up the stakes for the other assassin teams. They will know that their lives are also at risk."

"Very good," the general said. "Let's scare the bastards. Also, I think we should arm the Watch. The Watch guidelines should allow them to use their hunting rifles to pick off these guys. Otherwise, we are going to start taking some serious casualties … you can't expect our guys to take clubs up against pistols … and you know we have women in the watch, it's not all men."

They considered the truth of the General's point. Finally Professor Koch spoke, somewhat hesitantly.

"I think we have a problem here. The General is right, we will have some casualties as the Watch tries to capture the assassins. On the other hand, if we start shooting at them, we are likely to damage our reputation with the German soldiers. The SS, of course, is enthusiastically persecuting us. The Wehrmacht soldier, on the other hand, looks the other way more often than not. We get reports everyday of German squads shooting at groups of our people at very close range … and no one gets hurt. The only way they are not killing large numbers of our demonstrators is by deliberately missing. Also, I have numerous reports of Wehrmacht squads ignoring loads of food as it is smuggled into the city.

"I think we dare not shoot these bastards, even though I would like to, because we need the sympathy of the average German soldier … and we have that because he knows we aren't offering any violence toward him."

"I don't like it," the general protested. "We're asking unarmed men and women to go up against armed men who enjoy killing. We could have a bloodbath at any time."

"General," Christian said. "None of us like it. However, as you have taught me, Viking warriors do what is necessary, warriors take the risks they must. In this war, we are all warriors, the entire society is on the front lines of the battle. Shooting at the assassins would undoubtedly help us win that particular battle, but it might also lose us the war."

King Christian looked at the 12 members of the group and slowly … in several cases very reluctantly … everyone nodded in agreement.

Vald decided it was time to move to the next topic and asked for a report on the torture.

"The Gestapo seem to snatch people at random and then torture them for anywhere from half a day to, in a few cases, as much as five days. Most of the victims are released after no more than three days. If the victim breaks and starts naming friends, the torture stops and they are released as soon as they run out of names. As far as we can tell, the Nazis are making no attempt to arrest those named by the victims. The purpose seems to be to break our people and leave them with the self-loathing engendered by having named all of one's friends to the enemy.

"We know of 856 men who have been tortured and released. Forty-seven more were abducted within the last five days and have not yet been released. Another thirty-eight men were abducted more than a week ago and we simply have no information on them but we suspect they were killed."

"Can we endure?" Christian asked. "Can our people continue the resistance?"

"We have been monitoring people's reactions as best we can," Koch said. "Our worst problem, even more than the fear that the Nazis have generated, is that people are wearing out, they are tired. The daily hassles of trying to get food and water past the blockade, of doing without electricity, these are bad enough. When you add constant fear to the mix, people get exhausted. Perhaps the worst aspect of this is that the street crime makes people suspicious of their fellow Danes. Our biggest strength has been our solidarity and the street crime is seriously undermining this. So, a combination of exhaustion and loss of solidarity is becoming a very serious problem for us."

Koch stopped and seemed to be thinking. Finally he continued.

"There are several trends going on. With the decline in morale and the exhaustion of our own people, the big question is how long we can sustain our campaign in the face of the Nazi brutality. We're doing all we can to sustain our people. The press, Moellar's broadcasts, the ministers, all are helping ... for example my friend Kaj Munk is delivering strong sermons every week. I don't know if it is enough, but I don't know what else we can do.

"The SS and the Gestapo are becoming more brutal and more brazen. The big question here is whether we have any way to pressure them into less murderous behavior. With the public executions, we were able to use the world press. That is not working so well here ... the world press is not giving the story much prominence.

"We know that the Wehrmacht units are already resisting orders in some cases, such as failure to shoot demonstrators and laxness in enforcing the blockade. The main question here is how far and how quickly the Wehrmacht sympathy for us may go.

"Finally, and this is just speculation, the German High Command must be getting very impatient about Best's failure to secure materiel. He has managed to secure quantities of food-stuffs, but nothing else. At some point Hitler has to start asking himself whether it's worth all these troops to get some food. The really key question is at what point does Hitler decide Denmark is more trouble than it's worth and start pulling out his troops.

"Unfortunately, we have absolutely no information to help answer this question, all we have is speculation. On the first three trends, we have at least reasonable information, but on this one we have nothing except our own powers of reason."

Koch stopped talking and seemed to stare into empty space.

The silence went on for some time.

"That's all beside the point," an admiral said. "The Nazis absolutely destroy every army that they meet. Hitler is a madman but no army seems able to resist him. Hitler conquered all of central Europe without working up a sweat. Look at the facts. Hitler grabs us and Norway and then immediately invades France, Belgium, and the Netherlands all at once. Look at how quickly he succeeded:

Netherlands ... surrendered in five days.
Belgium ... gave up after 18 days.
Norway ... quit after 31 days."
France ... crushed in 42 days.

"Three fortnights to destroy France! The only European country that was considered equal to Germany in military power and it lasted barely a month and a half.

"Only Britain still resists and only because the English channel stopped the tanks. What do you think will happen to Denmark when Britain falls and Hitler really begins to pay attention to us? Britain is reeling and Hitler is preparing to invade and finish them. Afterwards, he will grind us to dust. We need to face reality and make some sort of accommodation."

Vald was stunned. The Admiral had articulated precisely his own worst fears. It's bad enough with only a few of the SS. For Hitler to focus his full attention on us … unimaginable. We could never survive.

For perhaps a minute and a half they considered the Admiral's comments. At length King Christian stood up and began to speak.

"Admiral. I want to thank you for brilliantly summarizing our situation. We must be realistic in our planning, and that means considering the worst case.

"However, I believe our good Admiral is overly pessimistic. Do not forget that Canada and New Zealand still stand with Britain. Given the ocean between them and Germany, Hitler will not easily overcome them.

"Winston Churchill is now the Prime Minister in Britain. Vald has met him and the man is a bulldog and a military historian. Under Churchill, Britain will resist and resist and resist.

"Equally important, Churchill has learned from France's mistakes. He now understands Hitler's 'lightning war' tactics and is preparing to counter them.

"Hitler may eventually conquer Britain but it won't be easy and it probably won't be soon.

"The really big question in all of this is what the Americans will do. Vald has spoken with Roosevelt several times and Roosevelt is itching to get the US into the war. Our own struggle, according to Roosevelt, is rapidly swaying American public opinion against the Germans.

"If the Americans come into the war, that will change everything. This war, for the first time in history, is a war of machines … tanks, trucks, artillery, ships, submarines, airplanes … these are the key elements in this war. Your industrial plant and raw materials are the primary means of fighting. And the American industrial might is vast, far bigger than Germany's. Hitler is truly a madman if he thinks he can beat the Americans.

"One more point about Hitler. The man has shown himself to be an egomaniac with grandiose ambitions. Unfortunately he is also a gifted demagogue and has total control over Germany.

"Men such as Hitler inevitably over-reach. His hubris dooms him. Sooner or later, he will make a fatal mistake. We can only hope and pray that his demise comes soon, before we are destroyed.

"To summarize our situation, as the Admiral pointed out, Hitler may subjugate all of Europe and then decide to crush us. Alternatively, Hitler may over-reach and fall, with or without the Americans having come into the war. We can only speculate as to which way things may go.

"So….How do we decide what to do?

"I can not order you into battle or to surrender. But I can tell you what I intend to do.

"I have been asking myself what my ancestors would have us do? I have been asking myself what my children and grandchildren would have us do?

"My ancestors were Vikings. Your ancestors were Vikings. Our Viking ancestors fought and sometimes we won and sometimes we died. But we bent our knee to no man.

"Life is very dear to me. The regard of my ancestors is more dear. The opinion of my children and grandchildren is more dear to me than life.

"My personal course is clear. As a Viking and your King, I shall continue to resist the Nazis. I shall continue to resist because I can not stand the thought of helping those I consider totally evil.

"Ultimately, each of us … and each of our countrymen … must decide how vigorously we will resist the Nazis.

"However, our choice to resist as a nation has already been made. Now we, this group, must not fail our people in leading and coordinating that resistance. We must not lose hope and must not lose courage. We must remember that we are Vikings.

"And we must lead as Vikings."

The King sat down and Vald thought he had never looked more the Viking warrior. Vald was the first to speak.

"We have before us both the best and worst cases for the course of the war. Given that we continue to resist the Nazis, we must answer two questions.

"How do we maintain our people's capacity to continue the struggle?

"What can we do to limit the Nazis ability to brutalize us?

"I think that we must now turn our attention to these two questions. I am open to suggestions."

The meeting went on for six more hours. As the day wore on, the room gradually became more and more cluttered with dirty cups, the remains of several large trays of sandwiches, and discarded papers. Slowly and painstakingly their new strategies emerged, assignments were made all around, and they adjourned.

Vald and the King left together as they had come. Vald was totally exhausted and marveled that the King, in spite of being 70 years old, seemed inexhaustible, even serene, in his will to resist their oppressors.

Chapter 43. The Will to Fight

The SS soldiers guarding Vald and the King were replaced by others, men whose attitude was even more venomous than the first group. The new guards were an additional burden for Vald … he felt that they wanted to kill him and were restrained only by their orders.

The Neighborhood Watch redoubled their efforts and the following night prevented several murders. In one case the Watch tried to capture the assassins but were seen too soon and the assassins used their pistols, killing one of the Watch members and seriously wounding two more.

In another case, the Watch spotted the Nazi car, with its lights out, slowly cruising a residential street. They watched it come to a stop right in front of their hiding place. As the Nazis got out of the car, the six men and three women of the Watch overwhelmed them and had them spread-eagled and helpless on the ground before they could react.

In three other cases, the Watch was able to scare the death squads away.

* * * * * * * *

Two days after the Freedom Council meeting, July 28, 1940, at 4:00 p.m. Vald and King Christian met on the steps of Amalienburg Castle. The four SS guards assigned to them followed. As planned, there were several hundred people in the square and at the windows of adjoining buildings, many of them with their forbidden cameras.

As Vald and the King reached their positions at the edge of the veranda and looked down the broad steps, two squads of Royal Guards moved to surround the four SS guards, standing very close to them.

"Move a muscle," a Royal Guard officer said, "and we take you down."

The King waited to see if the SS would react.

"At 1:30 p.m. today two German soldiers were executed for premeditated murder," Christian said. "These two men were caught in the process of attempting to kill an innocent man while he slept. They were tried in a Danish court of law, were found guilty of several of the murders that have occurred in Copenhagen in recent weeks, were sentenced to death, and were executed by hanging. The bodies will be delivered to General Best.

"There have been numerous murders of men sleeping in their beds in Copenhagen in the last two fortnights. These murders have been carried out by members of the German SS in an attempt to intimidate us.

"These murders, carried out at the order of General Best, demonstrate to the world that General Best and his command have lost all sense of decency, have lost all sense of honor. The German occupying forces, under the corrupt leadership of General Best, have descended into barbarism and can claim no place within the company of civilized nations. The behavior of the German occupying forces are a blot upon the proud traditions and honor of the German people.

"Despite the subhuman brutality of General Best's SS assassins, we will not be cowed. These assassins, skulking in the night time shadows, afraid to show their faces in the light of day, these cowards will be captured and will be brought to justice and will be executed for their crimes."

King Christian finished speaking, saluted his people, and walked back into the palace, accompanied by Vald. The Royal Guard stepped away from the SS soldiers and, after a moments hesitation, the four SS followed Vald and Christian.

Christian and Vald grinned at each other. The SS, caught by surprise and surrounded by the Royal Guard had not been able to interfere. They would get a serious chewing out from their superiors.

The text of the King's press conference had gone out over their secret cable in advance of the public announcement. Pictures of the event were distributed within an hour after the press conference. The papers the next day, both the illegal Danish papers and those in the US, Russia, Britain and elsewhere, carried stories, many of them on the front page.

* * * * * * * *

General Best was dismayed at the stories. The Nazi High Command, especially Joseph Goebbels, Minister for Public Enlightenment and Propaganda, will be furious. Thank god Ribbentrop had personally approved the assassinations.

Mid afternoon, three days later Christian again walked toward the front of his palace, his two SS guards close behind. As he stepped out the door onto the veranda, one of his guards reached for the King's shoulder and drew his sidearm.

Before he could complete either action, he was on the ground under two of the Royal Guards. His comrade suffered the same indignity. King Christian glanced over his shoulder, saw that his Royal Guard had immobilized the SS, and continued to the edge of the veranda. Once again there was a crowd of several hundred people in the square. Christian addressed the crowd.

"The Nazi SS and Gestapo have engaged in a systematic campaign of torture against innocent Danes. In the last two fortnights almost a thousand men have been tortured. Thirty-six are unaccounted for and we suspect have been killed.

"I have affidavits from one hundred and seventy-six of these men, detailing what was done to them and what the Nazis demanded of them. I also have photographs, documenting the torture done to them.

"The Nazis pretend that these men are engaging in illegal activities and demand to know who else is involved. The torture goes on until the victim begins naming names, supposedly of others engaged in illegal activity. However, the Nazis don't follow up on those named ... their real purpose is simply to spread fear and shame at having broken and named one's friends.

"This torture is another barbaric tactic of General Best to intimidate us and force us to support the German war effort. If General Best had a shred of honor, even a shred of decency, if General Best was a civilized Christian officer, he would not debase his office and his army in this shameful way. General Best sullies and dishonors a thousand years of proud German tradition. General Best will be held up to history as a war criminal and as one who committed crimes against humanity.

"We are here today to denounce these German crimes. We are here today to declare we will not be cowed. We are here today to vow that we will not be part of the German war effort. We are free Danes. We are Vikings and we will never bend our knee to a conqueror. We shall endure and we shall resist and we shall triumph."

King Christian turned to his Royal Guard, still pinning the struggling SS to the ground, and ordered:

"Disarm them. Strip them of their uniforms as punishment for attempting to lay their hands on your King. Then release them."

The Royal Guard hauled the SS to their feet, stripped them to their underwear and released them. Many cameras were very busy as the once proud SS went down the steps in their drawers. The newspapers had a field day with photos of the near-naked SS.

* * * * * * * *

General Best was enraged over the stories of the torture ... but the pictures of the humiliated SS officers ... the High Command will have my head.

Intolerable. This ends now.

"Two SS squads, in trucks," Best yelled. "Right now. And a car."

Best was in the car almost before it stopped.

"The Palace. Fast. Run over anything that gets in our way. DRIVE!"

Best went up the Palace steps three at a time, brushed past the Royal Guard without a word and barged through the door to King Christian's office, drawing his pearl handled .32 automatic as he did so.

* * * * * * * *

King Christian looked up from his desk and saw Best's contorted features and the pistol.

The impossible scene stretched out for what seemed to Christian to be forever but was probably only scant seconds. General Best stood there, with his pistol pointing at Christian.

Dear God. Is he going to shoot? Say something, anything, just say something.

"Hello General. I see you are upset with us." Voice sounds strained, too high.

Best continued to aim the pistol at Christian.

"You know, this is the room where General Himer killed my aide." Voice sounds a little better, keep talking, anything. "We have hidden cameras all around the room."

Best didn't respond, kept pointing the pistol.

Say something, defuse him. What to say? God, can't think.

Christian sat there, facing General Best's gun.

He's gone crazy, we pushed him too hard. He wants to kill me, he wants to shoot.

"Movie cameras are over there, others behind that picture," Christian said. Babbling idiot, I'm losing it. Is he going to shoot?

General Best smiled. It was a ghastly grimace, but was still recognizable as a smile. He holstered the pistol, stepped farther into the room, pointed at the King with the swagger stick in his left hand.

"My congratulations, King Christian. I wanted to see for myself if you were really as brave as your subjects claim. My threatening performance was quite good, was it not? You reacted quite well. Thank you."

With that, Best turned smartly and left the room, the tap-tap of the swagger stick against his knee audible as he went down the hall.

Christian was sitting there, head in his hands, when Vald rushed into the room a minute or two later. At the sight of him, Vald stopped and exclaimed.

"You're alright? Thank God. They told me Best was going to kill you."

Christian raised his head and took a long shuddering breath.

"I thought he would. I never, never want to see a face like that again."

A moment later Christian began to laugh, a high pitched crazed sort of laugh, but nevertheless a laugh.

"I would have been a useful martyr … but the photographers weren't ready, there would have been no pictures. I'm glad he didn't shoot, I'm really glad he didn't."

Two days later King Christian held a third press conference, this time to announce the execution of four SS assassins captured by the Neighborhood

Watch. Newspapers all over the world seemed fascinated by King Christian's continued defiance of the Nazis and gave the story prominent coverage.

Chapter 44. Struggle and More Struggle

The Neighborhood Watch groups added more members and began plotting the locations of the street crimes. Then they staked out the most popular locations. Within a week they had fifteen muggers, caught during or immediately after a robbery. Two of these muggers talked quickly and freely, almost boastfully, of their role in the robberies. Several others talked within a few days and the Watch soon had the full story, including the involvement of Clausen, the Danish Nazi Party, and Captain Eschmann.

A hurriedly convened meeting of the Freedom Council, attended by only half of its members, decided that the collaborators were engaged in treasonous behavior and should be executed. Eleven of the suspects were clearly known to each other and were implicated as part of the Danish Nazi Party. The other four seemed to be small time thieves who were merely taking advantage of the absence of the police.

The eleven collaborators were executed by hanging. The small time thieves were given the options of either joining the Watch or exile from Copenhagen under threat of death if they were found within the city. One left the city and three opted to join the Watch. One man was forced to leave after a week and the other two served honorably.

The underground press reported the execution of the eleven collaborators, the role of Clausen and the Danish Nazi Party, and the involvement of the German Army. The Watch caught another eight muggers the following week and subsequently executed them as well. Street crime decreased dramatically thereafter as the collaborators realized the German Army could not protect them.

The torture was the most difficult to deal with because people were grabbed at random, in broad daylight, and taken to Gestapo Headquarters where they were then tortured in secret. There seemed to be little the Danes could do to stop the tortures.

A mass demonstration against the torture was held in the square next to the Shell House, Gestapo HQ. The SS fired upon the demonstrators, killing ten and wounding dozens.

Killing the demonstrators generated world-wide publicity that enraged Hitler. He issued orders that demonstrations were not to be tolerated under any circumstances and, in a stunning show of illogic, cashiered the officer who gave the order to fire upon the crowd. Unfortunately for the Danes, they didn't know that the offending officer had been punished.

* * * * * * * *

Arne entered the square and approached the Gestapo HQ in Shell House at precisely two minutes before three p.m. As he walked across the square, Arne noted the steady stream of people converging from all directions. Arne and Tyge reached the sidewalk together and unfurled the large banner that read "Torturers work here". While they hung it from the building, Carin and Morten started their song:

> For the caged bird,
> for the tortured bodies,
> I sing your name, Liberty[1]

By the time they finished the first stanza of the song, they were 200 strong and growing as passersby joined them. Two minutes later an SS officer came to the door. He did a quick about face and they knew he was going for reinforcements. Four minutes after Arne and Tyge unfurled the banner, they finished the song and dispersed, scattering leaflets as they went. Three minutes later four squads of soldiers came into the square, moving at double time. The photographers in the nearby buildings captured images of the soldiers to go with their pictures of the demonstration. The picture of the banner on the Gestapo HQ ran in several major newspapers world wide and enraged General Werner Best. It did not amuse his superiors in Berlin.

The flash demonstrations were held several times a month, at randomly chosen times. The international press continued to be enraptured by tiny Denmark's defiance of all-conquering Germany and regularly ran front page stories on Denmark, much to the irritation of Hitler and his propaganda chief Joseph Goebbels.

* * * * * * * *

General Best decided there damn well would be no more press conferences. The publicity is keeping the High Command thinking about Denmark ... and me. Bad enough that the Danes continue to resist. Christian sure as hell isn't going to gloat about it to the world.

An SS squad of twenty-four men should do it. Especially if they shoot a few of the Royal Guard. Let Christian watch a few of his favorites die ... that will soften him up.

Idiot Hanneken howled he couldn't spare the troops. The fool doesn't seem to realize the danger to both of us. Maybe Hanneken wouldn't mind being sent to the front, but not me.

The summons to see Foreign Minister Ribbentrop arrived one day after Christian's third press conference. The fact that the summons was expected did nothing to ease Best's apprehension.

* * * * * * * *

Foreign Minister Ribbentrop didn't waste any time getting to the point with Best.

"The Fuhrer is losing all patience with the Danish situation. Hitler and Goebbels are both extremely upset over the publicity.

"Considering the number of troops we have in Denmark, the food you secure for us is not worth the trouble. The Fuhrer is wondering why we keep you on, why we shouldn't replace you? Frankly, Dr. Best, I'm wondering the same thing?"

Best wanted to remind Ribbentrop that he had enthusiastically approved their present course of action, but knew that would not help. He took a deep breath and plunged ahead. He had to make Ribbentrop understand that the dynamics created by a nonviolent defense were quite different from what they usually faced. He concluded by talking about the morale of the troops.

"My SS troops are rock solid," Best said. "Our Wehrmacht troops are another story. I have numerous reports of Wehrmacht squads firing on groups of Danes and not hitting anyone. This can only mean they are deliberately missing. In the blockade of Copenhagen, the SS are catching three times the number of smugglers as are the Wehrmacht, even though the SS make up less than ten percent of the patrols. Again, this can only mean the Wehrmacht are not really trying.

"General Ribbentrop, I at first didn't believe this, but our troops are being subverted by the Danes. The Wehrmacht troops are clearly not following orders properly, they are deliberately resisting orders. It is not overt, they go through the motions, but they are not trying."

Ribbentrop interrupted.

"How can the Danes subvert German troops? I don't believe it."

"General Ribbentrop, I understand your doubt. I too did not want to believe it.

The Danes offer no violence to our troops. They aren't shooting at us, they aren't even damaging our vehicles or weapons.

"In Denmark, these troops are being asked to help kill someone who is not threatening them in any way. They're refusing to kill the Danes. My Wehrmacht troops are rapidly being reduced to uselessness."

"But the SS," Ribbentrop protested. "The SS are still following orders properly?"

"Yes, General, the SS are still reliable. If I had 150,000 SS troops and didn't have to worry about bad publicity, I would easily solve the Danish problem."

Ribbentrop thought for a bit.

"Well, General Best, Hitler won't accept defeat so what do we do with these Danes?"

"I don't have enough troops. We are running the railroads, the post office, the telephones, truck convoys for food, and huge numbers of my men are doing nothing except securing food-stuffs. In order to get anything done in a factory, I have to maintain a massive presence throughout the entire plant. Our planning for this occupation did not anticipate any of this, so our manpower is totally inadequate."

"General Best, you are not going to get more troops. We have just overrun almost all of Europe and we still have to crush England. The troops you already have are all that can be spared."

Best hadn't really expected to get more troops, but he had to ask.

"The Danes have to be near collapse. I implemented the campaign of torture, assassinations, street crime, and destruction of important cultural symbols as we discussed in our last meetings. These are going well and are taking a heavy toll on the Danes. I expect them to break soon."

Best paused to collect this thoughts before continuing.

'However, as I said, we face an unprecedented situation and totally novel strategies. Given the High Command's orders to avoid bad publicity, my hands are tied … publicly, we either tolerate the Danes defiance or we give up and come home. The stern measures that would break them quickly are prohibited. We have no choice but to use stealthy measures and that takes a while. We must be patient."

When General Dr. Best ran out of air, he suddenly realized he had been holding his breath waiting for Ribbentrop's answer.

"General Best, we appointed you as Plenipotentiary to Denmark because we thought you a capable man. You are the officer on site, you are in charge, and you are responsible for making this work. Do you understand me? I expect you to solve the Danish problem and I expect it soon. More importantly, the Fuhrer expects you to solve this problem and get the materiel flowing to the Fatherland. That is all. You are dismissed."

General Dr. Best rose, snapped a salute, said, "Yes, sir," and departed. This is so unfair. Ribbentrop knows there's no solution to this mess. He'll make me the fall guy.

What a lousy philosophy. Hitler proclaims we are the master race. That means we always win, we can cut through any difficulty. If we fail at something, it means somebody doesn't deserve to be part of the master race. Son of a bitch! They're going to crucify me.

The Danes have to be getting tired. Have to find some way to buy time, the Danes will break soon.

Chapter 45. Lookout Duty

The moon was full but the clouds were so thick that you could barely see your own feet. Arne and Brigitte were the primary lookout team while a boxcar of vegetables was unloaded. A single road led to an area where six large oil tanks stood alongside the railroad, each tank about 30 feet high. Arne and Brigitte lay side by side on top of one of the tanks, watching the road. Any German patrol coming down the road would be visible long before it got to them. If a patrol came, they would use their torch to signal the team unloading the vegetables and all of them would disappear into the woods.

Some time after 2:00 a.m. Arne asked Brigitte a question.

"How are people holding up? Everybody looks sort of worn out."

"Our team? Everybody is tired, but I think we're okay."

"I'm tired, probably more tired than I've ever been. Greta and Morten have both lost weight. All of you have dark circles under your eyes. I wonder if I need to tell Prof we need a couple days off?"

"Maybe before long, but right now we're okay," Brigitte said.

A moment later she changed the subject.

"You played soccer?"

"Yes. As a forward."

"Tyge told me you were a big star."

"Maybe a little star," Arne laughed. "I was the leading scorer on my team ... but our team was not so good."

"That's not what I heard," Brigitte said. "The guys told me you were the fastest man on the team and the best player."

"Okay, you caught me. I am actually Denmark's greatest ever soccer player."

"Could I get your autograph, oh great and wondrous star," Brigitte teased. "And maybe even touch your royal hand?"

Arne held out his right hand and Brigitte extended her index finger to gingerly touch it. They dissolved into laughter.

"What about you, did you play sports?" Arne asked.

"No, just pick up games with my brothers and friends. Farm girls usually go straight home after school ... too many chores."

"You want to live on a farm, afterwards ... after the war?"

"Probably. Something very satisfying about working around animals and growing things. It's great for kids."

"So you're going to have lots of kids?"

Brigitte didn't answer, just squeezed his arm, hard and half raised her other hand in a shushing motion. Arne heard it then … at least one jeep… oh my God! Close. Can't see a thing. Where are they?

Arne rolled over, aimed his torch, and blinked it rapidly several times. No answer yet. Keep blinking. Come on, answer, damnit. There! One fast blink. Enough.

"Let's get out of here," Arne said. Brigitte was already at the edge of the tank, on her belly and looking over the edge.

"They're coming this way," Brigitte said. "They might have seen our signal."

Arne lay beside Brigitte and watched for the few seconds it took the jeeps to reach their area. The troops jumped out and spread out to encircle the group of tanks.

"The ladder," Arne exclaimed. He scooted to the other side of the tank and yanked their rope ladder up so that nothing showed from the ground. The clouds parted and the area was bathed in bright moonlight.

Brigitte stifled a gasp. "It's SS," she said.

Shit, we're dead. Those bastards kill everybody they catch.

Arne and Brigitte crawled toward each other and met in the middle of the tank.

Brigitte's hand found Arne's and held on. He rolled onto his side, facing her, and she came into his arms. Arne shifted position a little so he was lying on his back with Brigitte's head on his shoulder and his arms around her.

There was nothing to do except wait for the SS to find and kill them. A distant part of Arne's mind thought how much he would enjoy holding Brigitte like this under other circumstances.

Arne held Brigitte and waited. It'll take them a while to get to us. The rope ladder is the only way up here. Maybe they'll just check the tanks that have ladders. Please, God.

The moon went behind the clouds. They could hear the SS moving around and calling to each other.

A loud clank caught Arne's attention just as the clouds parted again. He looked to the left and went rigid. "Shhh," he hissed. "Look … over there."

Two soldiers on top of the tank next to them, perhaps a hundred feet away. Thank God our tank has some superstructure on top … maybe they won't be able to see us.

Arne forgot to breathe and neither of them moved while the soldiers remained on the nearby tank. They seemed to be taking a break, just standing there. Can hear their voices, what are they saying?

Finally! The two soldiers are gone. Lots of noise, sounds like the damned patrol is all around. My right arm is going numb.

They waited.

What was that? Sounded like a shouted command. More noise now.

The jeeps started! Are they leaving?

Arne rolled over and cautiously raised himself enough to look for the jeeps. Thank God! They're going. We're safe.

Brigitte was on her knees beside him, crushing his hand in hers. She started to cry and he put both arms around her.

"It's okay, don't cry," Arne said. Hell, I'm crying too. Stupid thing to say.

They held each other and cried.

When they recovered a bit, they climbed down and went to look for the others. Boxcar with the food is locked. No sign of anybody.

"They got away," Brigitte said.

"Let's get out of here," Arne said. "They might come back."

The rendezvous point was about a kilometer through the woods. They started out at a brisk walk, the trail easily visible in the bright moonlight. A little later, the moon was obscured and they couldn't see anything and were forced to stop.

Almost an hour later they reached the rendezvous. There was no one there.

"They gave up on us, think the Nazis got us," Arne said.

"What now?" Brigitte asked.

"We can either try to make it to a friend or just sit it out here," Arne said. "It's already 4:30 in the morning and it's not too cold. Let's just wait for dawn."

They found an evergreen tree where the ground was covered with old pine needles, soft and dry. They lay down, side by side and close together for warmth. Arne's jacket was under them and Brigitte's on top of them.

Brigitte's breathing slowed and she seemed to be asleep almost immediately. Arne lay awake for some time. Damn near died. Now I'm sleeping with Brigitte. What a night.

Chapter 46: Fleeing Copenhagen

The Nazis permitted people to enter Copenhagen but, to intensify the food shortages, banned anyone from leaving. Fortunately for the Danes, there were so many routes in and out of the city that the Nazis could not effectively patrol all of them.

August 12th was another cloudy, damp day when Arne, Greta and Morten met the twelve people they were to guide past the German patrols. The Jensen's were a young couple with four small children ranging from one to six years old. Mr. Jensen's parents and two aunts were also there. Two elderly men made up the rest of the group.

Arne looked them over and his heart sank. *Jensen Sr. looks awfully frail and he uses a cane. The aunts are fat, won't be able to go quickly. We'll have to carry the two smallest children. Well, we'll do the best we can … and pray a lot.*

"We have a couple of kilometers to go," Arne said. "Then we'll be clear of the German patrols. Not many patrols in this area, but we still have to be careful. Most of the time we'll be in pretty good cover. Greta and I will be scouting ahead and Morten will signal when you come forward, wait, or hide.

"This is the most important, this is the signal to hide," Arne said. Morten removed his hat. "You have to watch Morten, if he takes off his hat, you have a few second to get off the path and out of sight.

"The other two signals are pretty obvious," Arne said. He demonstrated waving them forward and holding his hand palm up for wait.

Mrs. Jenson spoke up. "What about you, what if a patrol sees you?"

"Well, Greta and I will be together and we will pretend to be lovers looking for a place to be alone."

Mrs. Jensen looked doubtful, "Does that work?"

"Most of the time it works," Arne smiled wryly. "With the Wehrmacht, it usually works. Just hope we don't run into an SS patrol."

"How will Morten know if you see a patrol?"

"Greta will lose her hat. Anymore questions? Just remember to stay alert and watch Morten. Don't do anything until he signals you. Okay?"

Everybody nodded and Arne and Greta started down the path. Morten stayed with the group for a minute and, before starting out, said, "Wait for my signal."

Arne and Greta reached the first turn in the path, saw that Morten was almost there and continued. Morten waited at the first turn where he could see both Arne and the group waiting behind him. When Arne and Greta reached the next turn he signaled the group to come. They continued in this fashion, with Morten maintaining an intermediate position between Arne and the refugees, for the next hour and a half.

Arne and Greta led their little group into a small barn. Arne spoke. "Is everyone doing okay?"

"My leg is starting to pain a bit, but I'll make it," Jensen Sr. said.

"The children are getting tired," Mrs. Jensen said. "How much farther?"

"Another half-kilometer gets us past the usual area they patrol," Arne said. "But I want you rested so that we can cover this last part quickly.

We're going to scout ahead. If everything goes perfectly, we'll be gone about half an hour. If we see patrols, we hide until they're gone. Don't worry if we take a while to get back. Oh, there's water here. Don't go outside, stay in here … be quiet and keep the door locked. Once in a while a patrol will go past here, but they never look inside."

Arne, Greta, and Morten slipped out and Mr. Jensen bolted the door behind them. They followed the path for a hundred meters and then turned and went up the hill on their left, picking their way through the trees. At the top of the hill, Morten climbed into a tall oak tree. Arne and Greta waited and presently Morten's voice floated down to them.

"All clear."

"Okay, we're off."

Arne and Greta hurried down the hill and continued up the path. After 300 meters, Arne waited while Greta crossed a large lawn and knocked on the door. Arne watched her enter the house. Several minutes later Greta raised a third story window and gave Arne the all-clear sign. Arne waved and trotted rapidly back the way they'd come.

Minutes later, Arne was at Morten's tree and out of breath from running up the hill.

"Morten, still all clear?"

"All clear. I don't see anything."

"Okay, I'm going to get them."

Running down the hill to the barn was easy going. Arne knocked on the door.

"Mr. Jensen. It's me, Arne. Time to go."

Jensen opened the door.

"There are no patrols in the area, but we need to move fast. Let's go."

Mrs. Jensen carried her baby and her husband had the two-year-old. Arne thought the five year-old boy and six year-old girl would be able to keep up on their own. Hope the aunts and Jensen Sr. can keep up.

They passed Morten's hill and crossed the open field beyond without incident. As they approached the house with Greta in the attic, the front door flew open and Greta and Mrs. Petersen, the lady of the house, both ran out, gesturing urgently.

"Quickly, quickly! There's a patrol," Greta called.

The Jensen's and their children broke into a run and were inside in moments, followed closely by two of the other men. The aunts struggled up the walk, badly out of breath but moving pretty quickly.

Jensen Sr., who was considerably behind the others, broke into a limping run but fell down, hard, just as he reached the edge of the lawn. Arne started back for him but Mrs. Petersen grabbed his arm.

"No time," she said. "Inside, now. Leave it to me."

Arne hesitated.

"Go! I know this officer," she ordered.

Arne turned and made it inside just before the patrol rounded the corner.

Mrs. Petersen dashed to the fallen man who was feebly attempting to get up. As she reached him, she looked up and seemed to see the patrol for the first time.

She smiled, beckoned to them.

"Herr Schmidt. Herr Schmidt, I need your help. My uncle fell and I think he hurt himself."

Herr Schmidt hurried up and looked at the prostrate man. His Danish was quite good.

"What happened? Are you alright?"

"My leg gave out. Bumped my head when I fell. I'm a little woozy."

"Herr Schmidt, can two of your men help him to the house?"

"Ya, we can, Frau Petersen." Sergeant Schmidt pointed at two of his men and they lifted the injured man to his feet. They carried him to the porch where they lowered him into a rocking chair.

"Herr Schmidt, I don't know how to thank you enough," Mrs. Petersen gushed. "Per is my favorite uncle but he is getting so frail, I was afraid he was badly injured. Thank you, thank you and God bless you."

Herr Schmidt blushed. "Oh, Frau Petersen, it wasn't anything. Good day."

Mrs. Petersen stood on the porch watching until the patrol turned the bend and went out of sight.

"Pretty friendly with Herr Schmidt, aren't you?" Jensen Sr. said.

"Damn good thing, too. He thinks I'm his buddy. I know all of his routes, everywhere he patrols," She shrugged. "We need to know what they're doing. An occasional cup of zichory and a little flirting is a small price to pay for the information." She started to go inside, then asked, "Are you okay?"

"I'm fine," he laughed. "I followed your line and faked it. Just have a gimpy leg. Getting old."

A half hour later Arne passed the group off to their contact who had arranged transportation to their respective destinations.

An hour later Arne, Greta, and Morten trudged toward the city with hand-carts heavily loaded with food. They were about half way back when Arne heard a German command from up ahead. They turned off the path and put their hand-carts behind thick bushes.

They waited for perhaps 30 seconds but heard nothing else. Arne began cautiously moving forward, keeping inside the bushes. A German patrol was stopped about a hundred meters ahead, right at the intersection of two paths.

Greta and Morten crawled up beside him and Greta whispered, "We wait?"

"I think we have no choice," Morten said. "There's no good way to go around them."

Arne motioned for them to follow and wriggled away from the patrol. There was a clearing stretching off to their left that would let them watch the patrol from a distance of almost two hundred meters.

"Let's go over there," Arne said. "We can watch them and they won't see us through the trees. It's far enough away they won't be able to hear us either."

Five minutes later Arne and Greta were lying on their bellies, side by side, watching the patrol through a screen of brush. Morten was thirty feet behind them, on the grass and falling asleep.

They lay there watching the patrol, talking only occasionally and neither minding the silences in between.

"Arne, how come you don't have a girlfriend?"

"I just don't, that's all."

"Hey, c'mon Arne. You're pretty cute … how come you don't give any of them a break?" She put her hand on his arm.

"Oh, I'll give the right one a break all right."

Greta didn't respond and they watched the patrol a little longer. Arne's work assignments frequently paired the two of them.

"I like being with you, Arne."

"Yeah?"

'You deserve a girlfriend, a girl who appreciates you." She gave his arm a little squeeze and smiled.

"Brigitte always seemed interested in Asger."

"Brigitte? Arne, you got a thing for Brigitte?"

Arne nodded.

"Let's be honest here," Greta said. "Brigitte's way out of your league, my friend. A lass like Brigitte gets a sports hero or a rich man, not somebody like you."

Arne didn't say anything, just plucked at the grass.

For long minutes neither of them spoke and finally the patrol formed up and marched off, moving away from their route. When the patrol was well away, they woke Morten, retrieved their hand-carts and delivered the food without further incident.

Chapter 47. Exhaustion

General Dr. Best summoned his personal SS unit and headed for Amalienberg Castle on August fifth.

"Wait here," he instructed the squad leader. "I will return shortly."

Best went directly to the King's office and brushed past the receptionist. The King was at his desk.

"I'm putting our flag, the swastika, on top of your castle," Best said. "You will no longer fly the Danish flag."

The old King digested this for several seconds before replying.

"I will send a Danish soldier to take the swastika down and replace the Danish flag."

"That Danish soldier will be shot."

"That Danish soldier will be me," Christian shot back.

Best regarded him, not sure he could believe his ears. *There is no end to this old fool's idiocy. God, how I want to shoot him. That would be the public relations disaster of all time.*

Best stared at the King for long moments, attempting to stare him down, but the old man sat there like a rock. Best finally dropped his gaze and walked out.

Best stopped just past the receptionist.

"Lieutenant, arrest everyone we see on the way out. Start with her." Best pointed at the King's receptionist. *That'll give the old fool something to grieve about.*

The SS snatched eleven Danes on their way out of the Palace. Best ordered death for all of them. *Christian and Vald will make formal complaints. We'll ignore them, deny we even have these people.*

* * * * * * * *

Gerhard and Jacob patrolled a different section of Copenhagen each day of the week. They made their rounds, were careful to see nothing worth reporting or interfering with, and exchanged pleasantries with those few Danes who acknowledged their presence. Their routine was undemanding and rather pleasant most of the time.

The weekly folk festivals continued, although the SS sometimes broke them up and pursued musicians. The musicians had so far eluded the SS, but several of them had lost instruments.

King Christian rode his horse through the streets of Copenhagen every mid-morning like clockwork, always by himself. It was a point of pride to Christian that he rode alone, with no bodyguard. In his mind, his bodyguard consisted of all of the Danes and that was enough for anyone. Besides which, he was a Viking and Viking warriors didn't use bodyguards.

The hard part for Christian was to see how gaunt his people were becoming. Everywhere he rode, the faces turned to him in greeting were cadaverous.

Vald came in every day and spent the day at his desk. Vald wanted … needed … to be useful and the SS prevented him from being part of the resistance, kept him from everything except the most routine of his work. He gradually sank farther into depression and despair. He spent long periods doing nothing at all, just sitting at his desk.

The SS assassination squads went out every night in search of victims and the Neighborhood Watch stalked the assassination squads. Sometimes the SS killed prominent Danes, occasionally the Watch captured the assassins, and sometimes the assassins killed the Watch.

The Gestapo continued to grab Danes off the street for torture but the Danes had adopted a policy of immediately reciting as many names as they could think of, so the Gestapo no longer even pretended to be interested in getting information from their victims. They simply tortured the victims until, somehow, it was decided to release them or kill them.

The blockade of Copenhagen entered its ninth week as August wound down, with all electricity, petrol, water, and food supplies cut off. The SS continued to kill those it caught bringing supplies into the city, but the SS patrols were few in number. The Wehrmacht troops barely made a pretense of trying to catch the smugglers.

Most Danes, even in the city, had their own vegetable garden and Copenhagen was now well organized to evade the blockade. Nevertheless, in the absence of large trucks, the sheer amount of physical labor required to keep everyone fed was exhausting.

Street crime continued but at a level considerably below its recent peak. For the first time in memory, the citizens of Copenhagen feared walking their streets and worried about their safety in their homes.

August in Copenhagen was sublime, with pleasant sunny days and cool evenings but Arne was not enjoying the weather. In an effort to bolster exhausted bodies and plummeting spirits, Arne was treating his entire group to breakfast. Carin read out loud from the lone menu.

"Omelets. With your choice of ham, mushrooms, or cheese. Pancakes. Bacon," she said. "Home fries and oatmeal."

"Oh my," Morten said. "Do they really have that?"

"Coffee is what I'm hoping for," said Tyge.

"I'll settle for near anything that will fill me up," Morten said.

The waitress came over and plucked the menu from Carin.

"We don't have most of that," she said.

"Coffee. Do you have coffee?" Tyge asked.

"Any eggs?" Carin said.

"Any meat at all?" Morten asked.

"Whoa. Slow down," the waitress said. "We have some potatoes and oatmeal. No coffee, not even tea."

This elicited a chorus of groans all around.

"Sorry. The blockade … Yesterday we didn't even have oatmeal."

"Okay," Arne said. "Look, just bring us what you can. We have a tough day ahead of us …"

"You know the portions are small, don't you? Our owner says we have to ration everything … I'm sorry, there just isn't enough …"

Arne looked around at his group and realized that this breakfast wasn't going to help. We're still going to be hungry. Already sick of potatoes and oatmeal. How long can we keep this up? Even Greta is slim. There were rumors that some people in Copenhagen had actually starved to death.

The entire month of August had been one long blur of hard physical labor for Arne and his team. Each day, every day, was taken up with a combination of transporting food staples into Copenhagen and helping to smuggle people out. My group … Hell, the resistance as a whole … is on the verge of collapse. I'm numb, too tired to care.

Part Three. Arresting the Jews

September 1940 through February 1941

Prof. Hal Koch Journal, September 8, 1940

Rumors of more madness. Duckwitz says they are seriously considering arresting all of our Jews. The Freedom Council refuses to take the rumors seriously ... they keep mindlessly repeating that <u>we</u> don't have a Jewish problem. As if our attitudes carry any weight with Hitler. They should read Hitler's own words in Mein Kampf. They should read the news reports on the concentration camps. Ah, ah, ah ... everyone is too exhausted to consider one more potential problem when we already face more than we can deal with.

Now Russia seems to have caught the madness ... they already have Finland and half of Poland and now they invade the Baltic states.

Best is wearing us out. The blockade of Copenhagen, the assassinations, the torture, the street crime ... all these are wearing us down. I really wonder how much longer we can keep up the resistance before we all collapse from sheer exhaustion. But we must not despair, God never asks us to do something beyond our capabilities.

Chapter 47. Judische Frage (Jewish Question)

General Best knew he was running out of time. Four months in stinking Denmark. Foodstuffs moving in a steady stream. A few minerals moving south. Couple thousand Danish Nazis joined the Wehrmacht. Another few thousand working in German factories. That's it. That's the extent of the good news.

Arms factories producing nothing usable. They would all die of old age before the shipyards finished a submarine.

Every damn week Ribbentrop complains that the cost of occupying Denmark exceeds the benefits. Terrorize the Danes into submission, he says. But don't get any bad publicity, don't do anything to get America to sympathize with the Danes, we don't want America in the war. Shit. I need a magic wand.

With 100,000 SS troops we could crush them. Wehrmacht troops are useless. Blockade was another failure, too few good troops.

Even the night-time assassinations failed. The Danes caught too many of the assassins ... and hanged them. Even the SS is afraid to continue that game.

The Gestapo tortures 20 or 30 Danes a week. The Danes stage their little five minute demonstrations in front of the Gestapo HQ two or three times a month and manage to generate some embarrassing publicity.

Street crime way down too. Danish Nazis are thugs, but the Watch caught lots of them. Hanging a few of them discouraged the rest.

Half of the Danes aren't working. How the hell are they managing to live. Damned government must have set up some system to subsidize them.

The bombing of the Tivoli Amusement Park was a master stroke. Fritz Clausen's idea ... even bumbling idiots occasionally have good ideas. Clausen said it was an important cultural symbol and he was right. Thousands of Danes visited the smoking wreckage after the bombing. Clausen planning to bomb several more sites.

The country has to break soon. Nobody can function like this for very long. But damn! Ribbentrop isn't going to wait. Have to do something to buy time.

His aide interrupted his reverie to announce the arrival of George Duckwitz, his shipping liaison for Denmark.

"George, so good to see you. How is your lovely wife? A drink? This is a very good schnapps."

"Annemarie is in good health, thank you. I have to decline your kind offer of schnapps, General, my stomach won't take it. How may I help you?"

Best poured himself a shot, downed it, and contemplated Duckwitz. Duckwitz has many Danish friends, including Jews. He may understand the Danes a little too well. Where do his deepest loyalties lie? Regardless, he will be candid.

Best caressed the silky rosewood of his swagger stick while he chose his words carefully.

"I am being pressured to deal with the Judische Frage (the Jewish question). How do you think the Danes will react if we arrest the Jews and deport them?"

"General ... that would cause major troubles. The Danes have no discrimination or prejudices against the Jews ... they are treated exactly like everyone else. Any action against them would unite the country against us."

"Surely the average Dane isn't going to risk himself for a Jew. I can't see anybody causing trouble, especially as it would be a crime to interfere with the arrests. Anyone who helped the Jews would be subject to arrest and deportation."

Duckwitz took a deep breath and looked away before answering.

"General, as you know, I believe it is morally wrong to single out the Jews. In addition, I think the Danes will act to protect their friends and neighbors."

"Do you think the Danes would use violence to help the Jews."

"I don't know about that. They might, I suppose. I'm sure they won't passively accept it."

Best thanked Duckwitz and ended the meeting.

Best considered the possible consequences of arresting the Jews. Maybe we could provoke the Danes into violence. Violence would motivate the Wehrmacht troops to do their job … instead of walking around with their eyes shut.

Or, arresting the Jews might be the straw that broke the Resistance's back. Maybe the Danes would ignore the arrests. If that happened … Danish solidarity would be no more.

Best felt a grim satisfaction. Either way, we win.

On September 8 General Best sent Ribbentrop a carefully worded telegram suggesting that it was time to deal with the Judische Frage in Denmark.

September 17 General Best received notice from Ribbentropp that Hitler had decided 'in principle" to carry out the operation against the Danish Jews. It remained only to work out the details.

The afternoon of September 17 Best's security agents, dressed in civilian clothes, broke into the Jewish Community Center and stole the membership lists for the Copenhagen Jews. Another group started combing the phone books for Jewish names. General Best received a promise of an additional 50 Gestapo officers to assist in carrying out the arrests.

The details of the raid clicked neatly into place. The Jewish newyear, Rosh Hashanah, falls on October first. Perfect, all the Jews will be home or with relatives. Catch all of them in one twenty-four hour period. Transport via the hospital ship, the Monte Rosa. Gestapo and SS officers to supervise the raid and the army provides the manpower and trucks.

Arresting the Jews buys at least several months time. The High Command will wait to see how this comes out.

If the Danes react with violence, the Wehrmacht will wake up and we'll grind them to pieces.

If the Danes react passively, that damnable King and pathetic little Prime Minister and everybody else will finally see the resistance is failing. Then they'll fall apart.

Best had two glasses of his favorite Schnapps before bedtime and, for the first time in many weeks, slept soundly and woke up feeling refreshed and confident.

Chapter 48. George Duckwitz

George Duckwitz was ashamed to be a German, ashamed that he had joined the Nazi party in 1932. Damn. Another summons from General Best. Talking to Generals guarantees trouble.

Hitler's crazy. All that nonsense about the Jews. Why in hell does Best make me a personal confidant. I keep disagreeing with him.

Perhaps Best wants my insights into the Danish character. The man is a canny politician ... but without a conscience. Assassinations and torture! My God, how have we sunk so low?

The formal dinners are the worst. Have to watch every word at these affairs of state. My Danish friends might think I'm selling out.

Duckwitz informed General Best that he wanted no part in a bureaucracy that would be judged by history as inhuman. He offered his resignation and asked for immediate transfer to another post.

Duckwitz answered his phone on September 12th. It was General Best, urging him to continue in his post. Several of his Danish friends and his wife also asked him to stay, arguing that he might be able to help the Danes if he remained.

On September 20 Duckwitz went to Stockholm and met with the Swedish Prime Minister, urging him to offer sanctuary to the Danish Jews. Upon his return to Copenhagen, he met with several Wehrmacht army officers to argue that the arrest of the Jews would be a blot upon their honor and that they should refuse to participate. His efforts bore some fruit.

Von Hanneken wired his superiors that he had serious reservations about the proposed arrest of the Jews. The German High Command wired back that Hitler had approved the action in principle and that they had only to work out some details before the arrests would be carried out.

Several other officers agreed to do what they could to help.

* * * * * * * *

Duckwitz received a visit from Major Klein, a close friend of many years.

"George, I am hearing very disturbing, very dangerous things about you."

"I'm not surprised ..."

"You are committing suicide. For nothing! Hitler has decided and there is no stopping it. My contacts in the Gestapo tell me they are watching you. You are already considered untrustworthy. Any further protests will get you in serious trouble, probably arrested."

"I'm sorry. Thank you for coming, for your concern for me. I can't do anything else. I will do everything in my power to stop the arrests."

That evening Duckwitz wrote in his diary that Major Klein left "as if he had just said his last goodbye to a cherished child that had been seized by temporary insanity."

The diary also said, "It is good that Annemarie shares my convictions. There will be no detour from the road I have taken. There are, after all, higher laws. I will submit to them."

* * * * * * * *

Duckwitz spent the next several days in frantically securing "legal" exit visas for a large number of his Jewish friends. These friends were given papers showing that they were now citizens of Sweden and most of them immediately took extended holidays in their new country.

Duckwitz had excellent contacts in the German Admiralty in Copenhagen and knew that they disapproved of the planned deportation of the Jews. At his urging, the Corvettekapitan Richard Camman, Harbor Commander for Copenhagen, pointed out to his superiors in the German High Command that the planned action against the Jews would take them away, for a long time, from their minesweeping in the North Sea. The High Command's response was that they had to continue the minesweeping ... and this meant they were not available to patrol the coastline or the waters between Denmark and Sweden.

Corvettekapitan Camman went further. During the last week of September, he arranged that all the patrol boats under his command were scheduled for repair in dry dock. This meant that there were very few German patrol boats available for policing the Oresund, the bay between Denmark and Sweden.

Kapitanleutnant Friedrich Wilhelm Lubke, chief of sea transport, was another old friend of Duckwitz. He learned of the plan to deport the Jews when he was ordered to ready the Monte Rosa, a hospital ship, to deport 5000 Jews. The captain of the Monte Rosa, Heinrich Bertram, was a friend of his. The two of them quickly agreed to pretend that the engines of the Monte Rosa were seriously damaged and that the ship could not be gotten ready in time. The German High Command was forced to send two other ships, the Devon and the Warthland, to pick up the Jews.

Duckwitz had done all he could to stop the arrests. He went to work each day at the normal time and put in a regular day. Wonder when the Gestapo will come for me ... I just hope they don't arrest Annemarie

Chapter 49: Three Days

Duckwitz walked into General Best's office in response to his summons on September 28.

Best came immediately to the point.

"George, the Jews will be arrested the night of October 1. By the evening of October 2 we will have all of them in custody."

Duckwitz didn't want to believe it. Why is Best telling me this? He knows how I feel about this. Damn! He's going to arrest me.

Best seemed content without a response and continued, eyes still downcast.

"I tried to stop it, but the Fuhrer has issued a Fuhrerbefehl (Fuhrer's edict). As you well know, there is no turning around once there is a Fuhrerbefehl. We have to carry this operation through to completion."

Duckwitz was unable to respond. Crushing me, can hardly breathe.

Best looked up and into Duckwitz's eyes.

"George, I know you think this is a bad idea ... I wanted to let you know I had no choice in the matter."

Duckwitz finally managed to find his voice.

"Thank you, sir. Will that be all, sir?"

"I'm sorry ... I just wanted you to know ... ," Best repeated himself

Duckwitz fairly fled from General Best's office. Three days! Arrests in three days. What the hell can be done in three days?

An hour later Duckwitz found Hans Hedtoft, the leader of the Danish Social Democratic party, in a meeting. He burst into the meeting room.

'Hans, I have to see you. Right now."

"George, what is going on? Can't it wait until we finish here?"

"No! It can't wait even a minute. It's life and death!"

Hedtoft and three other top officials went along to an adjoining room.

"Now the disaster is about to occur. The whole thing is planned in full detail. Ships are going to anchor in the harbor of Copenhagen. Your poor Jewish countrymen will be forcibly transported to the ships and deported to an unknown fate. It is scheduled for the night of October first, three days from now."

"Thank you for the news." Hedtoft seemed about to pass out.

A moment later, Duckwitz nodded and rushed from the room.

* * * * * * * *

Hedtoft and his friends took only a moment to decide on their course of action and hurried off in different directions. Hedtoft went to the home of the president of the Jewish community, Carl Bernard Henriques, a prominent attorney. Henrique's response to Hedtoft's news was simple.

"You are lying!"

Hedtoft responded that he was absolutely sure of the impending raid.

Henriques couldn't believe it. He had just come from meeting with the Danish undersecretary of the Ministry of Foreign Affairs who had been reassured by General Best that nothing was going to happen.

In desperation, Hedtoft told him everything he knew, including Duckwitz's role. Finally Henriques was convinced.

Hedtoft went next to the home of Rabbi Marcus Melchior, the chief Rabbi of Copenhagen.

"Rabbi, I am sorry to bother you," Hedtoft said. "General Best is planning on arresting all the Jews on Rosh Hashanah. You are to be arrested and sent to prison camps in Germany."

Rabbi Melchior didn't say anything, just turned and went and sat down in the living room, in his favorite chair. Hedtoft silently followed and sat opposite him in an overstuffed chair. Hedtoft waited, trying not to fidget while the rabbi sat there, fingering the tzitzis on his tallit. A moment later Melchior finally responded.

"They tried to arrest me already, about three weeks ago." He paused, seemingly lost in remembering. His right hand continued to finger the tzitzis.

"They came to our door in the middle of the night. Our oldest, my boy, started toward the door but I stopped him. We stood here, listening to them banging and shouting at us to open up. I didn't know what to do ... I have five children, most of them small ... couldn't run ... we just stood here, praying while the banging and shouting went on for several minutes. I was sure they would break the door down."

"What happened?" Hedtoft was leaning forward. 'How did you get out of it?"

"A miracle," Melchior chuckled. He stopped fingering the tzitzis. "The lady next door began to yell at them 'What are you doing? It's 2:00 a.m. The Melchiors aren't even here, they went on holiday, somewhere up north. Go away and stop bothering us.' And they did. They went away."

"That's all, they just went away?"

"They went away. The lady lied for us. We spent the next week with my brother, just in case, but they never came back."

"Well," Hedtoft said. "I'm afraid they are coming again. This time it's for everybody."

Rabbi Melchior thanked him, Hedtoft went on to his next stop, and Melchior began warning his friends.

The following morning, September 29, Rabbi Melchior was conducting the early service in the Copenhagen synagogue. Rabbi Melchior said his morning prayers and then announced to the congregation that the new-year services were canceled. He announced:

"I have very important news to tell you. Last night I received word that the Germans plan to raid Jewish homes throughout Copenhagen to arrest all the Danish Jews for shipment to concentration camps. They know that tomorrow is Rosh Hashanah and our families will be home. The situation is very serious. We must take action immediately. You must leave the synagogue now and contact all relatives, friends, and neighbors you know are Jewish and tell them what I have told you. You must tell them to pass the word on to everyone they know is Jewish. You must also speak to all your Christian friends and tell them to warn the Jews. You must do this immediately, within the next few minutes, so that two or three hours from now everyone will know what is happening. By nightfall tonight we must all be in hiding."

* * * * * * * * *

The evening of September 29 Duckwitz wrote in his journal. "It has finally happened and here, too, everything has gone to pieces. One has to try very hard not to lose one's composure and not to weep. Four years of hard work is for naught ... because of stupidity and unreasonableness. Now the inhabitants of the last country in Europe will hate us from the bottom of their hearts. It is very difficult to be a German."

Chapter 50. Chaos

Jorgen Knudsen was on his way to work September 29 when he saw friends stopping people on the street. His first thought when he found out about the planned raids was "Det kan man ikke – that is not acceptable!" He rushed to the nearest telephone booth, ripped the phone book loose and raced to the garage to pick up the ambulance he normally drove. Instead of going to work, he pored over the phone book, looking for Jewish names.

"Ah," Jorgen often talked to himself. "Goldschmidt is just down the street from here."

Three minutes later he pulled to a stop in front of the Goldschmidt residence, bounded out of the ambulance and ran to the front door where he leaned on the doorbell until an elderly woman opened the door.

"What is wrong? You can stop ringing."

"Oh, sorry, but there is no time. The Germans are going to arrest all the Jews, you must hide."

"What are you talking about? We have done nothing … why should they arrest us?"

"Look, you must believe me. The arrests are scheduled for Friday night, during Rosh Hashanah. You will be arrested and sent to concentration camps. Do you have non-Jewish friends who will hide you?"

"Non-Jewish? We have no one. My husband is ill and I am old. All of our non-Jewish friends are dead or moved away."

"Well then, you must come with me to the hospital. We can hide you there."

" I don't know … I have to talk to my husband."

"All right, let's go talk to him."

Mrs. Goldschmidt led Jorgen into the sitting room where John Goldschmidt was sitting. He immediately spoke.

"Rose. I heard everything. We must do as he says. The Nazis have been arresting Jews all over Europe and no one knows what happens to them after the arrests."

"Oh dear, oh dear. I never thought it would come to this. I have to pack, I have to get our things."

Jorgen asked, "How long will it take you to get ready?"

"I don't know, I don't know what to take. Oh dear."

Jorgen hadn't thought about this either, but he knew the hospital routines. "One small bag for each of you. No more. Just a change of clothes and your toiletries. No more than that."

"But our things. What will happen to all our things?"

"They will still be here. What's important is to save your lives. Now look, you go pack and I will return in an hour. In the meantime I will warn others. Now hurry."

With that Jorgen ran off and went to a Jewish home a few blocks away. An hour later, having warned several other families with friends who would hide them, he came back for the Goldschmidts. Mr. Goldschmidt was so frail Jorgen helped him walk to the ambulance and half-lifted him into the back. Rose got in with her husband and they drove away.

Jorgen stopped and picked up another old woman and then headed for Bispebjerg Hospital. Jorgen was halfway to the hospital when he turned a corner and saw the German checkpoint just ahead of him. There was nothing he could do … reluctantly he slowed and stopped for the troopers.

"Your papers, please."

Jorgen handed the soldier his ID and waited, dreading the next command.

"This seems in order. I'll check the back."

"Wait." He handed the soldier a face-mask, the same mask surgeons use during operations. "You'll need this."

The soldier automatically reached for the mask, then hesitated. "Why do I need that?"

"My patients have yellow fever. Very contagious, often fatal. You wouldn't want to get that. The mask might protect you."

Jorgen watched the soldier as conflicting emotions played across his features. Fear won out over duty and the man waved him through.

Jorgen drove straight to the emergency entrance, but parked a few feet from the door. He opened the little window to the back and said, "Wait here, I need to make sure the right people are at the desk."

Jorgen went inside and realized he didn't know any of the admitting clerks. He went up to the nearest one and asked, "Where is Hannah today?"

"She's here … must have stepped away for a minute. Can I help you?"

"No, thank you, I need to see Hannah."

Jorgen sat down to wait and nervously drummed his fingers on the arm of the chair. Just then Dr. Karl Koster, one of the surgeons and an organizer of the doctor's petition asking the government to oppose measures directed against the Jews, walked through the room. Jorgen was on his feet instantly, calling, "Dr. Koster, Dr. Koster."

"Yes? Oh hi, Jorgen."

"Dr. Koster, a word with you, please." Jorgen drew him into a vacant examining room and closed the door behind them.

"Jorgen, what's up. You seem very agitated?"

"I am. I have three Jews in my ambulance who need a place to hide … and I don't know any of the admitting clerks. Are any of them stikkers? Can we trust them?"

"Let me see … wait a minute." Dr. Koster went up to one of the clerks and they whispered for a minute. He was smiling when he returned.

"You saw? Bring them to her … she will register them under Danish names and give them a reasonable sounding ailment."

"Okay."

"Now, I have to go and make sure the hospital has something to do with them. You will be bringing more?"

"I think so. I only bring them here if they have no where else."

"Good. We have to help. Arresting our countrymen … Det kan man ikke – this is not acceptable.

Jorgen spent the rest of the day searching for Jews. He lost track of how many he warned and he made five more trips to the hospital before he finally went home late that night.

* * * * * * * *

Dr. Koster recruited Robert, a 17 year old boy, to canvass the immediate neighborhood of the hospital. Robert walked up and down the nearby streets, looking at the nameplates on the houses. If the name was Jewish, he rang the doorbell and talked to them. Sometimes they did not believe him. In most cases he persuaded them they had to flee and some of them went with him to the hospital. Robert turned them over to the receptionist.

All of the hospitals were connected with the central Visitationen Office which sent patients to the various hospitals. As Jews were brought in, they were distributed across all the hospitals and to departments within the hospitals, always with fake names and reasonable sounding diagnoses.

* * * * * * * * *

Arne and Brigitte and the rest of their team spent all of Thursday and Friday warning Jews and, for those who needed it, helping to find a place to hide. Saturday afternoon Professor Koch summoned them and gave them a new assignment.

"We did not anticipate that the Germans might arrest the Jews, so we had no plans. We're making this up as we go along.

"Most of the Jews are in hiding, out of immediate danger. We don't know how many were caught, but it seems that the majority have escaped.

"Now we must get them to safety, to Sweden. If they stay here the Nazis will eventually find them.

"We have to smuggle them across the sound … and this means money to pay fishermen and boat captains.

"We need to raise money, lots of money. I need all of you canvassing potential donors Monday morning."

* * * * * * * * *

Danish reaction to persecution of the Jews was swift. The day before the raids a statement by the Bishops of the Lutheran Church, the Danish state church, was delivered to Nazi leaders. The following Sunday, just after the raids, the statement was read from the pulpits of all Danish churches.

> "Wherever Jews are persecuted because of their religion or race it is the duty of the Christian church to protest against such persecution, because it is in conflict with the sense of justice inherent in the Danish people and inseparable from our Danish Christian culture…we shall fight for the cause that our Jewish brothers and sisters may preserve the

same freedom which we ourselves evaluate more
highly than life itself… We shall therefore in any
event unequivocally adhere to the concept that we
must obey God before we obey man."

Pastor Ivor Lange, the influential pastor of Frederiksberg Church, stated:

"Those who remain silent or disapprove by merely
shrugging their shoulders are no better than Nazi
accomplices…I tell you that I would rather die with the
Jews than live with the Nazis."

Christian Moellar wrote in the underground newspaper Frit Danmark,

"We have helped the Jews and we shall go on helping
them by all means at our disposal. If we desert them in
their hour of misery, we desert our native country."

Copenhagen University and University of Aarhus both voted to close
themselves down, beginning October 3 in protest. Numerous occupational
groups, including doctors, nurses, pastors, architects, students, sports club
members, teachers, and others all delivered petitions to Nazi authorities
protesting the persecution of the Jews.

Chapter 51. The Pundik Family

Herbert Pundik was 16 and in French class in the Metropolitan School in
north Copenhagen when the Headmaster interrupted the class. The
Headmaster consulted a sheet of paper and then called out, "Herbert
Pundik." He also pointed at a couple of other students and said, "Come out
into the hall. If there are any others of Jewish descent, you had better come
too."

"We have been warned that persecution of the Jews will soon begin,"
the Headmaster said. "You had better hurry home. The Germans may be
here at any moment."

Herbert ran back into the classroom and grabbed his books and pens.
The class was silent, but one of the boys gave him his boy-scout compass as
a going away gift and he rushed out and jumped on a streetcar.

When Herbert got off the streetcar instead of rushing straight home he
stopped at a newsstand and bought a couple of magazines. What am I
doing? I need to flee, not buy magazines.

Herbert ran home and burst into the family flat. His parents and two younger brothers were packed, dressed warmly and ready to leave.

"Where are we going?" Herbert asked.

"I don't know," Mrs. Pundik admitted.

"Lucas! His summer cottage," Herbert said.

"That seems our best choice. Lucas won't mind." Mr. Pundik said. "We'll take a cab."

"All the way to Gilleleje village?" Mrs. Punkik asked. "Do we have enough cash?"

"They might be checking the trains. We have no choice," Mr. Pundik said. "Herbert, take your bicycle to the cab stand and ask for our friend. He'll take us even if we don't have enough money."

The dispatcher assured Herbert their friend would be there before five that evening.

The Pundiks were packed and waiting … but the taxi didn't come. By 6:00 p.m. all of them were distraught. Finally at 6:35 p.m. Herbert, who had been watching his parents grow increasingly distraught, couldn't keep quiet any longer.

"He's not coming. We have to run, we have to go somewhere."

"Where? Where can we go?" Mrs. Pundik said. "We have nowhere to go."

"Something terrible must have happened to him," said Mr. Pundik. He polished his glasses on his vest for about the tenth time in as many minutes. "He wouldn't abandon us."

"We have to go," Herbert insisted. Father's size and good-natured banter usually kept all of them relaxed, but not this evening. The Germans might arrive at any minute … they had to do something, anything was better than sitting and waiting to be arrested.

"Yes," Mr. Pundik said. "For tonight, we hide in Orsted Park, in the woods. Mother, get food. Herbert, help her, Boys, you come with me and we'll get blankets."

Five minutes later they left their apartment and after a short walk were in the park. Almost immediately they found several others who were also trying to hide. Along with five others, they found a little glade almost surrounded by thick bushes. They settled down tfor the night. Herbert fell asleep listening to the soft voices of the adults trying to figure out how they were going to get out of the city.

* * * * * * * *

Mr. Pundik woke up early Saturday morning, stiff and cold. The dew was heavy and his clothes were damp. The Nazis won't have to do anything, in another day or two we'll all have pneumonia.

The morning was interminable, it seemed noon would never come. We have to do something … all of the water is gone and most of the food .

One of the others had a suggestion.

"The Municipal Hospital is just across the street. They would feed us."

"They might have stikkers," Pundik was dubious. He had his glasses in his hand, polishing the lenses on his vest.

"Well, we have to do something. Anybody have any other ideas?"

No one spoke for what seemed to be a long time.

"I'll go and see if I can find help." Pundik was afraid, but he felt he had to do something to care for his wife and children. "After dark, I'll go after dark."

He stopped polishing the glasses and put them on.

They were increasingly thirsty and hungry as the afternoon wore on. Nothing to do, not even a book to read. Can't even make any noise.

They sat, four adults insisting that the six children also sit quietly. Occasionally they whispered together, but mostly they just waited. Finally the day grew dim and then it was dark.

Pundik gathered up his courage and crept out of their hiding place, pausing only to reassure his wife that he would be careful.

Pundik was a city dweller. Hard to move among bushes at night.

He looked back. Came that way … or was it on that side? Gone five meters and already lost? I'll never find them.

He called his wife's name, not very loud.

"Here," she replied. "What's wrong?"

He went toward the sound and found them in a few steps.

"I'm not going to be able to find you in the dark. Everything looks the same."

"What do we do?"

"Come with me to the edge of the woods," Pundik replied. "You can wait for me there."

The tiny band crept through the darkness until they reached the edge of the woods. They were two blocks down from the main entrance to the hospital. Pundik turned to the group.

"Move back a little, stay hidden from the street. Wait there."

Pundik snuck along the edge of the park, just within the edge of the trees, until he was opposite the hospital. He spent a few seconds trying to ensure that no cars were approaching, then dashed across and into the hospital entrance.

Pundik stopped just inside the entrance. The receptionist was doing something with a file of papers. No one paid any attention to him. He walked over to the receptionist.

She looked up, smiled at him and asked, "May I help you?"

"Is it safe to speak candidly as a patriotic Dane? There are no stikkers around?"

"We have a couple of Nazi lovers here at the hospital, but we know who they are. Why?"

"I'm hiding … in the park." Pundik pointed across the street. "My family, a number of us. We need food and water … I hoped you might be able to help."

"Why are you hiding, are you Jewish?"

"Yes."

The young woman grabbed a sheaf of papers and shoved them at Pundik.

"Here, fill these out … not with your real name, make up stuff. Just look busy, like a patient. Sit over there and if anyone comes through, be busy filling out your paperwork. I'll get help."

While Pundik filled out forms, the receptionist was busy on the phone. A few minutes later a young medical student came down, spoke briefly to the receptionist and then approached Pundik.

"We can help. How many are with you?"

"There are nine of us."

"Hmm. Too many for you to carry food back for them. Go get them. We'll feed you and give you food for the morning. Tomorrow night you can come back. When you come back, go directly to the cafeteria, down that way. Pretend you're here to visit a sick relative."

Pundik was overcome. "Thank you, thank you." He almost forgot to look for cars before crossing the street to the park.

* * * * * * * *

Saturday night, while Pundik was fetching his group to eat in the hospital cafeteria, Dr. Koster and twelve others from the various hospitals were meeting at Bispedjerg Hospital. No one was quite sure, but it seemed that there might be as many as 1500 or 2000 Jews hidden in the various Copenhagen hospitals. The big question was what to do with them.

Everybody knew that the only possible long term solution was to get them to Sweden, but that meant a rather large-scale boat operation to smuggle them across the sound.

Koster spoke, "The Freedom Council is working on the problem, but frankly this caught everybody by surprise. For a few days we have to keep everybody where they are."

Two days later, the Pundik family was in the hospital, admitted as patients. Dr. Koster had a friend, Aage Bertelsen, in the Lyngby suburbs north of Copenhagen who was arranging transport to Sweden. Pundik informed the others that the plan was for them to stay in the hospital until safe transport could be arranged to Lyngby and thence across the Oresund to Sweden.

Pundik had no way of knowing that even as he spoke to his family and friends, that they were on the verge of being arrested. Several Wehrmacht units surrounded the hospital in preparation for searching it.

Chapter 52. Rabbi Marcus Melchior

Rabbi Marcus Melchior had a large family with five young children, ranging from an infant to a boy 12 years of age. After warning friends, they bundled the children into a taxi and went to the train station.

Mr. Nicolaisen, a Christian friend, offered them the use of his summer cottage north of Copenhagen. As they got on the train, it occurred to Marcus that they would be very easy to catch. All of them were dark and stereotypically Jewish in appearance. If the Germans were watching the trains, they would certainly be caught.

We should have taken a cab. Too late now.

He settled into his seat and began to pray while his wife dealt with the children.

Marcus and his family arrived at the cottage without incident Friday evening and entered with the key provided by Nicolaisen. The pantry was well stocked with staples and they enjoyed a simple but filling meal and went to bed.

Marcus voiced his hopes as he and his wife lay in bed, "This seems very peaceful. I think we will be safe here."

"I don't think I could stand it if they arrested us and separated us from the children," her voice was muffled with her face buried in his shoulder.

He held her close and rubbed her back.

"God will provide, God always watches over us."

The next morning they had just finished cleaning up from a breakfast of pancakes when there was a knock on the door. Mrs. Melchior clutched the youngest child tightly, eyes wide with fright. Marcus looked out the window and said, "It's okay, it's an old lady."

Crossing to the door he unlocked it. The old lady began speaking in a loud voice as soon as the door opened.

"Hans. So good to see you again. How is Mrs. Petersen? I brought you some of that jam the children like so well."

As she spoke, the old lady practically forced her way into the room and closed the door behind her, then stood peering out the window.

Marcus finally found his tongue.

"I'm sorry, I think you are mistaking us for someone else. We are not the Petersens and my name is not Hans."

"I know. That was for the benefit of the stikker who lives next door."

"A stikker? We're next door to a Nazi?"

"You are Jewish, aren't you?"

"Yes," he said. "We are."

"I thought so. You look Jewish. The guy in the next house is an ardent Nazi. He will betray you as soon as he gets a good look at you. And he knows my sympathies ... it would do you no good for me to take you in."

"What must we do? We have no other place to go."

"I have friends who will take you in, but I have to find someone the stikker doesn't know. Let me check ... I'll be back in just a little. Don't let him see you."

Marcus and his wife gathered up their few possessions and waited.

"Lets go into the trees in the back," Marcus said. "Just in case the stikker has already called the Nazis."

They gathered up the children and hurried out the back door. The high hedge between them and the stikker's house hid them until they reached the back of the lot and then they were in among the trees. Marcus led them farther into the trees until they found a sunny glade well away from the houses.

"Wait here. I'll watch for the old lady." Marcus snuck back toward Nicolaison's cottage. There ... that's the stikker's place. Can't see the lane from here.

He moved a few meters to the left. Okay, both houses, the lane in front. This should do.

He settled down to wait.

God in heaven! A German army truck. Soldiers running everywhere.

He began to shake all over, but pulled himself together, slid backwards until he was behind a big tree and then jumped up and ran to where his wife and children waited.

"Dear God," he panted. "The Germans ... we must flee."

Mrs. Melchior already had the baby in her arms and he scooped up the three year old. He looked at the other three and said, "We have to walk a bit. Be quiet and follow me."

Marcus had never hiked in a forest without a path. In a few minutes he was thoroughly lost. Have to keep going anyway, need some distance from the Nazis.

"I'm tired," the six year old said.

Marcus looked at his watch. Not sure what time we started. Must be close to half an hour, though.

"Okay, we can rest here," he said. "They're not following us."

Dear God, please let that be true!

"Stay close children," Mrs. Melchior said. "Keep quiet. We're safe as long as we stay quiet." She put the baby down to play in the grass.

Turning to Marcus, she held her hands palm up.

"I don't know," he admitted. "I don't know what we can do."

"Well, we can't stay here with the baby. We have to find someone to take us in."

For several minutes neither spoke. Finally Mrs. Melchior said, "We have to go back and find the lady who warned us. She'll have a place for us."

"Good. Good. But let's wait an hour to make sure the Nazis are gone."

They rested in the morning sun while the children climbed a tree and then found several interesting caterpillars which only the two oldest were bold enough to pick up.

Twice their parents told them to keep their voices down, but the woods were so peaceful and they seemed so isolated from the world that their fear of immediate discovery soon ebbed away.

The Melchiors were discussing how they might find the lady who had warned them when they were startled by a man appearing from behind a nearby tree.

Marcus leaped to his feet, interposing himself between the stranger and his family.

"What do you want? Who are you?"

"Easy, friend. Easy," the stranger replied. "I think we're in the same boat. I think you're hiding from the Germans, just as I am. Am I right?"

Marcus relaxed a little, "Yes, we're hiding from the Nazis."

The stranger turned and whistled. "My wife and two friends are with me," He explained. "My name is Eli." A minute later the other three, a man and two women, arrived.

"What are you going to do?" Eli said. "We adults can survive for several days, but it'll be a problem for the children."

Marcus explained their plan and Eli suggested that he and his friends scout ahead to make sure there were no Germans in the area. "Where is this lady?"

"That way," Marcus pointed.

"Well, we might as well get started."

Ten minutes later it was clear to Marcus that he didn't know where they were going. He told Eli the address to Nicolaison's cottage, but none of them were familiar with the area.

There was nothing to do but to continue blindly forward. When they eventually reached a road, none of them recognized it, none of them had the slightest idea where they were.

Eli's wife was very blonde and had blue eyes. She could easily pass for an Aryan Christian and she volunteered to go and make inquiries. They selected a hiding place which allowed easy access to the road without much chance of anyone seeing them coming out of the woods.

They settled down to wait once again. An hour went by and Eli was getting very nervous about his wife when she arrived.

"Oh, its all worked out. We're all safe."

Eli embraced her and kissed her, "I was getting so worried."

"It was easy," she laughed. "I walked around a little and saw a young man chalking the 'V' for victory symbol on a wall so I knew he was okay. I just told him we were hiding in the woods and needed help. He got me a place to stay and there's a taxi waiting for us."

Marcus could hardly believe it. "You have a place for all of us?"

"Three different places. One for each family. Now, Rabbi, you go first and the taxi will come back for the rest of us."

Mrs. Melchior and Marcus embraced her, shook hands with Eli and his friends and hurried to the waiting taxi and their unknown protectors.

Chapter 53. The Raids

A large number of troops were required to arrest 7500 Jews in one night, even when most of them lived in the city of Copenhagen. Every Gestapo and SS soldier in Denmark was mustered. In addition, fifty newly arrived Gestapo officers were on hand. At 4:00 p.m. on Friday October 1 the Wehrmacht units assigned to assist in the operation began to assemble. By ten p.m. everything was in readiness … the Gestapo and SS officers in charge of the various units, the Wehrmacht support troops, the convoys of trucks to transport both the German soldiers and the expected prisoners, and the two transport ships waiting to receive the Jews.

At 10:25 the detailed assignments were handed out. Each unit was given a list of specific individuals to arrest. At 11:45 p.m. the convoys began to move and rapidly fanned out across the city.

* * * * * * * *

Gerhard' and Jacob's squad and an SS squad were assigned to one of the new Gestapo officers. As they rode in the back of the truck toward their first victim, Gerhard asked Jacob, "Why do this? Why arrest the Jews?"

The older man just looked at him for a minute before replying, "You want the official bull? Or, maybe something else … ?"

"I know what the Fuhrer says about the Jews causing problems," Gerhard shrugged. "The Denmark Jews aren't causing problems far as I can see. So, why?"

"It's politics. Best needs to show Berlin something."

"Now we're arresting people to make a general look good ... "

Jacob didn't bother to reply. Been a soldier a long time, longer than most of these baby-faced officers. These gung-ho SOBs are a pain.

In another few minutes the trucks came to a stop and the troops closed off the entire block. Troopers banged on three different doors and called each family by name, ordering them to come out. There was no response. The banging and calling went on for several minutes until a neighbor came out onto his steps and called to them.

"What's going on? What are you doing?"

The Gestapo officer replied, "We're looking for these families, they've broken the law and are to be arrested. Go back inside your house."

"They're gone, you won't find them."

"How do you know they're gone?'

"They're friends and not so stupid as to wait for you to come get them. They're long gone."

The Gestapo officer strode onto the porch to confront the man. "Friends of yours? Perhaps you helped them escape? Perhaps I'll arrest you for interfering."

"They're friends but I didn't help them, I didn't have to ... many others helped them. I've done nothing except help you by letting you know they're gone."

The Officer and the Dane stood eye-to-eye for several seconds. Abruptly the Officer left and ordered his troops back to the trucks..

The next three stops were similar. They knocked on the doors, got no response, and eventually left.

"This is very strange," Jacob said to Gerhard. "How do you go to arrest somebody and just leave when they don't answer the door."

"I dunno," Gerhard said. "Doesn't make sense."

"Maybe they have orders not to break down the doors. "

"That make no sense," Gerhard said. "Why would we have those orders?"

Jacob had no answer and they rode in silence to the next stop.

On their seventh stop an emaciated, middle-aged man opened the door to their knock.

"Are you John Wiesenthal?"

"Yes. What is it?

"You're under arrest."

Two soldiers grabbed Wiesenthal by either arm and half walked, half dragged him to the nearest truck and forced him to climb inside.

Their next stop was the Jewish old age home beside the Copenhagen Synagogue. The soldiers burst into the home and fanned out to the various rooms. Within minutes they had 29 elderly residents, aged 60 to 90, and brought them into the synagogue.

One old lady was paralyzed and had been bedridden for years. Two of the SS troopers simply dragged her down the hall and across the lawn to the synagogue where they dumped her on the floor.

She lay there crying, unable to move, until two of the elderly residents straightened her out, put a pillow under her head, and calmed her somewhat.

"Do we have all of them?" Their officer asked.

"All but one. One of the swine cut his own throat when he saw us."

"Good. One less to deal with. Now ... let's find out where their relatives have gone. Question them."

The SS troopers were happy to obey this order. The evening had been almost a total failure so far and now they could vent their frustrations.

The old people of course knew nothing. Within minutes the SS were punching and kicking their helpless victims. The brutality elicited nothing save screams and crying.

Gerhard looked on with obvious dismay. Jacob strolled casually over to him and whispered, "Outside. Now."

They were no sooner outside than Gerhard bolted for the bushes beside the walkway and proceeded to throw up. Jacob stood there, waiting, wondering what his country was becoming.

The Gestapo Officer soon tired of brutalizing the old people and ordered them loaded into the trucks. As this was going on, several of the SS troops urinated in the synagogue. One of them went to the front of the sanctuary and stood there, spraying urine over everything he could reach.

* * * * * * * *

General Dr. Best organized the flow of information from the raid to come directly to him, rather than the normal procedure of having his staff assemble the data and then provide him with summaries. By 4:00 a.m it was clear that very few Jews were going to be caught this night.

So, Duckwitz did indeed warn the Danes. Seven thousand Jews in hiding. Their next step will be to try to get them to Sweden. Very good.

Next ... violence to protect the Jews or a collapse of Danish solidarity? We bought some time. Maybe the Wehrmacht gets off its fanny and does its job again.

General Best was the only one who knew that the massive raids had netted a total of only 248 Jews. All the rest were in hiding. At 9:00 a.m. General Best went to sleep and slept soundly until 2:00 p.m. that afternoon. He awoke refreshed. He was still quite optimistic.

* * * * * * * *

The day after the Rosh Hashanah raids, General Best issued a statement to the press:

> "As a result of measures taken by the German authorities, the Jews have been removed from public life and prevented from continuing to poison the atmosphere, for it is they who have to a considerable degree been responsible for the deterioration of the situation in Denmark through anti-German incitement and moral and material support for acts of terror and sabotage."

October fourth, three days after the Rosh Hashanah raids, General Best sat at his desk and reviewed the reports from his Gestapo and SS officers. In the three days since the raids we caught only 21 Jews? No violence yet. The damned Danes seemed to be cooperating to hide the Jews.

How could 7000 people just disappear? The Danes have to break. They have to break before Ribbentrop sends me to the front. Ribbentrop needs to be placated. Denmark being Judenfrei (free of Jews) should help.

Best sent Ribbentropp a very carefully worded telegram proclaiming Denmark as Judenfrei.

General Best turned his attention to the question of why they were catching such a miniscule number of the refugees. He quickly noticed some anomalies. All the Harbor Patrol boats scheduld for service at the same time … none of them available to patrol the Oresund between Denmrk and Sweden. And the Monte Rosa needs an engine overhaul just when we need it to haul the Jews. What bull!

The officers responsible for these actions provide the perfect excuse if anyone ever looks closely at the raids. Transfer them to the front. With any luck they won't survive to tell their version of the story. Replace them with Gestapo officers, men I can trust, men who will truly persecute these Danish bastards.

Best spent October fifth drawing up a plan to create a large number of squads, each of which would have either a Gestapo or SS officer and at least one or two Gestapo or SS troopers. The Wehrmacht troops won't dare to be too lax with properly motivated officers. Hanneken will resist the idea, but I can play Hanneken's neuroses.

Best's scheming was interrupted mid-afternoon by a telegram from Reichfuhrer SS Heinrich Himmler informing him that SS General Gunther Pancke would arrive shortly and would be the Supreme Head of the SS and Gestapo in Denmark. Best read the telegram and immediately wanted a stiff drink … or maybe half a dozen.

SS General Gunther Pancke! Shit. We watched each other claw our way up the ranks, over the bodies of other officers. It isn't fair. It's bad enough dealing with that idiot Hanneken. Pancke is smart. Tough to fool that bastard.

Pancke will command all the SS and Gestapo forces. All the good troops. Everything will be calculated to enhance his own career.

I'm Plenipotentiary for Denmark. All the responsibility and none of the power. It's just so unfair!

Pancke will be fanatical about catching the Jews. He'll put a lot of pressure on the slimy bastard Danes … they might break yet. If the Danes don't break, maybe Pancke gets the blame … ?

My record of service to the Fuhrer is second to none. "The Bloodhound of Warsaw" they called me. We killed more than 8,000 Jews and Gypsies.

Hitler himself approved my legal brief that genocide was legal if carried out efficiently, i.e., if there were no survivors.

They can't brush me off like some has-been! And, yet … that's what was happening. All my years of service and now it's down the toilet.

Best stifled a sob and then got stinking drunk.

Chapter 54. Kaj Munk

Pastor Kaj Munk was one of Denmark's most celebrated men. He was a poet, a playwright and the vicar of Vederso Church in Western Jutland. Munk had little faith in democracy and thought nations needed strong, heroic leadership. In the 1930's Munk had expressed admiration for Hitler and his ability to inspire the German people. He had publicly wished that Denmark had a similarly historic figure to inspire and unite the people.

Shortly thereafter Mussolini, dictator of Italy and Hitler's ally, used machine guns to slaughter, by the tens of thousands, Ethiopians armed with spears. Hitler began implementing his genocidal practices against the Jews and Gypsies of Poland and Czechoslovakia.

Pastor Kaj Munk, appalled, recanted his admiration for Hitler and wrote an open letter to Mussolini criticizing him for persecuting the Jews.

When the Germans occupied Denmark, Munk was an early and outspoken critic. He used his pulpit to regularly urge Danes to resist all demands from the Nazis.

Immediately after the raids against the Jews, Munk began interviewing Danes, asking them why they got involved in helping the Jews. The following quotes are taken from his notebook:

> "The hand of compassion was sometimes faster than the calculation of reason."

"The raids hit us like a bombshell. The university senate, which never does anything in less than months and months, took about a half hour to decide to shut down classes for a week in protest. Then all the students and lots of the faculty immediately went out to see what they could do to frustrate the Nazis."

"If we had stopped to think about it, we might have hesitated. For most of us, we were so outraged, it was so unacceptable, that there was never any question of helping or not. You just jumped in and did whatever you could."

"We doctors had already signed a strongly worded petition so we were already committed. The only question for us was how to help."

"Many of the clergy were already committed and the Bishop's statement crystallized that. Many of us immediately began issuing fake baptism certificates to Jews so they could pretend to be Christians."

"Nobody thought of Jews and Christians ... we were all just Danes, just people like you and me. These madmen had to be stopped and everybody I knew was helping."

"I am 19 years old and very naïve. I went around collecting money from everyone for the sealift. I thought that every Dane would help to the limit of their ability and it never occurred to me that anybody might be an informer."

"I was worried about informers ... I personally knew two Danish Nazis ... but I also had close friends who were Jewish and I couldn't just abandon them."

"We had friends and business associates who were Jews. My wife and I talked about it for about two seconds and decided we had no choice ... we had to do whatever we could."

"I was really afraid for my wife and children, but all my friends were helping, so I was sort of shamed into helping as well. Mostly I gave money, much more than I could easily afford, but my friends were actually hiding Jews in their homes … "

Pastor Munk delivered another fiery sermon on October fifth, castigating the Nazis for their persecution of the Jews. On October 10, 1940 as Munk sat in his favorite chair reading the Bible, his front door shattered with a loud crash.

Munk jumped to his feet just in time to be knocked down by an SS trooper, the first of several who charged into his living room. Stunned, he struggled into a sitting position.

"What is the meaning … ?" He got no farther before a soldier barked "Nein!" and forcibly pinned him to the floor by pressing the rifle's muzzle into his chest.

Munk lay there, barely daring to breathe. A minute later an officer strolled into the room.

The officer bent over a little and peered at Munk.

"The famous Pastor Munk. How are you feeling today, Reverend? Hmm? Not so talkative this morning, are you?"

The officer smiled and looked all around at his troops who smiled back. Munk thought they were pleased with themselves. The bastards are enjoying this.

The officer turned his attention back to Munk.

"Reverend Munk. You really should know better," the officer's tone was pleasant, conversational. "You look like a good Aryan. What has made you into a traitor to your race? What led you astray? Now you must suffer, now you will see the error of your ways."

The officer walked out the door. Two troopers grabbed Munk by his arms, dragged him outside and pushed him into the back of a truck. The troopers climbed in with him and the truck pulled away.

Munk discovered he still had his Bible in his hand. They'll torture me. I wonder if I can stand it?

The truck stopped. Munk was confused, We only went a kilometer, we're just outside my village.

Two soldiers dragged Munk from the truck and to the side of the road. A blow to the back of his knees knocked him onto his face. A hand grasped his hair and yanked him to a kneeling position.

Munk was shocked. I feared torture … it's going to be a bullet. The bastards!

His panic turned to cold rage.

"You think killing me will change anything?" He smiled at the officer. "My countrymen will sing songs for me."

The officer snatched the Bible from Munk and threw it down the road. Munk was still smiling at the officer when the bullets shredded his chest. The Bible lay in the road, seven meters from the body.

Prof. Hal Koch Journal, October 3, 1941

There are moments when I am overcome by love and admiration for my countrymen and this is one such moment. We had no plan and no preparation for saving the Jews and no one has any notion what is happening. All that is certain is that 7500 Jews disappeared overnight. My people, my crazy, wonderful Vikings rose up like an irresistible tidal wave and swept all the Jews into hiding. Those of us supposedly in charge did what we could, but we were almost irrelevant. The people, the ordinary miraculous Danes, they just went out and somehow, nobody knows how, THEY JUST DID IT. God is indeed still in charge and still creating miracles. Now I half expect that tomorrow the waters of the Oresund will part and the Jews will walk to Sweden.

Chapter 55. The Sealift

Safety for the Jews was only a few kilometers across the Oresund, the narrow bay separating Denmark from Sweden. In places the bay was narrow enough that rowboats or kayaks could be used. In other places the crossing was twenty or even thirty kilometers.

The illegal crossings were dangerous. Parts of the Oresund were mined and the rest was patrolled by the Germans. Boats caught smuggling Jews were confiscated and the crews imprisoned. Because of the heavy risk involved, including the very real risk of loss of livelihood for entire families, fishermen and boat captains alike needed to be well paid.

Saturday afternoon Professor Koch sent Brigitte and Carin to the suburb of Lyngby with a list of names to solicit for money.

The girls were more than a little nervous at their first stop, but Carin knocked on the door. A moment later the door opened and a woman greeted them.

Brigitte gulped and plunged straight in. "Are you the lady of the house? Oh, good. We're asking for money to pay for the Jews crossing to Sweden."

"How is that being managed? Moellar's broadcasts said there are thousands of Jews in hiding, that the Germans didn't catch very many."

"We don't know details, but the Freedom Council is working on arranging transport. I imagine it will involve fishermen and commercial boats. We expect it to be fairly expensive."

The lady gave them 30,000 Kroner, an immense sum, and told them to stop at every house on the block, that all of her neighbors would also contribute. An hour later, after stopping at six houses, they had 110,000 Kroner.

Every place they went gave them additional names. By dinner time, after four hours of canvassing they had almost half a million Kroner and were sitting down to a nice meal, courtesy of their last donor. In addition to the two girls, the group included the host and hostess and their seventeen year old son, Lars.

As they were finishing the meal, their hostess exclaimed.

"Oh, I just had a thought. Gerhardsens are having a party this evening. You really should go there ... they will have lots of rich people there."

"Really? You don't think they would be offended if we came to their party," Brigitte asked.

"Well, maybe initially. They'll get over it and you'll get lots of money. I would call them but the Germans might be listening. Look, their place is not too far. You can walk it in about 30 minutes."

Turning to her son, she asked him, "Lars, why don't you go with the girls? You know the Gerhardsens.."

The three of them left a few minutes later.

The 30 minute walk took them from dusk to full dark. Lars and the girls went to the kitchen entrance, where they were greeted by the sister of the owner. When they explained what they wanted, she took them to the living room and introduced them to Mrs. Gerhardsen. Then she and Lars went to see Mr. Gerhardsen and the men who were in the library with cigars and whiskey. A half hour later they met Mrs. Gerhardsen in the kitchen to count the money. They counted almost half a million kroner in cash and pledges.

The three young people sat there looking at their piles of money.

"I've never even seen this much money before," Carin said.

The other two young people had nothing to add, but Mrs. Gerhardsen just laughed. "This group can afford it. If you need more, come back. The Germans aren't going to get away with taking our friends."

"We need someone to drive you home," Lars said. "You shouldn't be out on the streets with all this." He turned to Mrs. Petersen. "Is there a doctor here ... or someone else with a permit to drive?"

"I don't think so ... I know a good cabby," she said. "I'll call him."

Following Professor Koch's instructions, Monday morning Brigitte delivered a cardboard box full of their million kroner to an address in Lyngby. From there the money went to Aage Bertelsen.

* * * * * * * * *

Aage and Gerda Bertelsen , along with a number of friends, began trying to help Jews reach Sweden even before the raids. Their first efforts were to secure, quite illegally, visas for visiting Sweden. Their house became the office for this project and almost 100 Jews were provided with the necessary papers to go to Sweden.

By the Sunday after the German raids, it was clear that they would never be able to secure enough visas to deal with the fleeing Jews. They quickly discovered friends were involved with organizing boats to smuggle people to Sweden from Humlebaek, about sixteen kilometers north of them. At the same time, their young friend David Levine was scouring the area for Jews.

David located the Jews, brought them to the Bertelsen house and from there they were hidden with neighbors until they could be transported to Humlebaek and across the Oresund. Aage was also in touch with Dr Koster at the City Hospital and was helping arrange passage for the Jews hiding in the hospitals.

Gerda greeted David's latest batch of refugees and David prepared to go out again. Gerda stopped him.

"David, when have you eaten?"

"I don't remember."

"Okay, sit down. You're not going anywhere until you eat."

"Thank you, Gerda, but I don't think you have anything I can eat." David was Orthodox and very careful about the dietary laws.

"David ... there must be something."

As the conversation went on, it became increasingly obvious that the vast majority of the food on hand was unacceptable. Eventually, Gerda discovered that egg yolks, red wine and a few other minor ingredients were permissible. From then on, almost every time she saw David, she forced him to sit still long enough to eat her special "kosher food."

By the following day, David's beard stubble was quite heavy and made his already swarthy appearance doubly noticeable. He looked Jewish ... he could have posed for one of the anti-Jewish posters used by the Nazi propagandists. When he arrived at the Bertelsen's with the latest batch of refugees, Aage took one look at him and exploded.

"Do you realize what you look like? You put yourself and all of us in danger with that beard."

"Okay. I'll shave. Only I have to go and get my razor."

"Where?"

"In my flat in Copenhagen."

"Are you crazy?" Aage glared at him. "You don't leave the house until you shave. Now, go in the bathroom and use my razor."

"Thank you, but unfortunately it is impossible."

"What do you mean, impossible how?"

"I cannot use your razor."

"This is stupid! And foolish. You'll get us killed!"

"I can't. Moses directed that you must not shave the beard … only cut it."

"You are normally clean-shaven." Aage said.

David admitted that he had an electric razor. "The electric razor doesn't shave, it merely cuts the whiskers."

"Moses allowed for electric razors?" Aage shouted.

David said nothing and Aage tried a different tack. As a Christian theologian he had occasionally studied the Talmud, the Jewish scriptures.

"Look, the Talmud says that in matters of life and death it is permissible to disregard the commandments of the Law."

"Ah, you are correct. All right." David got up, climbed the stairs and went into the bathroom. A few minutes later he came out, and from the top of the stairs, called out.

"Aage. I'm sorry, I can't do it."

Aage went to the foot of the stairs. David's face was covered in lather, with a few patches of bare skin, numerous bloody spots and black stubble peeking through the lather.

Gerda came in and asked what all the commotion was about. After hearing the story, she told Aage to go to a neighbor just down the street and borrow their electric razor. This solved the problem and David was soon clean shaven again.

* * * * * * * * *

Arne Sejr and his group were part of the network funneling the refugee Jews into Aage Bertelsen's organization, but everything was moving so fast that there was mass confusion.

Carin and Morten were sent to Birkerad, just north of Copenhagen, with instructions to go to the main square and meet a number of refugees, who were then to be sent to Lyngby and Bertelsen's group.

The square was full, at least a hundred people, in little clusters of four to eight. Most of them were swarthy, dressed inappropriately in winter clothes, and carrying suitcases. It was obvious they were Jews and were attempting to flee.

"One stikker, that's all it would take," Morten said. "If one stikker sees this bunch, we're lost."

"We better hurry," Carin said. "Remember the password 'Oil on the mountain.'"

They plunged into the square, calling "Oil on the mountain" at each group and stuffing them into taxis as fast as they could. Within the hour, everyone was safely away.

As the last taxi disappeared from view, Morten turned to Carin.

"Let's get out of here. Fast!" He began walking toward a major street, Carin at his side. A block away from the square they hailed a taxi and gave it directions to the outskirts of town. The cabby asked them if they had come through the square and then asked, "Did all the Jews get out of there okay?"

Carin and Morten, who had been keeping silent with some effort, both burst out laughing.

"Yes," Carin replied. "Thanks to all the cabbies."

"So, why are you going to that part of town? There's not much out there but woods."

Carin looked a question at Morten who shrugged and said, "We're going to need some cabs."

"We're going to search for Jews hiding in the woods," Carin said. "Can you arrange for cabs to drive past there every half hour or so?"

"Sure. We'll be happy to stymie the Nazi bastards."

Ten minutes later they reached their destination and arranged a couple of places for the cabs to stop and, hopefully, pick up groups of refugees. Carin was from a small town but had spent most of her youth with her Father on his fishing boat. She was only somewhat familiar with forests but Morten was an Eagle scout.

Carin went into the woods far enough so that she could barely see the road and Morten maintained a position a little farther in where they could see each other most of the time. They found people almost immediately and in the next two hours located four groups totaling twenty-seven in all. All of them were transported by cab to Aage Bertelsen's group in Lyngby.

Morten and Carin had no way of knowing that Aage and his group now had more Jews hidden in their neighborhood than they could transport out. Aage had to find more transportation, lots more transportation.

Chapter 56. Rabbi Melchior #2

The taxi picked up Rabbi Marcus Melchior and his family from the woods and took them to a house near the beach. The owner assured them they would be safe and that he would find them a boat to Sweden. He fed them and, apologizing for the cramped quarters, took all five of them to his one spare room in the back of the house.

Mrs. Melchior accepted the blankets and pillows he provided and looked at the rug on the floor.

"This will do fine," she said. "We can manage very nicely here. Thank you so much, I don't know what we would have done without you."

Their host shrugged off her thanks and asked if they were hungry.

"I'm starving," the nine year old said.

Before either of the Melchior's could respond, the man laughed.

"I bet you are," he said. "When did you last eat?"

"Days and days ago," the boy replied.

"Well, come then. Let's hurry and feed you."

After the meal, they settled down to wait while their host made inquiries, very carefully, because he was worried about stikkers.

* * * * * * * *

Four days later, their host took them to meet a boat.

The Melchiors found a whole group waiting for the boat, just inside the trees at the edge of the beach. Some found their way to the village on their own, others came by ambulance from Bispedjek Hospital, and the Danish Rifle Club fetched two from hiding in the woods.

The price for passage across the sound was 2,000 kroner per person. Five of the people didn't have nearly enough money. Marcus and some of the other adults urged everyone to pool their money and in this way there was enough to pay for all but two people.

Their host became agitated and told them to wait, he would be right back. He returned fifteen minutes later, beaming, and announced he had 9,000 kroner, just in case anyone else showed up who couldn't pay.

They waited there, half-hidden, for what seemed a long time. Marcus spent the time in prayer. Finally a fishing boat appeared.

Everybody got up and started moving toward the pier but the boat kept going.

"Something's wrong," Melchior's host called. "Back into the trees. Quickly!"

They ran, all pretense of quiet or caution gone until they were well into the trees and out of sight of the beach

Once again Melchior's host urged them to wait and slipped away through the trees.

Their host returned in a few minutes and said the Nazis were searching beach cottages in the area. They had to flee. They ran through the trees and down a little country lane. Several young men helped the three oldest until they were well away from the beach.

They split up into four groups and went to different homes for the night.

The Melchior's evening meal was only bread and soup, but it was very tasty. The next morning they went back to their old host's house because it was closer to the beach.

They waited in that one small room, coming out only to go to the bathroom, for two more days. The Germans were patrolling the beach area and had arrested several homeowners and three fishermen for aiding refugees.

They had to wait until the patrols left the area. Three more days passed so slowly Marcus thought time had stopped. They had nothing to do and little to occupy their minds except fear.

The children's moods alternated between clinging with fright and irritability at their enforced inaction. Mrs. Melchior had trouble sleeping and was exhausted from constantly trying to keep the children occupied and quiet. Marcus' prayers were starting to sound a little desperate.

On the evening of October tenth they were startled by a knock on the front door. They all jumped to their feet, ready to flee out the back, as their host answered the door. The visitor said, "Hello, I'm sorry to bother you, but I'm looking for friends of mine. Have you seen or heard anything about the Melchior's?"

The host, afraid of informers and not knowing any last names anyway, said, "Never heard of them. What's your business with them?"

"Well, they're fleeing the Nazis and I'm trying to find them to help them."

Marcus had his ear pressed to the door, listening intently, and he suddenly smiled and swung the door open. The rest of the family heard him exclaim, "Nicolaisen, my friend. How on earth did you ever find us?"

Nicolaisen gave a great shout and practically leaped for Marcus, but his cane slipped, his bad leg gave out and he fell at Marcus' feet. The rest of the family all came crowding as Marcus helped him to his feet. In an instant they were all embracing and laughing and crying.

Nicolaisen explained that he arrived at the cottage shortly after they fled and, not finding them, he went to see the lady that warned them about the stikker. Ever since, he had been going from cottage to cottage all up and down a ten-kilometer length of beach.

Nicolaisen was worried.

"I talked to a lot of people the last couple of days and the Nazis are all over the area. You have to get out, go to another area."

"Well okay," Marcus said. "Where do we go?"

"There's a group in Lyngby. I think you should go there."

"That takes us back to the outskirts of Copenhagen, that's closer to the Nazis."

"I know," Nicolaisen said. "But we're kind of at a loss here. The bastards are all over the place."

No one said anything for a while and Marcus and Mrs. Melchior, each in their own fashion, tried to keep despair and fear at bay.

"They won't expect that," Mrs. Melchior said. "Moving back toward Copenhagen. This Lyngby group has a good system?"

"My contacts tell me they moved hundreds of people to Sweden without losing anyone. They're good."

"Marcus," Mrs. Melchior took his hand in both of hers. "Let's do it, let's go to Lyngby."

"I'll get a cab," Nicolaisen stood up. "Get ready. I'll be back shortly."

* * * * * * * *

When the Melchiors arrived, the Lyngby group had almost three hundred Jews hidden in the immediate vicinity of the Bertelsen house. They also had arranged a small fleet of fishing boats and one larger boat to take Jews to Sweden.

The Lyngby group had been moving people as quickly as possible to take advantage of the strange absence of German patrol boats in the Oresund.

By the time the Melchior's arrived in Lyngby the German patrol boats were back, thus making the sealift more dangerous for all concerned.

With three hundred people to transport they needed more than taxicabs. They scrounged up lorries and packed people in them as tightly as they could. Some of the lorries were open, with three-foot sideboards. In these lorries, the people had to lie down so they weren't visible from the street. Marcus and his wife lay down and their children lay on top of them.

Packed in like sacks of potatoes, they made the ten-mile trip to Hamlebaek. By the time they arrived, the two youngest Melchior children had lost control of their bladders and both adults were wet from urine.

Finally they got to their destination and were again parceled out among various homes to await darkness and the fishing boats that would carry them across the sound. Marcus and Mrs. Melchior gratefully accepted the chance to bathe and wash their soiled clothes and settled in for a few hours of rest.

The villagers reported that there had been no Nazi activity that day and that there was a large boat waiting for the refugees. At midnight they gathered in a warehouse on a pier. A substantial ship, the Gerda III, sat at the far side of the pier, about 30 feet away. By midnight there was a large crowd of refugees gathered in the warehouse, including the Melchiors.

* * * * * * * *

Tyge and Henny, a local resident of Humlebaek, peeked out a grimy window at the Gerda III so tantalizingly close.

"See the guards?" Henny said.

Tyge watched two German sentries come together right in front of them, do an about face, march to the far ends of the pier about a hundred meters away, turn and come back again.

"How do we get past them?" Tyge said. "We can't get to the Gerda with them out there."

Henny just chuckled. "Those two get replaced in a few minutes … and the new ones are blind and deaf."

"Blind and deaf. What do you mean?"

"Some of our people have been chatting up the Wehrmacht. The two coming on duty don't want to see any refugees … they won't see or hear a thing unless we start setting off fireworks."

"Are you sure about this?"

"Ah, there are the new men. Trust me."

Tyge realized that he had no choice but to trust the local people, so he kept his doubts to himself.

Henny got the refugees lined up and instructed them to go on his signal. Marcus and his family were at the back end of the line.

"When I signal you, go as quickly as you can," Henny said. "You must be quiet about it. Now, the ones preparing to go stand here, out of the light, so you can't be seen from outside. When one group goes, the next one moves up. Any questions? Good. Get ready."

Henny eased the door open and Tyge realized they must have heavily oiled the hinges because they made absolutely no noise. Watching from the darkened interior, Tyge saw the guards come together just a few meters away, do an about face and start away. They were perhaps 30 meters away when Henny sent across the first three refugees, two young men and an old woman.

The two men, holding the old woman by either arm, almost carried her across the pier and up the short gangplank. All three of them were ushered into the shadows on the boat by a man that Tyge hadn't seen until then. The guards continued their walk to the end of the pier, wheeled about and returned.

Each time the guards walked to the end of the pier, another small group of refugees dashed across to the waiting Gerda III.

"I don't believe it," Tyge said. "How could they not notice? And how can you be so calm?"

"I told you," Henny said. "So long as they can pretend, they won't see anything."

All went well for some time until perhaps half of the crowd had made it across the pier and was on board the Gerda III.

Suddenly there was the sound of a motorcar and a moment later headlights illuminated the end of the pier. Tyge stopped breathing while a young couple finished their dash across the pier and ducked into the Gerda an instant before the headlights illuminated the area.

The motorcar stopped right in front of their door and a German officer emerged and motioned to the sentries. Tyge noticed that Henny had eased the door shut and now stood, rigid, looking out the window.

Tyge could make out only a few words but the officer seemed to be chewing out the sentries.

The officer got back into the motorcar and roared off into the night. The sentries waited until the motorcar was gone, then turned and faced the door behind which the refugees huddled.

"Snotty SS bastard," said one.

"Where the hell does he get off threatening us?" said the other.

"Well, you put him straight, proper told him that no Jews were getting across our pier."

"Yeah. Think he believed us?"

"Those SS bastards never believe anybody. He'll be back to check on us again."

"Right. Well, we better walk. Keep a sharp eye out."

The two sentries resumed their pacing up and down the dock. Henny motioned for everyone to begin moving to the other end of the warehouse. When they had moved through several rooms and could talk without fear of the sentries overhearing them, Henny explained.

"The SS came by and chewed out the sentries and spooked them. We can't go across that pier anymore tonight. We'll have to try to get you onto other boats. In the meantime, go back to wherever you were staying."

* * * * * * * * *

Rabbi Melchior was generally an optimist, but failing to get on board the Gerda alarmed him. He picked up his three year-old and tried to reassure his family.

"We are fortunate to have such friends, they make sure we're okay. We'll get on a boat tomorrow." Just then Henny came up to them.

"Rabbi, I have a boat for you. It will be uncomfortable, but it will get you to Sweden tomorrow."

"Ah, thank God. Thank you. See," Marcus turned to his wife. "God takes care of us and this nice young man is his helper."

The five Melchiors and four others followed Henny outside and down a side street. Henny stopped at a small house, rapped on the door, and told them to wait a minute while he went inside.

"Tarben, can you put nine people on your boat? The SS showed up in the middle of loading the Gerda III and I have lots of people that didn't get on board."

"Sure. Let's get them on board now and I'll deliver them in the middle of my normal fishing trip."

Tarben and Henny came out to where the refugees waited.

"This fisherman will take you," Henny said. "Go with him now to his boat and early in the morning, a couple of hours from now, he'll deliver you to Sweden."

They followed Tarben down a little alley to the beach and he rowed half of them at a time out to his boat. They all got into the hold which was somewhat slimy because it was normally used to hold fish. Worse than the slime was the smell, a mixture of fish and gasoline. Before he closed the hatch over them, Tarben explained in a whisper what would happen.

"I'm leaving the hatch partially open so you get some air. Around 3:00 a.m. I start for the fishing grounds. I'll take my usual route, so as to not arouse any suspicion. My fishing spot is very near the international border, so when we get there we make a short dash into Swedish water and you'll be safe. Sorry for the discomfort and the smell, but it will only be a couple of hours and then you will be safe. Good night ... oh, be quiet, sound carries over the water."

Marcus stretched out between the ribs of the boat, trying to adapt his body to the curve of the bottom of the boat. Four inches of water filled the bottom of the hold and wet his feet. Thank God the water isn't cold. Good, she's holding the baby.

He reached for the three year old and cuddled her to his chest. The boys look like they're asleep already. This hurts my back. Never be able to sleep here.

The noise of the engine startled him and Marcus realized he slept after all. Feet are frozen. My back is killing me, stomach wants to throw up ... petrol vapors making me sick. No matter, I'm happy, soon we'll be safe.

The boat started out at first light and traveled steadily. After an hour, Tarben looked in the hatch.

"Everybody OK? We're almost to my usual area ... another few minutes and we turn and dash to Sweden."

Mrs. Melchior reached over and squeezed his hand. "Marcus, we're really going to make it, aren't we."

"Yes love, we are," he replied. "We'll soon be safe."

She didn't answer, just shuddered and squeezed his hand.

A moment later Tarben appeared at the hatch again.

"A German patrol boat. Everybody quiet." His head disappeared and the hatch cover slammed shut, leaving them in almost total darkness. Several loud thumps followed as Tarben dumped something on top of the hatch.

Mrs. Melchior gripped his hand so hard that, through his fright and despair, Marcus wondered at her strength. He turned his head to caution the children to be quiet and saw their eyes wide with understanding and fear.

Marcus and the other refuges waited in the darkness for an interminable time that was probably only a few minutes.

The engine cut off and the k-thunk, k-thunk, k-thunk of moving through the waves was replaced by the gentle rocking of a boat at rest. Marcus' nine year-old had long since lost the contents of his stomach to seasickness but dry heaves threatened to overtake him. Marcus shook his shoulder and commanded, "You must be quiet."

They heard another boat and felt a bump as it pulled alongside. Then a strange voice commanded, "Stand aside for an inspection."

Tarben, sounding jovial, asked, "Can I offer you some coffee? Just made some fresh. Well, actually, it's only zichory."

"No, I'll just have a look around."

A moment later their worst fears were realized as they clearly heard, "Open the hatch."

Mrs. Melchior gasped. Rabbi Melchior held her hand and they waited for their doom.

The command was repeated, "Move this gear and open the hatch."

They lay there, frozen with fear, listening as something was dragged off the hatch and then one of the covers was thrown off and they were blinded by the sudden sunlight.

Marcus' eyes were tearing from the sudden light, but he could make out the German officer standing there looking at the nine of them.

No one moved and nobody said anything for a long minute.

"Nice load of fish," the officer announced. He turned away and in two steps was at the edge of their boat.

A few seconds later they heard his boat pulling away.

Tarben watched them go, then started his engine and headed straight for Sweden. Fifteen minutes later he called, "You're safe now. We're in Swedish waters."

They all came up onto the deck and clustered around him, giddy with relief. Marcus asked, "What happened back there? I don't understand it."

"I don't know. The officer was the only one who came … all his men were still on his boat … none of them could see into the hold. Maybe he had to go through the motions, but he … guess he had to show his superiors that he's trying, this lets him show a search."

Mrs. Melchior said, "Thank God it wasn't the SS."

Marcus nodded. "God watches over us."

Marcus studied Tarben, a small wiry man in his mid-fifties. He wondered why this man risked his life and his livelihood to help strangers. Tarben noticed the scrutiny.

"What's the matter Rabbi? Never seen a fisherman before?"

"No, I just was wondering how you risk everything for us, people you don't even know?'

Tarben snorted and held his hands up, palms out.

"See all those calluses? I pride myself on being tough. I can outwork men half my age. Now, how tough would I be if let these bastard Nazis scare me, huh?"

He turned back to adjust the wheel as if that explained everything.

Tarben dropped them in a small Swedish fishing village a half hour later. Marcus saw Tarben begin haggling with a local fisherman over a load of fish ... he needed to buy fish to prove he had been fishing if the Germans stopped him on the way home.

Swedish officials met the refugees, had them fill out some forms, and arranged food and shelter.

At least twenty strangers helped them to escape. Marcus never learned the names of most of their rescuers. God not only moves in mysterious ways, He inspired a lot of Gentiles to risk their lives for us.

Chapter 57. The Pundik Family #2

While the Nazis surrounded his hospital and were preparing to search it for Jews, Dr. Koster and his group were busy. Shortly after the Nazis showed up outside, a funeral procession of twenty-seven motorcars left the hospital. The deceased was a prominent businessman who had many friends, so all the cars were full. The Wehrmacht lieutenant in charge of the search party asked the funeral director a couple of cursory questions and then waved the funeral procession on its way. The Pundiks were in the sixteenth car. A total of 127 people, everyone else in the entire procession except for those in the first car, were Jews fleeing the Germans.

The ride to the Bertelsen's in Lyngby took only about 30 minutes, but Mrs. Pundik was complaining about stomach pains that seemed to rapidly get worse. They got there just in time to be loaded into lorries for the ride to Gilleleje, a village on the northern end of the island.

A Nazi patrol had been spotted nearby a half hour earlier and everyone was in a state of barely controlled frenzy.

Mrs. Pundik was in such pain that she could barely stand. One of Bertelsen's group was a second year medical student and he quickly decided she had appendicitis and had to return to the hospital.

"I'm going back with her," Mr. Pundik announced.

"No, you can't," Aage said. "Everything is arranged for the trip to Sweden. Mr. Pundik, you put your entire family at risk by returning to Copenhagen. We will take care of Mrs. Pundik, but you and the boys must go on. We will ensure you are re-united in Sweden."

Leaving Mr. Pundik to say goodbye to his wife, Aage ushered the three boys onto one of the waiting lorries. A moment later a neighbor rushed up to announce the Nazi patrol was two streets over and seemed likely to come this way.

The loading was completed in a mad rush and each of the four lorries drove off as soon as it was loaded. Mr. Pundik was hustled into the back of the nearest lorry and then discovered that he had no idea where his children or any of their luggage was.

* * * * * * * * *

Mr. Pundik wondered what route they would take. Shortest route to Gilleleje takes about forty minutes. Might take us longer. Packed in here like sardines, can't even sit down.

Shouldn't be taking this long … already been 90 minutes. Guess we're taking back roads. Oh, hell. Now we're turning around. Must be a checkpoint ahead.

Damn, lots of bumps, feels like a cowpath.

Two and a half hours now. Wonder where we are? Legs killing me, really wish I could sit down. Diesel fumes making me sick.

Somebody just threw up. Yech! Diesel fumes and sour vomit.

God help us, turned around again. Are we ever going to make it? Almost four hours now.

Urine! Smell of urine. Somebody peed themselves. Hope I can hold it.

This is going on forever. Not sure I can stand it.

Old lady just fainted … been almost six hours.

Another cow path! Are we there? Stopping …

* * * * * * * * *

Arne threw open the door where Pundik stood packed in among the others.

"Hurry," Arne said. "There are patrols nearby. You have to get inside as quickly as possible."

Arne and several local people helped them out of the truck and urged them toward nearby houses.

"Wait, I need to find my wife," a man protested.

"You need to get inside before the Nazis get here." Arne said.

Arne stopped to assess the situation. Local people urging, in some cases almost dragging, the refugees toward nearby houses. Refugees resisting, trying to find lost luggage and family members. Too much noise … people arguing, raising their voices. Madness. Going to get caught.

Arne grabbed two of the local men.

"Pass the word to your friends. Get them off the street NOW. We will re-unite families as soon as the patrols leave. Don't argue, just tell them the patrol is coming and get them off the street."

The men nodded and they and Arne passed the word.

Ten minutes later all the refugees were out of sight.

Except one.

Mr. Pundik was distraught and refused to go inside.

I lost my wife," Pundik said. "I lost my children. Now my pen. I can't leave it too."

He started to climb back into the truck to search for it.

"You're nuts," the driver said. "I'm outa here."

Pundik leaped into the back of the lorry and stood there wildly shaking his head "No. No!"

"Come, be reasonable," Arne said. "It's only a pen … it can be replaced."

"It's not just a pen," Pundik shook his head violently. "My wife gave it to me."

"I'm leavin," the driver headed for the lorrie's cab. "He can stay in there if he wants."

"Wait," Arne said.

The driver paused and Arne promised, "Just a minute."

He jumped up into the back of the lorry and used his torch to search. Almost right away he saw a little silk pompom that turned out to be attached to the end of the treasured fountain pen.

Arne and Pundik hurried after the rest and even discovered Pundik's children.

The next morning a schooner arrived in the Gilleleje harbor to take a load of refugees. Jews and their protectors rushed to the pier from all over the village.

Some old people, too frail to walk quickly, were carried to the pier and up the gangplank in handcarts. For about twenty minutes the area swarmed with people.

A man came rushing onto the pier and shouted, "A patrol is coming."

* * * * * * * *

The Pundiks and their host arrived in time to see the schooner cast off the ropes and begin to move.

"Let's run," Herbert said. "We can still catch it."

Mr. Pundik clutched Herbert's arm.

"No, son, the gangplank is gone … we wouldn't be able to get on board."

Just then the sound of several lorries being driven at high speed caused them to look around. Four German trucks roared past and, braking violently, stopped on the pier.

Transfixed, Pundik, his three boys, and their host stood and watched. German troops ran out of the trucks, urged on by a Gestapo officer. Too late. The ship's only a few meters from the pier, but it's out of reach.

Gestapo Officer Juhl , the officer in charge of the patrol, shouted for the Harbor Patrol. There were no patrol boats nearby. Juhl watched helplessly as the schooner and hundreds of Jews sailed away to Sweden.

The Pundiks went back into hiding, courtesy of a local family.

* * * * * * * *

Gestapo Officer Juhl swept back into town that evening just as several groups of refugees were moving toward the fishing vessels waiting to take them. Twelve Jews were caught immediately. Three fishermen were also arrested, their boats confiscated.

Officer Juhl systematically searched through all the houses of the village, beginning with those nearest the piers.

Danes of all ages raced through the village to spread the warning.

No one knew which houses hid Jews, so everyone had to be warned. The warning and an exodus of Jewish refugees spread outward from the village pier like the shock wave of an explosion.

The Pundik's host, on the far edge of the village, got the warning about twenty minutes after the searches began. The Pundiks grabbed their few possessions and went out the back door just in time to join a small crowd of perhaps twenty other refugees, led by one of the villagers.

They walked for nearly an hour, down back roads and across several pastures until they reached a large barn.

The first floor of the barn was full of dairy cows and the second floor was loaded with hay. The refugees would be hungry and thirsty, but burrowing into the hay would keep them reasonably warm until morning.

Shortly after four a.m. the farmer's teenage son woke them and announced that breakfast would be ready in fifteen minutes. He apologized for not being able to take better care of them and showed them where the outhouse was. He also suggested that the men simply go behind the barn to urinate so that the single toilet would not hold them up too long.

Several basins, towels, and soap awaited them on the porch and there was a hand operated pump just off the porch.

"When you finish washing up, come on into the kitchen for breakfast," he said. "If there is anything else you need, let me or my parents know. I'm going now to help get everything ready."

Mr. Pundik shook his boys awake and the four of them went behind the barn to urinate. Herbert seemed to think this was a grand adventure, but the two youngest boys were frightened.

"Dad, why are the Nazis chasing us?" the ten year-old asked.

"What will they do to us?" the fourteen year-old wanted to know.

Pundik's heart sank. He didn't want to lie to his boys, but he also wanted to reassure them.

"Our Danish friends aren't going to let them catch us. In a day or so we'll be in Sweden and safe." *Not a good answer, but the best I can manage.*

An hour later all twenty-two of the refugees were stuffed with eggs, bacon, hash browns, oatmeal and tea.

Pundik thought wistfully of coffee, now almost impossible to find since the Nazis had shipped it all to Germany. It was, however, very fine to have a full stomach. Even his youngest son seemed less fearful with a full belly.

They returned to the barn for another night. The following morning, after another big breakfast, their group and about sixty others were taken to the village.

They gathered in the back room of a restaurant near the pier, crammed in together while they waited for a ship to dock.

At ten a.m. the Gestapo returned and began searching the area around the pier. In imminent danger of being discovered, they were hurried out the rear door, and down an alley leading away from the pier. Four blocks away they arrived at the Gilleleje Church and rushed inside. Father Johan greeted them.

"We have a good hiding place for all of you. I'm sorry it will be uncomfortable, but it's the best we can do and still keep you close enough to get you on a ship as soon as the Nazis leave."

Pundik was beginning to despair, but he didn't want his boys to give up hope. He put his arm around the youngest boy's shoulder and said.

"This is like camping, isn't it? Sort of like training for the army."

"I don't like not eating," the boy said.

"The hay got inside my shirt … it's scratchy," the middle boy said.

"You guys are sissies," Herbert said. "It's good for you, toughen you up."

"Look at the bookworm talking. You're not tough," the middle boy said.

"Nea, nea, Herbert is a sissy," the youngest said.

Mr. Pundik shushed them, secretly happy that they were engaging in the bickering usual for brothers rather than worrying about the Nazis.

"Look," he said, pointing into the closet ahead of them. "We're going to climb that ladder into the attic."

They watched while a little old lady struggled to get up the ladder and was finally lifted the last few feet by the men who had gone ahead of her.

"I can't do that," the youngest Pundik announced. The ladder to the attic above the sanctuary was fully twenty-five feet long and, even to Mr. Pundik, seemed very high.

"I told you this was like training for the army," Mr. Pundik said. "Like a soldier, you have to do it even if you're afraid."

"Dad, I'm afraid of falling. I can't, I can't." The boy was pushing back into Mr. Pundik, physically trying to flee the high ladder.

Pundik knelt down, with his hands on his youngest's shoulders and looked into his eyes.

"Herbert will go first. Then your other brother. You and I will go up together and I will hold you. When we get near the top, the boys will reach down and grab you and pull you up. See, you won't be able to fall."

"I don't like it. You might drop me."

"Never! We won't drop you. You don't even have to look. Just let me guide you and you'll be at the top before you know it."

The boy looked doubtful and tears glistened in the corners of his eyes but he shook his head "okay".

Herbert scampered up the ladder easily, followed a little more slowly by the fourteen year-old.

Mr. Pundik positioned his youngest on the first rung, and stood behind him with his arms on either side.

"See, I'm going to be right here. You can't fall. Now take a step up and I'll move right with you."

They began moving and got a little more than halfway up before the boy looked down. He immediately froze.

"Okay. We're doing fine. Now look straight ahead, look at the wall right in front of you. No, no, don't look down. Look straight ahead. Look, I can almost touch the wall in front of me, see?"

The boy kept his eyes straight ahead, but didn't move. Pundik put one of his hands over the boy's and moved it up to the next rung.

"Okay, now your right foot … move it up a step."

They covered the next ten feet in this fashion, with Pundik literally talking the boy up each step. Two rungs from the trap door, Herbert reached down and grasped the boy's right arm. The middle Pundik son got the boy's left wrist.

""They have you, all you have to do is let go of the rung."

The boy kept his grip on the rung.

"Listen, squirt," Herbert said. "If you don't let go, I'm going to lift you by your ears."

The boy started to sputter a loud retort, let go of the ladder rung with one hand, and was hauled unceremoniously through the trap-door, suffering a long scratch down the left side of his ribcage in the process. He yelped at the pain but then was on the attic floor and Herbert had him in a bear hug and was speaking in his ear.

"Well done, oh littlest squirt. I had to say something to get you to let go of the rung."

By nightfall the attic was bitterly cold. Pundik and his children huddled together for warmth and were still cold. By midnight they were all shivering. Mr. Pundik began talking quietly to some of the other adults.

The entire group gathered together, standing very close together. Cuddling together, their body heat kept all of them warm. Even the outermost people were warmer than they had been and by taking turns being on the outside everyone kept reasonably comfortable.

The night seemed interminable. Standing up, pressed together for warmth, many fell asleep for short periods. Some of the children slept for extended periods, kept from falling over by the adults pressed around them. The sleeping children fell down in slow motion, so that after an hour or so they were folded up in a squatting position.

Morning came eventually. The buckets for going to the bathroom were nearly full and smelled terribly. Pundik's sons were all complaining of hunger and thirst, having had nothing to eat or drink for twenty-four hours.

Occasionally a young child began to cry and, if the parents couldn't quiet them immediately, a soporific was passed over to put the child to sleep.

Mercifully it was a clear day and the sun soon warmed the attic. The densely packed mob dispersed, people lay down on the wooden floor, and fell asleep. Pundik was exhausted and lay down as well, but his stomach rumbled and he was very thirsty. The discomfort kept him awake for perhaps thirty minutes.

Pundik came awake because someone poked him in the ribs. He opened his eyes to see a man with his fingers to his lips, signaling silence. What … ? Where are we? What's happening?

Oh. Church attic. Somebody talking, down below.

"I'm sorry, Officer, what did you say your name is?" It was Father Johan's voice.

"Lieutenant Juhl, Gestapo officer in charge of this area. Now stand aside, Father."

"Pleased to meet you, Lieutenant Juhl. Have you come to worship with us?"

"Father, don't play games with me. I told you. We need to search your church."

"As good Christians, you are most welcome to enter for worship or prayer. But this is God's house and no one may search it."

"Stand aside, Father, or we will remove you."

"I am sorry, sir, but God is my superior and I can obey none other."

There was a momentary silence before Juhl spoke again.

"If there are locked doors, you can open them for us or we will break them down. Your choice."

"You should have more regard for God and His house, Lieutenant. This is unbecoming for a German officer."

"Put him in the squad car, with a guard. I will deal with him later. Now let us see if our informer was correct about the stinking Jews."

Pundik waited, hardly daring to breathe. Doors opening and closing. Snatches of talk, can't make out the words.

Their trap door wasn't opened. Maybe they won't find it.

Pundik waited a few more minutes. Dear God, help us in our hour of need.

"The men found nothing sir." A soldier, reporting to Juhl.

"There must be an attic," Juhl said. "Did you find an attic?"

"No, sir. We found no access to an attic."

"Look at it," Juhl commanded. "It's got a steep gable roof. But the sanctuary, the main part of the building, has a flat ceiling. There's a large attic up there. Find the entrance and you'll find the Jewish swine."

Oh, dear God. He's going to find us.

After another few minutes they found the trap door leading to the attic, tucked away in the janitor's closet. Officer Juhl waited while his men found a ladder and one of them went up, pushed the trap door open, and shone his light into the attic.

"Lots of 'em . The attic is full of 'em," the soldier reported.

* * * * * * * *

A dozen troopers began herding the Jews to the ladder. The little old lady that had been pulled up the last few steps objected that she needed help to get down.

A large trooper gave her a violent shove and she fell into the open trap door. She fell all the way down and didn't move after hitting the floor. Juhl ordered two of his men to carry her out of the way and then ignored her, not even checking to see if she was alive or dead.

Pundik went down the ladder in a fog of despair. The youngest was so frightened by the Gestapo brutality that he completely forgot his fear of the height.

Officer Juhl released Father Johan and drove away with his trucks full of Jews.

* * * * * * * * *

One of Father Johan's deacons raced to Lyngby to warn Aage Bertelsen.

"Aage, eighty of our people were caught."

"What? How? How could that happen?"

"Near as we can tell some outsider saw too much and snitched on us to the Gestapo. They were hiding in the church attic and Father Johan tried to stop the Gestapo, without much luck."

"Oh my God, so they know Father Johan is involved."

"Yes, but funny thing. They didn't arrest him. Just let him go."

"Does the Gestapo know about us?"

"Can't tell, but Father Johan said they will get the story out of some of the refugees. The Nazis will find out about your group."

"Thank God we didn't give anybody any names … all they can tell the Nazis is the location. We'll move right away."

The deacon left to go home and Aage called an emergency meeting of three of his colleagues. He told them about the report from the deacon. After they finished asking him questions, he continued.

"Humlebaek has been our major port for a week now, but there are substantial problems with it, including four known informers in the town. The problem at Gilleleje seems to have stemmed from a visitor.

"We have to move our headquarters.

"Maybe we can fool the Nazis. We'll clean out the HQ, but a few files will get 'accidentally' left behind a file cabinet or a desk, with a few names and some references to transporting Jews through Humlebaek.

"I have a friend who has been posing as an informant for Officer Juhl. He'll report to Juhl the location of the old HQ and that we are planning to ship large numbers of Jews through Humlebaek in the coming week. While the Gestapo is watching Humlebaek, we will be going through Gilleleje."

"Juhl caught eighty of our people in Gilleleje," the oldest of the group objected. "That will encourage him to stay up there."

"Aage, is your agent convincing?" Another man asked. "Will he tell Juhl a good story?"

"Oh, yes. He seems all youthful exuberance, like a puppy dog wanting attention. He demonstrated his fanatical Nazi Jew hating routine for me and it is quite terrifyingly convincing. I think Juhl will be convinced that our man is a kindred spirit and totally trustworthy."

"Well, he can tell Juhl that we were badly shaken by his capture of our people in Gilleleje … which we were … and that we are shifting everything to Humlebaek."

A few more questions and comments finished the meeting and they separated to implement Aage's plans.

* * * * * * * * * *

While Arne and his group were working with Aage Bertelsen to help Jews escape to the north of Copenhagen, other groups were going through the fishing village of Dragor in the south. With a population of about 2,100 people, practically everyone in Dragor was involved with the rescue operation. Six or seven hundred Jews escaped to Sweden through Dragor during the first week of October.

A week after the raids, a Gestapo Officer replaced the commanding officer in Dragor.

The day after the Gestapo officer assumed command, on a cold, wet, and windy Monday evening at eight p.m., several taxis full of escaping Jews arrived at the harbor. At that moment a bus full of German soldiers arrived.

Within seconds, the soldiers were shooting. Several people were injured and more than a dozen Jews were arrested. Over the next three days, ten of the fishermen were arrested, their boats confiscated and sold at auction. Four of the local men were also arrested.

The Dragor villagers pooled their money and, as the Nazis auctioned off the confiscated boats, bought them and returned them to their owners. After six boats were returned, the Nazis caught on and destroyed the rest.

The Gestapo immediately began torturing the arrested men. Seven other local men promptly went underground, before the torturers could get their names. The Gestapo arrested another dozen villagers over the next week.

The soldiers patrolling the harbor were Wehrmacht, but the SS watched carefully so they were diligent. Dragor was effectively shut down as an escape route.

Chapter 58. Arne and the Stikkers

Arne was spending all of his time helping Jews escape. Haven't been to class in over a week. Well, most of my profs are also helping in the rescue. Should be able to catch up with classes after the rescue effort.

Ten p.m. already. Been up for almost two days. Time to rest.

Sleep came to Arne within seconds of lying down.

Banging, bang, bang … going on forever. People should be more considerate. Just go away.

The rude inconsiderate noise made him angry and that woke him.

Someone banging on my door. Calling.

Arne climbed out of bed and staggered to the door. He pulled the curtain back and saw Brigitte and Tyge. He opened the door. Oops! Dressed in my underwear!

Brigitte fairly burst into the room and seized him by the biceps, seeming not to notice his state of undress.

"Arne, you've got to get out of here. They're looking for you."

"Who's looking? What happened?"

"Tyge and I were at the student union when we heard two men asking about you. We watched them go around the center, asking different people. Finally, they got to us."

Tyge interrupted, "I told them I had heard about you, that you had written some crazy thing like the Ten Commandments. This encouraged them and they said you were a traitor and they were out to catch you. Said the Gestapo was offering a reward for you."

"Arne, too many people know you around the university," Brigitte said. "Quite a few know where you live. If they keep on, they're going to find you. You have to get out of here. Right now."

"Okay, okay. Where am I going this time of night?"

"Come to my place," Tyge said.

"You live all the way across town," Brigitte objected. "I'm much closer. Grab what you need and we can carry it to my place in ten minutes."

Fifteen minutes later they had two suitcases, a cardboard box and four pillowcases full of clothes, important papers, and a few keepsakes.

"Too much for us to carry," Brigitte said. "Tyge, go down and find us a cab. Arne and I will get everything downstairs so we'll be all ready when you get back."

Arne noticed Brigitte had taken charge. Fine with me. I'll follow her around all day.

It only took a few minutes for Arne and Brigitte to carry Arne's possessions down the one flight of stairs and to the front porch. Then there was nothing for them to do except wait for Tyge to return with the cab.

"Uh, Brigitte, you sure it's okay for me to stay at your place?"

"Of course. Why wouldn't it be okay? You have some dread disease or something."

"No, no, it's just I don't want to impose or anything."

"Hey, it's only for a few days anyway. I'll make you do the cleaning."

"I don't mind doing the cleaning. And washing the dishes."

"Arne, do you ever laugh about anything?"

"What's that supposed to mean?"

"I'm trying to make a joke about cleaning, and you take it so seriously you offer to wash the dishes."

"Oh. That was a joke?'

"Apparently not a very good one."

Arne let the silence grow around them. Going to stay in Brigitte's flat. Wow.

Eventually Brigitte spoke again, quietly almost as if she were speaking to herself.

"You know Arne, all of us admire you … and none of us know you. You always seem to be working."

Arne didn't know how to respond to this but was saved by Tyge arriving with the cab. They hurried to put all Arne's stuff in the cab's boot. All three of them rode to Brigitte's flat.

"How do we know the Nazis aren't looking for the rest of you?" Arne asked.

"Well, we really don't know, but it's not very likely," Brigitte said. "You're the only one of us who has a name. Everybody knows about Arne Sejr. I think the Danish Nazis want to get you because you're a symbol for the resistance."

"They weren't asking about anybody but you, Arne," Tyge said. "You're going to have to go underground, at least for a while."

Brigitte had the last word. "Tomorrow, early, Tyge and I will go talk to Professor Koch. You stay here and just stay out of sight. Tyge, its way too late for you to go home now. If you don't mind sleeping on the floor, the rug is pretty thick and I have lots of pillows."

In spite of his wonderment at being on Brigitte's couch, right outside her bedroom, Arne quickly fell asleep and slept until Brigitte called him for breakfast.

Prof. Hal Koch Journal, October 10, 1941

It's finally happened. Clausen and his bunch of crazies are after Arne. Fortunately for us, most of them are easy to spot and most people won't give them so much as a civil 'Hello'. But if they persist, they will eventually get the names of all of them … too many people know Arne's group. It's time for all of them to go underground, or at least to move and keep the new address secret. I wonder how long it will take for them to get onto me? I think it is safe to continue as usual for a little.

The reports of the SS with the group from Gilleleje Church are sickening. Beating old people because they couldn't climb the gangplank fast enough … what has happened to these SS men? How could supposedly Christian officers fall so low? And what are they doing with the Jews once they round them up and send them to these concentration camps? Surely the amount of slave labor they get out of them can't be worth the effort it takes to catch and keep them, especially with old people who are already frail and sick. Unbelievably, they took all the people from the old age home. It makes no sense.

I have never seen our people so outraged. Moellar is walking a fine line in his broadcasts ... simultaneously urging on the resistance and reminding people not to be provoked into violence. He must have said "the Nazis want violence from us" at least ten times in his last speech.

If there was ever any doubt about Hitler's mind, this insanity with the Jews settles it. Megalomaniacs like Hitler always over-reach, always make fatal mistakes. Right now he seems invincible. But the Greeks had it right, hubris always presages the fall. We just have to hang on until Hitler does himself in.

The rescue efforts are going unbelievably well. Clearly most of the Wehrmacht troops are not trying to catch Jews ... and some of the officers seem to be actively interfering. Things have been so chaotic it's hard to know for sure, but it seems that more than half of the Jews have already reached Sweden.

We know of eighty Jews captured from the Gilleleje Church and forty-three from various other places. We have no way of knowing how many others the Nazis may have captured in total, but we think it is relatively few.

God is with us. We have to continue doing our part, in spite of our fears and doubts. "Be strong and of good courage ... the Lord thy God, He it is that doth go with thee: He will not fail thee, nor forsake thee." Deu 31:6

Chapter 59. Going Underground

Professor Koch insisted that all of them move to new flats. In the meantime, he ordered that Arne stay at Brigitte's and not go outside until they could ascertain how diligently the stikkers were in looking for him.

Arne loved novels. Haven't had time for one in months. Now, can't go out ... nothing to do. Time to read! Brigitte has a nice collection ...

Three hours passed before Arne put the novel down. Gotta pee. Thirsty too.

He went back to the novel and finished it two hours later. What time is it? Hmm, forgot lunch, no wonder I'm hungry.

Arne rummaged around Brigitte's pantry and found some food. While he ate, he worried. Who's helping the Jews get to the boats? Are Brigitte and the others safe? Is Prof okay?

This is pointless. Probably bad for my health too. Find something else to think about.

Oh, codes for the Germans. Keep em busy.

Need a provocative message.

He wrote several short paragraphs.

It is urgent that the contents of this message remain secret from our oppressors. If they learn of our intent they will be able to foil our plans.

There are about twenty of us in on the plot so far. We hope to increase that number substantially before we act.

Remember that secrecy is crucial. If you talk to anyone outside of our core group all of our plans may go for naught.

Arne continued to write similar paragraphs until he had twenty of them. The twenty-first paragraph was this:

Children of the world unite. Parents should not be allowed to oppress us by enforcing bedtime. We shall unite and overthrow this oppression.

There. That should do it. Arne smiled.

Arne's next step was to develop a simple code. In this case he simply counted the letters in the first word of the paragraph and then used that number to shift the alphabet. For example, the first paragraph began with a two-letter word. So the code for that paragraph was that an "a" became a "c", the "b" became a "d" and so on. The final step was to invent a fictitious name and a non-existent address.

Arne was quite pleased with his letter. Hundreds or perhaps thousands of Danes were writing similar letters. The Nazis are obsessively thorough and will decode all of the letters, just in case …

He was sealing the envelope when Brigitte arrived.

"Brigitte. Hi. I'm going nuts cooped up here."

"Hi Arne, good news. We didn't see any sign of the stikkers looking for you on campus. And Professor Koch has a place for you."

Arne was elated about the stikkers but disappointed about the place … he wanted to be near Brigitte for as long as he could.

"Oh. When do I move? Can I get back to work?"

"You're stuck with me for a couple more days. Professor Koch recruited several students to simply be in public places and listen for the stikkers. The students think he's simply looking out for a Danish hero, namely you. He wants you to stay out of sight until they can make sure the stikkers have given up looking on campus. Your new place won't be ready for another day or so."

"Well, I hate to be penned up, but I think I can stand you for a little while."

"I'm really an ogre," Brigitte gave him a mock glare. "Have you eaten?"

"I ate one of your apples at lunch time."

"Is that all? Weren't you hungry?"

"Well, I got lost in a novel and sort of forgot about eating."

"Oh, yeah? I do that too … nothing disturbs me when I get into a good story."

"You've got a lot of great novels here, a lot of stuff I haven't read."

"Feel free. You're going to need something to keep you busy the next few days. Let's get some food. Can you cut up these vegetables?"

The next hour passed in a happy blur for Arne as the two of them worked together to cook and eat a simple meal. Arne learned a little about Brigitte's farm background and she got out of him that he had been a sprinter for the track team.

After dinner, over a cup of zichory, the talk took a more serious turn. Arne asked Brigitte, "I don't suppose Prof knows how far underground I have to go?"

"Not yet, Arne. That's what they're determining."

They both knew there were several different levels of going underground and it depended primarily upon how much effort the Nazis were putting into trying to catch you. At the deepest level, you fled to Sweden or England. At the other extreme, you merely moved to a new location and tried to maintain a low profile. In between, you might move every few weeks and adopt a new identity with each move.

Arne hoped he didn't have to go deep underground. Frequent moves and new identities take enormous energy. Keeps you from the work that needs doing.

Arne spent three days in Brigitte's flat. Each day they had breakfast and dinner together and spent much of the evening together. On the second night they had just finished dinner when Brigitte got up to get the coffee pot.

As she stood up, she passed a little gas with an audible pop. Arne paused, frozen, with his water glass halfway to his mouth. Brigitte noticed his reaction and snorted.

"You think girls don't fart or what?"

Arne sniffed a couple times and then began laughing.

"Your farts smell worse than mine."

Brigitte gathered her dignity.

"I do everything exceedingly well … even stink."

The two of them dissolved into laughter. The silence while they drank their zichory was a comfortable, companionable time. Afterward they read until dusk and then ventured out for a short walk. Arne was sublimely happy and wished he could stay with Brigitte forever.

The next day both of them were given new last names and ID cards to match and they moved into new quarters. Arne's place was four blocks from Brigitte's. The resistance work resumed and there was no more time for novels. Arne occasionally wrote another letter to befuddle the German censors.

Prof. Hal Koch Journal October 25, 1941

The Swede's tell us 6213 Jews have entered their country since Oct. 1. We know the Nazis caught a few hundred. We think there might still be as many as 1,000 in hiding, still trying to get to Sweden.

We are better organized than we were a month ago, but so are the Nazis. Duckwitz tells us the Wehrmacht officers who were most sympathetic have been replaced with SS or Gestapo men. Best sent the officers who helped us to the front. Duckwitz doesn't understand why the Gestapo hasn't arrested him. I think he is an angel sent to help us ... or perhaps merely under an angel's protection. God truly moves in mysterious ways.

Chapter 60. Morten and Carin

SS General Gunther Pancke was both efficient and brutal in searching for the Jews. He put all of the Gestapo and SS troops under his command into conducting systematic searches of the villages best situated to ferry the Jews to Sweden. Pancke was smart enough to avoid anything approaching a regular schedule for his search teams.

The resistance could never anticipate when a particular area might be searched. The only good news was that the blockade of Copenhagen, although never officially lifted, was de facto over because the Wehrmacht were the only ones left to enforce it and they put little or no effort into it.

Arne was settled into a new flat and was using a false last name but had taken no further measures to hide. As far as they could tell, the Danish Nazis were not putting any serious effort into finding him. His nightmares about Poul still tormented him, but occurred less often.

The nearby villages that had helped so many Jews to escape in the early days of the sealift ... Dragor, Kege, and Store to the south; Lyngby, Humlebaek, Rungsted, Vedbaek to the north ... these were heavily patrolled by the SS. Trying to escape through these villages was now terribly dangerous. As a result, they were moving the refugees farther from Copenhagen before trying to get them onto a boat.

Arne's entire group was assigned to work with Aage Bertelsen and the Lyngby group. They assisted upwards of seven hundred Jews to escape during the first hectic two weeks of the rescue. Now, a month into the effort, instead of dealing with twenty or thirty or forty Jews at a time, they were smuggling people out one or two or a family at a time.

The Danish Rifle Club conducted regular sweeps of the forests north of Copenhagen and was still occasionally finding refugees who fled from SS searches of neighborhoods where they were hiding. The hospitals still had a few Jews registered under Christian names. Numerous Jews were still secreted away with Christian friends or friends of friends.

As these Jews were located, Aage and his group arranged transportation to where a boat could be boarded. They used a group of trusted cabbies but also ambulances and delivery lorries.

The ambulances were perhaps the safest mode because when the Nazis stopped them, the "patients" always had some terribly contagious disease such as meningitis or black plague or yellow fever.

The riskiest part of most rescues involved the transfer of the refugees to the boats. A harbor with a pier allowed a refugee to simply walk out to a boat and get on board. Unfortunately there were a relatively small number of these piers and the Nazis closely watched those. The other alternative was to anchor off shore and get on board via a small rowboat.

* * * * * * * *

Just outside of the village of Alsgarde, 45 kilometers north of Copenhagen, Carin and Morten were pretending to be on a beach picnic on a fine sunny afternoon while they waited for a family they were to connect with a fishing boat.

"They're 30 minutes late," Carin fretted.

"Relax, they'll be here," Morten said around a mouthful of cheese and bread. "Don't you ever get tired of looking at the ocean?"

"Nope. I'm a fisherman's daughter, worked on my Dad's boat since I was ten."

"You aren't ugly enough to be a real fisherman."

Carin swatted him on the back of his head.

"Not ugly enough? By the time I graduated from high school my dad told everybody that I was not only the prettiest but also the hardest working deck hand in our village. I love the sea, working on the boat, everything about it. Look, I've still got the calluses."

"Never been on a fishing boat."

Morten studied her. Petite, very pretty … and amazingly strong. An enigma.

"You think the boat will wait?" Morten said.

"He's probably getting pretty nervous," Carin said. "This isn't a fishing spot, he has no good excuse for being here … and you can see him from kilometers away."

"How did you get assigned to our group?" Morten asked.

"I was trying to talk the villagers into getting guns to go fight the Nazis. When my father found out, he knew I was stubborn so he didn't argue, just suggested that I talk to the village mayor. The mayor sent me to Professor Koch and here I am."

Just then a young man came from the cottage and hesitantly approached them. Carin waved him on.

"Come on, we've been waiting for you. Call your family."

He turned and gestured toward the cottage. The door swung open and a young woman with a baby in her arms flew down the path to the man and the two of them ran to Carin and Morten.

"Captain must have been watching, the dingy is already coming in," Carin said.

The young man was thanking them profusely while his wife was asking if being out on the open beach was safe.

Carin and Morten didn't answer either of them because Carin was telling them they had to wade out and meet the dingy. All four of them headed for the shore and began wading out into the shallow water. After a hundred feet the water was only partway up their thighs and the young man said, "I wondered why the boat was so far out."

"He's as close as he can get without going aground," Carin said.

They continued to wade and finally met the dingy when the water was just above their waists.

"I was getting ready to leave you."

"Oh sir, we're so glad you didn't," the wife said. "We had to wait for a patrol to pass."

The wife handed her baby to the captain. Morten and the husband lifted the wife into the boat, then Carin and Morten boosted the young man into the boat.

"Good luck," Carin called. She and Morten immediately headed back as the captain rowed as fast as he could toward his boat.

Just as they got to the waters edge, a German army truck came onto the beach half a kilometer away. Carin glanced over her shoulder … the dingy was just reaching the boat.

"Run!" Morten yelled, and they raced for the shelter of the trees, thirty meters away, their wine and cheese forgotten on the abandoned blanket.

They reached the edge of the trees while the truck was still some ways off and Carin stopped momentarily to look at the boat.

The captain had started his engine and was underway. The young Jewish man was standing in the stern of the boat, holding the bowline of the dingy, apparently not knowing where to tie it.

She raced after Morten and the two of them ran deeper into the forest, where the truck could not easily follow. They heard a few shots and Morten grunted out between pants, "Shooting…at the boat."

Carin tugged on his sleeve, "Far enough ... walk."

They slowed to a walk and for a little while the only sound was their ragged breathing and their feet scuffling through leaves.

"I hope the husband had sense enough to lay down," Carin said. "He was standing up, holding the line from the dingy."

"It's probably all right," Morten said. "If the boat was still in range there would have been a lot of shooting."

"I don't like this daytime crap," Carin said. "Too damn easy to be seen."

"Yeah, think we should switch to night time pickups?"

"Hell, yes." She stopped. "We almost got killed today."

After discussing the situation with their colleagues, everyone agreed to switch to nighttime pickups. This was tricky because it was difficult for the boats and the shore parties to find each other without the use of lights. Lights, of course, made it easy for the Germans to find them. They solved the problem by choosing a new spot, selected because all involved could find it at night.

On October 29th, Carin and Morten were once more serving as beach liaison, this time for a middle aged Jewish couple. It was 1:30 a.m. and partly overcast, with only a sliver of moon. They were lying on their stomachs, where the beach met the woods, straining to see the boat. The Jewish couple waited in a nearby cottage.

"Boat's late," Morten grumbled.

"Only a little," Carin said. "This isn't the easiest spot to find from the water."

"You know these waters?"

"This is my water. My family is only a couple kilometers away … My father and I used to fish just off shore here."

"Okay, if this is your water, how does a fisherman find this at night?"

"Easiest way is to start at the village just north of here and then sort of ease on down the coast until you can just see the lights of the next village. Then you know you're here and you can look for the buoy we put out there."

Morten snorted. "You mean to tell me this pickup depends upon the captain finding a little beach ball sized buoy?"

"Well, also he's triangulating between some lights and the North Star … so he has a couple of things to look for. 'Course, the clouds kind of interfere with using the stars."

Morten just shook his head. "I guess I need a merit badge in seagoing navigation. I don't see him managing it."

"You're an Eagle scout."

"Yep," Morten said.

"You got a lot of merit badges?"

"Um, yeah, I was a pretty strange child. Couldn't do sports, had no friends. Then I got into scouting and loved it. Kinda came into my own as a scout, made a lot of friends. Got more merit badges than anybody in the region."

"Wow. I didn't know you were such an egghead. You're big enough to do sports."

"I'm big enough, and now I'm even coordinated enough. When I was a kid, I kept tripping over my own feet." Morten paused a minute. "I wouldn't admit this to just anybody, but I'm probably the biggest egghead you know. I like learning things."

Carin suddenly put her hand on his arm. "Shhh."

They listened intently for several seconds without hearing anything. Morten whispered in her ear, "What?"

She put her mouth close to his ear. "Thought I heard someone moving through leaves."

She cautiously rolled over and peered into the trees off to their left.

A moment later she heard it again and, on the other side, a torch snapped on, followed by two more, about fifty feet away. Almost instantly, several others flared to their right, but further away.

Morten bounded to his feet, dragging her upright, and raced for the heart of the woods. Carin heard shouted commands on both sides and the thud of booted feet racing toward them.

They ran thirty feet with Morten in the lead, dodging trees and trying to avoid losing an eye to the low hanging branches, when suddenly a figure appeared scant feet in front of them. Morten plowed into him, a gunshot sounded and Morten and the soldier both went down. Carin stopped, clutched Morten's arm and tried to heave him to his feet.

"Come on! Morten! Help me, I can't lift you alone."

Morten wasn't helping, wasn't trying to get up. He finally gasped, "Run." Again she tugged at his arm. "Carin, run! Ru … "

Carin bit off a sob and flew into the night. She ran, dodging around tree trunks and bushes. A second later the firing started and she was amazed at the loud "zinging" of the bullets past her head. Then she was overtaken by a feeling of weightlessness as a giant hand lifted her and carried her forward. She didn't feel anything as she smashed head first into a giant oak.

Prof. Hal Koch Journal, November 1, 1941

The Nazi bastards just left Carin and Morten. We had to search the woods to find them. The Jewish couple is missing and probably arrested. My God, my God! Your command to love thy enemies is very hard. At the moment I'm not capable of it.

I'm worried about Arne. He seems to think he is personally responsible for all of his group. We almost lost him when Poul was killed and now this.

Chapter 61. Studenternes Efterretniingtjeneste

Arne was waiting, sitting on the floor next to his office, when Professor Koch came into the hallway. Arne didn't respond to Koch's greeting.

"Arne, hello." Koch repeated. He unlocked his door and said, "Arne. Come in."

"Oh. Professor. Hi." He slowly climbed to his feet and followed Koch inside, where he slumped into a chair.

"What do we do? What do we do now, huh?" Arne stared at the table. "Poul. Carin. Morten. Asger freaked. What do we do now?"

Tears ran down his face and he began to pound his right fist into the table. Wham! Wham! Wham! The heavy table jumped with each blow.

Arne stopped pounding the table and scrubbed violently at his eyes with the back of his hand. For some time neither of them spoke.

"They were … all of you … like my own children," Koch said. "All of you, like my own children. I loved Poul. I loved Morten and Carin.

"Working with you has been one of the great privileges of my life. I am so proud of all of you. I'm heartbroken over Carin and Morten. I was crushed when Poul died … and I'm crushed again."

Arne looked at him and another tear ran down his face.

"You loved them too, didn't you," Koch spoke gently, quietly.

Arne nodded. They sat side by side for a while longer.

"Arne, we need a break, all of us. I want you to go away for a while, forget the resistance, forget everything and rest. I'm sending your whole group, what's left of it, for a holiday. When you are rested and somewhat recovered you come back and continue the fight. All right?"

"Okay, Prof," Arne said. "I wouldn't be much good for anything right now anyway."

"Where will you go, Arne?"

"Oh. I don't know. I can't go home … the stikkers are watching my folk's place."

"Hmm. Well, Bodil and I are going away for a bit too. Going to our cottage out in the country. Kind of rustic, but it should be peaceful and it's pretty. Got a nice little stream with lots of trout in it. Want to come along with us?"

"Thanks … Bodil might want you to herself for a change."

Koch laughed. "Yes, for the first couple of days. After that, she is always glad for something to keep me occupied. Come with us, Arne. We'll fish and take long walks in the country. My wife is a very wise, compassionate woman, she will help both of us."

And so Arne went on holiday with Hal and Bodil Koch. Brigitte went home to her mother. Tyge had no family and accepted Greta's invitation to go to her parent's home.

* * * * * * * *

Two weeks of rest and recreation allowed all of them to heal a little, but Arne wasn't ready to be a leader again.

Brigitte, Tyge and Greta went back to working with Aage Bertelsen on the rescue of the Jews. Professor Koch put Arne in touch with the underground students' information service, Studenternes Efterretniingtjeneste. This group gathered news from an enormous network all over Denmark, wrote it up, and distributed it to both the Danish underground press and the regular media around the world.

Arne's first assignment for the Studenternes Efterretniingtjeneste began with instructions to go to a particular café at 9:00 p.m. and meet a girl named Ulrike. He knew only that she was very tall, very thin, and would have a copy of Raj Munk's book of poetry. He was to ask her about Munk's political views.

When Arne entered the café he saw a girl reading in one corner. The book she had was Munk's poetry. He said, "May I join you."

She looked up at him but said nothing.

"Do you agree with Munk's views on democracy?" He asked.

"Hello," she smiled.

"Nice to meet you Ulrike."

She glanced around.

"We deal with hundreds, perhaps thousands of different people. None of us know more than a tiny piece of the Studenternes Efterretniingtjeneste so that the Nazis can't hurt us too much if one of us turns out to be an informer or is tortured into talking. For instance, Ulrike is not my real name and I have no idea what your real name is … nor do I want to know. After I train you, you will perhaps never see me again."

Arne digested this in silence while he thought about the implications of running a news gathering operation in secret.

"Okay. What must I do?"

"You're a courier. Reporters and photographers, most of whom we don't know, deliver their material to us via drop-points, one drop-point for each of them. Every day you'll make the rounds to see if there is anything to pick up. Then you'll take it to your contact person who delivers it to the office. That way neither the reporters nor you know enough to hurt us much if one of you is taken by the Gestapo."

"That's it. That's all I do?"

"That's it. It's a full-time job. How's your memory? There are a lot of drop-points. You want to be careful about putting things in writing. Here, look, here's my notes on where the drop points are."

Ulrike handed him a tiny notebook. Arne opened the book and saw these entries.

> 62. on the wings of angels
> 63. fallen heroes
> 64. most handsome cook
> 65. skinniest waiter

"These entries wouldn't mean anything for anybody else, but they remind me of the drop points. You have to develop your own reminders."

Arne paged through the little notebook. One hundred and nine entries.

"You go to over a hundred drop points every day?"

"Every day. Six days a week. Not on Sunday. You need a good bicycle."

"Mine is pretty decrepit."

"Um. I can get one for you. Meet me here at 6:00 a.m. tomorrow. Give some thought to your clothing and bring adhesive tape. We will go, oh, maybe thirty or forty kilometers by the end of the day. You'll need the adhesive tape when you start to develop sores … I had blisters all over my thighs and buttocks the first two weeks, I could hardly walk."

Ulrike started her rounds at 6:00 a.m., stopped for breakfast at 7:30 to avoid the worst of the morning rush, resumed the rounds at about 8:15 a.m. and made her drop of everything she collected that day around 3:00 p.m.

Arne's first day took considerably longer because at each stop he had to think of some unique descriptor that would help him remember but would not be a good clue for anyone else. At 5:15 p.m. they finally made their drop and Arne walked home, pushing his bicycle, legs aching and adhesive tape covering several tender spots on his buttocks and thighs. Arne stopped twice on his way home and chalked "V" on a wall.

The second day took even longer because Ulrike insisted that Arne try to remember each drop point. After each stop, Arne looked at his next notation and tried to remember what it referred to. He succeeded in about half of the cases.

Where he failed, he tried to think of a better clue and ended up changing quite a few of them. It was 6:25 p.m. when they finally finished.

Arne was exhausted and discouraged. Thighs feel like they're on fire. And my butt hurts. Not sure I'll ever remember all the drop points.

"You're doing well," Ulrike said in parting. "When I started, there were only fifty-seven drop points and we added the others over time … I didn't have to learn them all at once."

Arne thanked her and walked his bicycle home. Stopping to put "V" on a wall was such a welcome relief that he did it ten or twelve times.

It took three more days before Ulrike was satisfied that Arne knew the route thoroughly. By that time his leg muscles were becoming used to all the pedaling, but the raw spots on his thighs were very sore.

He gave up on removing the tape at the end of the day and just added more layers each morning.

Saturday, his first day without Ulrike and his last until Monday, he decided the layers of tape had to come off. He started to peel the tape off and stopped almost immediately. It hurt! Maybe a hot bath will loosen the tape.

After a half-hour of soaking, he tried again. Still hurt. The whole damn inner thigh is sore.

He gritted his teeth and yanked. Ouch. Only a third of the tape came loose.

Two more savage yanks and one thigh was free of tape. That hurt too much, gotta try something else. Maybe a good stiff drink.

He pulled on his clothes and walked a block and a half to the local pub. Three quick shots of whiskey later he went home and, thus fortified, managed to remove the rest of the tape.

He applied a soothing lotion to his mistreated thighs, drank a big glass of water, and fell into bed where he slept for ten hours straight.

With the resilience of youth, a day of rest had Arne feeling strong again. His thighs were still a little tender but with judiciously applied tape, they didn't bother him much when he made his rounds Monday. By the end of that week, Arne was feeling fitter than he had been since joining the resistance and he no longer needed the tape on his thighs.

The daily routine of picking up the news dispatches from the drop points was boring and seemed perfectly safe. No challenge there. By the end of the week he could think about Carin and Morten without feeling he was about to cry.

As Arne's rounds became familiar, he increasingly daydreamed of Brigitte ... he missed her and hoped she sometimes thought of him.

Nights were bad. One recurring nightmare featured an SS officer with a pistol that never ran out of bullets as he shot and shot and shot. The victims of the killer varied, sometimes it was Poul or Morten or Carin and sometimes it was another member of the team.

The dreams were emotionally devastating. Terrible guilt. All alone, never see Brigitte again. Just a nightmare, it's not real. Get a grip Sejr! How can a damned dream make you feel so bad?

Arne's third week as a courier passed uneventfully. He was increasingly bored with the routine, but in strange sort of way was thankful for it ... he needed a job that was not stressful. Finishing his rounds by mid-afternoon gave him plenty of time for novels. Every evening for the last several weeks was spent with a book. This Saturday evening was the same. Arne was on page seventy-two of a new novel when there was a knock on his door.

Arne's first reaction was fear. Nobody ever knocked on the door, it must be the Nazis.

The knock repeated. Got a happy little rhythm to it. Somebody is laughing. Can't be Nazis.

He threw open the door and discovered Brigitte, Tyge and Greta.

"Get your jacket, Arne," Brigitte smiled. "We're going out."

Arne was speechless. He hugged Brigitte, Tyge and Greta in turn. Still without saying a word, he ran for his jacket, abandoning them all on the landing.

"I'm so glad to see you." Arne had to stop himself from babbling. He missed all of them. Brigitte especially.

They did nothing very special that evening. Shared a meal. Reminisced about Carin, Morten, and Poul. Dried each other's tears. Caught up on what each of them had done since they were last together. Dawdled over zichory for several hours.

Late in the evening, Arne noticed that Greta and Tyge seemed to hold hands or just touch each other a lot. He finally looked at Tyge and asked, "Is there something about you two that I don't know?"

Tyge just smiled but Greta broke into giggles.

"Oh, I don't think it's official," Brigite smiled. "Tyge is planning his old age around Greta and hordes of children."

"We spent two weeks at Greta's parents," Tyge said. "When I had a minute to think, I realized that Greta was the most amazing girl I've ever known. After the first kiss ... " Tyge looked at Greta and stopped.

"I looked in his eyes one day," Greta said. "I just knew how he felt. Neither of us said a word. I just grabbed him and kissed him. It was the most wonderful kiss. And it led ..." Greta blushed.

"It led to more kissing and I don't intend to stop," Tyge said. He kissed Greta full on the lips.

Arne and Brigitte burst into applause. Soon thereafter they paid their bill and walked to Arne's flat.

Brigitte slipped her hand around Arne's upper arm.

"Do you think this will ever be over?" Brigitte said. "Will the Nazis ever go home and leave us in peace?"

They walked several more paces.

"I don't know, Brigitte. I do know I'm grateful for good comrades. I couldn't stand it without you and the others."

To comfort her or maybe himself, he slipped his arm around Brigitte's waist. Brigitte sort of snuggled into his side and he continued to hold her as they walked in silence.

The three of them walked Arne home and Arne watched their cab pull away. Felt awfully nice to hold Brigitte. Kind of surprised myself, putting my arm around her. She seemed to like it though. A nice, comradely gesture of support. Wish I could kiss her.

Greta and Tyge. Didn't see that coming, but they fit together. Nice. Why can't I have that with Brigitte?

Arne groaned inwardly and went inside to get his novel. It was a long book and he finished it as the sun came up. He made himself some breakfast and then slept the rest of the morning, dreaming of Brigitte gazing at him with eyes full of love.

He came awake, sometime after the dream about Brigitte, crying because a demon was taunting him about his stupidity in allowing Poul to be killed. The dream about Brigitte had faded away unremembered as dreams often do and he was left only with his grief and guilt about his three dead comrades.

Chapter 62. New Tactics

By mid-November, the initial flood of refugees had slowed to a trickle. According to the Freedom Council estimates there were perhaps five hundred Jews still left in Denmark. Aage Bertelsen and his group had transported over 700 Jews to Sweden and had an excellent system of safe houses, cabs, lorries and boats. SS General Pancke, however, was making the rescue effort increasingly difficult.

Tarben, at 53 years old, had been a fisherman all his life and owned his own boat. Only after his first trip did he begin to worry about the consequences of getting caught when he realized that his wife would have no income if he were arrested and his boat confiscated.

The incident with the German officer finding the Rabbi and the others in his hold reinforced the point. He knew an SS officer would never have let them go. For the rest of his trips, he charged 2000 kroner per passenger and the money all went into the special hiding place in the back wall of the cottage … just in case.

On the morning of November 4, Tarben set out with one passenger hidden behind a special panel in the cabin of his boat. He was half-way across the Oresund when the German patrol boat stopped him. He wasn't too worried because they had searched him several times without finding the secret panel.

The big German shepherd dog was something new. Tarben tried not to show his nervousness as the dog sniffed all around the hold. Then the dog's handler took it into the cabin. A minute later Tarben heard the splintering of wood and then the triumphant shout of the troopers as they found his passenger.

Tarben and the captured Jewish man were handcuffed and roughly tossed into the German patrol boat. Tarben wondered if he would ever see his beautiful boat again.

Tarben was taken directly to Gestapo headquarters and tossed into a tiny cell, too small for him to lie down and without furnishings of any kind. He spent a cramped night and toward morning, when his pleadings had no effect and he could hold it no longer, he finally voided his bladder and bowels in one corner. To complete his misery, he could no longer even sit down without soiling himself.

Around mid-day they came for him.

They led him to a larger room and, after removing all his clothes, bound him, naked, flat on his back on a long stainless steel table, with his arms stretched above his head. They left him there for what seemed a long time, long enough that his arms became very painful from the stretching and then finally went numb.

It was sometime in the middle of the afternoon when the Gestapo officer came to see Tarben. The officer spent several seconds examining Tarben, walking completely around him.

"I am Gruplietenant Specht and it is my job to find out who you work for."

Tarben noticed he was carrying a long flexible wooden rod and that he had a habit of tapping it against the palm of his left hand.

"What is your name?"

Tarben was silent.

"Come, come, Captain. We already know your name, I was just being friendly. I really would prefer being friendly, you know. But … if you refuse to cooperate my superiors will insist that I get nasty. You really wouldn't want that, it is very painful."

Tarben began to be very afraid but he remained silent while Specht circled his table.

"Now, Captain, what is your name?"

Tarben was silent.

The blow to the bottom of his feet was excruciating and Tarben involuntarily cried out.

"Perhaps you have an aversion to saying your name. Very well, who gives you your orders?"

Tarben was silent.

The blow to his feet was repeated so many times and so quickly the pain kept building, becoming more and more intense. Tarben screamed until he was hoarse and still the blows continued.

When the beating finally stopped Tarben was crying without even realizing it.

Specht's voice was pleasant, conversational, friendly.

"Now Captain Tarben, you really don't want any more of that, do you? The name of your superior, please."

Tarben cointinued crying but said nothing.

The flogging and questioning alternated for what seemed an eternity. When they unstrapped him and stood him on his feet, he collapsed from the pain. They dragged him to a cell with a bed but no mattress and a commode in the corner.

The next day the ordeal resumed. Tarben quickly lost track of the days. He broke his silence now and again to curse at Specht.

The beatings, rather than breaking him, hardened his resolve. Whatever they want, I won't give it to them. I'm a hard man. I'm tougher than anyone.

Tarben began to hope for death. They've destroyed my body. Never be good for anything again.

Tarben was in such a fog of pain that he didn't realize his guards were dragging him outside. The guards lifted him and threw him into the back of a truck. His head banged into the bed of the truck and he momentarily lost consciousness.

When he woke up he wondered why the sun was in his eyes. Then he saw the boots of the guards and remembered … a truck, going somewhere.

He wanted to know what was going on. So tired. Everything hurts. Maybe kill me now. That would be good, no more pain. … more pain might force me to talk.

Lots of money in the hiding place … family is okay. Sunshine feels good …

The truck stopped and Tarben tried to get out. He half-fell, was half-lifted out. He fell to the ground.

Grass. Always liked grass and sunshine. Time now. Shoot, damnit! No more pain.

The guards didn't make him wait.

They left the body there on the grass in the warm sunshine.

* * * * * * * * *

Aage Bertelsen was trying to adjust to General Pancke's new tactics. The German Shepherd dogs were being used every time a boat got stopped.

Aage had a special committee working on the problem. They came up with a powder made of dried blood and cocaine.

A dog would smell the blood, sniff at it, and get cocaine in its nose. After that the dog couldn't smell anything for some time.

Aage's people sprinkled the mixture on the gangplanks of all the boats and, when they had any Jews hiding in the boat, on the deck. After that there was no more trouble with dogs finding Jews on the boats.

Aage was also worried about people talking under torture. They tried to make sure people knew as little as possible, still anyone who broke completely would seriously hurt them.

They set up a fake office. Nobody worked there, but they kept lots of up to date information there, carefully chosen so that it wouldn't be very damaging. All the captains and field operatives were instructed that, if they were tortured, they were to hold out as long as they could. When they felt they were close to breaking, they were to tearfully reveal the location of the fake office.

If one of their people was caught, they would set up another fake office so the ruse could be used again.

Chapter 63. Endings and Beginnings

Arne's nightmares still came two or three times a week and they still had the same effect. He would wake up soaking wet, hoarse from screaming, and overcome with feelings of guilt and sorrow. On the mornings following a nightmare, he took to drinking wine until time to go out on his courier route.

Arne's routine seldom varied. After completing his route he went home, ate, and read another novel. While he read, he drank wine. It helped him sleep.

Ulrike had explained that if the Nazis ever figured out what he was doing and were smart about it, they would follow him and learn all the drop points. Then they would be able to lay in wait for the reporters and photographers. It was important, she emphasized, that he make sure he wasn't being followed.

Arne frequently forgot Ulrike's cautions. The job was boring. The only interesting thing about it was seeing how fast he could go, how hard he could push his body.

It always scared Arne when he realized he wasn't being cautious. He would obsessively look over his shoulder and double back on his route several times. This would last for a couple of days.

He never saw any sign of any one watching him and would soon begin to lose himself again in the drug of speed and tired muscles.

Arne never went out and never saw anybody except Tyge, Greta, and Brigitte who came by on Saturday nights once or twice a month. They were still working on rescuing Jews, but the numbers had slowed to a trickle.

One Saturday evening Arne answered the now familiar knock on his door and discovered to his mixed delight and alarm that Brigitte was alone.

"Hey. What happened to Tyge and Greta?"

"I'm glad to see you too. They went to see Greta's parents. You're stuck with just me."

"Well ... I'll do my best to put up with you. Where shall we go?"

"Lets just walk a while, okay?"

It was cold and felt like snow, but both of them had warm coats and hats. They walked a couple of blocks.

"Arne, Greta tells me you have a thing for me?"

"Yes." Arne could not meet her eyes.

"Yes, what?"

"I do, always have, since I first met you."

Brigitte caught his arm, stopping him.

"Why didn't you ever let me know?"

"Didn't think it would do any good." Arne shrugged. "You were always with Asger."

"Asger! A total pest, I couldn't get rid of him."

"I thought you and Asger ..."

"I tolerated Asger for the resistance, that's all."

Arne's eyes got big but he didn't say anything, just stared at her.

She finally leaned toward him and her lips found his.

He returned the kiss enthusiastically.

"You like me too?" Arne asked when the kiss ended.

"Yes. Wondered about you for a long time."

"Oh my god! All this time ..."

"All this time you were being dense ... and slow."

"Ah, I'm an idiot. An idiot in love." Arne kissed her again. A long kiss later he released her and they began to walk again, holding hands and both of them smiling.

"Feed me," Brigitte said. "I'm ravenous."

The rest of the evening passed in a delirious happy blur for Arne and culminated in a lingering and wholly satisfying kiss when he dropped Brigitte at her flat.

* * * * * * * *

Brigitte's schedule was erratic, but when she was free Saturday or Sunday, they were together. Arne relished her presence, it didn't matter what they did or where they went, so long as they were together, he was happy.

When they were apart Arne worried about her. Even his nightmares changed, although they still tormented him once or twice a week. Sometimes the SS officer shot Poul, Morten, or Carin but increasingly Brigitte was the victim. It took more and more wine for Arne to make it through to breakfast after the latest nightmare.

Part Four: End Game

March 1941 – End of WW II

Prof. Hal Koch Journal, March 20, 1941

Finally some good news on the war front. The British are not only hanging on under the Nazi blockade and bombardment, they and the Australians attacked the Nazi forces in North Africa and took Tobruk from the Nazis. The German armies are not invincible.

General Best must be pretty unhappy. Six months ago our resistance was on the verge of collapse from sheer exhaustion. Then Hitler's idiocy about Jews galvanized the entire country into action. According to the Swedes, more than 7,000 Jews made it into their country. Everybody forgot about their own troubles in the urgency to help our Jewish friends. We came out of it more united and stronger than ever. General Best turned out to be our motivator. Indeed God works in mysterious ways.

Bodil's counseling hasn't seemed to help Arne. She tells me six weeks of therapy is not very long, but Brigitte is very worried about him ... as am I. At least the valium is letting him sleep more regularly, but it doesn't seem to stop the nightmares.

We are going to win this struggle with the Nazis, but at what cost? Just in my group ... Poul, Morten, and Carin all dead. Asger slunk home in fear and defeat. Arne a psychological basket case. Brigitte, Tyge and Greta hanging on, but for how long.

The leadership, my God, my God. Vald looks like a corpse. I would have collapsed long ago if it weren't for Bodil and my faith ... every time I feel I can't go on, God renews me. King Christian has aged noticeably but he seems better than any of us.

When we planned a campaign of strategic nonviolence we never, in our wildest nightmares, imagined having to fight someone of Hitler's insanity.

Dear God, give us strength. And let America enter the war. Soon.

Chapter 64. Dansk Industri Syndikat

The Copenhagen branch of Dansk Industri Syndikat A. S. had a skilled workforce of 187 and normally churned out large quantities of high quality handguns, rifles and shotguns. The Nazis put them to work producing rifles for their soldiers.

The factory started a deadly dance of obstinate refusal to work for the Nazis. The factory was unusual only in that they managed to avoid any deaths among their management.

The first batch of 600 rifles took three times as long as normal to produce and all of them had crooked bores. They were worthless.

The shipment of unusable rifles resulted in the assignment of two engineers, one of whom was SS Lieutenant Hartung, and a squad of troops to the factory. Lieutenant Hartung announced that all rifles would be inspected upon completion of the bores and every crooked bore would result in the death of the responsible machinist. There were no more crooked bores.

Work proceeded on the rifles, albeit slowly. When the next batch of 600 rifles was ready, it was discovered that the firing pin was slightly oversize and stuck after each shot. In order to fire the rifle a second time, one had to remove the bolt and use a small punch to drive the firing pin back into place. The guns were taken apart and the firing pins sent back to the factory.

When the firing pins were ready, testing of the guns resumed. Lieutenant Hartung tested one of the rifles and was pleased that his first five shots were highly accurate. The second group was equally accurate and he almost stopped but decided to try one more group.

The third group was awful. Off to the right. Must not have been breathing right. Try another group.

Damn. Even farther to the right. Wait … a nice group, just all to the right. The sights must have moved.

Front sight off to the left. It's loose! Can move it with my fingers. More sabotage.

What else have they done? Tap the back sight a little … Shit, it moves too.

These fucking Danes aren't going to get away with this! We will have an end to these games. They will make good rifles!

Let's see the bolt. Works well enough … a rough spot, something not as smooth as it should be.

All the parts of the bolt seem okay.

The spring in the trigger mechanism … Where're the needle nose pliers? Stretch the spring a little. Okay. Stretch it a little more. Oh, crap! It stays stretched. They used soft steel for the spring. It'll fail almost at once.

Somebody must die!

They're clever … no records to show the responsible party. No matter. Kill a few … in secret.

Kill some supervisors in their beds. They'll get the message and won't be able to prove a thing.

Lieutenant Hartung dined alone that evening. Select somebody popular with the workforce. So many that deserve to die.

The production manager never shows any respect … love to kill him. But, no, we need his expertise.

Ah. The welding shop foreman was a doddering old fool but extremely popular. The entire staff treated him like their grandfather. A perfect target.

The assistant superintendent. The shop could function just fine without him.

Good thing I had my man follow these fools to their homes. False addresses only save them for a little while.

Lieutenant Hartung allowed himself a second glass of schnapps to celebrate the imminent slaughter of the two men.

* * * * * * * * *

Gregers Povelsen was worried. Supposed to watch and anticipate and plan … the wife claims it's mostly worrying … current situation warrants a lot of worry.

Gregers formal job at the Dansk Industri Syndikat rifle factory was as a janitor, but that was just a cover.

No one, especially the arrogant Nazis, ever paid any attention to a janitor. Gregers real job was that of Chief of Security for the plant. His job was to anticipate and counter the Nazi attempts to brutalize them.

While Lieutenant Hartung was testing the new rifle, Gregers picked up the cigarette butts that littered the area behind the firing range benches. Hartung's rage as he discovered the defects frightened him. He moved away.

Hartung will act to punish us. Only question is the form the punishment will take. It'll be brutal.

He hurried off to find the superintendent. Our top people need to be out of the factory, out of Hartung's reach.

Gregers' security committee had a meeting scheduled that day for 4:30 p.m., as they did each time a delivery of arms was made to the Nazis. Gregers' first question to the group was whether they had anything to add to his observations of Hartung, any clue or insight at all into what the Nazis might do to retaliate for the rifles' defects.

One man commented, "I was nearby when the sergeant dismissed the squad for the day. He didn't give them any special orders."

Another said, "I strolled past while Hartung, his aide, and the sergeant were in a huddle about thirty minutes ago. All I could hear was the aide saying something like '… late. What time should we expect you …'"

Nobody else had anything to add.

Gregers said, "I guess they aren't going to kill any of us .. at least not this time. But I tell you, Hartung was really beside himself when he discovered the spring was the wrong steel. He's not going to let it go."

They sat there and thought about it for a minute. A man who hadn't spoken so far cleared his throat.

"Tonight. Hartung is going to act tonight. He was telling his aide he would be late tomorrow."

They looked at the speaker and finally Gregers nodded, yes, yes, that made sense.

"OK, get word to the top people that they have to be out of their houses tonight and get the Neighborhood Watch people in place to try to catch the bastards in action."

* * * * * * * * *

Lieutenant Hartung still had a pleasant buzz from the schnapps when he got home at 7:15 that evening. He spent a pleasurable fifteen minutes touching up the already razor sharp edge of his favorite knife, listened to several of Wagner's heroic march pieces and at 10:30 p.m. set his alarm for 1:30 a.m. A half hour later he got up. Too keyed up to sleep.

He put Wagner on again. Can't sit still. Turn it off.

Knife's as sharp as I can make it. Revolver is loaded. Torch has fresh batteries. Crow bar for forcing the window. Clothes are dark. All identifying marks gone. Bicycle's dark colored, tape covers the reflectors.

By 11:45 p.m. he had checked everything twice. Everything's ready. Calm down, patience. Damn hand is shaking. Shit, man, cool it. Be okay soon as I get started. Waiting is hard part.

Two deaths will frighten the crap out of them. Going to be hard to hide my glee. Need to keep a poker face for a few days.

Only 11:30? Still too early.

Midnight! I'll ride by, see if he's asleep. No need to wait longer.

At 12:22 a.m. Hartung coasted slowly past the welding foreman's bungalow. No lights, the fool is asleep. Houses on both sides are dark too.

Vacant lot over there is dark. Leave the bicycle there, out of sight. Careful now, stay in the shadow of the hedge.

Okay, step through the light to the back porch, into the shadow again. Door's locked. Window too.

Good thing I brought the crowbar … work it under the frame … pry.

The bar slipped loose with a small sound of tearing wood. He glanced around.

It's okay, wasn't loud enough for anybody to hear.

Get the bar in further. Push! Wiggle it back and forth. Finally, that's enough.

He put some weight on the bar but the window latch held. He looked all around again and then put his whole weight on the bar. There was a loud "snick", loud enough to startle him, and the bar suddenly moved freely. He froze, then looked all around again.

Wait. Just wait a bit, make sure the old man didn't hear it.

Nothing. Ease the window up.

Hartung stepped through the window and into the room. Can't see a thing. Risk a quick flash of the torch. Kitchen. Door straight ahead.

No creaks from the floor.

Calm and focus. Going to be easy. Stupid Danes don't know who they're messing with. Slow and easy now.

It took Hartun twelve minutes to explore the bungalow and discover the old man's bedroom. There he is. Alone. Doesn't even have a woman. Pathetic old fool.

The old man was lying on his side, facing away, with one hand curled up under his chin.

Grab the hair, yank the head back.

Ah! Not enough hair.

An ear, then.

With his left hand, Hartung jerked the ear back and drew the knife across the exposed throat.

Wow! Amazing! What a fountain, at least two feet high.

He held the ear, with knife poised, until the fountain subsided. The old man's body jerked a few times but otherwise hardly responded to being killed.

Hartung carefully wiped his knife on the blankets. Nothing to it. The whole damn bunch will be weeping tomorrow.

Slowly and carefully, as soundlessly as he came, he went out the window and retrieved his bicycle.

Hartung could barely contain his feelings. Strong. Savage. A real warrior. The workers are going to shit themselves tomorrow.

He pedaled along at breakneck speed. He was soon out of breath and his legs burned. He slowed to a more reasonable pace and by the time he rode past his next target's house he had once again achieved a state of calm readiness.

House is dark. No vacant lot … that big tree is pretty dark. Hard for anybody to see the bike there.

Have to cross some open space. Everything dark nearby, nobody to notice me.

Back porch again. Door locked. Window too. Heavy curtains over the window, can't see inside. No matter.

The window lock yielded easily to his crowbar and made hardly any noise.

He had to lift the curtain and climb through at the same time and it was awkward. His upper body and right leg were through the window when he sensed movement just through the curtain.

He stabbed the knife straight ahead and hit someone, someone who cried out and moved away. Something struck Hartung a light glancing blow on the side of the head and he thought it was a club dropped by the person he stabbed.

He dived into the middle of the room, landed awkwardly on his side but rolled and came quickly to his knees, shaking off the curtain that clung to him. He crouched there, shifted the knife to his left hand, and drew his pistol. Torches snapped on and he swiveled desperately toward the lights. He was raising the pistol when something hit him in the head.

* * * * * * * * *

Gregers Povelsen's elation at the news of Lieutenant Hartung's death turned to grief and anger at himself when they discovered the shop foreman. A fucking failure! Who would have thought the bastards would kill an old man like that? He was my kid's godfather. How could I not protect him?

The club split Hartung's skull. Saved the trouble of a trial. I'm glad he's dead. How the hell am I going to tell my wife about this … she'll be devastated.

This job is making me old.

Now I gotta worry about German reprisals for Hartung. Won't be anything official, they won't admit one of theirs was an assassin. Some of us will die for it, that's for sure.

The factory will have a few days of peace until they send another jackal to replace Hartung. Maybe we use the time to replace our high-grade steel with some inferior crap.

Chapter 65. The Odense Steel Shipyard

The Nazis initially assigned six engineers, including SS Kapitan Schobel, to work with the shipyard. A month into the project, the Germans realized the shipyard had managed to produce essentially nothing, at least nothing that would work.

Another dozen engineers and three squads of soldiers were assigned to the shipyard. With eighteen engineers and three squads of soldiers peering over their shoulders, the shipyard had to at least pretend to be working industriously. The second month of the sub-building project saw a significant increase in the parts produced.

The third month of the project SS Kapitan Schobel realized that a lot of the finished products were being lost. His investigation revealed that parts seemed to disappear between leaving one shop and arriving at the next shop.

Kapitan Schobel spent two days observing, watching the process for routing parts. His three squads of troopers were standing around all day. Schobel replaced the couriers who transported parts from shop to shop with his troopers.

It took Schobel two weeks to implement a system of paperwork to control and record the flow of parts among the 14 different shops in the shipyard.

Seven days after implementing the new system, Schobel's engineers came to him and begged him to get some clerks to help with the paperwork. Eight of the engineers were spending full-time just dealing with the paperwork generated by the new system. No one was monitoring several of the shops.

Kapitan Schobel convinced General Best to send him ten clerks.

* * * * * * * * *

Knud Einstad had four different parts on his workbench. Each part was only partially machined and would eventually need more work from his station. Most of the last four days had been wasted in setting up for one part, doing just a little work on it, and then setting up for another part.

Knud knew he was playing a dangerous game. If one of the Nazi engineers stopped and seriously studied the parts and the respective blueprints, they would be able to see that he was wasting time.

Knud walked to the other end of the shop and picked up one of Kapitan Schobel's new forms. Back at his station, he started working on it. Scribble, make it hard to read. Oh, yeah … List several ways the part could be damaged. Takes lots of writing. Use incorrect code for the destination. Okay, all done.

Hmmm. Smear a little grease on it, make it harder to read. There. That'll keep a Nazi busy for a while.

Knud attached the form to the part, carried it to the far end of the shop, and put it in on the shelf marked "out".

Knud struggled to keep from smiling. The part needed to go about four meters across the room. The incorrect code would first send it to the other side of the shipyard, almost a kilometer away.

Knud spent the next five minutes doing completely unnecessary cleaning. He then walked back to get one more of Schobel's forms and went through the exercise of filling out a form for a second part.

Two more iterations of the form routine disposed of all four of the parts on his workbench. Wasted most of the morning. Not bad.

Knud went over to the Nazi engineer in charge of his shop and informed him he had nothing to work on. Having thus demonstrated his enthusiastic desire to be a good worker, Knud happily went back to his station and tried to think up some additional ways to gum up the works.

* * * * * * * *

Arne helped Tyge, Greta and Brigitte deliver several heavy boxes to the post office. The boxes were filled with books, each of which was gift wrapped and addressed to a German officer.

Kapitan Schobel received one of the gift wrapped books. Curious. No return address. Maybe it's from my mother?

The book title is "Fuhrerworte" ... the words of the Fuhrer. But the illustration! Hitler with a very large head and squinty eyes. On a white horse carrying a swastika banner. Heresy. Who would dare?

Inside, Hitler's speeches. No, short excerpts. Chosen to make him look ridiculous. These bastards dare to ridicule our Fuhrer! They should be shot.

This book, this "Fuhrerworte", is subversive. Can't be seen with it. Throw it away, no one can know I had it.

Am I the only one? Did others receive it?

Schobel eventually took it to his superior, claiming he found it.

Two days later he saw a news item in one of the underground newspapers boasting that they had mailed this abomination of a book to 2000 German officers.

* * * * * * * *

Kapitan Schobel was amazed at the amount of paperwork his routing system was generating, but fewer parts were being lost so he persisted. By the end of the second week of the new system he had a full time clerk assigned to each of the shipyard's 14 shops.

The third week of the new system he realized he didn't have enough couriers ... there were large backlogs of parts waiting for transport and, as a result, many of the workstations were idle, waiting for parts. Schobel went to Best and asked for more troops.

The meeting with Best did not go well. Best explained, in icy cold tones, that they were very short-handed, there were no 'extra' troops to be had, and that engineer SS Kapitan Schobel was damn well expected to get results with the troops he already had.

Kapitan Schobel called a meeting of his engineers.

"The shipyard is being very creative and quite effective in preventing any work from getting done.

"This is the basic problem as I see it. The shipyard is an extremely complex system. The production side has shops for planning, design, procurement, welding (several), machining (several), pipe fitting, electrical, hull assembly, and several others. No one person can grasp the system in its entirety. And since we are new to this system, each of us is still learning about the parts we are trying to supervise.

"The workers who have been in the shipyard for some time understand the details of its operations better than we. And that will be the case for some time to come, we can not hope to master the details anytime soon.

"Given the complexity of the shipyard, it is clear we can not control it or the workers by focusing on the details of what they are doing. There are not enough of us and we don't have enough hours in the day to deal with all the relevant details. The parts routing system that we implemented a few weeks ago demonstrates the problems with that approach ... we tried to control the system by focusing on some critical details and all that happened is that the Danes overwhelmed us with additional detail. That entire parts routing system was a mistake, one for which I accept responsibility.

"But we learned from our mistake. We can not win this by focusing on the details.

"We need to focus on results. We will define the results expected from each shop and each workstation. Failure to achieve those results will carry serious penalties.

"I need the four senior engineers to work with me to develop the initial hierarchy of parts. Then we will assign a set of parts to each of you, and you will work with the appropriate shops to assign responsibilities. In the meantime, those not helping me with the initial breakdown, try to see if you can identify the most troublesome of the workers. We will undoubtedly need to make an example of several of them."

A German submarine, with its diesel engines, ballast tanks and pumps, life support systems, torpedo tubes, and sound deadening mechanisms includes thousands of separate components. It took Schobel and his team two weeks to develop the set of objective results they intended to impose on the shipyard. In the meantime, without the engineers looking over the shoulders of the workforce, the already glacial pace of production slowed to very nearly a full stop.

* * * * * * * *

Knud Einstad was actually disappointed when SS Kapitan Schobel scrapped his new parts routing system and announced that they were going back to the old system. Oh well, we have other tactics we can use.

The new system was actually pretty simple: the Nazis had a list of some 8,000 parts or subassemblies and each was assigned to a particular person who was to be held accountable for that particular part being produced correctly and on time.

Oh boy, Knud thought, this is going to be fun. No provisions for scheduling the work. No rules for deciding priorities when more than one part needed work by the same machine. These idiots have no idea what they just handed us.

The flow of parts through the shipyard has several different levels of scheduling systems. The planning department first prepared some general priorities. These priorities dealt with the months remaining before a ship was to be delivered, the time various subsystems took to complete, and the sequence in which the subsystems were needed. These priorities were revised every couple of months for a typical ship.

Each shop superintendent took these priorities and made his own schedule. The shop schedules guided the craftsmen in the shops.

Knud and every other craftsman in the yard always changed their own part of the schedules. They had too. The officials in their fancy offices didn't know the idiosyncrasies of the shops. Something unforeseen always happened. The craftsman on the floor always had to make adjustments.

The system worked because the craftsmen knew what had to be done and who could do it and they continually made little adjustments to keep things moving along.

The Shipyard Resistance Committee met that evening. Every craftsman was instructed to act as selfishly as possible. Every one of them would demand priority for their particular part.

They would instantly have backlogs for some of the workstations. And whenever there was the slightest bit of discretion about where to route a part, it would be routed to one of the bottleneck stations.

Each of them would complain to the Nazi engineers that their part was going to be delayed, they couldn't get it through the bottleneck workstations.

The Nazis would then have the choice of accepting delays on the schedule or trying to manage the workflow. Delays were of course what the Nazis were trying to avoid, so the Danes were pretty sure the Nazi engineers would try to manage the workflow.

Managing the workflow, of course, got the Nazis right back into the morass of trying to deal with the details of the shipyard. All the workers had to do to slow things to a crawl was to simply defer to the Nazi engineers on all scheduling questions.

Knud, as a master machinist, was assigned responsibility for 17 different parts and 12 subassemblies. He spent seventy-five minutes looking through the blueprints for his products, then strolled past the other three master machinists in his shop and asked them to meet him in the restroom. A few minutes later they were all there.

"Looks to me like the number three milling machine could be a huge bottleneck," Knud said.

"I'm thinking the same," the oldest among them said.

The other two thought about it a minute and agreed.

"OK, we route as much as we can to that machine."

They left the restroom, one at a time and spread the word to the rest of the shop. That evening when the resistance committee met, each shop had identified one or more bottleneck processes that everyone was to try to use.

Two days later the shipyard had long lines of parts in the queues for the bottleneck machines and most of the other workstations were standing idle.

Knud and one of his friends staged a shouting match over whose parts would get priority on the bottleneck machine. The two of them stood toe-to-toe shouting at each other until their Nazi engineer came over to ask what the problem was.

Both of them answered him, at length and high volume. He finally made them take turns talking, then arbitrarily decided that Knud's part should go second.

Knud said, "Sir, all these other parts are also in the queue. My part is much higher priority than most of these."

"Well, then, put both of you ahead of these others. Let them wait."

This declaration brought forth a howl of protest from four other machinists. The four of them surrounded the engineer and all of them declared that their parts had higher priority than did Knud's.

According to all of them, moving Knud's part ahead of theirs would delay the entire submarine. The engineer was momentarily at a loss.

"Okay, okay. I'll establish the priorities," the engineer said. "Leave everything as it is until I get a chance to see what should go first."

Knud and his fellows began another chorus of "My part is top priority."

"Quiet!" the engineer shouted. "You'll get your priorities as soon as I get them ready."

The machinists grumbled but moved off to their respective workstations. Most of them managed to hide their smiles.

* * * * * * * *

The Nazi engineer trying to schedule Knud's workflow quickly realized he didn't have enough information to make good decisions, but he didn't see how else to schedule the work. He thought that simply doing it by first come, first served would be hopelessly inefficient. He set to work to figure it out.

By the end of the week the German engineers were doing little other than scheduling parts through workstations. SS Kapitan Schobel was working just as hard as all the other engineers to keep the work moving smoothly.

Certain of the workstations continued to experience large backlogs.

Schobel made a habit of walking through the various shops at random intervals and everyone was always busy. He took that to mean that their scheduling was reasonably efficient. Otherwise, he reasoned, there would be lots of idle time on some of the workstations and all of them were busy.

All the engineers were tied up doing scheduling. There weren't any knowledgeable observers to tell if the craftsmen were actually working or making toys for their kids.

Two months after taking over the scheduling functions for the shipyard, SS Kapitan Schobel reviewed the productivity figures. Productivity was even lower than the abysmal levels prior to taking on the scheduling.

Eight months wasted. Eight months ago this misbegotten shipyard was tasked with producing a submarine. A yard of this size should have been able to produce a submarine in four months.

There is a learning curve involved, perhaps the first one might have taken six or even seven months. Nevertheless, one should be done by now. But no, this piece of crap of a factory had accomplished nothing. There wasn't one major subassembly that he could point to and say "that's done." Not one.

Schobel began to worry that General Pancke might demote him. Damnation. I would demote me. This is ridiculous.

Schobel knew that he had made major mistakes in trying to manage the shipyard. Most of his fellow officers would have made the same or worse mistakes.

Remember your speech on the folly of trying to control the details of the shipyard. I was right ... we can't deal with all the details.

I didn't hang on to that insight. Scheduling the workflow was just another dive into managing the details. The Danes defeated us ... again! ... with overwhelming detail.

The bastard Danes must be laughing at us.

Well, okay, we can't manage the details. So how the hell do we manage the yard?

Well, one thing we can do. Eighteen competent engineers. Eighteen engineers can monitor significant chunks of the work.

We can punish those who deliberately slow things down ... but not killing. Maybe flogging. Yes! Public flogging!

This is important. Hope General Pancke allows me to carry it through.

Maybe go to Pancke and tell him what I learned. Maybe there is a general lesson.

Schobel considered the politics of his situation for a few minutes, then instructed his aide to set up a meeting with General Pancke in about a week. With any luck I go from the patsy who failed to the guru who showed how to whip a hostile workforce into shape.

* * * * * * * *

Knud Einstad was surprised and disappointed at Schobel's announcement. Dropping all the new systems? Going back to the original, to before the Nazis took over. What the hell are they up to? What are all these Nazi engineers going to be doing?

Two days later Knud stopped in the middle of machining a part. He took it off the milling machine and was setting up for another part when Schobel himself stopped at his workstation.

"Herr Einstad, what are you doing?"

"Just setting up to machine this part." Knud pointed to the part.

Schobel picked up the part Knud had just removed from his machine

"This part, Herr Einstad, is it finished?"

"No, it's not finished. It just needs to go to another station."

"I see, Herr Einstad. Where is the blueprint for it?"

Knud tried to look unconcerned. He waved a hand at his bench but made no move toward it.

"The prints are there, with those others."

He hoped Schobel wouldn't take the time to dig through the pile and find the right prints. Aw crap. He's looking for it.

After several minutes, Schobel found the correct diagram. He looked from the diagram to the partially machined part several times.

"Herr Einstad." He said. "You disappoint me. I had thought you a master machinist. Yet you make the mistake of a novice, of a rank beginner. This part needs additional work on the very machine where you had it. I can only conclude that you need more motivation."

Schobel was still smiling. He's happy he caught me. He's vicious … God, is he going to shoot me?

Schobel turned from Knud and waved over two of his troopers. "Prepare this man for a flogging in … ," he paused to consult his watch. "Prepare him for a flogging right here, right now."

Schobel stood there with that hideous grin. Shit! This can't be happening. A flogging. God, no!

They stripped Knud to the waist and tied him face down across his own workbench. The long thin piece of wood cut his skin and Knud screamed. He screamed again with every blow. They hit him ten times and then left him there, sobbing in pain.

Two more men were flogged and the obvious tactics for slowing down the work were abandoned. No one wanted a flogging.

* * * * * * * *

A week later it was still painful for Knud to move around, but he was recovering. The skin on his back was very tight and he moved slowly, afraid that any quick motion might re-open some of the wounds.

There was general agreement that the Nazi engineers could fairly easily spot the work-station slow-downs. They would have to rely on other tactics. Mis-routing of parts, losing parts, and deliberately creating backlogs were all easily done and were all difficult to pin down to any one person. Deliberately making parts slightly the wrong size was more dangerous but, especially with complex parts, was an option.

Using the wrong kind of steel was also a particularly useful tactic. The choice of steel for a given part involved designers, purchasing, and planners. The use of an inferior steel was not usually discovered until a part failed, and then it was too late to find out who made it.

Chapter 66. The Nazi Generals

General Dr. Werner Best remembered his arrival in Denmark. Expected it to be a soft job … good for my career. These crazy Danes are completely unmanageable. No one could have done any better. High Command treating me like a second-rate has been. Life is so unfair.

Hitler's losing it. Britain still hanging on and we don't have the navy to finish them off. Instead of finishing Britian, Hitler seems intent on conquering North Africa. God only knows why, nothing there but desert and more desert.

Duckwitz played his role well. Warning the Danes should buy me some leniency in case Germany is finally defeated.

Moron Hanneken has the Wehrmacht running the post office, the telephone company, and the railroad. The troops that weren't playing at running these enterprises were patrolling the streets … supposedly. The Wehrmacht is blind, deaf and mute. The Danes and the Wehrmacht ignore each other and the Danes do whatever they want. Fat lot of good the Wehrmacht does us.

General Pancke … he has the SS and the Gestapo … all the good troops. Pancke is no moron, but he's just now figuring out what we're up against. The fool thought he would whip the Danes into shape, that the Danes wouldn't stand a chance against him. Well, he's starting to learn.

That damn Moellar keeps telling the world that most of the Jews escaped. The High Command seems to be buying my story … If they ever check the numbers … God help me. Those treasonous Wehrmacht bastards who helped the Jews might turn out to be my salvation … blame the escape of the Jews on them.

Ribbentrop has to know that the assassinations stopped when Pancke took over.

Only the Gestapo torture and the Danish Nazi street crime remained of the original plan to brutalize the Danes into submission. And the Danes managed to cut the street crime way down.

The entire SS is trying to force Danish industry into producing war materiel. And it isn't working. Almost a year now and we aren't close to completing the first submarine. Finally a shipment of 600 rifles from the Dansk Industri Syndikat. Please, God, let there be no problems with the rifles.

The artillery pieces seemed fine. Until we fired them a few times. The steel was so soft that the guns were in imminent danger of blowing up.

Good for my career! What a joke. Personal survival, that's what counts. Surrounded with rival generals. Severely limited options.

One bright spot. We all have the same rank, confuses the accountability.

Hanneken is a fool … a perfect scape goat. Pancke is more formidable, but he's only now starting to understand the power of the Danish strategy.

My memos to Ribbentrop accurately predicted the failure of Pancke's tactics. Ribbentrop considers me a failure … but so are Pancke and Hanneken.

God help me if Pancke succeeds. If Pancke succeeds, Ribbentrop will destroy me.

Chapter 67. King Christian

King Christian was tired. The daily ride through the streets of Copenhagen, feeling the powerful horse under him, receiving the heartfelt salutes of the Danes … these were a tonic for him, reviving his spirit and body.

Today it wasn't working. Even my stallion is tired. The arch in his neck is still there and he's still lifting his feet high. Ears and tail are drooping a little. Both of us are drooping a little.

A year under the Nazis. Seems like forever. The bastards are wearing us down. Still, our casualties are small compared to a conventional war.

Christian leaned forward and rubbed the horse's neck.

"Good boy, such a good horse. You don't like the Nazis either, do you?" Christian said. The stallion straightened his ears and lifted his tail.

"That's it," Christian said. "Can't let the bastards know they're getting to us."

Pepped up the horse, who's going to pep me up?

Sit tall, damnit! Smile!

Christian smiled and saluted three Danish men on the sidewalk.

* * * * * * * *

Christian returned from his ride and went to Vald's office. He stopped in the doorway and studied his friend for a moment. Vald's lost so much weight, clothes just hang on him. Face is all sharp angles and creases. Cheekbones stick out. A year ago his hair was salt and pepper, now it's white, only the beard still has a little color.

The stress is killing Vald ... killing all of us, but killing him faster.

Thank God our guards are Wehrmacht now.

The damned SS read every paper and listened to every conversation. Made life impossible. Constantly in fear for your life.

The Wehrmacht ... they just go through the motions.

Vald looked up, interrupting Christian's reverie.

"Christian. I was just thinking about you."

"Hello," Christian said. "Can you come to my office for a bit?"

They walked to Christian's office and sat in the chairs under the window. Their four guards seated themselves in the chairs Christian provided for them, chairs that were at the far end of the very large office.

By keeping their voices low, Christian and Vald could talk without being overheard.

Vald and Christian had each managed to attend one Freedom Council meeting in the last year, but not at the same time. Christian wondered if Best had any idea how much it hurt to be isolated from the decision making. Hope not. Don't want to give him any satisfaction.

"Things are too quiet," Christian said. "What do you think they're up to?"

"I don't understand it," Vald said. "Best seems to be showing no initiative."

"Has the Freedom Council gotten a report to you lately?" Christian asked.

"Yesterday. Very little to add to the public reports. Wehrmacht troops basically going through the motions without bothering anybody. SS and Gestapo as fanatical as ever. The Council thinks having three Nazi generals works to our advantage in keeping their policies sort of fragmented."

"What about our people?"

"None of the key people betrayed or caught." Vald said. "Bertelsen had pneumonia but is recovering and getting ready for some R and R. Koch concerned that our people are wearing out, sites Sejr as an example. The kid is having terrible recurring nightmares and after doing a great job leading a field team basically collapsed into a psych case and now just doing courier work. Koch thinks we will have many more like that."

"Is there anything to be done about it?" Christian asked.

"Koch thinks R and R might help."

"Yes, good," Christian responded. "Can you let them know that I strongly encourage holidays. Now is a good time with everything fairly quiet."

"I will."

Christian leaned back, a far away look in his eyes. Vald waited, sipping his now cold coffee. He sent Christian's assistant for more coffee.

Christian talked, in a nearly normal tone of voice, about his horse. Vald played along. After a few minutes of desultory and trivial conversation, Christian again lowered his voice.

"I don't understand their lack of action. We have almost totally frustrated their plans … why aren't they trying some new devilry?"

"I don't know," Vald said. "But I'm thankful for it."

"Maybe Berlin is preoccupied with other matters and Best is just happy to be left alone?"

"Perhaps so. I don't see what else he could do to us without generating the bad publicity they seem to fear."

"You think we've beaten them?"

"Easy, quiet," Vald whispered. "I don't know. Best's behavior is bizarre. Warning Duckwitz like that made no sense. Now Best seems to be doing nothing. Pancke's fanatics are still harassing us, of course, but there aren't many of them."

The two of them sat quietly for a while, sipping their new cups of coffee.

"The big question is still the war," Vald said. "Is everybody going to fall before Hitler."

"I've never believed that. The man is a madman and, sooner or later will over-reach. The ancient Greeks got it right, hubris always presages a tragedy … and Hitler will destroy himself. We just have to survive until he falls. Pray that he falls soon."

Vald chuckled and stared at his own hands.

"It would be nice if he falls before I waste away to nothing."

Christian reached out and grasped both of Vald's hands.

"My friend, my colleague, my strong right hand. You are a Viking warrior. You and I have endured much and we'll continue to endure whatever is needed for our country and our people. The evil ones shall not win."

Vald met Christian's eyes and returned his grip.

Christian thought, we can do this. We can march through Hell itself if necessary. Pray to God it won't be necessary!

Chapter 68. Arne and Brigitte

Arne didn't like to go to sleep, the nightmares were too much. Each evening he read as long as he could, often falling asleep in his overstuffed chair.

After each nightmare he guzzled wine, straight from the bottle, as if he were drinking water on a hot day. Some mornings he started his rounds so drunk he could barely ride the bicycle.

On the mornings he was drunk, he slogged doggedly through the first hour or so like an automaton. Arne wouldn't have noticed a stikker or a Gestapo agent following ten feet behind him. At the end of the day, he was always filled with remorse at having been so careless, but he seemed helpless to change the pattern of behavior.

Arne's lifeline, the bright and shining light of his life, was the relationship with Brigitte. She came as often as her resistance work allowed and it didn't matter where they went or what they did. Her presence chased the demons away, at least for a time, and his sleep after seeing Brigitte was usually free of nightmares.

The first Friday in June, 1941 Arne fought his way out of a nightmare at four in the morning. It took a lot of wine to calm him down and he was thoroughly drunk when he left at 6:00 a.m. to start his rounds. An hour later he threw up. He fought a terrible headache until it occurred to him that he was dehydrated. The entire day was a blur of misery. He pedaled up to his building a few minutes before 5:00 p.m. and saw Brigitte sitting on the steps, waiting for him.

She smiled and came to him as he got off the bike. She threw her arms around him and kissed him.

"Arne, how come you smell like stale whiskey?" She pulled away and grimaced. "You're eyes are bloodshot. You look terrible. Are you sick?"

Arne shook his head.

Brigitte led him inside. She sat him at the table and started preparing zichory. When the zichory was ready, she handed him a cup and sat down next to him. She reached for his hand.

"Arne, what's going on? Are you okay?"

He struggled and finally spoke.

"The nightmares. The nightmares are driving me crazy. I keep seeing them getting killed. I can't stand it."

"Is that why you drink … to escape the nightmares?"

He nodded miserably.

"Does it help? The drinking, does it help?"

"Brigitte. I don't' know … ," he whispered.

"The nightmares … I feel so much guilt, so much sorrow … the nightmares always remind me it's my fault."

Arne clutched his chest and rocked back and forth.

Arne looked up and met her eyes for a moment.

"The drinking deadens the pain … for a little while."

Brigitte stood up and gathered Arne into her arms. She stood there cradling his head against her chest. They stayed like that for a long time.

Tears ran down Brigitte's face and dripped into Arne's hair.

"You need a bath," Brigitte said.

Arne didn't move.

"Okay, Arne, you're taking a bath." She unbuttoned his shirt and pulled it off. The shoes came next. She undid his belt and got him out of his trousers.

"Off you go … unless you want me to come in there and bathe you."

Arne seemed to wake up, looked down at himself clad only in his underwear and shuffled into the bathroom.

They went for a long walk, followed by a leisurely dinner. Afterward they stretched out on Arne's couch with Brigitte half lying on top of Arne. After a particularly passionate kiss, Brigitte slid down to the floor and sat there resting partly against the couch and partly against Arne's body.

"Arne, those kisses are dangerous. Makes me not want to wait for marriage."

"Um, me too." Arne sounded wistful, "We talked about it … I can wait."

She snuggled her head against Arne's stomach.

"I want to try something. I want to spend the night …no, don't look so eager, not sex. We agreed to wait for marriage and that's important to me. No, I'm thinking about your nightmares. You told me you were afraid you might hurt me during the nightmares … well, I don't think you would. I want to stay tonight."

He sat up, elbows on knees and his head in his hands. His voice was muffled as if coming from far away.

"I want to marry you, I want you beside me so bad … but I'm afraid." He raised his eyes to hers. "What if I hurt you? I couldn't stand that." The words came out as a strangled whisper.

"You're not going to hurt me."

"You don't know! The nightmares are so real. I'm trapped in them. I'm filled with rage and fear and guilt. Before I wake up, I'm acting on those emotions. I'm trying to kill the Nazi."

He looked at her helplessly, lost.

"I kill my pillow, it has been strangled so many times ..." He trailed off and shrugged. "I might strangle you."

"Okay, so maybe I can't sleep in the same bed with you. What about after you wake up? I could maybe help then, I could talk to you or just hold you?"

Arne managed a little joke, "I think you holding me is always a good idea."

"Maybe I could wake you up when the nightmare starts?"

"No, that's dangerous. I don't want you anywhere close."

"Well, how about if I just call you from the doorway?"

She finally wore him down. They agreed she would sleep on the couch and he would keep the bedroom door open. She stayed that night and again Saturday night and Arne had no nightmares. Sunday the two of them went to her flat and fetched some of her clothes and other necessities and Brigitte settled in as Arne's guardian angel.

Arne had no nightmares the entire week and by Friday was a little less afraid of going to sleep.

* * * * * * * *

"AAAAH!"

The anguished, guttural sound confused and frightened Brigitte. What's happening? Arne! A nightmare.

"Arne! Arne!" Brigitte stopped in his doorway. "Wake up. It's a nightmare. Arne! Arne!"

"AAAAAAH!"

Brigitte stepped to the foot of Arne's bed. He was thrashing around, arms and legs flailing.

Brigitte grabbed his foot and he instantly pulled the leg up, pulling her forward. Before she could recover her balance, Arne kicked out and hit her in the face, throwing her back. Brigitte crashed into the wall, banging her head painfully.

Her nose and the back of her head both hurt and her eyes were full of tears. I'm bleeding. Get up. What now?

Arne screamed again and thrashed around. He fell onto the floor.

"Arne! Arne!" He doesn't hear me.

She whirled and ran to the kitchen, returning a moment later with a glass of cold water. When the water hit him, he went rigid and then began to cry.

He's awake. Oh, God, blood dripping down my face. If Arne sees what he did ...

"Hold on, I'll be right back."

She fled to the bathroom. Wipe it off. Shit, my nose is bleeding like crazy. Cram some tissue paper in it.

"Damn!" It hurts.

Arne's still on the floor.

"It's alright, I'm here. Come on."

She pulled him up, got him onto the bed and lay down with him. Brigitte held him and crooned nonsense into his ear. The sobs gradually subsided.

The two of them fell asleep and didn't wake until half past six. As soon as Arne finished in the bathroom, Brigitte went in and stayed there until Arne left for his rounds. She was terrified that Arne would realize that he had kicked her.

* * * * * * * * *

Brigitte went to her doctor because her nose still hurt. The doctor took one look and asked her how she managed to break her nose. Straightening it was painful.

That evening Brigitte arrived at Arne's place at 5:24. Arne was already bathed and was in the middle of fixing dinner for the two of them.

He started to kiss Brigitte and stopped.

"What happened to you?"

Brigitte knew one eye was a deep purple color and swollen half shut. Her nose, although less swollen than the eye, was equally colorful.

"When I jumped up last night, I slipped and banged into the end table. Broke my nose."

Arne studied her face carefully.

"Brigitte, my toes are real sore … like I kicked something."

Brigitte didn't say anything.

"Look at me. Brigitte, tell me the truth … did I kick you?"

He looks so tragic. He mustn't know.

"No, no. I fell against the end table."

"So. How did I hurt my toes?"

"Arne, you were thrashing all around," Brigitte had it together now. " You kicked the bed or the wall or something. It's a wonder you don't have more bruises."

"Was I really struggling?"

"Arne, you looked like you were fighting for your life … you were jumping all around."

"I thought I was fighting, I thought I was there with the Nazis and Morten and Carin. It couldn't have been more real to me.

"Now do you see why you can't sleep with me, why I'm afraid for you?"

Brigitte thought her heart would break. *He looks so terribly sad. My poor Arne.*

"I'm still waiting for that kiss … just don't bump the nose." Brigitte was glad her lips weren't sore.

Prof. Hal Koch Journal, June 24, 1941

Now he's done it. I knew Hitler was insane. As a man of God I shouldn't rejoice when a madman sets out to kill additional millions, but Hitler actually betrayed Stalin and invaded Russia. This is the beginning of the end for him. Hitler will have no time for us.

Hitler has three fronts now: The battle of Britain continues, the Allies press the attack in North Africa, and now the Eastern Front against Russia. And Russia is vast, Russia will bleed and suffer and thousands will die but eventually the Russian winters will swallow the Nazi juggernaut just as it swallowed Napoleon and all the others who have tried and failed to conquer Russia. We just have to hold on.

Chapter 69. SS Kapitan Kurt Schobel

"I made a whole series of mistakes in managing the shipyard," SS Kapitan Kurt Schobel said at the beginning of his meeting with General Pancke. "I learned from those mistakes. I know what we have to do to coerce the Danish industry into producing for us. I know what the Danish pigs want us to do, and I know how to beat them."

SS Kapitan Schobel went on to describe, without sparing himself, how the Danes had sucked them into trying to manage the details of the yard and why that was not possible. He described his recent campaign in which his people focused on identifying and immediately punishing individual acts of defiance with a severe flogging.

General Pancke seemed impressed. He congratulated Schobel on his candor and his insights.

"Measure the productivity," Pancke said. "Prove that the new system is actually working.

"Prepare a memo, to go out over my signature, outlining these methods. I'm going to send it to all of our industrial liaison officers."

* * * * * * * * *

A month later Schobel had the productivity figures. The shipyard's performance improved dramatically.

Thirty-seven shipyard workers had been flogged and one machinist had a heart attack and died while being flogged. The floggings terrified everyone.

Christian Moeller railed against the floggings and the Danish underground newspapers reported on them extensively. The world press, however, seemed uninterested. Apparently mere floggings couldn't compete with the stories of major battles between the Allies and the Axis powers.

After Schobel's second briefing and the productivity improvements in the shipyard, General Pancke appointed Schobel to develop a training course for all of the industrial liaison officers. Suddenly, SS Kapitan Kurt Schobel was a star. He enjoyed his new job ... teaching others the benefits of flogging the Danes ... almost as good as watching a flogging.

Chapter 70. Schobel's Triumph

Knud Einstad was seriously depressed.

It looks like we'll finish a submarine. After fourteen months ...

Damned floggings. Everybody's terrified. No more stopping with a part half-done. No more 'mistakes' on sizes. No more mis-reading blueprints. No more changing set-ups after one part when the plan called for ten of them. Mis-routing of parts earned a flogging for both the sender and the recipient.

Working to the rules is a primary tactic now. Rules designed to slow the work.

Still managing large backlogs at some workstations and idleness at others. Still using the wrong steel a lot.

Thank God we produced extra of the sub-killers. Would be hard to make them now. Not too hard to install them, just have to be careful about the timing so they get covered up right away.

They'll get no use out of this sub.

The crew will die. Kids, just kids even if they are Germans. None of them will have a prayer. So now I become a killer of young men ...

* * * * * * * *

"If we kill the sub and its crew, the Wehrmacht troops may well lose their sympathy for us and start treating us as enemies," Professor Koch told the Freedom Council. "We can not afford to kill an entire submarine crew. It is morally wrong and it is tactically wrong."

"What do you suggest?" The Admiral demanded. "Do we just let them have a nice new submarine to sink Allied ships?"

"We let them know it's booby trapped. We give them just enough information so they realize the sub is unusable. Of course, we do that at the last minute."

Several people talked at once. Too many voices, each talking over the others.

No matter, the group accepts the idea. Only the details remain to be worked out.

* * * * * * * * *

The second week of October, 1941 the Odense Steel Shipyard completed a submarine for the Germans.

A partial set of blueprints and part of a memo had been "found" by one of their people posing as an informer and delivered to General Best. The fragment of the memo, which purported to be from a sub-committee of the Freedom Council, was labeled as page two and read as follows:

"… and finally, radio transmitters which will activate upon firing of torpedoes. If by some happenstance, none of the other devices destroy the sub, these transmitters will allow the Allied destroyers to quickly home in on the sub. Thus we not only prevent the Germans from getting another sub, we take the entire crew with it."

The blueprints were quite normal, showing a section of the bow of the sub, but were included in hopes of misleading the Nazis about the locations of the radio transmitters.

General Best studied the memo and the blueprints at length.

After a bit the tap … tap … tap … of the swagger stick on the desk intruded into his consciousness and he noticed that he was actually wearing a little round hole in the top of the desk.

His attention returned to the question of the submarine. Finally, after unconscionable delays, they were getting a submarine.

The High Command was pleased and looking forward to rapidly getting more. Pulling the plug on this sub would enrage everyone from Hitler on down. Worse, pulling the plug would remind everyone that the occupation of Denmark had so far been a dismal failure. Pulling the plug would reflect badly on his command.

If the sub was commissioned and then promptly lost in battle, it would be chalked up to the vicissitudes of war. No blame for its loss would accrue to him. No, he would let the sub be commissioned and take its chances.

General Best carefully shredded the memo. The blueprints were not incriminating and were simply tossed into the wastebasket.

* * * * * * * * *

The Freedom Council was concerned. The memo was delivered to General Best a week ago. The submarine now had a crew and was conducting sea trials. What was going on?

Christian Moeller announced to the world that the Germans would get no use out of the submarine because it was booby-trapped. He announced that the sub would sink on its very first combat mission and that the entire crew would die with it. He talked about the young men of the crew, their wives and sweethearts and children waiting for them, and he pleaded with the German High Command not to send these young Germans to certain death.

* * * * * * * *

General Hanneken, as was his custom, read a transcript of Moellar's speech and was enraged. Moellar was a filthy rabble-rouser, skilled at telling propaganda lies.

Ten minutes later, Hanneken began to wonder and called for one of his engineers.

"That filthy Moellar claims the sub is booby trapped and will sink the first time it goes into combat. How could that be done?"

"General, there are many ways, but perhaps the easiest would be to make it noisy. If the sub is noisy, the enemy can find it easily."

"Hmmm. How do you make it noisy?"

"Uh, the real question is how do you make it NOT noisy. There are so many things in a sub that make noise. We go to great lengths to make those things quiet."

"Well, I assume our engineers supervising the yard would see to that."

"Yes, certainly, General. That would be a major concern for them."

"Well, how else might it be booby-trapped?"

"Perhaps install a device that would make noise only when they dive, when they are trying to hide."

"Could you do that?"

"I'm sure we could, but I haven't really thought about it."

"What else?"

"Ah, mess with the center of gravity."

"What does that mean."

"Oh ... well. The center of gravity of the sub must be lower than the center of buoyancy. Otherwise the sub flips upside down and sinks to the bottom when it dives. Then it is irretrievably lost and everyone in it dies."

Hanneken was stunned.

"How do we check this?"

"There is only one way to check. You have to dive and see what happens."

Hanneken dismissed the engineer and went to see General Best. When Best dismissed his fears as groundless, he went to see General Pancke. Pancke listened and promised to assemble a team of engineers to look into the matter.

* * * * * * * *

The next day the engineers reported to Pancke that they had come up with numerous ways of fatally booby-trapping a submarine. The first part of their report listed five ways to ensure catastrophic and immediate failure. The rest of the report enumerated several ways to make the sub easy to kill.

Pancke read the report with growing dismay. He ordered the engineers to consider which of these might have escaped the attention of the engineers supervising the Odense Steel Ship Yard. He also put a team of engineers on checking the sub to find any hidden booby-traps.

Pancke then called the commander of the sub and told him not to do the first test dive that was scheduled for the following day. They wouldn't be doing any dives until his engineers had checked the sub thoroughly.

Chapter 71. Defects and Traps

Pancke's engineers prepared a preliminary report at the end of their third day studying the new submarine. General Pancke summoned Kapitan Schobel and several top aides to join him for the briefing from the engineers at 8:00 a.m.

The chief engineer reported the following preliminary findings:

- *Three hull plates were half the correct thickness and would probably burst if the sub dived below 150 feet. If the hull plates burst during a deep dive, the sub would flood so rapidly that it would definitely sink.*
- *Roughly ten percent of the rivets were such soft steel that they would probably rupture in any deep dive. This would sink the sub. Some of these rivets were in places that would be very difficult to replace because there was machinery or bulkheads in the way.*
- *The bearings on the main shaft to the propeller were made of very soft steel that would become noisy after a short period of use and would fail completely after perhaps a month of use.*
- *They found several other bearings also made of very soft steel.*
- *Overall, the sub is very noisy and will rapidly get worse as bearings go bad.*
- *No radio transmitter has been found. However, a radio transmitter can easily be hidden where it would be impossible to find until it started broadcasting.*

The sub is definitely a death trap and, at a minimum, the problems already identified must be fixed before it can used.

A cold fury built in Pancke while he listened to the briefing. At the end, it took him a minute before he trusted himself to speak. He finally had himself under control and asked the engineer.

"What is your recommendation for this submarine?"

"Well, sir, remember we have only begun checking it. We need more study before we have a definitive picture of the problems. So, it is hard to say."

"If you had to make a decision today, what would you say?" Pancke persisted. "Would you recommend junking it or salvaging it?"

"Sir, I don't know."

Pancke's voice was icy steel, "What did you check that didn't have serious problems?"

"Uh…" The engineer thought a minute. "The piping, sir, the pipes we checked were okay. The firing mechanism for the torpedo tubes were good. That's all, sir. Everything else has problems."

Pancke had a sudden insight. "Could the radio transmitter be in a pipe?"

"Yes, sir. If the transmitter was properly enclosed, it could be anywhere."

"The damned pipes are good because they don't want us checking the pipes … that's where they hid the traps."

"That's good, sir. That's probably right." The engineer grimaced. "But there are kilometers of pipes … and some of them are nearly impossible to get at. We would have to practically tear the sub apart to get at all the pipes."

Pancke stood up and glared. "I ask one more time. Would you junk the sub or fix it?"

The engineer wiped his brow before answering. "Sir, I would junk it. There are too many problems and we might never find the transmitters."

Pancke sat down, elbows on the table and head in hands. After a moment he sat back, once again the SS General. "Thank you for your very fine report. You and your men did a good job."

Pancke turned to Schobel. "Well, Kapitan. Any suggestions? You are the guru for dealing with a reluctant work force."

Pancke noticed that Schobel was pale, breathing rapidly and sweating heavily. *Now we will see what the Kapitan is truly made of.*

Schobel shuffled his papers. *Trying to gather his wits,* Pancke thought. *Pretending to be looking for something. The son of a bitch got us into this, let's see him get us out of it.* Pancke began drumming his fingers on the table.

"General, it is clear that we have, once again, underestimated the Danes." Schobel said. "Our policies of flogging for individual wrongdoing succeeded. We now have to extend that policy to the level of the organization. This sabotage was not carried out by an individual but by the shipyard working in concert, in a conspiracy. Therefore, we need to punish the shipyard as a whole. We need to flog, oh, say, twenty percent of the workers. That will put an end to their resistance."

General Pancke sat there with a thoughtful expression on his face. He finally said, "Okay. We flog lots of the bastards. We want them crapping their pants in fear ... "

Pancke went on to outline a plan to truly terrorize the shipyard.

Chapter 72. Floggings

Knud looked up from his workstation to see a Wehrmacht squad enter his shop. He was immediately terrified. *This is it. I hope they don't kill too many of us.*

The troops gathered everyone from the shop and marched them to the large open space in front of the docks. When Knud's group arrived, there were already hundreds of men lined up facing the docks. More arrived every minute. There were guards all around the area, one every few feet. In front of them, three SS squads and an officer waited next to the docks.

It took a half hour to get the entire workforce assembled. The SS officer, a Colonel, Knud thought, stepped up onto a small stage. His amplified voice boomed out at them.

"The Odense Steel Ship Yard was tasked to produce a submarine for the Fatherland. Each and every one of you had a responsibility in producing that submarine. You had a duty to fulfill in building that submarine. Instead of doing your duty, you willfully and criminally chose to sabotage the submarine. Because of your criminal acts, you will now be punished.

"The sentence for your criminal behavior is flogging. A roll of the dice will determine the number of lashes. Three dice will be rolled and the total of the three will be the number of lashes.

"This barrel has each of your names on a little slip of paper. I will draw names to determine who gets flogged."

Knud remembered his own flogging only too well. Dear God, don't let them draw my name.

The first victim was hustled forward, stripped to the waist, and bound to a sturdy post. The Colonel made a great show of rolling the dice but did not announce the result.

The trooper with the lash simply looked at the dice and nodded. He moved to a position beside his victim and struck the first blow. The skin split, blood flew, and the man screamed, a long, agonized shriek. Knud felt his knees begin to buckle and held on to the man next to him.

The next lash drew another scream and a second bright red line across the man's back, slightly below the first one. Knud was holding his breath, worrying about how many strokes the man would receive.

After ten strokes that seemed to take an eternity, the lashing stopped, the victim cut down, dumped onto the dock.

The entire grisly routine was repeated over and over. Each time Knud prayed that some other name, any one else, would be called.

By mid afternoon there was a long line of men lying on the dock. Some of them moaned and twisted. Some of them lay still.

Knud thought some of the victims might be dead. All of them are bleeding. The sea must be turning red.

Knud became numb, rousing only when another victim was selected. Each time he trembled and prayed his name wouldn't be called.

Eventually the sun went down and the Nazis turned on the lights. They took turns administering the lashes. The night wore on, past midnight and the floggings continued.

By the following morning Knud had lapsed into a state of semi-consciousness. What … ? Guys are moving away from me … ? No … my name!

No, no! No fair. Can't flog me a second time.

Knud's legs gave out and he sat down heavily.

Knud's oldest friend from the machine shop stepped forward, grasped him under the armpits and heaved him upright.

"Courage, Knud. Remember, you are a Viking. Walk up there and look the bastard in the eye. You are Knud Einstad, Viking warrior."

Knud shook himself and some of his courage returned.

"Thank you," he said.

He managed to walk steadily forward and stared the Colonel in the eye until they seized him, spun him around, and ripped his shirt off. They weren't gentle in tying his hands and hoisted him until he was on tip-toe, more hanging from the post than standing.

How many lashes? They won't tell me.

He lost track of the number of lashes almost immediately. Afterward, he lapsed into unconsciousness soon after they dumped him on the dock.

* * * * * * * * *

It was a week before Knud had the strength to return to work. Shufflling along like an old man. Slow and easy. Back is a mass of scabs. Any sudden movement might tear the wounds, start it bleeding again.

Shortly after he got to his work-station he began to feel uneasy. The feeling grew, but he couldn't tell why. Finally, mid-morning, he stopped work and just spent a little while looking around, wondering why he felt so strange. He walked around to say hello to a few of the other machinists.

Suddenly Knud knew. Every one was afraid. The entire shop is cowed. No one would look anyone else in the eye, they were all ashamed. All of them, avoiding me. We're defeated, beaten, afraid of the Nazis.

Everyone is actually working. No one was scheming, no one trying to slow the work. The Nazi bastards won.

Prof. Hal Koch Journal, December 15, 1941

Japan bombed Pearl Harbor! Hitler obliged by declaring war on the USA. The Americans are in the war.

The madness continues at ever-greater levels of violence, but it can't get much worse ... essentially the entire world is already involved in the fighting. Japan apparently decimated the American fleet in the Pacific, it will be a long hard struggle for the Americans to recover but they will. I can't see how tiny Japan can hope to defeat the USA in the long run.

Hitler's lightning war against Russia bogged down at the gates of Moscow and Russia is finally mounting a serious counter-offensive. Hitler will learn the folly of arousing the Russian bear.

With both the Americans and the Russians opposing him, Hitler can not prevail. Finally one can foresee the Nazis' defeat with some confidence.

I wonder how many more innocents have to die before the madness ends?

Chapter 73. Aftermath of the Floggings

Two days after the floggings, SS Kapitan Kurt Schobel was having a hard time maintaining his usual fierce expression. The shipyard workers are beaten curs … can see it in their posture. Can smell their fear. These pathetic Danes will cause no more trouble.

Schobel suppressed a smile and an urge to do a little victory dance. It was a hard fight, the Danes had been stubborn … but now they're beaten. And they know it.

The shipyard should produce a submarine every four months. General Pancke's engineers were taking apart the first submarine to learn all the tricks the shipyard had used. They would know what to watch for on the next one.

An occasional public flogging would serve to terrorize the workforce. Keep 'em in line.

* * * * * * * *

While Schobel was gloating, Gerhard and Jacob were discussing the floggings. Gerhard was appalled at the brutality and Jacob was telling him to keep his opinions to himself. Gerhard protested.

"I overheard four of our squad mates talking about the floggings. Three of them thought the floggings were wrong. The Danes aren't threatening us, only refusing to follow our orders. Of course, the fourth man wanted to shoot a bunch of them."

"Gerhard, Gerhard, Gerhard. Haven't I taught you anything? Look, the surest way to get in trouble is to talk bad about what some officer has decided. Keep your trap shut."

"I'm sorry Jacob, I remember what you told me. It's just that what we're doing is wrong. We kill and beat innocent people, people who haven't done anything to us. It bothers me."

"Bothers me too," Jacob's voice was so low Gerhard had to strain to hear him. "You noticed I can't hit anything I shoot at? And we never caught any smugglers. Gerhard, our job as soldiers is to survive the war, to survive the crazy officers. We do what we must … and as little harm as we can. Just be careful what you say. Our squad leader is okay, but some of these SS bastards will shoot you for the wrong opinion."

* * * * * * * *

Five weeks after the floggings SS Kapitan Kurt Schobel sat down to review the productivity figures for the shipyard. Fantastic. Productivity was slightly more than twice as high as it had ever been.

Schobel delivered the good news to General Pancke in person. They decided to administer similar lessons to all the other factories that were still resisting. Pancke detailed Schobel to organize the floggings.

* * * * * * * * *

General Dr. Werner Best thought the overall situation was becoming entirely too complicated. Pancke might just pull this off, might actually get materiel out of the Danes. Makes me look bad if he succeeds.

Hitler has entirely lost it. Fighting on three fronts at once. Against America and Russia. Madness. How the hell does Hitler expect to beat all of them at once? Tanks can't swim the channel to Britain, sure as hell can't get to America.

Russia is mounting offensive campaigns for the first time. General Motors and Ford will spit out tanks by the thousands. God help us.

If Germany loses, that leaves us at the mercy of the Danes. They'll hang Hanneken, sure as shit. Might hang me too. They know I ordered the assassinations. Can't prove it though. Thank God the Danes are persnickety about legal niceties.

I saved their Jews. Duckwitz will testify for me.

Can I sabotage Pancke? Should I?

Hitler's talk about Aryan superiority, the Fatherland's destiny, the thousand year Reich … the demented ravings of a total lunatic. He's doing us all in.

Hang on, hang on. Don't rock the boat, watch and wait for a little longer.

* * * * * * * * *

January 18th 1941 General Pancke received orders that he and most of the SS and Gestapo under his command, including Kapitan Schobel, were being re-assigned. The fighting with the Russians and preparations for the anticipated entry of the US forces required more men and officers. A handful of SS and Gestapo troops would remain in Denmark under General Best's command.

General Hanneken received orders, also on January 18th, that twenty percent of his men were needed on the Russian front. Gerhard and Jacob were quite relieved that they were to remain in Denmark.

Kapitan Schobel was enraged at the new orders. While he was no longer quite so happy with the shipyard ... he had noticed a definite change in the men's attitudes, they no longer carried themselves like beaten curs ... he was elated with the lesson they administered to the Dansk Industri Syndikat arms factory.

They had quite a few more 'lessons' scheduled. Now, just as they were finally winning, he was being pulled out. He consoled himself with the thought that the new manual spelled it all out in detail, he wasn't personally required in order to continue the program.

* * * * * * * * *

General Best assumed command of the remaining SS and Gestapo troops on January 20th. He never officially stopped the torture or the floggings or the street crimes orchestrated by the Danish Nazi party. He simply re-assigned the troops involved in those programs to other duties and failed to replace them.

General Best maintained the Gestapo and SS troops as General Pancke had, as a separate and self-contained command. This made it easy to keep an eye on them and to ensure they didn't commit any more atrocities.

Prof. Hal Koch Journal, January 20, 1942

The worst Christmas holiday of all times. Hitler's megalomania may have sealed his own doom, but that hasn't changed our situation one whit. Our people are beaten down with fear and exhaustion. Our factories are actually working for the Nazis ... actually working, slowly, but working ... the Odense shipyard is on track to produce a useful submarine. The floggings seem to have defeated us. Or maybe the floggings were just the last straw. One doesn't see much of the Viking spirit these days.

Chapter 74. A Visit to General Best

"This is crazy," Tyge said. "It's just too dangerous."

"No, no," Arne said. "I can do this."

"I don't see how," Brigitte said. "Just walk in and ask to see General Best. There's no telling what he might do."

"Wait," Arne said. "Wait. King Christian is sending a personal note, saying that he and Best need to talk."

Brigitte snorted. "So. That's supposed to help?"

"Good," Tyge said. "I understand. Delivering the note to Best is still too dangerous."

"I already promised Prof I would do it. I really don't think it's going to be a problem."

"Arne, If this stunt gets you hurt," Brigitte said. "I'll never forgive you."

"Brigitte …," Arne was momentarily at a loss. "Look, there has never been any physical danger for the Germans, not the entire time they have been here. They don't see us as a threat and they won't harm me. There shouldn't be any problem in getting in to see Best."

"Arne," Brigitte said. "If you get arrested, I'll kill you myself."

Arne put his arm around her shoulder but she shrugged him off and wouldn't look at him while they walked the several blocks to their flat.

The following afternoon Arne took a taxi to General Best's headquarters. He got out of the taxi, took a deep breath and walked up to the sentry at the entrance to the building.

"Hi," Arne said to the sentry. "I need to see your superior."

"Who are you and why do you need to see my superior?"

"I have information that General Best needs."

The sentry considered this, then stepped inside the building. He returned a moment later. "He'll be here shortly."

A lieutenant wearing the black uniform of the SS came out and looked at Arne..

"I have information General Best will want," Arne said.

"You can give it to me."

"Sorry," Arne replied. "My orders are to give it to General Best and no one else."

"You can't see General Best. Give me the information."

"I can't give it to you. It is for General Best only."

The lieutenant drew his pistol and pointed it at Arne. "Okay, be stubborn. You are under arrest."

"That won't work," Arne said. "I don't know what is in the documents so you can torture me all you want and it won't do you any good."

"We will just take the documents."

"Well, we thought you would do that," Arne said. "I don't have them with me."

The lieutenant seemed nonplussed. "What do you want?"

"I want to see General Best. I want his personal guarantee that I can deliver the documents to him and that I will then be allowed to leave without any danger to myself."

"Why would we do that? Who is sending these mysterious documents?"

"The documents come from the highest levels of the Danish government. I am instructed to tell you that General Best will be extremely interested in them. He will be very displeased if they are prevented from reaching him."

The lieutenant searched Arne carefully, then told him to wait and went for his superior.

Arne talked to a captain, a colonel, and then General Best's aide, repeating each time more or less the same discussion that he had with the lieutenant. Finally, two and a half hours later he was ushered in to see General Best.

Arne followed the aide into General Best's office. Best was reading a sheet of paper and didn't look up for several minutes. Putting me in my place by ignoring me.

"What is this nonsense?" Best leaned back in his chair and studied Arne.

"For your ears only," Arne said. "Sir."

"My aide can hear."

"Sir," Arne said. "My orders are very explicit. Your ears only. It comes from the highest levels."

"Very well," Best said. "'So young … you intrigue me so I will humor you." He dismissed the aide with a wave of the hand.

Arne waited until the door closed behind the aide.

"I was sent by King Christian. There is a document he wants you to have. He instructed me to tell you that this is an unofficial contact. He asked me personally to deliver the message rather than use a government official."

"Okay, what is this message."

"I don't know and I don't have it with me. My instructions are to ask you for your personal guarantee of safe passage, in writing."

"Very well. Bring the documents and give them to my aide."

"I'm sorry, sir. My strict instructions are that I have to put the documents into your hands only. No one else is to see them."

Best shrugged.

"Bring me the documents. You have my word that you will not be harmed."

"Sir," Arne took a deep breath. 'My instructions are to get a written pass from you, a document that instructs your men to escort me to you and that promises me safe passage to deliver the documents. I have been told that I will not be given the documents until I have that statement in writing from you."

Arne waited, watching the annoyance in Best's face, and discovered a moment later that he was forgetting to breath.

Best abruptly leaned forward in his chair, snatched a pen and paper and began scrawling a note. A minute later he shoved the note across the desk to Arne. Arne picked it up and read:

January 20, 1942
The bearer of this note shall be searched, then escorted to
me. He is not to be harmed in any way and has my personal
guarantee of safe passage into and out of Shell house.
General Dr. Werner Best

"Does that satisfy your 'Instructions'?"

"Yes, sir. Thank you."

"Bring the documents tomorrow afternoon. Now get out of here … you are an impertinent pup."

The following afternoon Arne presented his note to the sentry at Shell House. He was searched and promptly escorted to General Best's aide. The aide glanced at the note, then led Arne into General Best's office.

Neither Arne nor General Best said anything. Arne handed him the package and turned to leave. The aide, caught by surprise, leaped to open the door for Arne and followed him until he reached the sidewalk.

Arne walked off down the street.

Chapter 75. The Viking Awakes

Knud stood there in the middle of the shop and remembered his first flogging. So much pain and fear. The second time, I shamed myself. Prayed it would be someone else. Almost fainted when they called my name.

Sorry excuse for a Viking!

Probably the only one to get it twice.

And here I am, wondering how to fight the Nazis again. Must be a slow learner. Too stupid to be afraid.

Why no more fear? Should be afraid.

He walked back to his work-station and did a little work. Wonder how we might help the guys get past their fear, remember they're Vikings?

Knud held a meeting for his shop that evening. About half of the men came, a total of 12 of them. After making sure everyone had a beer, Knud started talking. He told them how terrified he had been and how he prayed that his name wouldn't be called. He told them how he fell down when his name was called and how his friend helped him up and restored his courage. He told them that being flogged was the worst pain he had ever experienced.

"I'm still here. The pain is temporary and now it's gone. I'm ashamed I was so weak while they were flogging us but now I remember who I am. I'm a Viking. I fell down … now I'm up again, ready to continue the fight. I may die but I won't give up."

Knud looked at each man in turn. About half met his gaze, at least for a second or two. The rest wouldn't even look at him. Knud asked them a question, very softly, so softly they had to strain to hear him.

"What about you? Were you terrified? Were you praying that some one else's name would be called?"

Slowly, hesitantly, the men began to talk. Knud listened and when they ran down he asked another question. Gradually they processed their fear and shame. By the end of the evening they remembered they were Vikings. They regained their courage. They were ready to resist the Nazis again. Carefully. Cautiously, but ready to resist again.

After the men went home, Knud sat on his porch, drinking a beer. The men of my shop do us proud. What about all the other shipyard workers?

How on earth can we deal with all those frightened men? Perhaps the Freedom Council can help? All it took for my gang was an evening of sharing. The Nazis haven't won yet.

Chapter 76. King Christian and General Best

General Dr. Best was not terribly surprised by the documents given to him by Arne. The main document was a memo that outlined the legal strategy for prosecuting him for multiple counts each of murder, kidnapping, and torture.

The cover letter pointed out that the strategy could be implemented as soon as the war ended, assuming that Germany surrendered and General Best was still in Denmark. The cover letter also mentioned that the likely penalty, if Best was convicted on even a fraction of the charges, was death by hanging.

What surprised General Best was that the King decided to give him the memo. Christian's note read:

"We need to talk. In person. Christian"

Best was a lawyer and as such appreciated the legal reasoning that went into the memo. It was obvious that some very competent people had worked on the document. If Christian's purpose was to scare him, the memo was a resounding success.

Best had no doubt that Germany was going to lose the war ... they couldn't fight the entire rest of the world, even with Japan's help. The only real question was whether or not he would still be stuck in Denmark. What could he do to insulate himself against the kind of legal action so carefully outlined in Christian's damnable memo.

He called his aide and instructed him to set up a private meeting with the King.

* * * * * * * * * *

General Best arrived precisely on time and was immediately ushered into King Christian's office.

"Good morning General Best. Thank you for coming."

"My pleasure, King Christian. What can I do for you?"

"Perhaps a walk in my garden? It is a beautiful day although rather cold."

King Christian put on his coat and the two men strolled out to the garden and walked down a path among the evergreens.

General Best remained silent, waiting for Christian to take the lead, although he was bursting with impatience to know what Christian was up to. They strolled along for perhaps five minutes before Christian got down to business.

"General Best, I think we both know that Germany can not win this war, it cannot defeat England, Russia and America all at once."

"For the sake of argument," Best said. "Let us assume you are correct."

"Fair enough," Christian said. "When Germany surrenders, you personally will be in a rather delicate position. You will be prosecuted for murder, among other things."

"I committed no crimes," Best said. "I merely followed orders while attempting to minimize the deaths among your people.

"Without me the casualties among your Jews would have been much higher. Duckwitz's warning allowed you to save almost all of your Jews. I managed to stop Hanneken's executions in the town square. Admittedly, it took a while to stop him, but his rank is equal to mine so I couldn't just order him to stop, I had to convince the High Command to make him stop."

Best stopped walking, turned towards King Christian and stood there with his hands palm up and outspread to either side. Christian thought he looked like a penitent asking forgiveness.

"General Best, the business with the Jews was most instructive. We are very appreciative for your warning. However, my legal people tell me that we have a strong case against you personally for the night-time assassinations, the torture, the deaths of our people during the curfew protests, and the deaths in quite a few factories. You are the responsible authority and you bear responsibility for the actions of your subordinates."

"I did not command those troops." Best protested. "General Hanneken commands the Wehrmacht and General Pancke commanded the Gestapo and SS."

"General, I have no wish to argue with you or to convict you of these crimes. I merely remind you of the legal argument my lawyers have prepared. Assuming you are still in Denmark when Germany finally surrenders, you will be put on trial. I can assure you of that."

Christian stopped walking and looked General Best in the eye. A moment later he continued.

"I personally agree that you have a strong defense. I wanted to chat with you today to see if we could not further strengthen your defense."

"What do you want from me?" Best asked.

Christian strolled on down the path for about ten steps before answering.

"I want to minimize the damage we do to each other. Your Fuhrer will fight to the bitter end, he will not stop until Germany is totally depleted, stripped of men and materiel. He is unlikely to release us … he will hang on to everything until it all goes smash. That means we are stuck with each other while this tragedy plays out to its bitter end."

Best did not reply and they walked in silence for some time.

"King Christian, I can offer this. We continue as we have been, the shipments of food must continue. The small shipments of iron and other minerals must continue. That, I think, will keep Hitler from thinking much about us. You, for your part, must not interfere with the shipments of food and raw materials," Best looked at Christian and the King nodded his head in agreement. Best continued.

"General Pancke and most of the Gestapo and SS are gone … the remainder are now under my command and I can assure you they will behave themselves. The Wehrmacht under General Hanneken have not been bothering you and I can promise that will continue."

"Very good, General."

"Christian, now look here. This is delicate. If your newspapers or Moellar begin trumpeting 'Victory' or any such nonsense, Hitler might well get angry and order retaliations. Then we would be in for it. If that happens and I don't carry out his orders, I will be replaced. The replacement would be more bloodthirsty than I. Both of us would lose."

"I understand," Christian said. "We will continue much as before. However, since the torture and assassinations have stopped, we have no reason to hold the flash demonstrations that have been so embarrassing to the High Command. I think we can simply co-exist, with minimal damage to each other, while the war winds on to its bloody conclusion. At the end, at your trial, I will testify on your behalf ... if you can keep your end of this bargain."

Best stopped and held out his hand. The two men shook hands and the deal was consummated.

When General Best returned to his office a half-hour later he re-assigned to regular duty those squads that had been shadowing Prime Minister Stauning and King Christian. These squads were not replaced.

Chapter 77. Brunch with the King

March 2, 1941 Eminent Professor Hal Koch arrived five minutes early for his meeting with Prime Minister Thorvald Stauning and King Christian.

Vald and the King arrived together, promptly on time, and greeted Koch warmly. Koch reported that everything, the entire country, was quiet and peaceful. All of the SS and Gestapo had been pulled out of the factories and replaced by a much smaller number of Wehrmacht troops. The few remaining SS troops were all assigned to securing foodstuffs.

Koch leaned back, took his eyeglasses in his right hand, and spoke.

"It's really strange. You see the German soldiers, we're still occupied. The soldiers ignore us and we ignore them. It's like we're two nations, sharing the same space but determined not to interact."

"Let me tell you," King Christian said. "General Dr. Best and I had that little conversation we planned. It went very well."

"He didn't protest?" Vald said. "He agreed Germany can't win the war?"

"Even that," Christian said. "He understands his position and is frightened about a trial. He wants to keep things quiet."

"So, we have won," Koch said. "Finally. It's over."

"Unless Hitler, somehow, decides to focus on us," Christian said. "Best was worried about Hitler. He emphasized that we have to keep things quiet, so we don't attract Hitler's attention."

"Hitler is overwhelmed," Koch said.

"Right," Vald added. "It would take a lot to attract Hitler's attention while trying to fight a war on three separate fronts."

"Agreed," Christian said. "Nevertheless, there is little to gain by pushing Best around. We should just be quiet while Germany exhausts herself."

"The Freedom Council meets in two days," Vald said. "We can work out the details there. We'll find a low key way of saying Germany is finished, we won, everybody relax and don't make waves."

The talk then turned to how the Danes were doing. Koch spoke.

"You remember what I told you about young Sejr? The debilitating nightmares and the drinking?"

Vald and Christian both nodded and Koch continued.

"Bodil has been seeing Sejr on a weekly basis and he is getting better, but it is a long slow process. Bodil tells me there are at least hundreds of others, perhaps more, having similar problems. Some of them are ashamed to admit their problem, so there may be many more. Bodil wants some kind of public health program to try and find these people so we can provide help."

Vald said he would talk to the relevant legislators to get a program enacted.

"For a year now, Vald said, "our shipyards and many of our factories have been operating without any income, drawing on government funds to continue in business. Similarly, large numbers of our people have been drawing government funds while on strike or working full-time for the resistance. As you know, this means the government has been hemorrhaging red ink. It's time the Freedom Council revisited this issue."

"You have a recommendation?" Christian asked.

"Just that it's time for Parliament to take up the issue," Vald said. "I want to ask the Freedom Council to charge Parliament with addressing the issue. Seems time to get them back to work."

Eminent Professor of Theology Hal Koch searched around for his reading glasses, found them on the table to his left, put them on, and sat there looking over the top of the glasses at his two companions. A year ago Vald had been just slightly overweight with brown hair that was beginning to turn grey … today he was so thin he was little more than skin and bones and his hair was almost completely white.

King Christian didn't seem to have lost any weight, he still had the ramrod straight, trim figure he always had, but his face was much more deeply lined than it had been a year ago.

Koch lifted his hand, fingers extended, and looked at it. The fine tremors he had two weeks ago were gone. The fine edge of exhaustion threatening all of them was gone as well. He thought this was the most relaxed any of them had been in more than a year.

Chapter 78. Arne and Brigitte

Arne's nightmares were down to less than one a week. Recovering from a nightmare was still a hellish process of climbing out of a deep, dark pit of despair and pain.

Arne no longer drank to recover from a nightmare, now he held fast to Brigitte. Even with Brigitte holding him, stroking his face, whispering in his ear, even so the path back was always difficult.

Brigitte and Arne were walking one beautiful Sunday afternoon, neither of them speaking, simply enjoying walking and being together. Brigitte stopped at the top of a hill and asked him a question.

"Do you think it's been worth it?"

"What? Has what been worth it?"

"The resistance? Our struggle against the Germans ... has it been worth all the deaths and pain?"

"I wouldn't have met you without the resistance."

"Um. Well, imagine we could have met anyway, would it still have been worth it?"

"I had to do it. I would have lost myself if I hadn't at least tried to resist the Germans. So yeah, I guess for me it was worth it."

"I guess for me too ... I didn't really have any choice."

"I kinda lost myself anyway," Arne turned to her. "I'm not the same. I was sure about most things, self-confident and I always knew what was best. Now, now I'm not. I'm always second-guessing myself. I'm more afraid.

"I used to be very trusting ... I used to have an innocence ... The Nazis took that from me, now I see evil around me. I don't like it, but I see evil in people."

Brigitte didn't say anything, just kissed him.

* * * * * * * * * *

"Arne, we need to get married," After six weeks of sleeping on Arne's couch, Brigitte was fed up.

"I can't." He looks so tragic.

"I want your children. I want you. I want to get married."

"How can I marry you? I can't even sleep in the same bed with you."

"Arne Sejr, I don't care. We're getting married. Now!"

"I want to, Brigitte. I want it more than anything in the world, but ... what about the children?" He was whispering now, a hoarse, strained whisper Brigitte could barely hear.

"I might hurt our children ..."

Brigitte gathered him into her arms.

"Hush, hush, my darling Arne. It will be all right, we will be all right. We are getting married. I'm not letting you get out of it. We're getting married and we're getting our own place and we'll buy two beds. I'll be with you."

Brigitte felt him relax and knew she had won. They stood there for a while, arms entwined and bodies pressed close.

"Bodil says you're getting better. She says you're going to be okay. Arne, even if you never get over the nightmares, I'm not letting you go. We'll manage somehow."

Chapter 79. The End of the War

World War II dragged on for four more bloody years until Japan and Germany were finally totally spent.

Denmark and the occupying German troops under General Dr. Werner Best managed to largely ignore each other while the war dragged on. Hitler committed suicide in his bunker and atomic bombs obliterated two Japanese cities. Japan and Germany both surrendered unconditionally.

General Hanneken was recalled to Germany before the end of the war and escaped from Danish justice.

General Dr. Werner Best was immediately arrested upon Germany's surrender. A Danish court sentenced him to death for his role in war-time atrocities. However, his death sentence was soon changed to a twelve-year prison term and he was actually released after only three years. He lived quietly until his death in1989.

The Danish Jews and policemen arrested by the Nazis were incarcerated at Theresienstadt Concentration camp, the infamous way stop for the gas chambers. Most of the people sent to Theresienstadt were killed, but the Danish people, government and private citizens alike, kept up such a steady stream of inquiries and care packages of food that all of the Danes sent there survived the war and returned home afterwards.

Rabbi Melchior stayed in Sweden until the end of the war, where he was the head of the Copenhagen Synagogue-in-exile. At the end of the war, he and his family were able to pick up their lives again in Copenhagen.

Knud Einstad never worked on a submarine after the war, but he did continue to build ships and later helped build oil-rig platforms.

Professor Hal Koch and Bodil Koch became national heroes for their roles in the resistance. Bodil served in Parliament from 1947 to 1968. Professor Koch died in 1963 and Bodil almost ten years later in 1972.

Prime Minister Thorvald Stauning didn't survive the war, dying peacefully in bed on May 3, 1942.

King Christian Rex suffered a fall from his horse near the end of the war and broke his hip. His health declined thereafter and he died April 27, 1947 at the age of 77, revered as a national hero.

Greta and Tyge married, bought a house near Greta's large and boisterous extended family and had hordes of children and grandchildren..

Arne and Brigitte married but slept in separate beds for the first six months. One day Brigitte bought a double bed and gave away their two small beds. When Arne protested Brigitte simply ignored him and he, having gained a little wisdom from living with her, knew when to surrender.

Arne's nightmares became quite rare and, even when they did occur, they were less devastating and eventually merely left him a little sad.

Brigitte's first child, a girl, arrived nine months to the day after Germany's surrender. A boy followed a year later and the third and final child, another boy, was born two years after that.

Brigitte and Arne visited Greta and Tyge frequently and the children of both couples began thinking of each other as cousins. Hal and Bodil became unofficial grandparents for both families. They all took holidays with Hal and Bodil in their country cottage. After a time the three families worked together to enlarge the cottage.

Asger became an alcoholic and died just two years after the war ended. Bodil declared him a victim of the Nazis just as surely as were Poul, Carin and Morten. They erected a stone monolith, with a brass plaque bearing the four names, behind the Koch's cottage.

The end.

* * * * * * * * * * * * * * * * * * *

NOTE: I am frequently asked "How much of this story is true?" or "Which of these characters were actual people?" The short answer is that quite a bit of it is true and many of the characters are real. My website provides more detailed answers to these and some related questions. It also provides the references used in writing the book.

My website: www.barryclemson.net

---

[1] The following lyrics, which I used for Arne's flash demonstration, are actually taken from the theme song used by the Chilean demonstrators to protest the torture carried out by the Pinochet dictatorship:

> For the caged bird,
> For the tortured bodies,
> I sing your name, Liberty

Acknowledgments

The idea for this book grew directly out of my experience more than 40 years ago with the young civil rights warriors of SNCC, the Student Nonviolent Coordinating Committee. Fannie Lou Hamer wasn't so young but inspired all of us. I worked on voter registration in Biloxi, Mississippi alongside incredibly courageous local people including Dickie and Benny and Curtis and Roger and especially Arthur Lee Jacob … and lots more whose names I can't remember after all these years. The black people of Mississippi taught me the power of nonviolence, that it is more powerful than guns or hate.

SNCC showed that nothing is so powerful as a people committed to a just cause. The practical strategies and tactics needed to apply that understanding to national defense came from Gene Sharp and his colleagues.

My wife and helpmeet, Mary, is a pastor with the quaint notion that her job is not to make the congregation comfortable but to stimulate their spiritual growth. This means that everyone gets offended on occasion and sometimes all of them are angry at once. Mary's unflinching dedication to telling the truth while under fire is a continuing lesson in courage. Her example, encouragement, and support sustained me during the long struggle to complete Denmark Rising.

The members of the Norfolk Writer's Meetup prodded, cajoled, and whipped me into a passable fiction writer. Sarah Albertini-Bond, Teresa Csorba, Deborah Clark Ebel, Richard and Rose Earls, Alex Johnson, Frieda Landau, Doug Phinney, and Joelle Presby all provided major assistance in my education and in critiquing the manuscript through several iterations. Lauran Strait provided invaluable editorial assistance. Because of all this marvelous help, the book eventually became a pretty good novel. The remaining literary shortcomings are entirely because I am a slow learner, not because of any defects in their teaching.

Barry Clemson
Norfolk, VA August, 2009

Dr. Barry Clemson

I grew up in Alaska. Part of that time we lived 20 miles from the nearest road, went to school by dogsled, and had outdoor toilets (imagine twenty below and going in the middle of the night!). I had mountains, lakes, and wilderness as a playground and as a young boy frequently went on solitary hunting trips.

My friends and I dammed up creeks and built a cabin on the mountainside (well… half a cabin before we got distracted), all before I was old enough to be interested in girls. Even today, after fifty years of living in cities, I still think (totally unrealistically!) that I am a mountain man.

At age 16 we moved to Penn State University and I saw my first TV, telephone, and elevator. Over the next few years, both parents, an uncle, and three siblings all attended Penn State while I started an academic journey that took me through separate degrees in science, politics, and management.

In 1964, in the middle of my undergraduate work, I joined almost a thousand other Northern students as part of the Mississippi Freedom Summer assault on the segregated South. I stayed in Mississippi until April of 1965 and during that time was attacked by both civilians and a policeman, was threatened by a couple of mobs and by a man with a rifle, and was arrested. God must have been watching me pretty closely, because although I thought I was about to be killed several times, I was never even injured.

My "career" has taken me through a dizzying array of different roles including custom manufacturing, community development, university teaching & research, software development, carpentry, and (since retirement in 2006) writing, both fiction and essays. For a long time, this odyssey through all these careers puzzled me, but I recently realized that all of it was God's way of preparing me for writing fiction which explores the uses of strategic nonviolence.

My wife of twenty-plus years and I have children, grandchildren, and one great-grandson. All four of our parents are still living (my parents live in a rural part of Alaska).

Now, in retirement, I am busier than ever. I work with system scientists from around the world on questions of surviving the mess we humans have made of our world. I am part of a healing prayer ministry, I tend my vegetable garden, and I try to get my city-born wife to love the wilderness ("No, the bears aren't going to eat us and there are no snakes in Alaska!").